Praise for Carol Goodman and *The Widow's House*

"Carol Goodman is, simply put, a stellar writer."
—Lisa Unger, *New York Times* bestselling author of
The Red Hunter

"Blends a perfect gothic premise . . . with modern mysterious twists. . . . I couldn't put it down but I didn't want it to end."
—Wendy Webb, bestselling and award-winning
author of *The Vanishing*

"Foreboding and moody. . . . As you're pulled deeper into its crumbling corridors and gothic history, you'll never guess where its true threats lie."
—Miranda Beverly-Whittemore, *New York Times*
bestselling author of *Bittersweet* and *June*

"Goodman expertly melds the psychological thriller and academic mystery into a compelling story."
—Associated Press

"Goodman pushes the needle over into the red zone and keeps it there through page after page of suspense."
—*Chronogram*

"[Goodman] offers puzzles and twists galore but still tells a human story."
—*Boston Globe*

"Goodman combines gripping suspense with strong characters and artistic themes. Those who read Anita Shreve or Jodi Picoult are likely to become fans."
—*Library Journal*

"Goodman specializes in atmospheric literary thrillers."
—*Denver Post*

THE OTHER MOTHER

THE
OTHER
MOTHER

CAROL
GOODMAN

WILLIAM MORROW
wm *An Imprint of* HarperCollins*Publishers*

P.S.™ is a trademark of HarperCollins Publishers.

THE OTHER MOTHER. Copyright © 2018 by Carol Goodman. Excerpt from THE WIDOW'S HOUSE © 2017 by Carol Goodman. All rights reserved. Printed in the United States of America. No part of this book may be used or reproduced in any manner whatsoever without written permission except in the case of brief quotations embodied in critical articles and reviews. For information, address HarperCollins Publishers, 195 Broadway, New York, NY 10007.

HarperCollins books may be purchased for educational, business, or sales promotional use. For information, please email the Special Markets Department at SPsales@harpercollins.com.

FIRST EDITION

Designed by Diahann Sturge

Library of Congress Cataloging-in-Publication Data

Names: Goodman, Carol, author.
Title: The other mother : a novel / Carol Goodman.
Description: First edition. | New York, NY : William Morrow, [2018]
Identifiers: LCCN 2017042257 (print) | LCCN 2017046186 (ebook)
  | ISBN 9780062562654 (ebook) | ISBN 9780062819833 (hardcover)
  | ISBN 9780062562647 (softcover)
Subjects: LCSH: Mothers and daughters—Fiction. | Motherhood—
  Fiction. | Psychological fiction. | BISAC: FICTION / Suspense. |
  FICTION / Contemporary Women. | GSAFD: Suspense fiction.
Classification: LCC PS3607.O566 (ebook) | LCC PS3607.O566 O85
  2018 (print) | DDC 813/.6—dc23
LC record available at https://lccn.loc.gov/2017042257

ISBN 978-0-06-256264-7
ISBN 978-0-06-281983-3 (library edition)

18 19 20 21 22 LSC 10 9 8 7 6 5 4 3 2 1

To my mother, Marge, and my daughter, Maggie, who together taught me everything I needed to know about being a mother

Warning to Women with Postpartum Obsessive-Compulsive Disorder

Women with postpartum OCD (obsessive-compulsive disorder)—having intrusive and disturbing thoughts, sometimes about harming their child—are advised NOT to read the first-person stories until after they have recovered. Women with OCD often "borrow" from others' intrusive thoughts—that is they read or hear of someone else's intrusive thoughts and then they start having those thoughts as well. If you suspect you have OCD, speak to your medical professional about this and, if necessary, receive treatment before reading any of the stories in this book!

Understanding Postpartum Psychosis: A Temporary Madness, Teresa M. Twomey, JD

THE OTHER MOTHER

"Can you tell me when you first thought about hurting your child?"

"It was a few days after we'd come home from the hospital. I was carrying her down the stairs . . . there's a steep drop from the landing and when I looked over it I suddenly had this . . . *picture in my head* of myself lifting her over the banister and *dropping* her."

"And did you ever do anything like that? Deliberately drop her . . . or hurt her in any other way?"

"No! It was just a thought. I'd never hurt my baby . . . in fact, I did everything I could to make sure I didn't hurt her . . . to keep her safe."

"What exactly did you do to keep yourself from hurting her?"

. . .

"Ms. ■■?"

. . .

"Ms. ■■, what did you do to keep your child safe?"

PART I

Chapter One

She's crying again.

I don't know why I say *again*. Sometimes it seems as if she's done nothing but cry since she was born. As if she'd come into this world with a grudge.

"We're almost there, sweetie," I call to her in the backseat, but she only cries louder, as if she can recognize my reassurance for the lie it is. The truth is I don't know where we are or how far we are from our destination. The last time I looked at the map app on the new (cheap, pay-as-you-go) phone, it showed our location as a blue dot in a sea of endless green. As if we'd fallen off the map of the known world. When we crossed the river there was a sign that said WELCOME TO THE LAND OF RIP VAN WINKLE. I feel as if I've fallen asleep and woken to an unrecognizable world—only who sleeps with a crying six-month-old?

"Do you want your ba-ba?" I offer, even though she just finished a bottle half an hour ago. I root around in the diaper bag on the passenger seat but find only an empty bottle. Hadn't I made up two at the last gas station? Or had I been distracted by the woman in pressed corduroy trousers and Burberry jacket who'd eyed me microwaving a bottle with that

Why-aren't-you-breastfeeding-don't-you-know-bottles-will-rot-your-baby's-teeth-and-lower-her-IQ look. She was holding the hand of a toddler who had an iPhone in his other hand, his eyes glued to the screen.

At least it won't rot her brain, I had it in mind to say but instead out popped, "Isn't it hard traveling with kids? We've been driving for hours! My husband's away on business and I'm relocating for a new job."

Burberry Jacket eyed me up and down as if she didn't think I looked very employable. In my ratty old sweatshirt, grimy jeans, greasy hair pulled back in a sloppy bun I suppose I didn't. I should have left it at that but I had to add, "—as an archivist at a private library."

Her eyes widened, either because she was impressed or thought I was crazy. The latter, most likely, from the way she clutched her electronics-besotted son closer to her. *Archivist.* How stupid could I get? She'd remember me. When she saw my picture in the paper—

It won't be in the paper, I told myself for the hundred and seventh time (I'd been counting) since we'd left. I'd made sure of that.

I drove away from the gas station repeating all the reasons I didn't have to worry: I'd ditched my old phone and bought a new one with cash. I didn't tell anyone except Laurel about the job and Laurel won't tell. I haven't passed a car in the last fifty miles. I'm in the middle of nowhere, just me and a crying baby—

She's stopped screaming. I'm not sure how long it's been since she stopped. Since Chloe was born I sometimes lose little bits of time like that. *Mommy brain*, Esta, the leader of the mothers' support group, called it. *It's a hormonal thing.* I angle the rearview mirror to see Chloe's face but the car is so dark

I can't see her at all. I don't know how to find the dome light and there are no streetlights on this country road to illuminate the interior. It's so dark and quiet in the car it's almost as if she isn't there.

Of course she's there, don't be ridiculous, I tell myself, but already I can feel the thought taking root in my brain. *Bad thoughts,* my mother would say, *stick like burrs. You need something to make them go away.* A couple or six shots of whiskey is what she used. Sometimes when she got home late from her job at the bar I'd hear her muttering to herself, *Leave it!* like her brain was a dog who'd picked up a piece of garbage on the street.

Leave it! I'd tell myself on all the sleepless nights I lay awake imagining that Chloe had stopped breathing or that she had been stolen out of her crib. *If you keep going into her room, Daphne,* Peter would say, *she'll never learn to sleep on her own.*

Leave it! I say now. *She's in the car seat. She's just sleeping.* But I can't leave it. Instead I remember a Schuyler Bennett story that had been one of my favorites in college, the one called "The Changeling." Like many of her stories it was borrowed from an old piece of folklore. In it a woman who believes her own baby has been stolen by fairies carries the changeling through the woods to leave it on the fairy hill. She waits all night, listening to the sickly wail of the child, until at last at dawn she sees the fairies come and leave a healthy baby in its place. She lifts the plump but strangely quiet baby into her arms and carries it home. The baby seems to grow heavier and heavier in her arms until at last when she comes out of the woods she looks down and sees that what she carries is a log of wood and she knows that she has given up her own baby to the fairies and brought home a changeling instead.

Maybe you'd feel better, Peter had said, after skimming the story from the book on my night table, *if you didn't read such morbid stories.*

Now I can't shake the idea that when I reach the house I'll find an insensate lump of wood strapped into the car seat—or nothing at all. Maybe I left Chloe at the Quickie Mart. Maybe— the thought makes my mouth go dry—she was never in the car at all. I try to reassure myself by going over the details of leaving the house, carrying her out to the car . . . but all I can see is me sitting in the car, writing in my journal, getting ready to go in to get Chloe. I can see myself getting out of the car, going up the front path, but then the picture goes blurry, like a film out of focus. *Mommy brain,* like Esta said, *hormones*—but when the film comes back into focus I can see myself walking back down the path holding Chloe's car seat. I can see myself putting her in the back of the car. So it's ridiculous to think she's not in the car.

Still, I call her name. There's no response.

Because she's asleep, I tell myself, not because she's stopped breathing.

Leave it! I tell myself.

Once I get an idea in my head, though, it's very hard for me to let it go. *Intrusive thoughts,* Esta said, *get worse with stress,* and I've certainly been under a lot of stress these last few weeks. Hiding what I was doing from Peter, applying for the job with Schuyler Bennett without him knowing, then worry- ing that she would call and tell me she'd changed her mind, she didn't need an archivist after all. Hadn't it been too good to be true? The ad had appeared on the library job site as if it had been left there just for me. *Archivist wanted for author, must love books and be willing to relocate. Room and board included.* And when I found out it was Schuyler Bennett, one of my favorite authors, it really had seemed too good to be true—

Usually that's because it's not true. Peter's voice is so real in the car I almost believe that he's sitting in the passenger seat next to me. That he's been there all along. I can even hear what he'd say next. *You have to be realistic. No one's going to give you a job with your background—*

But then I see the sign. WELCOME TO CRANTHAM. POPULA-TION 4,300. A half a mile later there's a sign pointing to the village center. *After the sign for the village,* Schuyler Bennett had said, *you'll pass the entrance to the hospital. The turnoff for the house is a mile up on the right.*

I see why she mentioned the hospital. The entrance is the most noticeable landmark I've passed in an hour. Two brick pillars and a wrought iron arch with the name Crantham spelled out in large black iron letters. The Crantham Retreat for the Insane, it was called when Schuyler Bennett's father was the head doctor there in the fifties and sixties. Of course it's not called that anymore. Now it's the Crantham Psychiatric Center.

Don't worry, Schuyler Bennett had said when she mentioned the hospital's proximity to her house, *they take a very genteel class of patient there these days—celebrity rehabs, anorexic teen-agers, overworked executives. You don't have to worry that any serial killers will get out and make their way over.*

I had laughed, knowing that was *exactly* what I'd be think-ing about from then on.

The turn comes up so quickly, I almost miss it. The only sign is a mailbox with a number on it, no name.

I cherish my privacy, Schuyler Bennett had said. *I ask that you not divulge any details about the job to your social circle.*

Social circle? Ha! Who would I have told? The other mothers in the support group? I'd told Laurel, but she hadn't paid attention. No one knows where I am. As I make the turn into the narrow, unlit drive that climbs steeply upward it occurs to me that if I drove off the side of a cliff right now no one would know what had become of us.

Not that I would do that. I would never drive off a cliff, plunging Chloe and me to our fiery deaths.

Leave it! I tell myself.

We climb steeply up through deep pine woods, the trees so close they brush the roof of the car with a whispering sound. At the top of the drive is a stone house with a tower. It looks like the castle in a fairy tale—or in one of Schuyler Bennett's stories.

I pull into the gravel drive. A light has come on in the doorway and I can see the silhouette of a woman behind the glass. For a moment the outline, with its stooped back, looks like the cardboard cutout of a Halloween witch, but then as the woman comes out the door I see it's just that she has a limp and is leaning heavily to one side with a cane. She's much older than her last author picture but still I recognize her as Schuyler Bennett, come out herself to welcome us.

I turn quickly to check on Chloe. In the light from the door I can see her clearly, her face sticky with tears and formula, sound asleep in the car seat. After my morbid fantasy of her being gone I'm almost surprised to see her and for a moment she looks like a stranger. Then I feel a swell of relief followed by the familiar pang of guilt, as if imagining her gone were the same thing as *wanting* her gone.

I turn back around and roll down the window. Schuyler Bennett sticks a crooked hand in and says, "You must be Laurel."

I can feel a hysterical response bubbling up to my lips: *Yes! That's who I must be!* But all I say is "Yes, that's me."

Daphne's Journal, June 11, 20—

It wasn't supposed to be like this.

That's what I said in group today and Esta said there are no *supposed-tos* here.

"*Supposed-to* is society telling us what motherhood should look like. Most of you are here because you didn't measure up to that *supposed-to*. We're here to say to hell with *supposed-to!*"

She actually pumped her fist and there was a smattering of applause and a chorus of *yeahs*—practically a cheering session for the sleep-deprived postpartum crowd. It all made me feel just exactly how I felt in third grade when I asked during a dental hygiene lesson if there was some other way besides brushing to remove the gooey white stuff that collected between my teeth and Miss Dubovsky led the class in a round of "Brush! Brush! Brush!" (She could have told me about flossing instead!)

Chastised. That's how it made me feel. Since this is my journal—Esta suggested we keep a journal in which to write down all the things we're afraid to say out loud—I may as well tell the truth. So there, Esta, your little motivational speech made me feel chastised.

But then one of the other mothers—the blond Valkyrie in $300 True Religion jeans who looks like she was doing Pilates *during* delivery—said, "I'm with Daphne here. I didn't think I'd be spending my baby's first few months feeling homicidal."

"Can you tell us whom you're feeling homicidal toward?" Esta asked, blinking at the Valkyrie. I noticed she hadn't fobbed *her* off with a slogan, but then the Valkyrie didn't look like she was used to being fobbed off.

The Valkyrie didn't answer right away. She crossed one long leg over the other and I noticed that her toenails were painted bright red. Who had time to get a pedicure with a baby at home?

There was a palpable tension in the room. So far all anyone had admitted to was feeling a little blue and maybe "even a little angry" at our progeny when they kept us up all night and spit up in our hair and cracked our nipples with their insistent hungry mouths. But then she smiled, cool as a cucumber, and said, "Right now I'm feeling homicidal towards whoever designed these fucking chairs."

We all moaned in sympathy. All our backs hurt. We could all agree on that.

AFTERWARD WHEN WE were all heading to our cars Valkyrie sidled up to me and said in such a casual aside I wasn't sure she was talking to me, "I was going to say I feel homicidal toward my husband for signing me up for this loony-tunes circus."

I hid my gasp with a laugh. "My husband signed me up too," I admitted in a conspiratorial whisper. "He's been so worried about me he even offered to babysit."

She snorted and rolled her eyes. "Please. Make him pay for a babysitter next time." She gestured to a young girl wheeling a white-bonneted Orbit stroller (the same one I'd seen advertised in *Parenting* for over $700) along the shaded edge of the parking lot. "That way we can have a playdate afterward."

"How old is your baby?" I asked, cucumber cool myself. *A playdate!* I wanted to jump up and down. Valkyrie wanted to have a playdate with me! I hadn't felt so excited since Todd Brill asked me out in the tenth grade.

"Four months and still screaming through the night, the little bitch."

This time I wasn't able to hide my gasp. I'd never heard anyone call her baby a bitch! I really didn't know what to say to that, but then she was already taking long-legged strides across the asphalt toward the keening cry of the baby, calling, "Here

I am, here's Mommy—" And then, in an altogether different voice, to the babysitter, "Has she been crying this whole time? Why didn't you come get me?"

"She only started when she heard your voice," said the girl, a wide-eyed naïf who looked all of sixteen, looking nervously between me and her employer.

"Figures," my new friend said. Then she swooped the baby up in the air, surprising her mid-cry into silence, and making my stomach drop as she held the wiggling baby at arm's length over the hard pavement. "I'm Laurel, by the way, and this little imp"—she gave the startled baby a playful little shake—"is Chloë."

"That's so funny," I said, "my baby's Chloe too."

"Really," she said, arching one perfectly plucked eyebrow (*who has the time to pluck her eyebrows!*), "I guess we're fated to be friends then."

Chapter Two

"Y ou must be exhausted," Schuyler Bennett says.

"I'm really sorry we're so late," I say. "Some last-minute things came up . . ." *Like driving to Laurel's that last time. I hadn't planned on that.* "I didn't know you'd wait up."

She waves a crooked hand (*Arthritis*, she'd told me on the phone, *can't so much as lift a pen these days*) in the air. "When you get to my age, you don't need much sleep. Billie would have been here to greet you too but it's her grandson's birthday so I gave her the night off."

"Billie?" I echo, wondering if this is someone I'm supposed to have heard of.

"Mrs. Williams, my housekeeper. The one I suggested could watch Chloe for you?"

"Oh!" I say. "That's so generous. But I'm sure I can find day-care in the village—"

"Nonsense. Billie used to be a nurse, plus she's raised five children and fourteen grandkids. She was over the moon when I told her there was a baby coming to stay." She looks toward the rear seat, where, miraculously, Chloe is still sleeping. "And such an angel."

"Thank you. She is . . . at least while she's asleep—" I bite my lip to make myself shut up and then remember that *normal* mothers complain about their children. It's not like I called her a bitch the way Laurel would.

Schuyler Bennett doesn't seem to have made anything of my criticism of my baby. "Well, you'd better get her inside before she wakes up." She turns to lead the way back and I shoulder my handbag and the baby bag and unhook the car seat. The stroller attachment is in the trunk, but it wouldn't be easy to push it over this gravel. Besides, I don't want Schuyler Bennett to see how little luggage I have and think it's strange that I've arrived for a six-month stay with only one suitcase. Better I get it later.

Before I close the door I grab the baby blanket lying next to the car seat. It's soaking wet. For a moment I stand holding it, trying to figure out how this happened. Did I spill that second bottle on it? Did Chloe's diaper leak on it? But when I touch her diaper it's dry. I leave the blanket on the car seat to deal with later and turn to join my new boss. She's waiting at a different door from the one she came out of. "The tower has its own entrance, so you'll have your privacy," she says, unlocking the door and limping into a narrow foyer. "This door"—she points to a door on the right—"leads into the main house. You're welcome to come through anytime, use the kitchen, sit in the parlors. Of course you'll have full access to the library on the second floor, but please make yourself at home in the rest of the house as well. It's just me and Billie rambling around like a couple of dried-out peas in a pod."

"Thank you, that's so generous . . ." I'm repeating myself. But what else can I say? *You've saved my life. I don't know what I would have done if you hadn't taken me and my baby in?*

She waves away my thanks. "Save your thanks until you see the library. When the university offered to buy my papers I knew I'd have to get someone I could trust to sort through it all." She turns around in the doorway and fixes me with a hawklike gaze. Now that we're in the light I can see how sharp the bones of her face are under her thin, papery skin. Her short silver hair barely covers her skull. She had mentioned something about being ill and now I wonder if she was in such a rush to hire me because she doesn't have much time to get her papers in order. "And I'm really thrilled to have gotten someone with your credentials."

Laurel's credentials, I think, my face going hot.

"And I'm thrilled to get a chance to work with my favorite author, Ms. Bennett." At least that part is true.

A hectic blotch appears on her face. Have I embarrassed her? She turns away to open the door. "Please, call me Sky— everyone does—and come on in. You'll see I didn't lie about the apartment being small."

The apartment *is* small, and oddly shaped since it's the bottom floor of the octagonal tower. There's a sitting area with a flowered couch and coffee table, a tiny kitchen, a bathroom, and a bedroom with a double bed. In the middle of the space is a spiral staircase that coils up to the next floor, its smooth wooden planks suspended on a skeletal iron frame that makes me feel uneasy just looking at it.

"My father saw patients here when I was a girl," Schuyler— Sky—says, as if that explained the apartment's size or its odd shape.

"He was a doctor at the hospital, right?" I ask, more to show that I remember what she told me on the phone than because I want to think about mental patients in my new home.

"The *director*," she says, as someone else might say *king* or *president*. "I'm afraid you'll have to wade through a good deal of his papers. They're all mixed up with mine and some of the records will have to go to Crantham . . . actually, I have an idea about that, but we can discuss all that tomorrow." She must see how overwhelmed I am. She never mentioned her father's papers in our conversations. The idea of going through the files of a psychiatrist makes me queasy; I've had enough of madness in the last few months to last a lifetime.

She's gone on to describe the layout of the house. "The study on the second floor of the tower connects directly to the library, which I can reach by elevator in the main house. Shall we meet there tomorrow at, say, ten? Will that give you enough time to settle in?"

I'm not sure that I'll ever "settle in" here, but I manage to say "That will be fine" in a voice that doesn't sound like my own. It must be the right voice, though, because Schuyler—*Sky*—smiles and says, "Yes, I think it will be."

It's only after she's left—hobbling out of my door and crossing the foyer to the door to the main house—that I realize why the voice hadn't sounded like my own. It's because it sounded like Laurel's voice, which I've apparently appropriated along with her credentials and name.

AFTER SCHUYLER BENNETT leaves I carry the car seat into the bedroom and put it down on the floor. Chloe stirs but stays asleep. I'm tempted to leave her in the car seat but I know that's not good for her growing limbs (*Excessive time in a car seat can put a strain on your baby's developing spine*, one parenting blog had cautioned. *Straps on car seats may cause strangulation*, another had warned). Which means I'll have to deal with the bed.

I'd told Schuyler Bennett I didn't need a crib because Chloe slept with me. I'd braced myself for a lecture on the dangers of co-sleeping, which Peter had been adamantly against, but instead got "That sounds like an eminently sane arrangement."

What I hadn't told her was that the arrangement I'd come up with in my home had involved stripping the bed of pillows, putting the mattress on the floor, and shoving it up against a wall. That won't be possible here. The bed's on a heavy cast-iron frame with peeling (no doubt lead-based) paint that I can already imagine Chloe eating. It sits squarely in the middle of the room. Even if I could budge it I'm not sure it would fit against the angled walls.

She won't fall off the bed this one night. It's the same reasonable voice I'd heard before. Laurel's voice. It scares me a little to be hearing voices again, but if I have to have a voice inside my head, Laurel's wryly sensible tone is the one I'd choose. *But then*, I hear Laurel say, *all the voices sound sensible at the time.*

I LAY CHLOE down in the middle of the bed, put a couch cushion on one side of her (after checking that it's firm enough that she can't suffocate against it), and position myself like a human parenthesis on the other. I dump the half dozen ruffled and embroidered pillows on the floor so she won't suffocate on those either. She wakes briefly and stares at me, her eyes strangely wide in the dim light of the yellow duckie night light I'd brought with us.

Like an alien, I'd thought when she first came home from the hospital, as if she'd just arrived here from another planet. Eventually I had grown used to her. I hadn't thought of her like that for weeks, but now, perhaps because we're in this strange place, she looks new to me again. Even the strawberry mark on her nose has gone. The pediatrician said it would fade away, but seeing it gone gives me a pang. How long has it been gone? What other changes have I missed? How well do I know my own baby?

But then she reaches out a chubby hand and grabs a lock of

my hair while she sucks her thumb and I feel my heart contract.

That'll ruin her teeth, some of the other mothers would say, but I'd never had the heart to deny her such an easy means of self-comfort. If it worked for me, I'd try it myself. She drifts off to sleep after a few minutes and I try to follow her. *Sleep when the baby sleeps*, all the books tell you, but what the books don't tell you is how the silence of the long nights fills with sounds imagined and real. At home it would be the stealthy footstep of a burglar, the window latch opening, the crackle of electrical wires spreading fire through the walls. I'd made poor Peter get up countless times to check for burglars and loose wires. *Aural hallucinations*, Esta told us, *are a common postpartum phenomenon and not necessarily a sign of postpartum psychosis*. Here there's the whisper of all those pine trees, the hoot of an owl—and a step on the spiral staircase.

I freeze, hold my breath, tell myself it's just the wood settling in an old house—and hear it again. I imagine those stairs coiling like a snake up to . . . what had Schuyler Bennett said was up there? A study connected to the library. I imagine the length of the old stone house stretching out. Was there a locked door between the upstairs tower floors and the rest of the house? The thought that someone could wander from the house down into my apartment was disturbing. But who could it be? Schuyler Bennett said it was just her and the housekeeper in the house and the housekeeper was away visiting grandchildren.

Then I remember the proximity of the mental hospital and hear Sky's voice. *You don't have to worry that an escaped serial killer will get out and make their way over.* Why is it that sentences that begin *You don't have to worry* are always the ones especially designed to produce exactly that effect? I can vividly

picture an escaped lunatic—a woman with a gaunt face, unkempt hair, wild eyes, and an inflamed hatred of babies—
prowling on the floor above.

Leave it, I tell myself. It was just Schuyler Bennett come to
the library to get a book—

A creak, sharp as breaking glass, strafes through my nerves.
No, it can't be Schuyler Bennett. She might be in the library,
but she couldn't manage those stairs with her limp. I hold
my breath to listen, tensing my whole body. *The reason some
women experience aural hallucinations*, Esta had gone on to
explain, *is that Mother Nature has made our hearing extra-acute
so we can hear our babies' cries in the night.*

Mother Nature is a bitch, Laurel had whispered conspiratori-
ally to me. *Why didn't she give new mothers something useful,
like larger bladders or husbands who might actually change a
diaper?*

I hadn't wanted to admit to her that Peter *did* change Chloe's
diapers or that I found Esta's explanation reassuring. Maybe it
meant I wasn't going crazy after all. Maybe—

I hear the creak again. There's definitely someone on the
stairs. I get up, careful not to disturb Chloe, and pad barefoot
into the sitting room. Light spills down the spiral stairs like
water cascading over flat stones. The stairs are empty but now
I hear another sound coming from the floor above—a ruffling
sound, like wings. Maybe there's a bird trapped in the room
above.

Once when Chloe was only a few weeks old a sparrow got
into the house. I'd taken the screen off a window to get a wasp
out—several wasps, actually. They'd made a nest under the
roof and were getting into Chloe's nursery somehow. I was terrified one would sting Chloe and she'd turn out to be allergic
and go into anaphylactic shock.

Call the exterminator, Peter told me. But I was afraid they would use chemicals that would hurt Chloe, so I'd devised a system of waiting till the wasps, drawn by the light, landed on the windowpane, at which point I'd whisk them out with a dust mop.

Then one day I forgot to close the window and a sparrow flew in. Once in the enclosed space it panicked and flew wildly back and forth, slamming into closed windows and walls. I tried to use the mop to guide it out but that just increased its panic—and mine. Every time it hit a wall or window I felt my own heart slam up against my rib cage, as frightened as that stupid bird. It didn't help that Chloe was shrieking. The sound of her crying, that damned bird flying around, it had all made me feel . . . trapped.

But I wasn't trapped, I remind myself as I start up the stairs, gripping the narrow iron banister, placing each foot carefully on the smooth, slippery wood; I'd gotten out. As I come up onto the second floor I see that the room is a windowless octagon, lined floor to ceiling with books. The only furniture is a circular table with two heavy carved chairs pulled up to it. There's a lamp on the table but it's not lit. The light and the sound are coming from the next floor.

The stairs leading up to the top of the tower are narrower and made of iron instead of wood. The spiral is so tight I feel like a snail squeezing my body into a new shell. By the time I ooze through this corkscrew I'll be contorted into its shape, molded into something new.

What I am, when I get to the top, is dizzy from going round and round. The room spins like a top—an eight-sided glass top. This is where the light was coming from. A full moon shines through the open skylight and wide plate-glass windows. When the room stops spinning I see that the view stretches for miles over hundreds of wooded acres. That sea of green on my phone has been transformed into a silver forest. I might be Rapunzel up in her high tower with only my own hair as an escape plan. It takes my breath away seeing how far I've come.

This is what you wanted, a voice says. Laurel? Myself? I can no longer tell the difference. But somehow I *can* finally breathe. I've done it. I've gotten away. I've escaped. And that sound—

I cross to a rough wood table under one of the windows. It's just a ledge really, but someone has used it for a writing desk. There's a notebook lying open, pages white in the moonlight, turning in the breeze from the open window. That's what was making the ruffling sound. Not a bird, just these pages.

Still, as I approach the book, I half expect it to dart out from under my fingertips like that damned sparrow that had finally bashed itself to death against the bars of Chloe's crib. Peter had come home to find me sitting on the floor with the dead bird in my lap, Chloe screaming in her car seat.

The image is so disturbing I look away from the book—out the window—and notice that the woods below are not unbroken. I can make out some buildings below, a stately brick Victorian structure with two wings and a clock tower at its center, the clock face glowing like a second moon. It sits in a network of meandering paths and smaller buildings. It looks like a college campus or a country club, but it must be the hospital. I stare at it for several minutes, looking for the *escaped lunatic* of my imagination, but the grounds are so quiet I would think it was deserted if not for the smattering of lit windows and pathway lamps. *Celebrity rehabs, anorexic teenagers, overworked CEOs*, I repeat to myself. All as harmless-sounding as "postpartum depression." Nothing to worry about.

I look down at the book and read the spidery script.

. . . and when she came out of the woods she found that what she carried was a senseless lump of wood . . .

It's a handwritten draft of the changeling story. Schuyler Bennett must have written it here, looking out over all these acres of woods, like the woods the girl in the story has to walk through. Like the woods I've driven through with Chloe—

Chloe. The name intrudes as insistent as a baby's cry. Suddenly I have that terrible feeling I had in the car that I have left her behind. Did I put a cushion on the other side of her before I left the room? I can't remember. What if she's rolled over and fallen off? What was I thinking, leaving her alone on a bed?

I rush down the two flights of stairs, the iron staircase shaking under my weight, the wood one groaning like a bereaved mother. I trip over the last step and go sprawling across the floor, crashing so loudly that Chloe will surely wake up.

But she doesn't.

Because she's fallen to the floor and cracked her head open.

I crawl the last few feet to the bedroom, seeing it: her dazed, lifeless eyes staring up, her fragile skull cracked open like an egg, blood matting her fine, dandelion-fluff hair—

She's there. On the floor. Unmoving. I lunge for her, a scream rising in my throat, and clutch—

—a frilly boudoir pillow. Chloe is lying on the bed, thumb in her mouth, her other hand splayed out like a pale starfish against the dark sheets. Her eyes flick open as I land too abruptly on the bed and she lets out a frightened wail. I cradle her in my arms, rocking her and crooning, "It's all right, baby, Mama's here. It's all right. It's all right."

I say it over and over again until I'm not sure who I'm trying to convince, her or me.

Daphne's Journal, June 18, 20—

This day has been like a roller coaster!

I felt much better at support group today. Esta talked about how it's normal not to bond immediately with our babies and we shouldn't feel like it made us any less of a mother. That made me feel better because to tell the truth I've been feeling guilty that Peter seems so much more attached to Chloe than I am. I mean, it was hard because she was born early and had to stay in the NICU for three weeks, and it was so scary, seeing her in that incubator with all those tubes attached to her. So I felt a lot better talking about that.

Afterward I walked back to the parking lot with Laurel. I was kind of hoping she'd suggest a playdate but then I realized she expected me to have a babysitter already. She gave me the name of one and said maybe we could have a playdate next week. I was feeling really good about that but then when I got home I found Peter sitting outside on the porch. I was terrified! It was like that moment in cop shows when the woman opens the door to policemen and *knows* her husband is dead. For one thing, ours is not a porch anyone sits on. It's a place for seasonal decorations and packages to shelter from the rain. He was sitting on a straight-backed chair he'd pulled out from the kitchen.

"What's wrong?" I asked right away. "Where's Chloe?" I tried to get past him into the house but he blocked my way.

"She's fine," he said, holding up the baby monitor. "She cried for two hours straight. I had to come out here for air."

"You left her when she was crying?"

"There wasn't anything I could do for her, so yes."

"Did you try feeding her?"

He just looked up at me, clearly exasperated. "I would have," he said slowly, as if he were talking to a child, "but you didn't leave any bottles or formula."

I knew that couldn't be true—I remembered carefully preparing two bottles and leaving them in the refrigerator—but still I felt a hot flush of shame at the thought that I'd left my baby without any food. What kind of mother does that?

Of course I immediately ran inside and opened the refrigerator, only where I thought I'd left the bottles was a container of yogurt and a half-eaten banana, which I remembered putting back after my breakfast. There were two bottles in the sink, but they were dirty and caked with curdled formula. When I opened them the smell of spoiled milk hit me in the face. They couldn't have been the bottles I made up before I left the house.

I looked in the cabinets and the pantry for formula. Hadn't I just bought a new case? It was true that I hated buying formula. I had wanted to breastfeed but because Chloe was born early the doctors said she would expend too many calories nursing. I'd tried pumping milk for a while but my nipples cracked and bled and by the time Chloe got out of the NICU she was already used to formula and the bottle.

Peter had been really nice about it. "This way I get to feed her too," he'd said. And he'd been true to his word, getting up in the middle of the night for her two A.M. feeding even when he had to be at work in the morning. I knew that the least I could do was remember to buy the formula and keep the house stocked with clean bottles.

I went into the nursery. Chloe was sleeping on her stomach in the crib, her face red and tear stained, her playsuit damp. I wanted to pick her up but I didn't want to wake her before I'd made up a bottle for her. I looked under the changing table and found a sample of powdered formula that had come with some diapers. It wasn't the brand we used but it would have to do.

I went back into the kitchen and started scrubbing the dirty bottles. Peter followed me in, leaned against a cabinet and stared at me.

"Why didn't you drive to the store and buy formula and bottles?" I asked, concentrating on washing the bottles to keep my voice steady. I never knew what might set Peter off. He'd told me once that his mother had been very critical and that whenever anyone criticized him he heard her voice. It was why he'd decided to run his own business instead of working for a company.

When he didn't answer right away, I looked over and was shocked to see that he was crying. "She was crying so hard, I didn't want to take her out," he said.

I didn't know what to say. It wasn't the first time I'd seen Peter cry. He had cried when Chloe was born. *He really loves her,* I'd thought. To be honest, I'm a teensy bit jealous of that instant attachment he made to her. There are even times when I wonder if he loves her more than I do.

I felt so bad that I kept my eyes on my hands in the sink. They were red from the hot water. "I'll bring her next time," I told Peter. "Some of the other mothers do, with their nannies."

Well, *that* was the wrong thing to say! Peter's face got as red as my hands.

Peter snorted. "Their *nannies*? Now you want a nanny?"

"I could hire a girl from the college for a few hours. Laurel says—"

"Laurel?"

Of course he wanted to know who Laurel was, so I told him she was one of the mothers from the group and that she had given me the name of a babysitter she used sometimes.

"Did she say who was going to *pay* for this babysitter?"

"It's not expensive," I said.

"You have no idea what our financial situation is," he snapped back.

That was true, sort of, though it was also because Peter didn't involve me in our financial decisions. When I first met Peter I thought he must be rich. Not that it mattered that much to me, although I *was* tired of the twentysomething hipsters who wore flannel shirts and thought grabbing a falafel from a stand was a date. Peter was older. He wore suits and took me to nice restaurants, places I'd never be able to afford on a school librarian's salary. He was the first man I dated who talked about wanting children. When he told me he ran a hedge fund I was sure he must be rich. Of course, that's what everyone thinks. But it turned out that his fund was small and he said he didn't charge a big commission because he wanted his investors to earn as much as they could so they'd recommend other investors. In time it would all pay off and we *would* be rich, but in the meantime it was important to *look* like we were doing well but not to spend unnecessarily.

I didn't want to hear this lecture again or start an argument about money. I just wanted to hold Chloe and feed her. Leaving Peter behind, I went back into the nursery. I changed her first. Her diaper was heavy and her playsuit was soaked through. She started screaming while I changed her, holding her limbs rigid with rage. I was always afraid I would drop her when she threw these tantrums so I sat on the floor with her. She wouldn't take the bottle right away and then when she did, she drank so fast she choked and spit up.

I really didn't know what to do then. Should I get up to clean her? But then I was afraid that Peter would say something about how I'd made Chloe sick. So I just used my shirt to clean her off. I rocked her until she fell asleep. I knew I should put her down in the crib. The books say you shouldn't let them fall asleep while drinking because the formula pools in their mouths and rots their teeth. They'll wake up with gas later and they'll always need to suck to fall asleep. But I knew that when I put her down I'd have to go into the living room and face Peter. We'd have to talk about why I had forgotten the bottles. This wasn't the first time I'd had a lapse like this. Since Chloe was born I've been so forgetful. I can see Peter watching me, worrying that I'm not fit to take care of Chloe. Sometimes I think he might be right.

But the big surprise came when I finally put Chloe down and came out of her nursery. Peter was in the dining room setting the table with Chinese takeout and a bottle of wine. I'm not supposed to mix alcohol with my medication, but I didn't care. The wine was his way of apologizing. He has a hard time saying he's sorry. *My mother used to make me stand up in front of everyone to make a formal apology whenever I made the smallest mistake.* One of the reasons he wanted children, he'd told me on our first date, was that he wanted to be a better parent than his parents had been. I understood that all too well.

So really what this whole episode has taught me is that I should be grateful for having a husband who cares so much about being a good father. Some of the women in the group said their husbands won't even change a diaper. I should have apologized for forgetting to leave the bottles. I should have told him that it wasn't the first thing I'd forgotten and that maybe there is something really wrong with me—but before I could say any of that he held up the big shapeless woven bag I use both as a baby bag and my handbag. I hadn't gone anywhere without Chloe for so long they'd become one and the same.

"Look what I found in your bag," he said holding it open for me to see.

I didn't need to see. I could smell it. Sour formula. I'd put the two bottles I'd made up in my bag instead of leaving them in the refrigerator. As I leaned over the open bag I could see myself doing it. Preparing the bottles and putting them in the bag as I'd do when I was taking Chloe to the park or a doctor's appointment.

I looked up at Peter and saw he was grinning. "I guess this was your subconscious telling you that you didn't want to leave Chloe behind."

"I guess . . ." I was going to tell him there's something wrong with me, that maybe I shouldn't be on my own with Chloe, but then he held up a piece of paper. It had Laurel Hobbes's name on it and the name and number of the babysitter she had recommended.

"I called your friend's babysitter. She's going to come with you to your next group meeting. If you like her, maybe we could see about having her come a few days a week."

For a moment I just stared at him, wondering if he'd called the babysitter because he knows that there's something really wrong with me and he doesn't want to leave me alone with Chloe. But then I realized I was just being paranoid. He was trying to do something nice for me, to take off some of the pressure of being a new mother. And a babysitter *will* help. I won't have to worry about being on my own with Chloe and I can spend time with Laurel. I need a friend—another mother—to talk to. Which reminds me—I should set up that playdate!

LATER.

Like I said, this afternoon has been a real roller coaster. I went from being so scared when I saw Peter on the stairs to being angry at him that he left Chloe to cry, to ashamed that I'd left him without bottles. Esta says it's normal to feel these emotional swings postpartum. It's just hormones. Well, hormones or not, now I feel really happy. I texted Laurel to thank her for recommending the babysitter. I added (casually) that I hoped we could hang out after group next week. She texted me right back with three emojis: a crying baby, a glass of wine, and a happy face. I think that means yes!

Chapter Three

We both sleep through the night. It's the longest I can remember sleeping since giving birth—since months before, actually. I'd started having trouble sleeping when I was pregnant. The books said that was normal; pressure on the bladder, hormone surges, anxiety about the birth could all be causes. But the books hadn't said anything about feeling invaded, as if an alien vampire were sipping the blood from my veins. And I didn't feel comfortable saying *that* to my obstetrician, who'd already prescribed me antidepressants when Peter told him I cried all the time.

After Chloe was born I was afraid if I really gave myself up to sleep I would wake to find her dead. That's how all the stories I read on the Internet went—*I had my first good sleep since the baby was born and when I went into the nursery she wasn't breathing*—

Shouldn't I be worried about that now?

But I'm not. Even though in the dim light I can't really see her color, or hear her breathing over the patter of rain on the windows, I believe that Chloe is breathing. She seems . . . *heartier* to me, less vulnerable, and I suddenly realize why. It's because I'm thinking of her as Laurel's Chloë and I don't think anything bad could happen to *her*.

Chloe stirs and opens her eyes, blinking at me as if I'm the stranger, her mouth working. Before she can cry—I don't want Sky Bennett awoken the first morning to a crying baby—I snatch her up. "It's all right, baby, let's get you changed."

She seems startled to be swept up into the air. I sway-walk her into the sitting room and balance her on my hip while I mix the formula and microwave her bottle. While the bottle is warming I take her on a tour of the sitting room. There's not much to see: a faded overstuffed chintz couch, a rocking chair, a coffee table strewn with a few local magazines with names like *Cabin* and *Country* clearly meant for weekenders from the city. I try to sit down in the rocking chair but abandon it as Chloe begins to squirm. This room is suffocating; she needs fresh air.

I grab the bottle out of the microwave and open the door— and am startled as the facing door swings open at the same time.

The first thing I notice about the woman in the doorway is her size. She's easily six feet tall and well over two hundred pounds. In her plaid flannel shirt and jeans she could be a lumberjack, but no lumberjack on the planet would have that haircut. It's a horrible cut for a woman of her size—or for any woman over six years old, for that matter. Chopped to a point that falls between chin and ears, fanning to the sides like the pages of a waterlogged book, and clipped back in two strips that show gray streaks and dark roots beneath a cheap orangey dye. She is not what I would have imagined when Sky said she had a housekeeper named Mrs. Williams, but that must be who she is because she's stretching out her arms toward Chloe while making a high-pitched sound meant, I think, to be encouraging.

I tighten my grip on Chloe and remember an image from a dream. Not my dream, but one Laurel said she had repeatedly when Chloë (*her* Chloë) was born. *I'm in a mental hospital and they've come to take Chloë away from me. A nurse stretches out her arms and they keep growing, moving toward me even as the nurse herself stays perfectly still, it's just those awful rubbery arms coming to snatch Chloë away from me. And I know once they do, I'll never see her again.*

The woman has the air and capable, no-nonsense manner of a nurse, and I have the horrible thought that she has come from the mental hospital to take Chloe away from me because I am unfit. It's all I can do to keep myself from backing away and slamming the door in the woman's face. Instead I say, "She's a little shy of strangers."

"Oh, she won't be shy of Billie," the woman—Billie, I'm guessing—croons. She comes closer and scoops Chloe right out of my arms. I brace myself for a scream but Chloe only stares up at the big woman. "There, you see!" Billie's looking at Chloe but clearly talking to me. "Babies love me. And I bet you need a bit of a break after the long drive up here."

She tears her eyes away from Chloe to give me a quick once-over. "Why don't you have a nice soak while I give little missy here her breakfast." She plucks the bottle out of my hand, efficient and bossy like the nurses in the NICU when Chloe was born. "Miss Bennett will be waiting upstairs for you in the library when you're ready."

Without waiting for an answer Billie turns and leaves me standing in the doorway, my arms empty and curiously light.

BILLIE IS RIGHT that I need to clean up, but when I go into the bathroom I'm startled to see that the big claw-foot tub has no shower attachment. I don't really like taking baths—have avoided them since I fell asleep and nearly drowned in one once—but there's no choice. I turn on the taps and watch the water rise with a sick sense of apprehension, as if the water might leap over the edge of the tub and drag me down into its depths.

It does feel good, though, when I finally lower myself in. I soak away all the days of grime and fear, scrubbing at my skin with the brand-new loofah and rosemary-mint soap that's been left for me. The only scary moment is when I tip my head back to wash my hair and my ears fill with a roaring that sounds like someone screaming. For a moment, I can't move. My limbs feel frozen. I'm convinced I'll drown in here.

I come up gasping for air, splashing water over the rim of the tub. I use a chipped China ewer to rinse my hair after that. I pour scalding-hot water over my head again and again until my hair is clean and the last echo of that scream is gone.

Only when I'm wrapped in a towel do I remember that all my clothes are still in the trunk of the car. I can't bear the thought of putting my discarded dirty clothes back on, so I wrap myself up in a terry robe that's hanging on the back of the bathroom door. There's a pair of slippers too. I feel like I've come to a spa, one of those places that Laurel was always talking about. *We'll get the husbands to watch the babies and go to Canyon Ranch for a weekend.*

When I come out into the living room I find that my suitcase and stroller have been brought in. Which means I forgot to lock the car last night.

I have a moment of panic. Was there anything in the car that would give away my identity? I borrowed the suitcase from Laurel, so it has her monogram on it. LSH. Laurel Sutton Hobbes. The car *is* registered in my name but I've hidden the registration, along with my license and passport, at the bottom of Chloe's diaper bag inside a package of Huggies.

I look for the diaper bag and realize it's gone. Billie must have come in and taken it. Of course she'd need diapers for Chloe. How could I have been so stupid! If she uses that pack of Huggies, she'll find Daphne Marist's driver's license, registration, and passport—along with the packet of papers I took from Peter's desk. God knows what she'd make of that! She'll take it all to Schuyler Bennett, who will only have to make a few phone calls to determine that the woman sleeping in her guesthouse isn't who she says she is. She'll kick me out and probably call the police.

I'm starting to sweat under the terry robe. I strip it off and get dressed. The clothes I packed only a few days ago feel foreign to me—creased and stale smelling and too big. I must have lost weight since I packed, I tell myself, but still they feel like they belong to someone else. Someone who actually thought she could get away with this preposterous ruse.

I look at my watch and see it's nearly ten. Should I go up to the second floor to keep my appointment with Sky Bennett or should I grab Chloe and get the hell out of here? But where on earth will I go? Back to Peter? He'll take Chloe from me. He'll sue for divorce and full custody. He'll have me declared an unfit mother. He could even have me arrested for kidnapping.

So I climb the spiral stairs, around and around, like a rat on a wheel. When I come up into the second floor of the tower I find Sky Bennett sitting at the table, a china teacup at her elbow and papers spread out in front of her. I'm so certain I've been found out that I fully expect to see my own license and passport and the packet I took from Peter's desk, but when I get closer I see that these pages are yellowed with age and the photos scattered among them are sepia-toned. They're from a past older than mine.

At the sound of my step, Sky looks up. "There you are. I hope you slept well. You *look* worlds better. Billie says your baby is a treat. She's taken her out for a walk in the stroller so we'll have plenty of time. I hope you don't mind if we get started right away. I've been up since dawn looking through old things. I thought we'd get the *juvenilia* out of the way. Tiresome as it may be, it's the underpinning. It's what makes us who we are, isn't it?"

I see, as I pull out a chair, that she's really expecting an answer. What in the world am I supposed to say? I think of what my childhood and Peter's made us into. Peter's parents were so strict that he's a bit of a perfectionist. And I grew up with an alcoholic single mother, so of course I've made a botch of being a mother myself. But then I remember a line from one of Sky's books. "It's the stories we tell about ourselves that make us who we are," I say.

Schuyler Bennett's face lights up. "Oh, I did know you were the right one for the job! Sit down and let me tell you a story."

Daphne's Journal, June 25, 20—

I am in love!

A few years ago the object of my affection would have been the latest in the string of underemployed actor/bartender/ losers I dated before I met Peter, but today it's the nineteen-year-old sophomore Vanessa Lieb, whom Laurel recommended to babysit. She's made everything so much easier. First of all, she immediately reorganized Chloe's diaper bag.

"You should get one like Laurel's," she told me. "It has all the right pockets."

The right pockets! Who knew that was all I needed to make motherhood manageable!

Then she changed Chloe and got her in her car seat so I could "get myself ready" for group. I'd actually thought I *was* ready, but I used those ten minutes to brush my hair and change the shirt Chloe had spit up on for something a little nicer—a floaty gauze top I ordered last week from Anthropologie. I hid the package from Peter when it came because he's been going on about money again, but really, I *need* some new clothes. I still don't fit into my pre-pregnancy stuff and I'm sick to death of my maternity clothes. Anyway, the top was on sale and Laurel was wearing something like it last week, so . . .

I felt so much better freshened up and I didn't have to worry about getting spit up on again because Vanessa got Chloe out of the car seat too. She knows Laurel's babysitter, so she waved at her in the parking lot and they went to take the babies to the park while Laurel and I went into group.

The other mothers were talking about how forgetful they've been and I was going to tell the story about forgetting the bottles last week, but I felt a little embarrassed. But Laurel talked about how forgetful she'd been lately and I thought if someone as put-together as Laurel could admit to being "a little out of it" I could tell the story of the bottles. And then another mother told about how she sat through a whole luncheon with her nursing flaps unbuttoned and her tits hanging out and we all laughed. "It's mommy brain," Esta said. "A perfectly natural response to fluctuations in hormones." What a relief it was to hear her say that!

It really helps to hear other moms' stories so I don't feel so crazy and alone. There was even a mother who said that she heard voices sometimes, telling her things. You could have heard a pin drop in the room.

"Well, what do the voices say?" Esta finally asked.

"Don't forget to sterilize the baby bottles; don't drink coffee before you nurse, those kind of things."

We all breathed a sigh of relief. "Well," Esta said, "it sounds like a very sensible sort of voice."

"Sure," Laurel whispered in my ear. "All the voices sound sensible at the time."

I had to keep myself from laughing!

Afterward we all piled into Laurel's Lexus SUV and went back to her house and guess what? Laurel lives in our neighborhood. Her house even looks a lot like ours. When I commented on it she said, "Isn't it awful? All these ticky-tacky suburban boxes. I never thought I'd end up living in Westchester."

"Me neither!" I said, not mentioning that it was a lot fancier than anyplace I thought I'd ever live. Her house is fixed up a lot nicer on the inside than ours is. Everything's done in pale sand and bone colors. There's even white carpeting, which I'd be terrified of getting dirty but maybe Chloë (I found out that Laurel spells it with an umlaut. I told her I'd thought about using one but I was afraid all her teachers would resent it) doesn't spend much time in the living room. Laurel sent Va-

about it and gave me another glass of wine. It turns out we have so much in common! We're both orphans, for instance. Of course, I never knew my father and my mother died driving home drunk from the Dew Drop Inn on Route 9 and her parents died when their private jet crashed into the Alps as they were returning from a ski trip to Gstaad, but still the end results were the same. As Laurel said, *We were both alone in the world so we latched onto men who promised security.*

Of course, her parents left her a gazillion-dollar trust fund and my mother left me a closet full of tacky dresses and her collection of feathered roach clips, but still . . . we even both went to library school. I got my library degree at SUNY Albany and worked at a school library and she got her undergraduate degree at St. Andrews and her *archival* degree at the University of Edinburgh, then interned at the National Library of Scotland. But as Laurel put it: *Quelle surprise! We both wanted to put the world in order after it had fallen to pieces.*

We're practically the same person! We even look a little alike—at least, Laurel thinks so. I mean, I'm not as tall or thin and my hair isn't as blond, but when I pointed all that out Laurel said, "So the only difference between us is heels, a good colorist, and a couple of baby pounds?" Which made me laugh.

I even told her the story about the bird that got trapped in Chloe's nursery and she said, "Well, of course you freaked out! It made you realize how trapped you feel being saddled with a baby!"

We had so much to talk about, we totally lost track of time and Vanessa had to remind me that she had to get back. Laurel called a taxi for us and while we were waiting for it her husband, Stan, came back. And that's something else we have in common; we both married older men. I think Stan might even be older than Peter—he certainly *looks* older but maybe that's

nessa and Simone (that's Laurel's nanny—she's actual
France! Only Laurel would have an actual French au pai
the playroom, where there are a gazillion toys, most of
are way too old for our four-month-olds, so we could have
"mommy time" to ourselves.

We sat on a big white couch and we talked about everyth
It's been so long since I talked to anyone like that—not si
college, when we'd all stay up late in our dorm rooms talk
about books and the meaning of life. Laurel and I didn't ta
about the meaning of life, though. We started by telling eac
other our labor stories. Laurel had a really bad time because
she had morning sickness, then preeclampsia, and had to be
on bed rest and they had to induce labor. I told her about how
Chloe came early and how scary it was. When I told her how
the doctor had said right in the middle of my labor that she
might end up with cerebral palsy Laurel said, *What an asshole!*
Which sort of shocked me because I hadn't thought of it like
that. I told her how guilty I felt because I'd worked through my
pregnancy and I was on my feet a lot.

"Well, whose fault was that?" she asked. "Whose decision
was it to keep working?"

I started out telling her how Peter and I had both agreed
it was best I work until my delivery so I wouldn't be dipping
into my maternity leave, but then she asked me what Peter did
for a living and when I told her he managed a hedge fund she
laughed. I started explaining about "low fees" and it being a
small fund, and how Peter had had such a strict upbringing he
was really nervous about money, but she just shook her head
and said, "Bullshit, he just sounds cheap. I'm sure there's plenty
of money. You have to stand up for yourself. Look at where giving in got you."

Which made me cry a little. But she was really, really nice

because he dresses more old-fashioned. He seemed nice and he didn't get mad that we were sitting around drinking wine in the middle of the day while the sitters took care of the babies. He seemed to find it funny and he even offered to give Chloë her bath.

I had the taxi drop Vanessa off at her apartment first so it was really late by the time we got home. When I saw Peter's car in the driveway I was worried that he was going to be mad that I'd left the car in the church lot and that I was late and dinner wasn't ready and the house was a mess. And sure enough the minute I walked in he started in with *Why are you late?* and *Where's the car?* I was about to say I was sorry but then I thought about what Laurel said about it being Peter's fault I'd worked through my pregnancy and about men being cheap so instead of apologizing I said, "This is the first friend I've made since Chloe was born and I really like her, so please don't ruin it."

His eyes got big and I thought he was going to explode, but instead he said, "I was just afraid something had happened to you and Chloe. I've been sitting here imagining you driving off the road or driving onto the train tracks like that woman in Valhalla last year. I've had the news on to listen for any traffic accidents. Then when the I saw the taxi pull up . . ." He turned away.

So then I felt really bad. It must have been scary for Peter when I got so depressed after Chloe was born and now to see me so forgetful. And it *was* a terrible story about that poor woman who drove onto the train tracks by mistake—not half an hour from where we lived!

I told him I was sorry and that I'd never forget to call him if I was late again. I also made a mental note to myself to avoid train crossings from now on.

Chapter Four

At first I am so worried about Billie finding those papers in the diaper bag that I can barely pay attention to what Sky Bennett is telling me, but as she launches into the story of her childhood I get so caught up in it that I forget all about Billie finding my ID and exposing me as Daphne Marist. I forget all about Daphne Marist and Laurel Hobbes altogether. I guess that's what a really good story does—it makes you forget about yourself for a while.

And Sky's is such an amazing story—like something out of Dickens! Her father was the director of Crantham from the late forties through the early seventies. They moved here from New York City.

"Imagine what a shock that must have been for my mother! One minute swanning through teas and dinner parties on the Upper East Side and the next stuck up here in the wilderness."

I'm having a harder time imagining living on the Upper East Side, but I don't say so.

"But in those days a wife went where her husband's job took her, and this was an important opportunity for my father. It's hard to remember now that everyone's on Prozac that in those days the only place for the mentally ill was in the big hospitals—

many of which were just awful. Little more than prison work-houses! But Crantham was different. It was founded in the 1870s on the principles of 'moral treatment' for the mentally ill. Have you seen the grounds yet?"

. The question startles me and for a minute I think she's try-ing to catch me out in a lie—that I'm not who I say I am—but then I remember the view from the tower. "I went up to the tower last night and saw the grounds from there. It looks like a college campus . . . or a country club."

"Exactly!" she says, clearly pleased. "The grounds were de-signed by Calvert Vaux and Frederick Law Olmsted." She pauses, as if waiting to see if I recognize the names. I recog-nize Olmsted, but it takes me a moment to realize that the per-son she is calling Calvert *Vox* was the one I'd always thought of as Calvert *Voe.*

"Didn't they design Central Park?" I say, thinking this is something Laurel would know.

"Yes," Sky says, giving me an odd look. Maybe it's so obvi-ous that I shouldn't have said anything. I'd noticed that with Laurel sometimes, like you were supposed to know that the Orbit stroller was the one to buy but you weren't supposed to bring up the fact that Kim Kardashian and Kanye West had one. Maybe Calvert Vaux and Frederick Law Olmsted were the Kimye of their day. "The founders of Crantham wanted their patients to enjoy the same restful environs as Central Park. There was a croquet lawn and dairy farm, a chapel and a little theater. It was like a quaint English village. I loved running around it."

"You had access to the grounds?" I ask. "Wasn't that danger-ous? I mean, they were still mental patients."

Sky gives me a reproving look. Should I not have said *mental patients?* What else am I supposed to call them? "My father felt very strongly about setting an example of trust and community. He actually wanted to live on the grounds, but my mother drew the line there so my father had this house renovated for us. My father had a path built that went directly down to the grounds and he installed a back gate—I'll have Billie show it to you later; it's been years since I was able to navigate it—and I would follow him down every day. When he was treating patients, I'd go see the cows in the dairy and talk to my favorite patients. There was a famous poet who left poems for me in secret hiding places and an old woman who believed she was Marie Antoinette, who taught me French, and an artist who painted my portrait . . ." Her eyes glaze over for a moment as if she is seeing her younger self, and then she jerks herself to attention and begins rifling through the papers. "Here—" She extracts a sepia-toned photo of a group of men and women decked out like Russian peasants dancing around a Maypole. "That's from the Founder's Day Fete and this"—she plucks a printed program from the pile—"is from the Annual Dance. As you can see it was a very fairy-tale atmosphere."

"And therefore important to your formation as a writer," I say.

She smiles, my Vaux-Olmsted gaffe forgiven. "So you see why I'd like all these documents included with my papers." She waves a crabbed hand behind her and I take in the stack of file boxes that I hadn't noticed when I came in. There must be at least twenty.

I pause, confused. Hadn't she said last night that she wanted her father's papers to go to the hospital? I don't recall her saying anything about organizing them as part of her papers. But then maybe I've misunderstood or forgotten something she said. I feel a flush of heat in my cheeks, followed by an icy prickling across my scalp. What if all those baby hormones have washed out all my brain cells, and I'm not actually capable of doing this job? I can feel her waiting for my response, the silence growing heavy.

When in doubt, repeat what's been said to you, Laurel once told me. *People love to hear their own words.*

"You want me to include your father's papers in yours?" I say, making it halfway between a question and a statement.

"Yes," she says, smiling.

I return her smile, my equilibrium regained, and ask, "Is there anything in particular that you want me to focus on?"

She sorts through the pages on the table and picks out a formal portrait of a middle-aged man wearing a dark suit and sitting stiffly at a desk with a bookshelf and a bust of Freud behind him. He has the same square face and light eyes as Sky, but on him the features look even more intimidating. "I would like my father's legacy preserved," she says. "People today . . . they hear 'mental asylum' and they picture *One Flew over the Cuckoo's Nest* or something out of a Tennessee Williams play. They see the man who ran such a place as a soulless bureaucrat. I'd like to tell a different story about him."

"I understand completely," I say. It's the truth. I understand, better than I could say, wanting to rearrange the facts to tell a different story.

When Sky leaves I stare at the stacks of boxes and realize I have no idea what an archivist does. I was a school librarian. I specialized in knowing the titles of every Judy Blume book ever written, reshelving the Nancy Drews in series order, and retaping the bindings of the Twilight books. My Intro to Library Science class had covered the archiving of private libraries as a career option but our professor said such positions were rare so I didn't take the follow-up class. There was nothing rare about me.

Not like Laurel, who had gone on from her archival degree at the University of Edinburgh to work as an assistant to the rare books librarian at the National Library of Scotland. She'd spent a summer cataloguing the private library of a laird in Perthshire . . . *recording every boring letter his grandfather had written about fishing on the Tay*, she had told me. *I had to record what box it came from, what it said, if it mentioned anyone famous, then store it in an acid-free folder, and then make a directory . . .*

I try to remember more details, but I can't. But I do recall Laurel saying she used a software package for archivists. Maybe I could download it.

I take out my laptop and the first thing I see on my desktop is a program called ArchAngel: "A Complete Data Management Program for Archivists." *Eureka!* I feel like shouting. Laurel told me about the program when I started asking her questions about what archivists did, but I'd forgotten that she had downloaded it for me. She'd even included her own files. All I have to do is follow the system she used for the laird in Perthshire.

I make a new file for Schuyler Bennett. When I save it I look back at the desktop at the folder labeled "journal." That's the journal I'd started keeping in the mothers' support group, as per Esta's advice. I was so dutiful about keeping it, as if writing everything down could keep my fears at bay.

I open the journal to the last entry I wrote, just yesterday. It seems so long ago that I was sitting in my driveway, typing furiously before I went in to collect Chloe and leave. I picture myself walking up the front path to my door and, just like last night in the car, my mind shies away from it. Like there was something I don't want to remember—

Leave it, I tell myself. Now is not the right time. If Sky comes back I have to look like I've made a start. I have to look like I know what I'm doing. I have to look like *Laurel*.

I haul the first box onto the table. It's sealed with packing tape, and scrawled across the top is *Crantham Retreat 1948*. I stare at the old name for several moments thinking that's what I've found here—a retreat. Then I go to find a knife.

The first box is full of bound notebooks all with the same leather covers, stamped with an insignia of a tower that resembles this tower. When I flip through them I find that they're all full of the same old-fashioned script.

I select one to read more carefully. The date on the first page is August 21, 1951.

> M.E. responding quite well to E.C.T. therapy. Plan to continue course of treatment for six more weeks.
>
> H.J. exhibiting signs of paranoia again. Delusion that he is being held in a German concentration camp persists. Query: Better to play along with delusion or confront patient with reality?
>
> Dinner of roast beef, asparagus, and potatoes. B. continues to complain of isolation. If only she had as much to engage her as I do! Suggestion that she run a knitting circle with the patients met with scorn. "Do you want me to end up with a needle in my eye?" she asked. Suggested basket weaving but she responded she'd rather stick a needle in her own eye. Query: Why do women make everything so difficult?

So Morris Bennett had his own difficulties at home. "B." must be Sky's mother (I make a note to look up her full name). The dry, amused tone corresponds to the picture Sky drew of him, as does the unhappy wife. I couldn't help but sympathize with her, being relocated to a new home all while trying to please a finicky husband. I remember when we first moved in together Peter picked at everything I did, from how I folded towels to how I put glasses away in the cabinet, but he would always phrase it as a suggestion.

Don't you think these towels would look neater if you folded them in thirds? Wouldn't you spend less time rewashing glasses if you put them back top down so they don't get dusty? If Dr. Bennett was anything like that, I don't blame her for thinking about putting a needle in someone's eye!

I begin ordering the books by date, writing the date of the first entry and the last on a slip of paper that I insert in each one. I catch stray remarks as I do, observations on the progress and regression of Dr. Bennett's patients (always designated by initials), dinner menus, weather reports (a lot of blizzards), and the continued sparring of husband and wife—which the doctor hoped would be solved by the birth of their first child.

> I can only hope that B. will find the occupation and comfort in a child that she has failed to find in me.

I flip through to find the entry for Sky's birth and find it on December 28, 1953, the final entry of that journal.

> After twenty hours of difficult labor B. was delivered of a baby girl. Mother and child are doing well, although B. understandably much exhausted and confused from the sedation. Have suggested we christen the child with B.'s name in the hope it will endear the child to her.

What a strange thing to say, I think. Why was he afraid that his wife wouldn't love their new baby? And why did he think giving her the same name would help? It must be a male thing. Peter said that if we had a boy he'd like to name him Peter, but I never in a million years wanted another Daphne. It would have felt like the baby had taken everything from me, including my name!

Abandoning my record keeping, I search through the journals for the next one, curious to know if Morris Bennett's fears were grounded. But there's no journal that begins in January 1954. The next in chronology I find begins in March of 1954. Either one's been lost or Dr. Bennett took a pause in writing. That's surprising after the years of regular entries but not as shocking as the first entry. Gone is the dry, reserved tone.

> B. continues to worsen. She has become obsessed with the notion that the baby is not her own. She believes that I have switched our child with one belonging to one of my patients. I can only conclude that these delusions are a result of puerperal insanity. I've engaged a nurse in the village to take care of the child and another to watch B. when I am not able to. I am afraid that if this goes on I will have to admit B. to the hospital, but I am reluctant to because of how it will reflect on my authority. Even though it is clear that she is raving I do not relish the thought of my staff hearing her accusations that I have impregnated one of my patients and foisted it upon her. I can only hope that this delusion is a temporary one and that B. will accept our child as her own. Meanwhile, the child's piteous wailing seems to follow me everywhere I go

in the house, even to the top of the tower, which seems to
act as a funnel for the sound.

The description of a baby's cries funneled through the tower
is so eerie that I can almost hear it. I look up from Morris
Bennett's journal and realize I *do* hear it—the sound of a baby
crying as if it had been preserved in the tower over the years—

Or Chloe is somewhere in the house crying for me. How
long have I been here?

I look at my watch and see it's after noon. Two hours that
I've dreamed away over Morris Bennett's journals, not even
once thinking about Chloe. It feels like a disloyalty. After all,
how much do I know about Mrs. Williams? What kind of a
mother gives her child over to a woman she's met for all of five
minutes? How do I even know that the woman who showed
up at my door this morning *is* Mrs. Williams? Maybe she's an
escaped patient with a fixation on babies.

The crying grows louder. I can't tell where it's coming
from. Morris Bennett was right—the tower *is* like a funnel
for sound. I get up and turn in a circle, not sure what direction
to go in. Down the stairs to my apartment? But as I approach
the spiral stairs the sound grows fainter. It must be coming
from the main house.

I push open the door and find myself in a long book-lined
corridor that stretches into the shadows, like a corridor in bad
dreams that goes on forever. That's another of Laurel's dreams.
In this one she's put Chloë down in a room in an enormous
house and then forgets where the room is. She wanders down
the long corridors, hearing her crying, unable to find her. Just
as I do now, groping my way down the dim hallway, trailing my
hand along the ribbed book spines until I reach a wide staircase. The crying is definitely coming from downstairs. I head

down, the wooden steps creaking under my feet. The stairwell is paneled entirely in the same dark honey-colored wood, as if it had been carved out of the surrounding forests. It smells like pine and woodsmoke.

I pause at the foot of the stairs, listening for the sound of crying, but it has become unnaturally quiet, as if the house is holding its breath. I look into a parlor full of faded chintz settees and divans drowsing in mote-filled patches of sunlight like big cats. This must be the parlor I'm "welcome to use" but it doesn't look like anyone has used it for years. Even the faces looking out of the framed photographs on the tables and the oil portraits on the walls look as if they're uncomfortable. As if they are patients waiting for a doctor. One face in particular draws me over the threshold. It's a portrait hanging over the mantel of a young woman painted in bright primary colors. It's jarringly modern for this old-fashioned room. The face, while beautiful, is painted in broad, primitive strokes of green, yellow, red, and blue, each feature somehow separate from the rest as if they might fly apart into a dozen separate pieces. At the bottom someone has written "For Elizabeth, my girl of many faces." Elizabeth, I recall, is Sky's mother's name. Perhaps this was done by a family friend, which explains its place of pride over the mantel. The woman in it does look familiar—

The cry wrenches my attention away from the painted face and all the faces in the framed photographs look at me reprovingly, as if to say, *Why are you dillydallying here while your baby cries?*

I follow the cry down another hall and through a swinging door into a bright, modern kitchen. Billie is standing at the counter straining carrots through a sieve and Chloe is ensconced in a bouncy chair. She waves her arms in the air at the sight of me and I go straight to her, feeling a queasy mixture of relief and guilt. "Mommy's here," I say, scooping her into my arms and pressing her to my chest. "Don't cry, Mommy's here." But there's no need to tell her that; she isn't crying, at least not now. To Billie I add, "You should have come and gotten me if she was crying." As soon as I say it I hear the echo of Laurel's voice chiding Simone in the parking lot.

But Billie doesn't look offended by my sharp tone, she only looks confused. "I would have," she says, "but she hasn't cried all morning."

Daphne's Journal, July 7, 20—

Laurel was right that all I had to do was be more honest with Peter; everything has been much better since I told him how important Laurel's friendship is to me. Really, it was all my fault. Peter's been nothing but loving and supportive since Chloe was born; how could I expect him to know what I wanted when I didn't know myself? I can't even blame him for not hiring a babysitter, because I'd told him I hadn't wanted one. I mean, that was because when he first suggested it I thought he was criticizing me for not being able to take care of Chloe myself. But now I see how paranoid that sounds and how much better it is to have some help. Peter even said I could have Vanessa watch Chloe so I could go out to lunch with Laurel. And he wasn't mad when Laurel suggested I join her health club, even though it's way more expensive than the gym I used to belong to.

"It's important you look and feel your best," Peter said.

Which made me realize I've really let myself go. I still haven't lost all the weight I gained while I was pregnant. Peter hasn't said anything about it, except once when he said he was just a little disappointed because I'd been so fit when we met. When I told Laurel that, she said that was a really passive-aggressive thing for him to say and what did he expect? *Pregnancy is like having an alien take up residence in your body.* But then I told her it wasn't really Peter's fault because I had never told him how hard I used to work to stay thin, running three miles a day, counting calories, measuring portions. I had to give up running when I started spotting in my second trimester and my OB/GYN said I had to eat more. I still feel guilty that my running and being underweight might have caused Chloe to be premature. But once I stopped counting and measuring everything I kind of went a little overboard. And then after Chloe was born

I just felt so overwhelmed and the medication the doctor gave me makes me feel so bloated and groggy.

"What you need is to feel in control again," Laurel told me.

So we've been going to Laurel's health club every morning. It's so relaxing! We take a yoga class and then run on the tread-mills and get massages from this dreamy guy named Bjorn and then have lunch in the café. I always order exactly what Laurel is having because I figure, hey, it's working for her! At first I was a little shocked at how little she ate—kale salad with sunflower seeds and plain hot water with lemon juice—but then she told me that the antidepressants *she's* on actually suppress her appetite. She gave me a bottle so I could ask my doctor about prescribing them and left a few in it so I could try them. Now I don't feel hungry at all! I've lost 5.2 pounds and I have so much more energy! I don't even mind when Chloe wakes me up at night, it's like I really don't need that much sleep anymore.

We usually go straight back to Laurel's house after the gym to play with "the two Chloes" as Laurel calls them, but today Laurel took me to her hair salon. She said I needed a new haircut to go with my new figure. She spent a lot of time talking to the stylist and colorist about what would look good on me. I'd always just gotten a blunt cut because I don't like the feeling of hair hanging around my face, but Laurel said a little layering would give me a lift and I would get used to it. "Just you wait," she said, "a good haircut is better than an antidepressant."

And she was right! The minute I saw myself I felt like a new person.

She was right about something else too. We really do look alike. Especially with my new haircut. We could be twins!

Chapter Five

I search Billie's bland and guileless face for any sign of deception and find none. Then I look at Chloe. She has the kind of fair skin that blotches when she cries, but her plump cheeks are as smooth and unblemished as a porcelain doll's face.

"I thought I heard . . ." I begin.

"Were you in the tower?" Billie asks, filling a spoon with bright-orange strained carrots. I'm so distraught that I don't even mention that I haven't started giving Chloe solid food yet.

"Y-yes," I answer. Where else would I be? Wasn't that where I was supposed to be?

Billie nods and holds the spoon to Chloe's lips. Chloe purses her mouth like a baby bird. "There are strange sounds in the tower. When the wind blows it plays those spiral stairs like a xylophone."

"I heard a baby crying, not a xylophone."

Billie smiles at Chloe and makes a chirping sound that makes Chloe chortle. "It can sound like a baby. Dr. Bennett saw a patient there once—a poor distracted soul—who said she could hear her lost baby crying. She was sure they were keeping her baby in the tower. One night she escaped—"

"Escaped? How?" I demand, alarmed that my vision of an escaped lunatic might be a real possibility.

"Don't worry," Billie says, hearing the panic in my voice, "this was back in the seventies; they've improved security since then. And this woman was crafty. She waited for the guard at the back gate to turn around and she clobbered him over the head."

"She was able to overpower him?"

"Madwomen have surprising strength," Billie answers placidly, all the while smiling at Chloe and making encouraging faces to keep her eating. "Especially a woman who thinks her baby's life is at stake. See, she'd developed the delusion that Dr. Bennett was experimenting on her baby—ridiculous, of course; Dr. Bennett was a saint!—but you can see where the idea came from. Imagine if you were surrounded by men in white coats always probing, asking questions, dispensing drugs and electric shock—"

"Electric shock? They gave that to women who—"

"Had the baby blues?" Billie says, her face still arranged in the cheerful expression she'd assumed for Chloe's benefit. It makes her seem as if she thinks electric shock was a treat. "When I worked at the hospital . . ."

"Wait. You worked at the hospital?"

"Why, yes," she says, looking surprised I didn't know. "Didn't Sky tell you? I was a volunteer there before I went to nursing school. Dr. Bennett noticed me and helped me pay for nursing school and then to get my first job . . . anyway, what was I saying? Oh yes, the way they treated the patients back then . . . it wasn't always a pretty sight. Especially what happened to this poor soul. They gave her so many electric shock treatments she forgot her own name. No wonder she became deranged and began to imagine that they were experimenting on her baby."

I shudder. In my worst moments I hadn't imagined any-thing so diabolical—only now I *do* imagine it: a helpless infant strapped to an operating table, a white-coated doctor approach-ing with a scalpel—

Leave it!

I shake myself to get rid of the awful picture but it has lodged there now, a piece of grit that will grow inside my brain.

Billie smiles at my expression. "So you see how she was driven to get out and search the tower. She hit the guard over the head—poor old Herb Marcus, he was never the same afterward—and made her way up the back path to the house . . ."

I see it as Billie tells the story: the madwoman from my imaginings last night, unkempt, hair loose and matted, wild eyes, bare feet—*surely they gave them shoes in the asylum,* a reproving voice points out—creeping up the hill toward the tower, all the while hearing her baby's cries. I see her finding her way in through the downstairs apartment where Chloe and I are living and climbing the spiral stairs, turning around and around in a tight coil as convoluted as her own mad delusions, hearing her baby's cries all around her in the wind and the creak of the spiral stairs. And when she got to the top of the tower and didn't find her baby—

"What did she do?" I cry so sharply that Chloe stops mouth-ing her carrots and lets some dribble out of her mouth. "When she didn't find her baby?"

Billie grimaces. "Ah well, she found a doll the doctor kept for some kind of demonstrations he did, a model, like, the kind that came apart."

"Oh no!"

"Yes." Billie nods. "The poor woman thought they'd taken apart her own babe. She gathered it up and jumped from the top of the tower."

I stare at Billie, horrified, while she cleans Chloe's face off with a washcloth as placidly as if we'd been talking about the weather. "That was the end of the doctor seeing patients in the tower. And the end, really, of the doctor. He never was the same. And the poor woman—"

"Didn't she die?" I ask, somehow more appalled at the thought of surviving such an episode than of her dying.

"No, she broke her leg in the fall and was crippled but she survived. In fact . . ." Billie looked up at me, a strange light in her eyes. Something almost . . . *triumphant.* "She was much better after that, as if the shock of falling shook some sense into her."

"Oh," I say. It's not the ending I was expecting. "And her baby?"

"What baby?" Billie asks. "The poor soul gave her baby up at birth. The baby in the tower was all in her head."

EVEN THOUGH IT'S time for lunch, I don't have much of an appetite after Billie's story. I change Chloe myself and rock her until she's ready to go down for her nap. Billie has set up a cot in the kitchen where she can watch her while she cooks dinner so I can go back to work. "Unless you need a rest yourself," she says.

"No," I say, thinking I'm unlikely to ever rest again with that awful story revolving in my brain. "I want to make some notes on the journals I indexed this morning." On my way out of the kitchen, I shoulder the diaper bag. "I'll just go refill the diapers."

"No need. I've got some here for when my granddaughter's visiting. I just took the bag to check they were the same size and to see if you had another baby blanket. The one in the car was sopping wet."

"Oh," I say embarrassed that I'd left the wet blanket in the car. "I'm sorry you had to bother."

"No bother. It's hanging up in your bathroom."

"Thank you," I say. "I'll go into town to pick up some more diapers."

But once again Billie waves me off, telling me she's already put it on the house shopping list. I leave, feeling a little useless. Back in my apartment I go into the bathroom and find the blanket hanging over the towel rack. Billie must have bleached it, because all Chloe's blankets were pink and this one is white. Then I look closer and see that where her name is embroidered there's an umlaut over the *e*. This is one of Laurel's blankets. She must have left it at my house . . . or we got them mixed up during one of our playdates. Just like I accidentally took her diaper bag, which I open now.

I dig out the packet that contains my own ID and the envelope I'd taken from Peter's desk. They're just where I left them, hidden in the folds of the bottom diaper, only hadn't the IDs been on top of the envelope? I stare at my driver's license. The four-year-old picture doesn't look much like me now, and it feels like a relic of another life. Daphne Marist's life. Daphne Marist was weak. When her husband threatened to take her child away from her she ran away instead of defending herself. Laurel wouldn't have run away; she would have stayed and fought. Far better to be Laurel Hobbes than Daphne Marist from now on.

I pick up the envelope I'd found in Peter's desk. It's thick, ivory-colored, the kind of envelope that would have held a wedding invitation, discolored where tape had held it to the underside of his desk drawer. I found it because when I opened the drawer to find a stapler the drawer had stuck. Which had seemed odd because Peter never tolerated anything broken. If a faucet leaked he tightened it. If a lock stuck he oiled it. If a door dragged over the carpet he took it off its hinges and sanded it. *You're lucky*, another mother in group told me, *I have to nag my husband to fix anything.* I had thought I was lucky too, until Peter started eyeing me as if I had a few screws loose.

So I took out the drawer to find out why it stuck.

I slide out the two items now to look at them again. One is a photograph of a little boy, maybe three or four years old. His hair is cut badly and he's not smiling. It looks like a school picture, only more institutional. The boy is glaring at the camera, square chin clenched, head tilted slightly to the side so that he's eyeing the photographer sideways. That would have sealed the likeness if I needed anything else to convince me that the picture is of Peter, but I hadn't needed anything else. The square jaw, the mole just below his left eye, the expression of distrust. Yes, this was my husband as a boy. Although I'd never seen a childhood picture of him I knew him immediately.

When I turned it over I'd found the words *Thomas Pitt, age 3* written in precise handwriting. Why had my husband, Peter Marist, been called Thomas Pitt?

The photograph is as much a mystery as the other document: the last will and testament of Laurel Hobbes, naming Stan as trustee of all Laurel's money left in trust to Chloë. I have no idea why Peter has a copy of Laurel's will, but I know from the fact that he has hidden it that he wouldn't want anyone to know he has it. Nor, I am guessing, would he want anyone to know about Thomas Pitt. The note I left for Peter said: "I have the picture and the will. I'll show them to the police if you come after me." They're my insurance policy.

But I need a better hiding place.

I look around the apartment. I could duplicate Peter's method and tape the envelope to the underside of a drawer, but I don't trust meticulous and efficient Billie not to poke around my stuff. So I tuck it in my back pocket and head up the spiral stairs. Surely there's someplace in the study, with its boxes of papers and files, where I can secure one slim envelope.

As I climb the stairs I think of Billie's story about the deranged mother come to rescue her baby. What kind of a story was that to tell a new mother? But then I remember that the nurses in the NICU could be a bit sadistic. When Chloe was five days old, an IV clamped to her skull, blue veins pulsing in the blue bilirubin lights, a masked and gowned nurse force fed her because, she told me, she was too frail to expend the energy it would take to breastfeed.

And yet she was not too frail to scream and fight the tube going down her throat. Her face was red, her tiny fists clenched. Surely she was expending more energy like this than if she were in my arms and at my breast. I suspected the nurse was doing it to punish me because the last time I'd fed Chloe she'd taken too long to finish her allotted formula. It was my fault. My fault my baby was crying. My fault she was in pain. My fault her life was at risk.

I'm standing in the study now, tears pricking my eyes, but I'm not myself anymore. I'm the lunatic mother searching for her lost baby. Where would she look? There's no place here to hide a baby.

I climb to the next floor, to the top of the tower. In the daylight the room is ringed by blue sky and floating clouds. It's like being in a hot-air balloon, floating untethered to the ground. I wonder if that's what that mother felt when she stood here, clutching a broken doll she thought was her child. Did she think the only way she could be free was to leap into that endless blue?

Peter told me a news story once about a woman who jumped out of a high window, her baby strapped to her chest. She had developed the obsession that she'd harmed her baby, that he was hopelessly impaired, and that it was all her fault. She couldn't live with the guilt—or leave her child to lead a damaged life. So she decided to take both their lives. When she landed, though, her body absorbed the blow. She died; her baby survived and went on to live a normal life. The idea that her baby was damaged had been a delusion. Peter wanted me to see what could come of always fretting about Chloe, but after I heard that story I'd become terrified of standing near windows, afraid that I'd take it into my head that Chloe was damaged and I'd leap to my death.

When I shared the story with my group, Esta took me aside. "It may be better if you don't tell stories like that," she said. "Some women who may be suffering from postpartum OCD are very . . . *suggestible*. They may hear a story about another mother with delusions and begin to think that they are suffering from those very same delusions."

"You mean," I'd said, "that delusions may be *contagious*?"

"Well," Esta had said, looking flustered, "I wouldn't have put it like that, but basically, yes. I would recommend that you stay away from reading accounts of other mothers with postpartum psychosis and perhaps . . ." She had hesitated, looking uncharacteristically unsure of herself. "Perhaps this group's not the right place for you."

"You're kicking me out of the group?" I exclaimed. "But it's the only thing holding me together!"

She'd looked a little alarmed and then her face had softened. "I guess I could just try to monitor what you're exposed to. I'll bring it up in next week's group—without naming any names—that we should all refrain from lurid horror stories about women with postpartum psychosis."

"Like the one I just told," I'd said.

"Exactly," she'd replied.

I step closer to the window to see if I've gotten better, and hear a floorboard creak beneath my foot. I stop and test it with the toe of my shoe. It rocks a little. I kneel down and run my hands over the old worn planks. They're wide and weathered, worn in the center of the room as if someone had paced over them. The one I stepped on is definitely loose. I dig my fingernails in between two boards and pull up the loose one. Dust motes fly up into the air, catching the light. I cautiously reach my hand down into a shoebox-sized space, a perfect hiding spot. A silverfish scuttles away, sliding through a crack at the bottom. Clearly it hasn't been used in years—if it ever was.

I put the extra set of car keys with my monogram on the fob into the hiding space. Then I take the envelope out of my back pocket and lay it next to the keys. I keep my hand on it for a moment, picturing the little boy in the photograph. I feel a pang at leaving him here. Even though I know the boy is Peter, there's something in his expression that expects just *this*—being abandoned.

"It's only temporary," I say out loud.

When I take my hand out I brush something loose from the rough wood, something silky that sticks to my sweaty skin. I flinch, thinking it's another silverfish, but it's not. It's a pale-pink ribbon, frayed and faded with age. Like something that might have belonged to a baby doll.

Or to a baby.

Daphne's Journal, July 8, 20—

Sometimes I wonder if it's only mothers' hormones that change when a couple has a baby. Peter's been really nervous and touchy lately too, like he's on super-high alert like I am. Take what just happened tonight. It all started with my new haircut. I was nervous he wouldn't like it or he'd guess how expensive the highlights were, but he loved it! He said it made me look ten years younger.

I should have just said thank you and left it at that but something about how he said it—like I must have been looking old and haggard before the haircut—made me say, "Like a college girl? Too young for you."

Right away I knew I'd said the wrong thing. His jaw tightened and he gave me one of his sideways looks. Sometimes I forget how touchy Peter is about his age. When we first met at the gym I thought he was in his early thirties. I was surprised when I saw on his driver's license that he was in his forties. I'd made a joke about it later and he'd gotten angry that I'd looked at his license. He was right, of course, I shouldn't have been snooping in his things, so I apologized and we made up.

I couldn't help noticing afterward, though, how he never makes any reference to his childhood. Nothing that would clue you into how old he is, like the TV shows he watched or where he was on 9/11 or the sports teams he grew up rooting for. I'd known him a year before I found out he'd gone to a state college way upstate. He says he doesn't like to mention it because the people he works with all went to fancy boarding schools and Ivy League colleges. He's proud he's a self-made man and that he started his fund with seed money that his landlady gave him to manage. And he should be proud of it! He traded a tiny fund up to a small but respectably sized one in only ten years and he did it all on his own. He says, though, in the finance world it's better to look like you've always had money, not like you've had to scrape and claw your way into it.

So he was probably just feeling a bit testy when he told me that maybe I was too young for all of this. He had his arms open wide as if he meant our nice Westchester house, the living-room furniture I'd picked out of Pottery Barn and the curtains from Country Curtains. I thought it was all the height of suburban luxury until I saw Laurel's white carpeting and Roche-Bobois sectional and custom-fitted window treatments. Now I think our house looks like a child's playhouse version of adulthood, like the dream house a teenager would design by cutting pictures out of a magazine—like I did as a teenager when my mother was working nights at the Ramada Inn bar. It even looks like a teenager lives in it: couch cushions askew, mugs on the tables, dust coating everything. When Peter and I decided I would stay home, we'd agreed to do without a house cleaner. After all, if I'm home all day I can theoretically do the housecleaning. Only I never seem to get around to it.

I told him I could do better with the house, but he shook his head.

"I don't mean the house, Daph," he said with that tired, patient look he gets when he's explaining something—like how our taxes work—that he thinks I should already understand. "I mean Chloe. I mean being a mother. Maybe you're too young for all the responsibility. Maybe I rushed you into having a baby because I wanted one. Maybe that's why you keep forgetting things and leaving your stuff everywhere. You're acting out your resentment."

"I don't resent Chloe!" I said. I'm afraid I might have shrieked, because Peter winced. Or maybe he winced because it was so obviously a lie. I *do* resent Chloe—her constant crying, her tantrums, her demands. But that doesn't mean I don't love her. Does it?

"It doesn't matter," I told Peter. "She's here now and I'm managing just fine . . ." But my voice wobbled on *fine* and that made it sound like I was anything but fine, so I added: "And you're here."

He looked away and didn't say anything. I got a terrible feeling in my chest that was so bad that I wondered for a moment if I was having a heart attack. For a minute I was certain Peter was planning to leave me. And what would I do if he did, if he's had enough of my tears and forgetting things and the house always being a mess and me being fat? How could I manage on my own?

But that was just me freaking out. When he looked back at me his face was softer. "Yes, thank God for that. You'd never manage on your own."

"I feel terrible for the single mothers in the group," I told him, feeling relieved.

"I'd never let that happen," Peter said. He held out his arms and I stepped into them. I could feel how tense he was. The argument had scared him too. He was probably just as afraid of me leaving him as I was of him leaving me.

"I really am doing better," I murmured into his chest. "It helps to have the group—and Laurel as a friend."

"I'm glad you've found a friend your own age. Maybe we should invite Laurel and her husband to dinner."

I immediately felt like all the breath had gone out of my chest. Laurel? Here? Meeting Peter? I'm not sure what scared me worse—her seeing where I live because our house is nowhere near as nice as hers or her meeting Peter because, well, I've said some things about Peter to her, just venting really, but what if she let something slip and Peter guessed what I've told her?

But of course I couldn't say any of that to Peter. He was trying to make up for the argument. And this would be a way to show that I really was mature enough to handle being a wife and a mother. "I guess," I said, "but what would I cook? I haven't made anything more ambitious than mac and cheese in months!"

Peter said he'd get steaks for the grill and we could hire Vanessa to come watch Chloe and help. So what could I say but yes? I texted Laurel to see if she and Stan can make it this weekend. I made it sound really casual and added an emoji of a cocktail glass and a hamburger.

She texted back a yes and three cocktail glasses.

I texted back four and then she sent back five and the blotto smiley face. So I think it will probably all go fine. Peter's been so sweet since our fight. He even gave Chloe her bath. I could hear him talking to her while I was texting Laurel. I'm really lucky to have a husband who's so involved. I have nothing to worry about. He'd never be able to bear being parted from Chloe.

Chapter Six

I spend the rest of the afternoon looking for the woman who jumped out of the tower in Dr. Bennett's journals. I know it's not really a part of my job, but I can't help it; I have to know what happened. Billie said that she had been a patient in the early seventies, so I put the earlier journals aside and skimmed through the journals from that time period. I found her in the spring of 1971.

Admitted today, E.S., 19 year old woman, of above-average intelligence, sound constitution, and good family, with puerperal delusions and impulsive behavior. Claims not to have known she was pregnant. Gave birth in college dorm room and abandoned infant in a dumpster, but believes baby has been stolen from her for purposes of medical experimentation. Sedative administered, bed rest and hydro-therapy recommended.

The poor girl. How could she not have known she was pregnant? But I remember that in college there were stories about girls who didn't realize they were pregnant, who thought they'd just gained the freshman fifteen and then gave birth in the dormitory bathroom. The idea had haunted me through my freshman year when my periods were irregular and I'd put on *twenty* pounds (I'd never had access to so much food!). But when I got pregnant with Chloe I wondered how anyone could be pregnant and *not* know it. How deluded would a person have to be?

But then, there were things I'd turned a blind eye to that seemed awfully obvious now.

I comb through the rest of the journal looking for any entries regarding E.S. There's one at least every week, but they aren't particularly illuminating. Or hopeful.

> E.S. refuses to talk during sessions. Her behavior
> becoming more erratic: hair-tearing, self-mutilation,
> weeping. Convinced that baby was taken from her
> because there was something wrong with it—

I feel a weird tingle in my veins reading this. It sounds so much like the woman who jumped from her NYC apartment— or like the fretting of the mothers in the support group. *Her head is shaped funny. He's not smiling. Is it normal to cry this much? She hasn't rolled over yet. He's got a rash.* All the baby books with their developmental charts and milestones and what-to-expects made it sound like there was one normal, but babies were as maddeningly different as grown-ups. And what must a newborn baby have looked like to a scared teenager alone in a dorm room? She must have thought she'd given birth to a monster. No wonder she'd abandoned it—and no wonder she was haunted by the specter of what had become of it.

I go back and read through all the notes Dr. Bennett's made on E.S., trying to glean more of her history, but his notes are curiously opaque. But then, I realize, this journal is meant only for himself. He would have kept a file on E.S. at the hospital. I wonder if I could ask for it.

But why? I hear a voice say in my head. Laurel's voice. I don't really have an answer, only that I can't stop thinking about E.S. and wondering how her story must have affected Sky. E.S.'s story is so much like the "Changeling" story that Sky must have known about it. In fact, I may have found the origins of the changeling story.

I'm so lost thinking about E.S. and the changeling story that Sky has to come tell me it's time for dinner. "I'm glad you're engaging with the material, but I don't expect you to live up here." She smiles so I know she's teasing. "Or never eat or see your baby again."

"Oh! I suppose Billie must want to go home."

"Only if she could take Chloe with her. She's smitten. You'll have to tear your baby out of her arms."

I laugh the way you're supposed to laugh when people make jokes about stealing your baby. You are *not* supposed to shriek or call a cop or tell them, *Fine, take her.* I busy myself stacking the journals so Sky won't see these thoughts flitting across my face.

"It looks like you've made good progress," she says.

"Your father's journals are fascinating—and I can see ties to your writing in them. In fact, I was thinking . . ."

"What?" she asks when I hesitate.

"Well, you *did* say you wanted to tell a different story about your father, so I wondered, if you were planning to do that maybe you'd like for me to pick out some sections from the journals that I think relate to your writing."

Sky takes so long to answer that I'm sure I've overstepped my bounds. After all, she'd hired me as an archivist. I was supposed to put order to her personal papers, not speculate on the origins of her writing. What possessed me to make such a suggestion?

Not what. Who. It's just the kind of thing Laurel would come up with. And Laurel wouldn't back down even with Schuyler Bennett staring at her as if she were sprouting horns.

"Actually," Sky says, "I think that's an excellent idea. Have you found anything along those lines?" Her voice shakes on the last words and I realize how personally charged this material must be for her. Why would she let me poke around in the secrets of her past?

Because she hired you to do exactly that, a voice says in my head. Laurel's voice.

She hired me to put her papers in order, I counter.

This is how you bring order to chaos, by tracing it back to its source.

"Yes," I tell Schuyler Bennett, "I came across this one patient that your father treated in the early seventies—a young woman suffering from postpartum psychosis who'd developed the delusion that her child had been stolen from her." I don't mention the story Billie told me or that I'd spent the afternoon searching all of Dr. Bennett's notes on the case. "It reminded me of your changeling story and I wondered . . ."

"Wondered what?" Sky asks, eyebrow arched.

"I wondered if your father ever talked about this case to you."

"I was abroad in the late sixties at a boarding school in the French Alps, and then I went straight on to college. I don't remember my father talking about that case."

"Oh," I say, crestfallen. "I guess I went off track . . ."

"But then, maybe I've just forgotten. It was a long time ago. You should keep looking at his notes on that case. Type them up for me and I'll have a look. Except . . ."

"Except what?" I ask.

"Well, that's not really the job of an archivist."

Here it is. I have overstepped my bounds. She must realize now that I'm not really an archivist. I'm not even Laurel Hobbes. I prepare myself to apologize, but before I can she says, "But that's not really what you are, is it?"

All the breath goes out of my lungs. She knows. "I can explain . . ." I begin.

She holds up an authoritative hand. "There's no need. I saw it as soon as I met you. After all, it takes one to know one."

"One what?" I ask.

"A writer, of course. You have the instincts of a writer. I could tell right away. And the way you've put together this story : . . well, to tell you the truth I *have* been thinking of writing a memoir, but I wasn't sure I was up to it . . . but if I had someone to help me . . ."

"You mean you'd like me to help you with your memoir?" I ask, incredulous.

"Yes, if you wouldn't mind. Of course, I'll adjust your salary accordingly."

I resist telling her that I would do it for free. "I'd like that very much," I say.

"Good." She raps her knuckles on the table and then starts to stand up. "I'll make an appointment for you with Dr. Hancock at Crantham."

"An appointment with a doctor?" I ask, my voice high-pitched, all my scholarly calm gone. "But why?"

"For background on the hospital," she says. "You'll need it if you're going to help me with my memoir."

WE EAT DINNER on the terrace watching the sun set over a long ridge of mountains to the west. The mountains look unreal, like pieces of tissue paper layered over one another in deepening shades of green and blue.

The terrace is artfully situated so that it gives the best view of the mountains while obscuring the view of the hospital. I imagine Sky's mother landscaping the terrace to conceal her husband's line of work. I imagine dinner parties where the conversation centered around the lovely view—as it does now. Sky, her face rosy in the reflected light of the sunset, waves her gin and tonic shakily at the mountains, naming peaks and the number of times she and her father climbed them. She'd been a 3500er by the time she was nineteen, "although my father always contested my claim to Peekamoose, because I'd become so enraged at something he said I stormed down the mountain before we reached the peak."

"Do you remember what you were arguing about?" I ask as I struggle to debone the brook trout Billie produced for our dinner. This is something I imagine an assistant memoir writer would ask and I'm hoping it will distract Sky and Billie, who have both skillfully deboned their fish, from my clumsiness.

"Ha!" Sky barks the one syllable laugh I'm becoming accustomed to. "What *didn't* we argue about? The Vietnam War. Civil rights. Women's liberation. Mostly the latter. My father expected me to do everything a boy would—shoot, climb mountains, go to medical school—but he was convinced that most women were 'congenitally unfit for the full responsibilities of the workplace.'"

"I suppose that wasn't unusual for the time," I say, finally freeing the trout's spine from its flesh. "He saw women at their worst in his line of work. In fact . . ." I hesitate, not sure I want to go down this road. But then, how long could I avoid it? ". . . he seems to have specialized in women with mood disorders, especially postpartum mood disorders." I glance at

Chloe, who's sleeping peacefully in her stroller. She'll be up all night after such a late nap, but it's so nice to be able to eat dinner in peace that I don't have the heart to wake her.

"Does that bother you?" Sky asks. I look toward her and see she has transferred her attention from the faraway mountains to me. The sun has slipped below the ridgeline, turning the papery mountains into a singular black cutout. Sky looks like another cutout, dark against the smoldering sky.

"No," I say quickly. Too quickly. "Why should it?"

"I just thought, being a new mother yourself. It can't have been easy these last few months . . . especially being a single mother."

I have to remind myself that is what I'd told her in the emails we'd exchanged. It hadn't even felt like a lie. *We might as well be single mothers for all the help our husbands give us,* Laurel had said. I'd thought that Stan was actually quite helpful, and I'd felt a little guilty eradicating him from Laurel's curriculum vitae.

My husband and I have separated, I had written, *and I'm looking for a place where I can work and live with my six-month-old daughter.*

"Oh," I say now, spearing a morsel of white-boned flesh and imaging what Laurel would say. "Do men ever really help out with babies all that much?"

But Sky doesn't take the bait. "So you didn't experience any postpartum depression?"

I think about the days after Chloe was born, while she was in the NICU, in a plastic incubator, attached to tubes and wires like a science experiment. What would "depression" have looked like? I'd felt an aching sadness and guilt. But then I remember that was me—*not* Laurel.

"No," I say with a certainty born of Laurel's confidence. "I think I just felt . . ." What had Laurel said that first meeting? Not the part about feeling homicidal, but later. ". . . like I lost track of who I really was. That my identity had been swallowed up by the idea of Motherhood with a capital *M*." *Motherfuckinghood*, Laurel sometimes called it. "That's why I felt it was so important to apply for this job. When I saw your ad, I thought, This is perfect." I pause because I can feel myself tearing up. I don't have to fake this part; seeing that ad on the library job site had felt like someone had tossed me a lifeline when I was drowning. "I knew that getting back to doing what I was good at would be my way back to myself again."

I look up. Sky holds my gaze and then gives me a curt nod. On anyone else it would be a dismissal but on her it's an affirmation. "Well, then, it's a good thing I placed that ad."

AFTER DINNER CHLOE wakes up fretful, so I take her for a walk around the garden. The Orbit stroller handles the gravel like a BMW hugging the Autobahn (it really *was* worth the ridiculous price), and the gravelly sound soothes Chloe. It's nearly dark but the garden holds the last light like a jar holding fireflies. The glow lingers in the orange flowers shaped like Chinese lanterns, and in the real Chinese lanterns suspended from glossy-leaved trees, and soaks into the marble statues of mournful women with bowed heads. The path curves through a shrubbery, emerges at a marble fountain where a woman perpetually pours water from a vase, and then plunges back into a hedge maze.

The path turns back on itself so often I lose all sense of direction. I stop at a particularly lugubrious statue of a veiled woman, her features smeared by her stone cloak, and look around for the house, but the shrubbery is too high and the sky has faded to the uniform violet of twilight. I have the ridiculous notion that the rest of the world has vanished while I looped around the garden, but then a light appears high above me and the tower springs into view like a lighthouse. I am a sailor lost at sea glimpsing shore. My breath evens and, looking down at Chloe, I see that she is also transfixed by the light in the sky.

"Home," I say experimentally, and she gurgles back at me as if agreeing.

I follow the path, which soon comes out at the front of the house. Billie is kneeling in the perennial border, deadheading chrysanthemums, a basketful of withered blooms beside her muddied knees.

"Just thought I'd get these before I left for the night," she says. "How's our little miss?"

I peer around to the front of the stroller to see that Chloe has fallen asleep again. "She'll be up all night," I say.

"Maybe not, the air up here is good for sleeping. I bet she sleeps straight through."

"Has Sky gone to bed?" I ask.

"Gone to bed, but she'll be up all night writing. That's when she gets her best work done."

"I hadn't realized she was still writing." I look up at the tower room and notice that the light has gone out. "Does she work up there?"

Billie, who has gotten to her feet slowly and is brushing dirt from her knees, stares at me. "She hasn't been able to get up those stairs in years."

"Of course, I wasn't thinking," I say hastily. Billie gives me a look like she agrees with me. *She doesn't think much of you,* I think, only it's Laurel's voice saying it. *She thinks you're a bad mother for letting someone else watch your baby.*

But then Billie smiles and says, "You weren't to know." She

straightens Chloe's blanket. "You'd better get her inside before she catches a chill from the damp."

As soon as she says it I feel the chill in the air. I shiver and turn to go inside, but then I look up at the tower again. If Sky couldn't get to the top, and Billie has been down here working in the garden, who turned on the light?

AFTER CHLOE IS settled in bed with sturdy couch cushions on either side of her, I search downstairs for a switch that would turn on the light in the tower. I can't find one, but that doesn't mean there isn't a remote switch in the main house. Sky Bennett has the air of someone who is used to being in control. Maybe it's being the daughter of a doctor. I imagine Morris Bennett wielding his power over the fiefdom of Crantham. It was like a little kingdom, the way Sky described it, with its dairy farm and workshops, complete with the feudal manor on the hill and a watchtower to guard against invading barbarians.

Except one of those barbarians had made it past the blockade all the way into the keep. The thought of that madwoman creeping up the spiral stairs in search of her lost baby makes my skin prickle. Even though it was forty-five years ago, somehow now it is paired in my mind with the light going on in the tower. I know I won't sleep tonight unless I go up there myself to make sure there's no one there.

I climb the stairs barefoot, trying to make as little noise as possible. I think of what Billie said about the wind playing the stairs like a xylophone. It *does* feel like I am inside an instrument. I'd felt like this during my pregnancy too, as if my body had been taken over in service of something bigger.

Like demonic possession, Laurel had said, *or having that thing from* Alien *inside of you.* Only to me it had felt more like being swept up in a riptide, being carried farther and farther from shore.

When I reach the top I find the room as I left it earlier today. The book is still on the desk, still open to the changeling story. The overhead light has a string suspended from the fixture. It's not impossible that it's wired to a switch elsewhere, but that seems unlikely. I pull the string, flooding the room with such bright light that I am momentarily blinded. When I turn it off again it takes several minutes for my eyes to adjust to the darkness and even then a ghostly afterimage of the light blinks in the darkness.

Only it's not an afterimage. I step closer to the window to make sure and see it again. Down below, somewhere on the grounds of the Crantham Psychiatric Center, a light goes on and then off again. Someone is signaling back.

Daphne's Journal, July 10, 20—

I should be cleaning up from the dinner party but I have to write this down to figure out what happened.

It all started out really well. I made these fancy cheese sticks from a recipe I got off the Internet and put out candles and the new throw pillows I bought last week with Laurel at Home Goods (funny how even though Laurel is rich she still likes shopping for bargains) so it all looked really nice. Vanessa came early so I could take care of all that while Peter got the grill going. He was in a really good mood. He told me how nice everything looked and I realized that all the tension between us is just from the stress of having a new baby and Peter being worried about money, which is only natural for a man who's just had a baby. I could tell from how relaxed he's been about spending money lately that the fund must be doing better, and now that I've got Vanessa to help and Laurel to talk to I'm more relaxed too. I think we were just going through a rough patch and that things are going to be all right now.

Vanessa watched the babies so we could just sit and have our drinks and enjoy ourselves. I felt like we were two couples in *Mad Men*. Laurel wore these really cute capris and a Tory Burch top and sandals that made her look like Betty Draper and for once I didn't look drab next to her because I was wearing the Comme des Garçons shift I got at Barneys last weekend. It was on sale and I never would have gotten into it a month ago before I lost so much weight.

We started out with Expat cocktails, which Laurel said is what she drank at school in Edinburgh, but then the boys wanted beer and I opened a bottle of Prosecco for Laurel and me.

"Better Prosecco than Prozac!" Laurel said as her toast. Which made Peter laugh even though he used to glare at me

every time I took a drink because I'm not supposed to mix alcohol with the medication I'm on. But Laurel says it's okay to
have a drink with the pills she takes, so since I'm taking hers
now I decided I could have a few drinks. Besides, Peter was
having such a good time he never batted an eyelash. He and
Stan really got along. They talked about sports (I had no idea
that Peter knew so much about football!) and then work stuff. I
thought Laurel would tune out and we'd talk about something
else, but it turns out Laurel knows a lot about finance. She
was right in there with the boys talking about IRAs and annui-
ties and where to get the highest yield. I guess it makes sense
because she has so much money, although she said something
about it being all tied up in trusts.

"Laurel's parents were rather conservative fiscally," Stan
said, and I thought he looked a little unhappy. It made me
remember that he was a lot older than the rest of us—at least
ten years older than Peter, I think—and I felt bad for him and
went to get him another beer. When I came back Laurel was
telling a story that had both men laughing.

". . . and then she said that delusions could be catching and
maybe this group wasn't right for you."

My face got hot and I felt a little dizzy because she was obviously telling the story about what Esta said to me, which I'd
told Laurel, but *in confidence*. I really didn't like her telling it to
Stan and Peter—especially Peter, who would be worried about
me if he thought I was telling morbid stories at group. But then
Peter asked, "And what did you say back to her?" and I realized
that Laurel was telling the story as if it had happened to her.

Laurel said, "I told her that I'd never heard anything so ridiculous and if she ever said anything like that to me again I'd
contact the APA and have her license revoked."

"Good for you," Peter said. "You can't let these people push you around. They think a couple of initials after their names makes them better than the rest of us."

I knew Peter didn't think much of psychologists. I'd asked him once if he'd go to one and he said it wouldn't do any good because he could too easily fool any psychologist into thinking whatever he wanted them to believe. But I was afraid that Stan and Laurel might think this was a strange way of looking at things. Laurel was grinning but Stan looked concerned. "Maybe this woman's really not helping," he said.

"Oh, she's all right," Laurel said. "Besides, it's the other women who make the group valuable. Look at how great I've felt since I met Daphne."

That made me feel so good I almost cried! And I instantly forgave Laurel for stealing my story—because of course that's what she'd done. She'd taken the story I told her about what Esta said to me and made it her own. Only she'd given it a better ending. She added what I should have said back to Esta, which, if you think about it, was her way of defending me.

"Yeah," I said, "Esta doesn't matter; the group's been good because I've met Laurel through it."

"So," said Peter, "maybe now that you two are friends you don't need the group—or Esta—anymore."

This really surprised me, especially after the whole talk we'd had about me being too young for the responsibility of taking care of a baby. But Laurel loved it. "I'll drink to that," she said, holding up her glass. "We'll have more time for the gym." She winked at me and mouthed, *And massages.*

I smiled back at her and then looked at Peter. He was smiling too. I thought that seeing me give this party had made him realize how much better I am. I glanced at Stan, but he was looking down at his phone. "Sorry," he said, "there's a crisis in the Asia office."

Peter said Stan could use his computer if he wanted, which really surprised me because Peter never likes anyone to get anywhere near his things. He must really like Stan. Laurel and I stayed out on the deck drinking Prosecco while Peter and Stan went into Peter's study. It kind of surprised me that Peter wasn't leaving Stan alone to make his call, but afterward Peter told me Stan asked him to stay to give him advice on some financial point, which I could tell made Peter feel good.

Anyway, while the men were away Laurel and I drank more than we should have. Thank goodness we had Vanessa there in case the babies woke up. I wouldn't have trusted myself to pick Chloe up. And I really didn't want to do anything to change Peter's mind about how well I was doing.

At ten P.M. I sent Vanessa home in a taxi and offered to get Stan and Laurel one but Stan said he'd only had two beers. While I was talking to Stan, Laurel went in to get Chloë. I should have realized she was too drunk and made Stan do it but I wasn't thinking—I'd really had too much myself!—so when Laurel came back out carrying the car seat, I didn't realize at first what was wrong. I almost let her go but then I noticed that the baby blanket was about to slip off and when I went to tuck it in I saw it was one of Chloe's. I knew because it was pink and had her name on it without the umlaut and Laurel *always* makes sure no one *ever* forgets the goddamned umlaut! I was going to let it slide but then I looked more closely at the baby in the car seat and realized it was *my* Chloe!

I think Laurel saw it at the same time because she tried to make a joke out of it. "Whoops! Wrong baby!" she said, taking Chloe—*my Chloe!*—back to the nursery. "Just checking to see if you would notice the difference."

Stan and Peter were too busy talking by the door to notice what had happened. Which was good, because I don't think it was a mistake or that she was testing me. I think that for a moment—just a moment—she had decided that she wanted *my* baby instead of hers.

Chapter Seven

For the next few days I try to put that blinking light out of my mind. I resist the urge to go to the top of the tower and signal back. I do *not* ask Billie or Sky if they see flashing lights coming from the mental hospital. I am aware of how crazy it sounds to think that a mental patient is trying to hail me from her cell. And if I know how crazy it sounds that means I'm not crazy. Right?

Instead I work hard on sorting through Sky's papers. Although all I really want to do is read Dr. Bennett's journals I spend the bulk of each day ordering Sky's journals, making up files in acid-free folders, which I'd asked Sky to order in advance, for manuscripts, drafts of early stories, and correspondence. There are decades' worth of letters from 1975 to the present, letters to and from her agent, her editor, and her hundreds of fans (she kept carbon copies of her own). I notice, though, that there's no personal correspondence. No friends. And that all the paperwork—journals and letters—dates from 1975. There's nothing from her boarding-school or college days, which I suppose makes some sense as far as archiving her professional papers, but since she's asked me to assist her in writing her memoir I ask her if she has any material from this period.

"The trunk I shipped back from Europe was lost," Sky explained when I asked her about it. "Which I always took as a sign that I was starting a new life when I came back here. That's when I started writing. Who needs a past when you have an imagination?"

I thought the answer was a little glib, the kind of aphorism she used to fob off reporters—and I suspected the truth lay in her father's journals. I've organized them chronologically now and bookmarked all the sections that mention E.S. so that I can reread them. I save them for late in the day and read them in the cool of the study on the second floor of the tower.

> E.S. still fixated in her delusion that her baby was taken
> from her because something was wrong with him. She
> believes she is responsible for the child's congenital
> abnormalities. I asked her if she was afraid the child was
> mentally unfit because of her current mental instability.
> She laughed and replied, "That's rather a Catch-22,
> isn't it? You think I'm crazy because I think my baby had
> something wrong with it, but the only sane explanation
> for my belief involves admitting that I'm crazy."

I laughed myself over E.'s response. It was clever and obviously the product of an educated woman (at least one who had read Joseph Heller's *Catch-22*). But I stopped laughing when I read Dr. Bennett's next lines.

> E.S. is always at great pains to demonstrate her
> intelligence and education to me but I fear her native

craftiness impairs our progress. She is always looking
for a way out of our discussions instead of a way into
her problems. I have moved our meetings to my home
office in the tower in the hope that the more informal
setting will make her lower her guard and engaged
a private nurse to accompany her to and from the
hospital.

I imagine E. as she is being brought up the hill. She'd be
wearing the shapeless pajamas and canvas shoes I've seen in
pictures of the asylum from the seventies, accompanied by a
private nurse like a lady-in-waiting, ushered into a medieval-
looking tower. She must have felt like a peasant girl being
brought before the feudal lord to be punished for stealing a
crust of bread. I admire her for maintaining her composure.

Today E. asked me why I didn't just show her that her baby
hadn't been damaged. I asked how I could do that without
producing the child and she responded that I could show
her medical records, adoption forms, pictures.
   "What makes you think I have those?" I asked. She
responded by waving her hands around in the air. "Look!"
she cried. "Look at all these books and papers you've
assembled. You've built a fortress of paper to keep the
world out!"

I looked at the books and files lining the eight walls of the
study—even the door leading to the main house was behind a
bookcase. E. was right; Dr. Bennett had erected a fortress of
paper. What had he said to that? I looked down at the journal
for his response.

I waited until she had calmed down and lowered her arms.
"And yet, I invited you in."

But E. had an answer to that too. "Only as a prisoner."
She picked at her hospital clothes with her fingertips. Her
nails are chewed to the quick, her cuticles ragged and
bloody.

"And if I let you wear your own clothes?" I asked.
"Would you feel less like a prisoner then?"

"A little," she replied, "and even less if we could meet
up above, where at least I could see the sky."

I conceded to both of her requests. I instructed the
matron that she was to have her own clothes to wear–
belts and shoelaces excepted. I granted, too, her request
to have a bit of red ribbon to tie up her hair, although
I made sure it wasn't long enough to constitute a
strangulation risk. I confess I am curious to see what she
does with the ribbon. She seems to have an obsession
with it.

I thought of the pink ribbon I'd found in the hiding place.
Might it have been red once? Had E. put it there? Did it have
some connection in her mind with the baby she lost? I remember one of the mothers in the group saying it was an old-
fashioned custom to tie a red ribbon on the baby's crib to ward
off the evil eye. Had E. hidden the ribbon in the place she
thought her baby was being kept?

I promised E. we would meet on the top floor of the tower
from now on. I am hopeful that both concessions will
give her a sense of control again and that she won't be
as compelled to hold on to her delusions about the child.

> I will, of course, have locks installed on the tower room
> windows. The nurse will remain in the study below us,
> available at a summons to come to my aid should it be
> necessary.

I put down the journal and look up, as if I expect to hear the doctor and his patient in the room above me, as if I am the private nurse listening for a summons. Instead I see only sunlight pouring down the spiral staircase and hear only the creak and groan of the metal stairs when the wind blows. I get up and climb up the stairs. It hadn't occurred to me to open the windows—hadn't one been open the first night?—so I'd never noticed if they had locks on them.

When I get up to the top floor I'm startled to see that the sun is already low in the sky. I've lost track of time reading in the room below without windows. It *was* a fortress of paper, obliterating the outside world. But up here the world opens up; there's so much light and air! And yes, a window is open, the one over the makeshift desk. I lean over the desk to inspect it. The window opens by pushing out at the bottom. Heavy copper locks are on the top sash of each window and a metal rod is attached between the sill and the bottom sash to keep it from opening more than ten inches. I look around the room. All the windows have similar protective measures. How could E. have gotten out?

Maybe Billie made up the whole story. I've learned over my first week here that Billie has a taste for the sensational and macabre. She delights in following tabloid news stories about domestic violence, prison breaks, and alien abductions. I caught her one afternoon reading aloud to Chloe a story about a woman in Queens who drowned her five-year-old son. *She doesn't understand a word of it*, she assured me when I objected. I'd thought of mentioning it to Sky, but I didn't like to complain when Billie was so helpful with Chloe. Besides, Chloe obviously adores her.

Still, I can imagine Billie inventing a story about an escaped patient throwing herself from the tower. All the ingredients are there—lunatics, mental hospital, medieval-looking tower— like flour, eggs, and butter laid out on a kitchen counter. Who could blame her for mixing them together and making a cake? It wasn't her fault if the story has lodged in my brain. There's no Esta here to warn her about impressionable types.

The more I think about the story the more improbable it seems, especially that part about the woman surviving and being cured. I'm glad I didn't tell Sky that Billie's story was what inspired me to read her father's journals. I'm not sure why I've kept this from her except that I suspect it makes me seem less like a serious archivist and not the kind of person she would want assisting with her memoir.

I push the window as wide as it can go and look down. Below is the flagstone terrace where we ate dinner. A person landing on that hard stone would do more than break her leg. I pull my head in—but something yanks me back as if a hand has grabbed my hair and is dragging me out the window. But of course it's only my hair caught on the edge of the window frame. Still, I feel the blind panic of being trapped. I've always been a little claustrophobic.

I jerk my head back but my hair is too entangled. Fighting back hysteria, I wriggle my hand out the window and feel along the window frame to where my hair is caught. I think it must be snagged on the rod or the lock but it's tangled in the wood itself, which feels rough and sharp-edged. As if the window had grown teeth.

Don't think about teeth, I tell myself as I untangle my hair from the sharp, splintery wood.

One of the mothers from group had shared this dream: *I dreamed I was pregnant and my baby died inside me. Only it turned into a zombie and started eating its way out of me.*

That's absurd, Laurel had scoffed, *babies don't have teeth in the womb.*

Which did nothing to stop that image of a fetus gnawing its way out of my womb from haunting my dreams.

My hands are bloody and sweat-slicked by the time I free myself (I think of Dr. Bennett's withering observation of E.'s hands—as if she could have had a manicure while in the asylum!), my face streaked with tears. I've lost a handful of expensively colored and highlighted hair showing brown at the roots. There are splinters under my fingernails and a long scratch across my cheek. My reflection in the window shows someone who's been through a street fight. I look like the lunatic of my imaginings.

I glance away from that frightful apparition, down at the offending window. Strands of my hair still hang from the splintered wood. Peter would never have tolerated such shoddy workmanship. And even though Sky doesn't come up here— can't come up here—I hurriedly pull my stray hairs from the wood. As I do, I see how my hair got caught. There's a long crack in the wood that looks like it was once repaired with wood putty. The putty shows white against the wood where the paint has worn away. I can clearly trace the crack back to where the rod is clamped into the window. There's a deep hole just to the side that's been filled with putty, as if the rod had been ripped out once and then reaffixed to the unbroken wood. As if someone had shoved the window open and broken the restraining rod in order to jump out.

Billie's story is true.

At least the part about E. jumping. I'm not sure about the part where she survived and got better.

WHEN I GET back downstairs I page through all the references to E. in the journals but I find no reference to her jump from the tower. Instead the journals abruptly end in 1973. The last entry is about E.

> E. much calmer today. Medication seems to be having
> good effect. I am optimistic that she is at last emerging
> from her mania.

And then she hit Herb Marcus over the head, crept up the hill, and threw herself from the tower.

It must have been a shock to Dr. Bennett, such a shock that he hadn't been able to continue his journals. As if he couldn't face his own smug assessment and how wrong he'd been. What had Billie said? It had been *the end of the doctor.*

But had it been the end of E.? Was Billie right? Had she survived? Had she gotten better, perhaps gone on to live a full, rich life, recovered from her *puerperal mania?* I've been so tied up in her story that I feel an urgency to find out, as if my own fate were tied to hers.

Or maybe I have postpartum OCD like Esta said and I'm so *suggestible* that I've tied E.'s story to my own. That I'm susceptible to her delusions—

But I don't think anything is wrong with Chloe—

Although she has been sleeping a lot lately—

Or that anyone is trying to steal her from me.

Except Peter. Who was. Or Billie that first day. But I no longer think that.

No. I'm drawn to E.'s story because of her intelligence and resilience. Who wouldn't be? There's nothing wrong with wanting to know what happened to her. In fact, it's part of my job. I'm not just the archivist; I'm helping Sky write her memoir and I feel certain that this is a vital part of Sky's history.

I'll tell Sky that I'd like that appointment with Dr. Hancock—and that I'd like permission to see the records of the patient E.S. whom Dr. Bennett treated from 1971 to 1973. I'll also ask her if she remembers E.S. E.'s fall from the tower precipitated Dr. Bennett's decline and subsequent retirement. Even if Sky was abroad she must have heard something about the incident. And when she came home to take care of her father, the house and hospital staff must have made reference to it. E. might even have still been a patient. Sky might have met her.

I go down to my apartment to freshen up before dinner. I dress in navy capris and a white button-down shirt and put my hair up in a twist. The layers I got from Laurel's stylist have begun to grow out and I can just scrape it all into a bun with the help of a handful of bobby pins. Pulled back, the brown roots show more. It makes me look more like my old self—less like Laurel. Maybe that's a good thing. Maybe I don't need her anymore.

Or maybe I've incorporated all she had to teach me and I just don't need to look like her anymore.

The thought gives me confidence as I walk onto the terrace. Sky is sitting in the big wicker peacock chair facing the setting sun. Chloe is in her playpen batting at a new mobile Billie must have gotten for her. I pick her up and take a turn on the terrace with her until Billie hands me a gin and tonic. I put Chloe back and take the smaller wicker chair next to Sky as Billie sets the table. Although I've been here only a week the routine makes it feel as if I've been here months. I haven't felt this at ease since . . . Well, I can't remember ever feeling so at ease. So comfortable in my own skin.

"How did your day go?" Sky asks.

"I've made a lot of progress," I tell Sky, "but I've hit a bit of a wall. Your father's journals end in 1973."

Sky nods as if this is to be expected. "When he stopped seeing patients. He retired a few months later."

"I'd like to find out more about the patients he was seeing at the time. Do you think Dr. Hancock would give me access to their files if I met with him?"

"Well, they *are* confidential, of course," Sky says, taking a sip of her drink. "But if I gave my permission I think it might be possible. You'd have to read them there, though. Would you mind spending part of the day down at Crantham?"

The question takes me by surprise. It feels like a trick question. I'm not sure what the right answer is. Does wanting to spend time at a mental hospital seem strange? Or does an aversion to it seem stranger? And what about Chloe? I see so little of her already.

As if in response to my concern Chloe holds up her arms, but before I can get up Billie swoops in and picks her up.

"If I can come back up for lunch to see Chloe I won't mind," I say.

"Of course you can come back up for lunch," Sky says. She drains her glass and smiles. "It's not as if you're being *admitted* there."

Daphne's Journal, July 23, 20—

I'm worried about Laurel. First of all, she took Peter's idea about quitting group seriously.

"What do we need them for?" she told me. "They're a bunch of losers. Do you really need to hear Alexa Hartshorn go on about how she's afraid she's a bad mother because she drank a cup of coffee before she nursed little Junior? Have you seen her lump of a baby? He could use a good shot of espresso. And I'm sick to death of Esta's sanctimonious, goody-two-shoes prattle. Honestly, telling me I shouldn't tell scary-mom stories because it might infect the 'more vulnerable mothers.' Like I'm Typhoid Mary."

That's another thing. Esta told *me* to stop telling scary-mom stories, *not* Laurel. When she told the jumper story at the party as if she had heard it first I didn't think much about it. I mean, everyone does that, right? Retell a story you've heard without saying where you heard it. No big deal. But there have been other things since. Retelling things Esta said to me as if she said them to her. Taking bits and pieces of my past and acting like they were hers. For instance, I heard her telling a woman at the gym that her baby was born prematurely. She told her how devastating it had been to watch her baby being force fed through a tube. But that didn't happen to Laurel; it happened to me.

I'm beginning to think that she has that OCD thing Esta told me about: she hears a story and then she begins to think it's *her* story. The worst thing is that Esta was right about the jumper story; it's really gotten to Laurel.

It started right after the party. We were at the salon having mani-pedis and she told me she was afraid there was something wrong with Chloë—*her* Chloë.

"I've never told anyone this," she whispered as if the Ukrainian girls scraping our feet would even understand, "but when Chloë was two months old, I left her on the bed and she rolled off. She hit her head so hard she threw up. I think she may have gotten brain damage."

"I'm sure she's fine," I said, remembering I'd told Laurel a story of doing the same thing with my Chloe. "She seems completely normal to me."

"But she's not rolling over on her own and your Chloe is." She was so agitated she jerked her foot and nearly kicked Svetlana in the face.

"Well . . ." I started to say something reassuring but she added, "And your Chloe was a preemie. She should be behind my Chloë developmentally."

I know it's silly but this made me a little angry for my Chloe. The doctor said I shouldn't worry if Chloe was behind on developmental milestones because of her being born early, but it was hard to listen to other mothers bragging about their babies rolling over and even sitting up already and to have to keep saying, "Well, she was a preemie." It felt good to have *my* Chloe doing something before Laurel's Chloe-with-an-umlaut.

So I just made a very concerned face and said, "Hm, maybe you should have her checked out." Which is practically the worst thing you can say to a mother.

Then I felt bad about it because Laurel took her Chloë to the hospital and had them run a battery of tests on her—even a CT scan. They didn't find anything but Laurel said she thinks they did but that they won't tell her because they're afraid of what she might do. That's when I found out about Laurel's history of mental illness. She told me that she had a breakdown when she was in college and again when she was in grad school. Then when she was pregnant she got really depressed and took some pills. She said she was just trying to get some sleep, but Stan brought her to the hospital and said she had tried to kill herself.

"That's how he became my mental-health conservator," she told me the last time I was at her house.

I didn't know what that was, so she had to explain it to me. I was kind of shocked, because it made it sound like Laurel really wasn't able to take care of herself. But I didn't want to make her feel bad, so I said, "I'm sure he just wanted to make sure he could help you if you were incapacitated. Like a power of attorney . . . Peter had me sign one in case something happened during delivery."

"But you don't have any money, so it doesn't really matter!" She was so loud that Simone, who was watching the Chloes in the yard, looked up. "I've got my inheritance. It's all in trust, of course, which drives Stan crazy, but with this conservatorship Stan could take all my money if I were in a coma."

I just stared at her, trying to think what to say to calm her down, and I noticed for the first time that she had these really dark circles under her eyes. "Are you getting any sleep?" I asked.

Her eyes widened the way they did in group when someone said something she thinks is stupid. "Why do you ask that? Are you saying I sound crazy?"

"No, no!" I lied. Because, really, she *did* sound a little crazy. "You just sound . . . *stressed out*. And I know what it was like when Chloe wasn't sleeping through the night."

Her eyes practically bulged out of her head. "You mean she is *now*? You didn't tell me that." She said it like I'd been keeping state secrets from her. The truth was I hadn't told her because I knew she'd be jealous.

"Oh, it's only been for a few nights." I laughed, trying to sound casual, but it came out sounding a little hysterical. "I didn't want to jinx it. And all I meant was that everything seems worse when you're overtired. You know, like when the Chloes act up when they haven't had their naps."

"I'm not a baby," she said frostily, getting up from the couch. "Sim, would you bring my Chloë in? I think it's time for her nap. I wouldn't want her to get cranky."

I tried to apologize, but Laurel pretended she didn't know what I was talking about. She got all remote, which I'd seen her do with Esta and some of the other mothers. *Ice bitch*, I heard Alexa Hartshorn call her once. But she'd never acted that way with me. I cried all the way home and it upset Chloe so much that she cried too. So there were the two of us just wailing away! I had to sit in the car a few minutes to get my composure back, because if Peter saw me like that he'd make a big fuss about it. Once when I cried in front of Chloe he said it was really bad for her to see me cry.

While I was spritzing my face with an atomizer Stan came out of the house. He was wearing his golfing outfit—a Ralph Lauren shirt and khaki shorts—and I remembered that he and Peter had had a golfing date. Seeing his skinny legs and knee-high socks I realized how ridiculous Laurel's fears were. I felt kind of sorry for Stan.

I dried my face and put on my sunglasses and got out of the car. Stan came up right away to help me with Chloe's car seat and carried it to the door. What a nice guy, I thought. He really didn't deserve a crazy, suspicious wife. I wanted to do something to help, so when we got to the door I told him I was worried about Laurel. I told him all about the jumper story and how she'd been talking about something being wrong with Chloë and that I was afraid she might have "internalized" the story.

Stan listened to it all very seriously, his head bowed, like he had the weight of the world on his shoulders, poor guy. When I was done he looked me right in the eyes (although since I still had my sunglasses on it was more like he was looking a little to the right of my eyes) and he touched my arm. "Thank you for telling me this, Daphne," he said. "I've been worried about her too. She—she has a history."

"She told me," I said, so he'd know he wasn't betraying Laurel's trust. "She said she was diagnosed with bipolar disorder."

He smiled, but it was a really sad smile. "That's what she tells people. But her diagnosis is more serious that that. She has BPD—borderline personality disorder."

"Oh!" I said, wondering if that was really worse. I don't know anything about borderline personality disorder, but the word *borderline* sounds kind of scary, like being balanced on the ledge of a tall building. "I didn't know."

"She's really good at hiding it," he said, looking away. "You wouldn't guess, for instance, that she's tried to kill herself twice."

"She told me taking those pills was an accident," I said.

"And cutting her wrists, did she say that was an accident too?"

That really shocked me. "Why would someone like Laurel try to kill herself? She's so beautiful and smart and . . ." I was going to say *rich* but stopped myself and said, "and so confident."

Stan smiled, but sadly. "That's what I thought when I first met her, but then I realized that it was all a show. It's part of her sickness. She can seem like a totally different person because when she's sick she *is* a totally different person. To tell you the truth, I'm not sure who the real Laurel is. Sometimes I think there is no real Laurel."

Which really scared me, because if there's no *real* Laurel, who the hell have I been friends with all these weeks?

Chapter Eight

I had planned to drive to Crantham, but when Billie comes to pick up Chloe she tells me she's already arranged to have a guard meet me at the back gate.

"I thought you'd want to walk," she says, bouncing Chloe up and down in her arms. "To get a feel for Dr. Bennett's routine."

"Yes, I guess that's a good idea," I say slowly, "only I thought I'd drive into town afterward to pick up some things."

"What do you need?" Billie asked. "I'll put it on my list."

The truth is I wanted to refill my—or rather, Laurel's—prescription for antidepressants but I wasn't sure how that was going to go. And I wasn't going to entrust that errand to Billie. So I list a few innocuous items like tampons, deodorant, and toothpaste. There's not much that isn't provided here. My kitchen is restocked regularly with tea and milk and cereal and I eat lunch and dinner with Sky and Billie. I haven't had any reason to leave the house since I came, which is probably for the best. Even though I've given Peter a good reason not to follow me, he could have reported the car as stolen. It's safer that I stay off the roads.

I change my shoes and follow Billie's directions to the back path. I miss it twice, so overgrown are the hedges that flank it.

The stone steps are nearly covered by moss. Two steps in and I'm in the deep shade of a pine forest. It's like entering a tunnel. How often does anyone take this path? Billie arrives every morning in a rusty old Honda Civic. Sky certainly can't manage it. The gardener obviously never sets foot on it. I should turn back and take the car, only I'd feel a little foolish if Billie saw me. And there is something . . . *alluring* about these woods—a haunted quiet that reminds me of fairy tales. Here is another clue to the stories that Sky wrote. She'd grown up surrounded by a forest, like a fairy-tale princess.

So I take a deep breath of pine-scented air and set off. The mossy stone steps give way to a path covered with dried pine needles that glow golden in the green filtered light. The only sounds are birdcalls and the wind sifting through the treetops. It's peaceful. I can imagine Dr. Bennett girding himself for the day ahead in the restorative calm. It must have been hard to see patients like E. who had so much potential but were hopelessly entangled in the workings of their misfiring brains.

As soon as I think of E. it's her I imagine on the path. Climbing up here to reach the tower where she thought her baby was being held, hearing her baby's cries in the sigh of the wind—

A sharp cry suddenly cleaves the slanted sunlight. I turn around so fast the trees spin, a kaleidoscope of branches and leaves, shards of light and dark. Something flits across the tilting sunbeams. I listen, but all I hear is my own ragged breath and stuttering heart. Even the birds have gone quiet, as if frightened by that horrible cry. Has a patient escaped from the hospital and hidden herself in the woods? It happened once; who's to say it won't happen again. She could be prowling through the woods now, looking for someone to attack for her civilian clothes.

A drop of sweat snakes down my back, sending a chill down

my spine. My skin prickles all over. The silence of the woods—so peaceful a moment ago—feels ominous now.

Panic, Laurel told me once, *comes from the name of the Greek god of nature, Pan, because of the sudden irrational fear that could strike a man in the woods.*

That's all this is, I tell myself, a panic attack. There's no lunatic prowling in the woods waiting to pounce on me. There's only me.

AT THE BOTTOM of the path I find a ten-foot-tall mesh fence with razor wire on top and WARNING! ELECTRIC FENCE! signs posted every couple of feet. There's also a locked gate. Clearly no mental patient has broken through this barrier. The uniformed guard standing on the other side doesn't look like he'd let a crazy woman hit him over the head. He's young, well over six feet tall, broad shouldered, muscular, and armed with a Taser. The eyes he trains on me are sharp and alert.

"Ms. Hobbes?"

It takes me a moment to remember that's who I am and to get over the surprise of his knowing my—or Laurel's—name, but then I remember that Billie has set this all up. "Yes. I'm here to see Dr. Hancock—Schuyler Bennett set up the appointment?" I'm instantly annoyed with myself for repeating what he must already know and for letting my voice go up at the end. As if I wasn't sure why I'm here or who I'm supposed to be.

"Can I see some ID?"

Has he picked up on my insecurity? Or has he seen my picture on a Missing Persons Alert? When I don't immediately produce my wallet he adds, "Just SOP, ma'am. Standard operating procedure."

"Oh—" I fumble for my wallet in my bag and produce Laurel's driver's license. Will it still look like me with my brown roots showing? "It's an awful picture."

The guard looks down at the picture and then up at me. I have time to notice there's a brown freckle in the white of his eye and a small scar dividing his right eyebrow. When he narrows his eyes, little crowfeet appear at their corners and he looks older than I first thought—thirties rather than twenties.

"Thank you, Ms. Hobbes." He hands me back my wallet. "Hospital policy."

"Of course, Officer . . ." I crane my neck to read his badge and I'm startled by what I read. "Marcus? That's the name of the guard who was attacked by a patient in the seventies."

The guard grimaces as he unlocks the gate. "My father. And the family claim to fame."

"I'm sorry," I say. "I grew up in a small town too. Everybody knew me as Tammy-the-town-drunk-some-people-shouldn't-ever-have-kids's kid."

He winces and grins at the same time, which makes him look somewhere in between the callow youth and seasoned veteran. Like a guy who's seen plenty of trouble but hasn't completely given up on people. I've made a connection with my confession but, I realize as I step through the gate, I've slipped up. I'd given him a piece of my own past instead of Laurel's.

OFFICER MARCUS, WHO tells me to call him Ben, gives me a tour on the way to the Main Building. "There's the laundry and the power plant. The hospital still produces its own steam power. That's where the dairy was." He points to a peeling red barn. "But it got too expensive to run. It produced enough milk and cheese and butter for the whole facility back when there were more than four hundred patients. They kept chickens too, and grew their own vegetables."

"Like a medieval village."

"Yeah," he says, "only populated by crazy people."

"And doctors," I add, "and nurses."

"Who do you think I was referring to?"

I laugh, although the idea that this place was run by crazy people makes me feel cold all over. "What did people say about Dr. Bennett?" I ask.

"Oh, he was like a god to the town for a while back in the sixties. He built the hospital up with his new and improved methods of treating the insane. Brought in a better class of patient too, socialites with drinking problems, the unruly pot-smoking teenagers of the rich, burnt-out executives . . ."

"You make it sound like a country club."

He shrugs. "I haven't been to many country clubs, but we do have our own golf course." The path, which has been winding decoratively through landscaped lawns, has led us to a rise that looks over a green golf course. A man in baggy pants and a tattered sweater vest is leaning over a ball with a club. As we pass he swings the club back and then forward toward the ball—but stops just before it makes contact. He shouts something incomprehensible and then swings the club back again and repeats the same aborted swing accompanied by the same shout, which should be "Fore!" but is actually, I hear now, "Fuck!"

"That's Mr. Simmons. He used to be a big deal at Lehman Brothers. Thank God for the sub-prime fallout. We were down to less than a hundred patients before 2008."

"What happened to Dr. Bennett's kingdom?" I ask.

"He retired. Then private insurers and Medicare stopped paying for long hospital stays. Then someone invented Prozac and the rich found other ways to treat their own. We're mostly a rehab clinic now with a few of the old guard in attendance."

I think of the blinking light I'd seen from the tower. "Are there any dangerous cases?"

"Most of these poor souls are so medicated, they wouldn't be able to punch their way out of a paper bag, but there's always one or two who tongue their meds and suddenly decide to do a runner. They can be surprisingly strong—and fast."

I look around at the gently curving paths, the landscaped grounds, the pairs of people strolling or sitting on benches. Beneath the bucolic calm there's a simmering sense of danger, like what I felt in the woods, a panic sizzling beneath the quiet. Looming over the pretty landscape is the Main Building, an imposing brick Victorian pile with a central clock tower, green mansard roof, and two wings. It looks more like a fancy college than a mental hospital, until I look up and see the bars on the windows. Nothing is quite what it seems to be here, I think, and then I hear a voice in my head reply, *Neither are you.*

BEN MARCUS TAKES me through the lobby, where I have to sign in at a security desk behind thick glass, and up an elevator that requires two sets of keys to operate. When we get off the elevator, the hallway is painted a perfectly pleasant shade of yellow. Framed paintings—modern abstracts with floating blobs of color—line the walls and the carpet is thick and clean. There's nothing institutional about it at all, but still I feel as if I can't breathe. "Don't worry," Marcus says, "the center of the building is only for administrative and doctors' offices. The patients are in the wings, and the doors to the wings are locked and guarded."

"What makes you think I'm worried?" I ask.

"You look a little green," he says, not unkindly. "Everybody does their first time."

"Yeah," I admit, "it feels . . . claustrophobic somehow."

"It took me a while to get used to it too."

I shudder at the thought of getting used to such a place and turn my attention to the paintings lining the wall so he won't notice my reaction. The paintings are no comfort, though. What had first looked like abstract blobs of color I see now are pieces of a face rearranged in random patterns: a nose floating beside an ear, a lock of hair curled like a seashell beside closed lips. Each picture by itself would be disconcerting enough, but viewed together they create the effect of a body splintered into a million pieces. As if the artist had been trying to reassemble the features of someone he had lost.

"One of the patients did those."

"What?" I ask, startled by Ben's voice.

"The paintings. They were done by a painter who was here in the sixties. He was famous. I guess that's why Bennett keeps them, but I've always thought they were kind of creepy."

I turn away from an eye staring up from a breast. "Did he end up here because of these paintings?" I ask.

"Oh no," Marcus answers. "He painted rather ordinary portraits before he got here. Maybe this was always inside him or . . ."

"Or what?"

"Or maybe he went crazy after he came here. I've always thought that if a person wasn't crazy when they got here, they would be soon enough."

Before I can think of a response to that, Ben Marcus knocks on the door at the end of the corridor and opens it. "I'll be out here to take you back," he says as I step through the door.

I almost say, *Thank God!* and *Please don't leave me here!* but instead I say thank you and walk in.

Dr. Hancock, a white-haired, tan man in his sixties, rises from his desk to greet me. "Ah, Miss Hobbes, so nice to meet you. Sky has been singing your praises." He shakes my hand and shows me to a comfortable chair in front of his desk. "Would you like something to drink? Tea? Coffee?" He waves to a sideboard set with a water carafe and an electric kettle.

"Some water would be nice," I say, sinking into the plush chair. "I walked over."

"Did you?" he asks, his eyebrows shooting up. "Good for you. I've always envied Dr. Bennett that commute. I drive from Garrison every day."

I flinch. Garrison is only a few towns north of where I live. What if Dr. Hancock knows Laurel or Stan? Crantham feels so isolated that I'd forgotten how close the real world is. "That's a long commute," I say to cover up my reaction. "You must be very dedicated."

He shrugs. "My wife wasn't willing to give up the amenities of the suburbs and the proximity of our grandchildren. After what happened to Mrs. Bennett I thought it was better to yield to her needs."

"What happened?"

"Oh, I thought you knew . . ." He looks at me suspiciously as if my not knowing about this means I'm not a real archivist. *Remember, you're here to ask the questions*, I hear Laurel's voice say in my head. *Don't let this officious prick rattle you.*

"Sky hasn't talked much about her mother," I say, hoping my use of my employer's first name will put me back on better footing. "Why don't you tell me?"

"I'm not surprised Sky doesn't talk about it. She was only seventeen when her mother killed herself. Hanged herself. It was a terrible thing."

"That *is* terrible," I say, thinking that at least my mother had the good grace to die in a drunken car accident that left a little wriggle room as to her intentions. "Did you know the family then?"

"Only slightly. I'd met Dr. Bennett when I was doing my residency at the Hudson Valley Psychiatric Center over in Poughkeepsie. Dr. Bennett was a consulting psychiatrist there. When he retired he personally recommended me for his replacement. He was quite the imposing figure. I've always hoped Sky would write about him. I gather that you're assisting her in her memoir?"

"Yes," I say, gratified that Sky has mentioned this to him. But of course she would have to explain my interest in E.S.

"Well, I'm glad you're here to help. I worry about Sky all alone up there in that big old house."

"She's got Billie," I say, looking up at the doctor. Instead of going back around behind his desk he's perched on its edge. I suppose he means it to be informal but I feel like he's hovering over me.

"Ah, the inestimable Billie! Loyal to a fault. Did you know they've known each other since they were children? Dr. Bennett hired Billie's mother to look after Sky's mother when she was suffering postpartum depression, and she would bring along Billie. They practically grew up together. Billie would lay down her life for Sky, but she doesn't exactly provide intellectual companionship. But you! St. Andrews and the University of Edinburgh! Quite impressive! What made you decide to go to school abroad?"

I'm still trying to parse Billie's history—she'd mentioned that Dr. Bennett helped her through nursing school but not that she and Sky had grown up together—so the question about *my* history catches me off guard. Luckily, Laurel's answer pops out of my mouth. "Edinburgh had the best archives program . . .

and after my parents died I wanted to start over where no one knew me." Just exactly how Laurel had said it. She always had two reasons for everything, and when she gave you the second one she also gave you the feeling that she was confiding in you.

"Eminently sensible," Dr. Hancock said, leaning back and crossing his arms over his chest. "One of my son's friends did the program at Edinburgh. Maybe you knew him . . . Todd Walsh?"

I pretend to consider whether I know Todd Walsh before shaking my head. "I had my nose stuck in my books," I say, and then, to ward off any more biographical questions: "I'm afraid I'm a bit of a workaholic. Right now, I'm totally engrossed in Dr. Bennett's journals and his accounts of his patients. Sky said you might be able to help me with that?" I end with a little lilt in my voice and cross my legs. Which is what Laurel would do.

I see Dr. Hancock pretend to not look at my legs and then he smiles. "I can't actually give you a patient's file, but, for an old friend like Sky, I think I can bend the rules a little bit and . . . er . . . give you some information. Who was it you were interested in?"

"A patient with the initials E.S. Admitted 1971, suffering from postpartum mood disorder, possibly postpartum psychosis. She may have tried to kill herself. Dr. Bennett's journals end in 1973."

"Hm." Dr. Bennett rubs his chin. "I came on in 1973. I think I do remember . . . hold on . . ." He goes to a file cabinet and opens a drawer. While I wait, I look at the books on his shelves: thick volumes of the *DSM* editions one through five bound journals of the American Psychiatric Association, and, looking out of place amid the scholarly tomes, *The Collected Stories* of Schuyler Bennett.

"Here she is. Edith Sharp. Nineteen years old when admitted. She had a breakdown her sophomore year at Vassar. She gave birth to a baby in her dorm."

"Yes, that must be her. Dr. Bennett said she gave birth in her dorm room."

"The dorm bathroom actually. Her roommate found her in the bathtub nearly bled out."

I wince and close my eyes as if I could protect myself from the image, but instead my brain is flooded by a wash of red. I see a woman in a bathtub full of blood, the blood seeping over the white porcelain rim. *Leave it,* I tell myself.

I open my eyes to banish the image. "That's awful," I say, blinking to clear the red film that still clings to my eyes. "But I thought . . . from Dr. Bennett's notes . . . that she abandoned her baby in a dumpster. He doesn't mention anything about a roommate."

"Yes, well, apparently the roommate went to get help and while she was gone Edith dragged herself out of the tub and—in the middle of a snowstorm, no less—carried the baby to a dumpster."

"Why?" I ask. Dr. Hancock looks confused, so I try to clarify. "I mean . . . she knew her roommate had gone for help. She must have known she'd be found out."

Dr. Bennett smiles. "You're reasoning like a rational person, Ms. Hobbes, and Edith Sharp was anything but rational at that point. In fact, when she was discovered putting the baby in the dumpster she maintained that the baby was her roommate's baby, a delusion she maintained for some time. I'm surprised that Dr. Bennett doesn't write about that in his journal. It's all here in her files, and it's by far the most interesting element of the case—a true case of BPD mirroring, although it wasn't called that at the time."

"BPD?" I ask, remembering that this is what Stan had said Laurel had.

"Yes, she had what would be diagnosed today as a borderline personality disorder—a difficult disorder to diagnose precisely because the patient may present with wildly different affects at different times. Someone with BPD has no stable sense of self. He or she will latch onto others and mimic their personalities. And that can lead to dissociative episodes during which the ill person may believe himself or herself to be someone else—even having no memory of the episode afterwards. The shock of giving birth triggered a dissociative episode in Edith. She may have experienced a blackout. When she came to, she believed it was her roommate who had had the baby."

The idea of being so far gone as to imagine yourself another person is so unsettling that for a moment I'm silenced. Then it reminds me of something Stan said about Laurel being a totally different person when she was sick.

"You . . . you mean she started impersonating her roommate?"

Dr. Hancock stares at me a moment before answering. "I wouldn't have put it like that, but I suppose you could say it was a form of impersonation. Only it was entirely unconscious. Someone suffering from BPD may not be aware that they've adopted another person's personality. They don't recognize that they've changed, because they don't recognize who they are."

I'm thinking about what Stan told me about Laurel, but Dr. Hancock misinterprets my expression. "I know it's hard to grasp. Picture it like this." He holds his hands up, thumbs extended, making a frame in front of my face. "Imagine looking into a mirror and seeing a total stranger. Edith had no self to cling to. The traumatic episode made her 'mirror' her roommate's experience. She came here fixed in the delusion that her roommate had given birth, and that the roommate had disposed of the baby because there was something wrong with it, an impression no doubt born, if you'll forgive the pun, from the memory of what the newborn premature baby had looked like."

I shudder, picturing Chloe when she was born—tiny and shriveled and bloody. "And what happened to Edith?"

"She tried to kill herself by jumping from a window in Dr. Bennett's study." He shakes his head. "Of course, it was foolish of him to see a patient off-site. It was lucky she survived."

"And was she better after that?" I ask, my voice betraying how desperate I am for a happy ending. Dr. Hancock stares at me. He must see that my interest is no longer academic. When he answers, his voice is gentle, though, as if breaking the news to a child that there is no Santa Claus. "There is no cure for BPD," he says, "but the dissociative episode was finally ended. The patient was able to accept that she was the one who had given birth . . . or at least . . ." Dr. Hancock hesitates.

"At least what?" I ask.

"At least she was able to convince her doctors she had given up the delusion. Patients with BPD are notorious for 'tricking' their doctors. It may be that Edith Sharp simply adopted another imposture."

I don't understand. "Of who?"

"Of herself," Dr. Hancock answers, "but herself *cured*."

Daphne's Journal, August 1, 20—

I'm waiting for Peter to get off the phone so he'll watch Chloe so I can go over to Laurel's and I think it's a good idea to write down what's been going on to get it clear in my head.

I still haven't heard from Laurel since we had the fight. At first I was so angry I didn't care. All I had done was tell her there was nothing wrong with her baby and suggest she get some more sleep and she'd jumped down my throat. I assumed she'd apologize—send me a text with a sorry-face emoji and a cocktail glass and act like it was no big deal. I assumed I'd forgive her. But she didn't text or email or call. I even checked my spam to make sure I hadn't missed anything. Nada. Zilch. Not even a sorry-face emoji.

Then I started thinking about what Stan had told me about Laurel having BPD and trying to kill herself and I started worrying about her. I know how suicidal thoughts can get lodged in your brain, especially when you feel trapped. It had happened to me right after Chloe was born. I started hearing the words *I want to die* in my head, as if someone else was saying them. They were the first words I'd hear in my head when I woke up in the morning, the last when I lay down at night. *No you don't,* I'd tell myself. *You should be happy. You have a beautiful baby and a loving husband.*

I don't deserve them, the voice would answer.

You can't leave Chloe, I would argue back.

Maybe she would be better off without you, the voice would counter, or once, ominously, *Then take her with you.*

One day Peter found me asleep in the bathtub. It scared me half to death, waking up in cold water, Peter's hands on my shoulders. I was so startled, I thought he was trying to push me under the water when of course he was trying to do the opposite. I thrashed around and soaked the whole bathroom, and the carpet in the hallway. Peter was so upset. *What kind of a mother kills herself, leaving a child behind?* he shouted. I tried to tell him that it was just that I'd been so tired that I'd fallen asleep, but then Peter held up an empty bottle of sleeping pills. "Then why did you take these?" he asked. I didn't remember taking the pills, but I must have because I felt so groggy. I must have finally succumbed to the voices.

That's when I started going to the mothers' support group. I stopped taking baths too. I haven't heard the voice since. But now, thinking about Laurel, I remember what it was like and I feel terrible about the way I acted. I told Peter about it and he surprised me by being really sensitive. "It sounds like she really can't help the way she acts," he said. "Maybe you're being too hard on her. It's a shame to let the friendship go when she's been such a positive influence."

So of course that made me feel really bad. I even called up Esta and told her how Laurel was acting and she said that yes, Laurel might have BPD, but I should worry about myself and not "overproject." Whatever that means. For a therapist she's not very helpful! So I looked up BPD on the Internet and I was surprised to find all these blogs by people who have BPD talking about how hard it is to make and keep friends and advice pieces on how to cope if someone you love has BPD and I realized it was a sickness like alcoholism or postpartum depression and it really isn't fair to judge Laurel, because Peter was right. She really can't help the way she acts. No more than I could help listening to that voice that told me to take the pills.

Also, I found out the reason Laurel reacted to me like she did. It's because I'm her Favorite Person. That's a special phrase for people in the BPD community and it means a person whom the BPD idealizes. I know that might sound a little vain, but I can see it now. Even though I admire Laurel so much there's a lot that Laurel envies in me—like the fact I put myself through school without a lot of money, and how I lived on my own before I met Peter. All her taking me to her gym and hair stylist and the stores where she shops was kind of her way of making me over in her image so that she could see herself in me. Even her being competitive with Chloe's progress shows she really wanted to be like me. But the thing I learned from the blogs is that if a BPD's Favorite Person disappoints them, if they fail to live up to expectations, then the BPD turns on the FP and gets really angry with them. They devalue them. That's what Laurel is doing with me.

Which is really sad when you think about it.

I talked to Peter about it and he agreed I should go over and talk to her again. He even said he'd watch Chloe as soon as he got off the phone. So I've been writing this while I've been waiting for him. I've also been looking up archivist jobs on the Internet. I thought it might be good for Laurel to see that there were lots of options for her. And there were! I was surprised at how many I found and how interesting they sounded! Lots more glamorous than the school librarian job I'd had. There were a couple in the city and one in California at the Huntington Library and one in Philadelphia at a place called the Library Company. Of course, it would be hard for Laurel to do those, but still, with her money I guess she could up and move if she wanted to. There was even one in Vermont that I might be qualified for, but Peter would have a fit if I said I wanted to move to Vermont. I printed out the listings and put them in one of the pretty decorative folders Laurel and I had bought together at the fancy stationer's in town and I'm all ready to go. . . .

Peter's still on the phone so I think I'll just take Chloe with me. I feel a little nervous but also good about it. It's time I stopped thinking about just myself. For the first time since Chloe was born I feel like I'm really in control.

LATER.

Okay, that didn't go so well and now I'm really scared.

I got over there and Simone answered the door. When she saw me she stepped outside and closed the door behind her.

"Did she call you?" she asked.

I told her no and explained that I was worried about her. Simone shook her head and for an awful moment I thought she was going to send me away, but then she said how Laurel had been in an awful state and she was worried about her and Chloë. "I told Mr. Hobbes she should not be left on her own."

"Are you afraid she might hurt Chloë?" I asked.

Her eyes got all glassy and she put her hand on my arm and nodded. I could see she was too upset to talk. And I also realized how young Simone is and how hard it must be for her, living in a foreign country. When I asked if she would keep an eye on Chloe when I went in to see Laurel she said yes, but she begged me not to tell Laurel that she had let me in, because she might yell at her later.

I'm not sure what I expected but I never thought a person could change so much in a week. Laurel was wearing a pair of sweatpants that I thought must have belonged to Stan, because I was pretty sure she didn't own anything so baggy. She was sitting on the couch flipping through the TV channels, only her eyes were so glazed I don't think she was really seeing anything. Her hair was hanging around her face, lank and greasy like she hadn't washed it in days. Her skin was so white I thought for a moment she must have a facial mask on, but then I saw the dark rings under her eyes and smudged eyeliner and realized she probably hadn't even washed her face since I was here last. When she looked up at me, she barely seemed to register my existence. Like I was just another channel on the television. I sat down on the edge of the couch and noticed a smell. At first I thought it was the couch but then I realized it was Laurel.

"Hey," I said after a few minutes. "I came by to see if you were all right."

She made a sound, like a little croak, but then I realized it was a laugh. "And what do you think?" she asked, still staring at the television set. "Do I look all right to you?"

"No," I admitted. "You look like shit."

She laughed harder at that, so hard she started coughing. I offered her the half-filled water bottle on the coffee table but she waved it away. "Stan mixed that for me. It's supposed to have electrolytes and stuff in it but it tastes like shit. I think he's trying to poison me."

"Why would Stan do that?" I asked.

"To get my inheritance," she replied. Then she grinned, which looked all wrong on her face. "But he's in for a surprise. I've changed my will so he's no longer Chloë's guardian, so he won't have control of the money."

I was so shocked that I couldn't say anything right away but then I remembered what I'd read about people with BPD. Once their Favorite Person fell from grace they were completely devalued. Maybe Stan had been her FP once and now she was devaluing him. "He must know that," I said, trying to talk to her logically. "So why would he poison you?"

"Good point," she said, taking the bottle from me and taking a swig. "Maybe he's just trying to drive me mad so he can take Chloë away from me and have me committed."

I started to argue with her but then I saw that's what she wanted. Whatever I said she'd find some flaw in it. So instead I said, "So why are you helping him?"

She stared at me for a minute. I thought she was going to get angry at me, but she just tilted her head and smiled. "You know, you're smarter than you look."

I wasn't sure if I should be angry or flattered by that, so I just said, "I've been told I look a lot like you."

This time when she laughed it sounded like a real laugh and then she started crying. "Maybe not so much right now," she said. She was right; we don't look that much alike anymore. The funny thing is that with her roots grown out, the dark circles under her eyes, and the couple of pounds she's put on, she looks like the old me—the me before I met Laurel. It's like we've switched places.

I moved closer to her on the couch and touched her arm. "Hey," I said, "you've got so much going for you. You could go anywhere. You have enough money."

"It's protected even from me," she said. "If I tried to leave, Stan would have me declared incompetent."

That didn't sound at all like Stan, but I knew it was better not to argue with her. "Then get a job," I said. "If I had your credentials I'd apply for one of those fancy archival positions. I saw these . . ." I handed her the folder of job ads. She paged through them listlessly then let the folder slide into the gap between the cushions. "Don't you see? It would be a way out. You could start over. Find yourself again."

"What do you mean *find myself*?" she asked suspiciously.

I realized I couldn't say I'd been reading about people with BPD or she'd know that Stan had told me, and that would just make her more paranoid. "I've been reading . . . about women with postpartum depression. Like us. Sometimes we can feel like we've lost touch with who we are . . . it can feel like we've lost ourselves."

She turned her head and looked at me—*really* looked at me—for the first time since I'd come in, her eyes traveling up from my new Tod's loafers to the New Religion jeans and boho Anthropologie top and Kate Spade diaper bag (with all the right pockets) to my artfully tousled and highlighted hair.

"Look at you," she said. "You're the one who's lost yourself. Why don't you apply for one of these jobs if they sound so great?"

"I don't have the credentials," I said, determined not to be hurt by her words. "You do."

"Then use mine," Laurel said. "You've taken everything else that was mine. Why not take my name too?"

I knew it was just her sickness talking, but still it stung to hear her put it like that. She'd encouraged me to go to her hairdresser and buy the diaper bag with all the right pockets and dress like her. But with her looking at me like that I saw how pathetic I was, how ridiculous it made me look. Like some kind of wannabe.

"Okay," I said, getting up. "Call me if you want to talk. If not for your own sake, then for Chloë's."

She laughed again, but it was that strangled sound that really wasn't a laugh at all. "Maybe she'd be better off without me. Maybe I should walk into the Hudson with rocks in my pockets like Virginia Woolf."

It sounded so much like my own voice—the one that had urged me to kill myself—that for a moment I was sure it was my bad voice talking, not Laurel. But then I looked down at Laurel and realized that her head must be full of those bad voices.

"Laurel," I said, "you wouldn't . . . you're not thinking of hurting yourself, are you?"

She looked up at me, startled, her blurry eyes focusing for the first time since I'd come in. "What would make you say something like that?" she asked in a hoarse voice I didn't recognize.

"It's just that Stan said . . ."

"What?" she snapped when I hesitated. "What did Stan say?"

I realized I'd made a mistake. If I told her that Stan told me about her suicide attempt she'd feel betrayed, but if I didn't—and she *does* hurt herself—I'd never forgive myself. The second option seemed worse. "He said you tried to kill yourself. It's nothing to feel ashamed about; I did it too, just after Chloe was born. I just felt so overwhelmed and tired. I just wanted to sleep. I don't even think I meant to. Maybe you didn't mean to either." I could hear myself babbling and knew I was about to start crying, so I shut up.

Laurel stared up at me, her mouth literally hanging open. "Did you tell anyone about this?" she asked finally. "About my so-called suicide attempt?"

"Only Peter," I said. "And he was so sympathetic. He urged me to come over—"

"Get out," she said, so quietly that at first I thought I must have misheard her. Then she got louder. "GET OUT!!!"

I was so surprised I jumped. Then I grabbed the folder off the couch and ran to the door. I was crying so hard I couldn't see. I had to put down my bag and the folder to wipe my eyes. Simone brought Chloe and held her out to me. For a moment I just couldn't take her. Laurel's words were ringing in my head. *Maybe she'd be better off without me. Maybe she'd be better off without me.* It felt like the words had gotten stuck in my head and I couldn't hold Chloe until I had shaken them off.

"Leave it!" I said out loud.

Simone stared at me like I was crazy. Like I'd been talking about Chloe. I didn't know how to explain so I just grabbed Chloe and my diaper bag and walked to my car. I cried all the way home, Laurel's words going through my head over and over again. *Maybe she'd be better off without me, maybe she'd be better off without me.* I think for the first time I really understood what it meant to lose your mind and it made me scared. What if that happened to me? What would happen to Chloe? I knew I'd never hurt her in my right mind but what if I wasn't in my right mind? What if those voices came back, like the ones that had told me to take the sleeping pills and drown myself in the tub? What if *this* time I took Chloe with me into the tub? *It would be better*, a voice said, *to kill yourself first.*

Which made a certain kind of sense.

I thought Peter would be out when I got home but he wasn't. He was waiting for me on the porch.

"What's the matter?" I asked because he looked like he'd gotten bad news. He had his laptop in his lap so I thought it must be something in the stock market. He turned it around so I could see the screen. It took me a few minutes to realize what I was looking at—the screen was open to the job site where I had looked up the archivist jobs for Laurel. It was my laptop he was holding, not his.

"What are you doing with my laptop?" I asked. It came out angrier-sounding than I'd meant it because I was still so on edge from seeing Laurel.

"I was having trouble getting online so I was checking to see if the problem was with my computer or the modem—I didn't think you'd mind. I was surprised to find that you were looking at jobs, especially ones so far away."

"I was looking for Laurel," I said.

"Why would *she* be looking for work," Peter scoffed. "She's loaded."

"I thought it would make her feel more independent. You know it can be dispiriting being home all day with a baby without any intellectual stimulation."

"Is that how *you* feel?"

I started to deny it but then I realized that maybe it *was* how I felt. "Maybe," I said. "A little. Would it be so bad if I went back to work? You're always saying we're tight for money—"

"We're doing fine right now," he snapped. He hated when I put it that way. *We've got some cash-flow issues* was his preferred terminology, but I was damned if I was going to say that. "And how would it look if a hedge-fund manager's wife was working at the local school's library?"

"Lots of rich women work."

"At prestigious jobs, not as school librarians."

I felt my cheeks burning as if he'd slapped me. When we met he'd seemed charmed that I was a school librarian. When had it become something to be embarrassed about? But he was right. It wasn't the kind of job a rich woman would do.

"I've been thinking of getting an archival degree." As I said it I realized it was true. I wanted to do more than shelve Nancy Drews for the rest of my life.

"So, you *were* looking at those jobs for yourself."

The way he said it, like he'd caught me out in a lie, lit something in me. A spark of anger that I hadn't even known was smoldering. "And what if I had been? What if I'm tired of being lectured about money all the time? I could work, make my own money, be independent—"

"You'd better think carefully about what you're saying," he said in a voice so low I could feel it rumble in my bowels.

"Or what?" I asked, that spark flaring into flame. "I'm Chloe's mother, mothers always get custody."

"Not mentally ill ones."

I felt like I'd been slapped. "I-I've just had some postpartum depression."

"You tried to kill yourself," he said. "You're on antidepressants. If you try to leave me, I'll sue for full custody and I'll make sure you never see Chloe again."

I felt like I'd been punched in the stomach. I couldn't say anything. Peter stared at me for another moment and then he got up and reached for Chloe's car seat. I stepped back and nearly fell off the porch. He grabbed my arm to steady me.

"I'll take Chloe in and give her a bath," he said. "You try to get a hold of yourself."

I hadn't even realized I was crying. I ran upstairs and locked myself in the bedroom and cried and cried. And then I started writing all this down so I could figure out how things had gotten so out of hand. I hadn't even been thinking of leaving Peter—

Or had I?

Those jobs in Vermont and New York do sound awfully appealing—

Not that I would ever take Chloe away from Peter. I know how much he loves her, which is why he got upset when he thought I was trying to take Chloe from him—

What if he takes her from me?

Writing all this down isn't helping. I think I need to talk to someone. I'm going to try calling Laurel.

I'M REALLY SCARED now. I went to look for my phone in Chloe's diaper bag but I couldn't find it. I searched the bag again and found a wallet, only it wasn't mine; it was Laurel's. I just stared at it, trying to figure out how Laurel's wallet had gotten into my diaper bag. Then it came to me. I'd taken Laurel's bag. Hers had been sitting by the door. I must have picked up hers by mistake.

And then a really scary thing happened. I heard Laurel's voice in my head saying *You've taken everything that was mine.* It was like she was right there in the room with me. It made me think that Peter might be right. I *am* mentally unfit to take care of Chloe. I'm the one who has lost myself. I'm the one who's hearing strange voices in my head.

Then I heard Laurel's voice say *He's going to take her from you* and *You have to get away before he does.*

The scariest thing is that I think the voice might be right, but I can't help also remembering what Laurel said about hearing voices: They all sound sensible at the time.

Chapter Nine

I leave Dr. Hancock's office feeling shaken. I don't know what I'd been expecting. To find Edith Sharp had lived a happy, productive life, raised five children, written a memoir about her brush with madness and her miraculous recovery? I'm beginning to see that no one who is brushed with madness is left unscathed. Just hearing Edith Sharp's story has left me with blurry vision and a splitting headache that feels like an alarm going off in my head. An insistent wailing cry—

There *is* an alarm going off—a deafening siren. When I step out of Dr. Hancock's office the receptionist is standing at the window fingering her pearls. Ben Marcus is nowhere in sight. "What's going on?" I ask. "Where's Officer Marcus?"

The secretary gives me a startled look. "An alarm's gone off in C Ward. It's—"

Before she can finish, Dr. Hancock comes rushing out of his office. "Code Red!" he barks to his secretary. She turns as white as her pearls.

"What does that mean?" I ask, but Dr. Hancock and his secretary are already walking away. Dr. Hancock turns back to snap, "Stay put!"

Two more doors open in the hall and two doctors in white

coats come out and join them in their hurried flight to the elevators. Then I am alone in the reception room staring at the painting of the disembodied eye.

Which isn't very comforting at all.

I go to the window to see what the secretary had been looking at. The retired Lehman Brothers golfer is waving his golf club over his head while two orderlies in white scrubs try to placate him. Is that the Code Red? But the secretary said the alarm had gone off in C Ward. Isn't that one of the wings in this building? Ben Marcus said that the doors between the wards and the central part of the building are locked and guarded. So I have nothing to worry about.

So why had Dr. Hancock and his secretary looked so worried?

And how long am I supposed to wait here like a sitting duck? At the very least Dr. Hancock should have suggested I sit in his office. If he'd had the time I'm sure he would have thought of it. He left the door open. . . .

I let myself in, close the door behind me, and lock it. The snick of metal makes me feel instantly better. I pour myself a glass of water and sit down in the plush comfortable chair. I look again at the bookshelves, at the framed diplomas, at the file cabinet . . .

The drawer from which Dr. Hancock had taken out Edith Sharp's file is slightly ajar. Would it really do any harm to look at it? After all, Sky had given her permission. And I need something to keep my mind off that infernal siren.

I open the drawer. The file is still sticking up so I'm able to pluck it out quickly, upending the file behind it so I'll know where to put it back. I flip it open, being careful that nothing falls out. The first thing I notice is a photograph of a young woman stapled to the inside of the folder. She's wearing a neat hairdo—

bangs, shoulder-length hair curled under, a headband—that looks like it might have been popular in the sixties—or the early seventies if you were a conservative proper girl.

A scream rends the air and I nearly drop the folder. It sounds impossibly near, practically in the room. But that's only because it's coming from the open window. Still holding the folder, I cross to the window. Outside I can see a woman running from the building, a uniformed guard chasing after her. She is wearing loose gray pajamas. Her hair is a white nimbus floating over her head like a cloud, and as she runs up the slope of the golf course I have the impression that the cloud will bear her aloft into the air. I watch, willing it to happen, but then the guard—Ben Marcus, I realize—catches up with her and grabs her around the waist. She spins around and for a moment they look like they're dancing. But then I see her face. She's looking up into the air as if she were expecting help to come from above. Her gaze falls on me at the window and our eyes meet for a second before Ben Marcus tackles her to the ground. I flinch, but whether in sympathy for the impact of her hitting the ground or the impact of those wide green eyes I'm not sure.

On the ground, the woman continues to struggle. Ben Marcus is trying to hold her down, and it looks to me like he's trying to do it without hurting her. Another guard who's come onto the scene loses patience and Tases her. I look away as her body jerks, not wanting to see more, and realize that now that she's been caught Dr. Hancock may be back soon.

I hurry back to the file drawer but before I put the folder away I open it to look at the photo one more time. The young hopeful girl in the picture with the old-fashioned hairdo, sweater set, and graduated pearls couldn't be more unlike the bedraggled fleeing woman with the wild nimbus of hair and lined, weathered face, but the eyes . . . the wide green eyes are the same.

THAT NIGHT AT dinner I don't mention the attempted escape. I'm still trying to sort out what I saw. More than forty years have elapsed since Edith Sharp was admitted. Was the escapee really the girl in the picture? And if she *is* Edith Sharp, why did Billie say she got better? And why didn't Dr. Hancock say she was still at Crantham?

I focus on Chloe, spooning carrots into her mouth, singing the ridiculous little choo-choo song that Billie uses to get her to eat, burping her afterward and walking back and forth on the terrace until she falls asleep. Finally, though, when she is asleep, there's no reason not to put her down. When I look up from her stroller, I see that Sky is watching me.

"I hear that there was an incident at the hospital today," she says. "It must have been frightening for you."

"Not nearly as frightening for me as for that poor woman," I say, adding, "I saw her from the window. She looked . . . *terrified.*"

Sky clucks her tongue. "Poor lamb, she thinks it's 1971 and she's being punished for having had premarital sex."

"You know her?" I ask.

"I know *of* her," Sky says. "She was one of my father's last patients. Edith Sharp."

"But I thought . . ." I look over at Billie, who's placidly cutting her steak into tiny pieces. Edith Sharp must be the woman Billie told me about who jumped from the tower and got better, but for some reason Billie must not want me to let Sky know that we've talked about her. Maybe she doesn't want Sky to know she was talking about a patient.

"What did you think?" Sky asks.

Should I mention the story Billie told me? But if Billie doesn't want Sky to know she told me that story, I don't want to embarrass her. After all, she *is* taking care of Chloe. "I guess I just never imagined that she might still be here. She was suffering from postpartum psychosis and that's usually temporary."

"Usually, but not always," Sky says. "Sometimes postpartum psychosis occurs in women with previous histories of mental illness—bipolar disorder or borderline personality disorder."

"That's what Dr. Hancock said Edith had—borderline personality disorder. He said she gave birth in her dorm bathroom but convinced herself that it was her roommate who had the baby."

"Well," Sky says. "I suppose such a terrifying occurrence could unhinge a person." There's a tremor in her voice that makes Billie look up from her carefully shredded steak.

"This is not very pleasant dinnertime conversation," she says with a reproving look at me.

"I'm sorry," I say, thinking that I wasn't the one who brought it up. It reminds me of when Esta chided me for telling the jumper story. "I didn't mean to upset anyone."

"It's all right," Sky says. "Living in such close proximity to a mental hospital I've seen and heard worse than poor Edith's story. And besides, you see it proves your thesis."

"It does?"

"Yes. I *had* heard of Edith's case. It must have influenced my writing of the changeling story and I simply forgot about it. I imagine that once I'd made it into my own fictional story I forgot all about the source. I think you should continue exploring Edith's case. I'll tell Dr. Hancock to make a copy of the file for you."

Billie looks up at this, caution on her face. I don't blame her; I'm sure that releasing a patient's file to non-hospital personnel must violate any number of legal and ethical codes. But I don't really care. I'm still smarting from Billie's remark about "inappropriate dinner conversation" and I'm childishly glad to have Sky siding with me. Most of all, though, I want to find out more about Edith Sharp.

I DREAM ABOUT her that night. Edith is running in front of me, her white hair glowing like one of the lanterns in the gardens, and I'm following her through the hedge maze. Then we're climbing the spiral stairs in the tower, going up and up for so long I feel like we're climbing to the moon.

"We need to get the right view," Edith says without turning around. When we get to the top floor, there's a huge claw-foot tub where the desk used to be. I can hear water dripping into the tub, but I can't see the surface because it's too high. "We need to get the right perspective," Edith says, walking toward the tub.

I freeze on the top step, unable or unwilling to follow her. I don't want to see what's in that tub.

I look down and notice that the floor is wet. The hem of Edith's pajama bottoms is darkening in the water as she walks toward the tub. Water is dripping down the stairs, pinging on each metal step, making a sorrowful music.

"A water dirge," Edith says.

I look up despite my urge not to. She is standing beside the tub, facing me, but she's no longer the old Edith; she's the girl in the photograph, neat hair, headband, sweater set, graduated pearls. She's motioning to the tub like a campus tour guide. Like it's a stop on the tour I can't miss.

I wade through the water, which is surprisingly warm—like bathwater, which I suppose it is—until I am standing beside the tub.

"We need to get the right view," Edith says, stepping aside so that I can see what's in the tub. It's a woman lying just below the surface of the red-tinged water, her face oddly peaceful, turned to the baby cradled in her arms.

I jerk awake, my arms flying out to grasp something—

The baby. I'm trying to grab the baby in the dream and pull her out of the tub but there's nothing to hold on to. My arms collapse on empty air.

The baby is gone.

I come fully awake, tangled in sweaty sheets, alone in the bed. Alone.

Chloe is gone.

I sit up, pulling the sheets apart, looking for her. The cushion is still propped up on the other side of the bed. Did she somehow slide under it and fall off the bed? I push the cushion aside and crawl to the other side of the bed, then slither to the floor. I paw the dusty floorboards, peering through the dark for Chloe. I need light. But when I stand up the room spins and when I try to turn on the lamp my fingers are too slick with sweat—as if I'd really just plunged my arms into a bathtub—

The bathtub.

It was just a dream, I tell myself, but I'm already running, flinging open the bedroom door. Across the living room I can see that the bathroom door is open. A wedge of light spills out onto the floor like a blade that cuts off the air in my throat.

I didn't leave that light on, I tell myself as I wade across the room through air that has turned heavy as water. *I didn't carry Chloe into the bathroom. I didn't run a bath and put her into the tub.*

The worst story anyone told in group was told by a mousy little woman named Judith who said she'd heard of a woman (a friend of a friend, as if this were a sort of postpartum urban legend) who was so afraid of hurting her baby that she would sleepwalk at night and move her baby to places where she would be safe. She'd wake up and find her baby under the bed, in the laundry hamper, and, finally, in the car seat in a running car in the garage, where the paramedics found him, dead of carbon monoxide poisoning. She'd been dreaming, Judith told us in a breathy whisper, of taking the baby to the doctor to find out why he kept crying.

When I reach the bathroom, the tile feels wet under my feet but that could be because sweat is pouring off me. Even though I am shaking with cold. I cross to the tub, look down, and there she is. My baby. My perfect, plump, chubby-armed baby lying at the bottom of the bone-dry tub.

Chloe is swaddled in blankets and sleeping peacefully, but when I scoop her up she awakes and cries out as if angry to be taken from her comfy tub-bed. I squeeze her to my chest, rocking her back and forth, not sure who I'm trying to comfort with the motion. "It's okay," I tell her as I take us both back to the bedroom. "I'll never do that again."

Even, I tell myself, *if I have to never sleep again.*

Daphne's Journal, August 7, 20—

Ever since the argument Peter's been acting as if nothing happened. He's been really nice, checking with me to see if I need anything when he goes out and offering to watch Chloe for me.

Maybe he feels bad about what he said . . . or maybe he's just being nice because he's afraid I'm going to take Chloe from him.

Just like you would be if he tried to take Chloe from you, the Laurel voice, which has taken up permanent residence in my head, points out.

But he won't do that as long as I stay here and act sane.

Only what if he really thinks I'm a danger to Chloe and decides he has to take her from me for her own safety? Would I be able to stop him? Would I be able to convince anyone that I'm sane? I keep thinking of all the terrible things I admitted in group and to Laurel, all the "intrusive thoughts" I've had about dropping Chloe over the banister, drowning her in the bath, leaving her in the car—how would that look to a judge? One of the women in the group who was going through a divorce said that you never knew how a judge would rule in a custody case.

And I don't have the money to hire a lawyer.

I think I should look again at those job ads. As long as I'm dependent on Peter for everything I'm completely in his control. Not that I'd take a job far away, but if I could find one nearby, start part-time, save up . . . I'm going to look now . . .

WELL! THERE WEREN'T any openings for school librarians nearby, but there was one for an archivist. It's working for an author who needs someone to archive her private papers. A six-month position in a country estate in the Catskills, room and board provided, which means I could bring Chloe. But here's the really amazing thing about it. The author is Schuyler Bennett!!! Practically my favorite writer! It feels like a sign!

Only of course I wouldn't get it. Laurel could, with her credentials. I could show it to her . . .

Or I could apply for her. That would show her that she had options . . .

I DID IT! I even made up a new email account. I came up with ArchAngel, which I thought of because of the name of the software package Laurel showed me once. I had to add a number, so I used Laurel's birthday. Then I wrote an email to Schuyler Bennett. I had a copy of Laurel's résumé that she'd given me when I told her once I wanted to polish up my résumé, so it wasn't hard to talk about my (her) work experience. Then I had to say why I wanted to work with her and that wasn't hard either. Schuyler Bennett *is* practically my favorite writer, so I just told her that. When I looked at what I'd written so far I saw how Laurel and I together made the perfect candidate for the job. It's a shame we can't do it together. But I can't imagine Peter going for that. Besides, I'm doing this to show Laurel that she has options.

I thought of just leaving it there and not saying anything about having a baby. *Who's going to hire a single mother with a baby*, Laurel had said. But then what was the point of showing Laurel that she could get the job if it wouldn't work with Chloë? So I added: "On a personal note, I am recently separated and have a six-month-old baby. I realize this might present difficulties but I assure you I will find child care and work twice as hard for this opportunity. Your stories of women persevering through difficult times have been an inspiration to me."

I deleted and retyped the last line three times. It sounded a little pleading, which isn't how Laurel would sound, but then part of Laurel's problem is that she's too proud to ask for help. So I retyped it a final time and hit Send.

I immediately felt a little sick. What if Schuyler Bennett could tell right away that I wasn't Laurel? What if she somehow got Laurel's phone number and called her? I really should tell Laurel what I've done—and besides, I still have to return her diaper bag.

I JUST GOT back from Laurel's house. I tried calling but it just went to voicemail and said her mailbox was full. So I called Vanessa to come watch Chloe and I drove over there. I was surprised when Stan opened the door because it was the middle of the day. Then I felt scared, remembering what she'd said—that Chloë would be better off without her. "Is Laurel all right?" I asked.

"Why wouldn't she be?"

I didn't know what to say right away. After all, it was Stan who'd told me that Laurel had BPD and had tried to kill herself. "I just wondered because she's not picking up her phone and she didn't seem . . ." I hated to say anything bad about her, especially given all the stuff she'd said about Stan the last time I saw her. But that had been part of her delusional thinking, so I said, "She wasn't in good shape when I saw her last. It made me worry . . . about what you told me."

"She's much better now," Stan said coolly. "And frankly . . . well, I think she's better off not spending time with you anymore."

I was so shocked you could have knocked me over with a feather! I think I just stammered something about not understanding and then Stan said, "I've discussed this with Esta and we agree that you're not a good influence on Laurel right now.

It may not be your fault, but your own morbid delusions about your child are giving Laurel . . . *ideas.*"

"*My* morbid delusions?"

"Yes, that you're afraid you might hurt her. That you've thought about killing yourself and taking her with you. That you have a recurring nightmare about sleepwalking and leaving your baby in the car or drowning her in the bath—"

"That was Judith who told the story about the car! And the part about the bathtub—that was only a thought. Esta calls them intrusive thoughts. I'd never—"

"No? Peter told me that you tried to kill yourself in the bathtub. The last thing Laurel needs is someone planting those kinds of ideas in her head. Laurel is very impressionable."

"Laurel? Impressionable?" I scoffed. I'm afraid I may have laughed then. I could see by Stan's face that I must have looked a little crazy. "Laurel's the one who's impressed herself on me! She's the one who's always telling me how I should do my hair and what to wear and what to think."

Stan's expression changed then. He almost looked like he felt sorry for me, but then his face hardened and he said that was my problem. He asked me not to come by anymore and he closed the door in my face.

I stood there like an idiot for a couple of minutes. I even tried looking in the window to see if I could find Laurel, but all the blinds were drawn. Laurel always had them open. The house was dark and quiet, like a tomb, or a prison. I suddenly had the conviction that Stan was holding Laurel prisoner inside.

And then I remembered the bottle of water Laurel had been drinking the last time I was there. *Stan mixed it for me*, she'd said, *with electrolytes and shit. I think he's trying to poison me.*

I'd thought she was crazy, but what if she had been right? What if he was drugging her to have her declared incompetent so he could gain control over her money? I stared at the house for another few minutes trying to figure out what to do. Go to the police? They'd never believe me. They would think I was crazy.

I got back in my car and sat there gripping the steering wheel, my hands shaking so hard I was afraid to drive. Thank God Vanessa had Chloe. *Vanessa.* She had Simone's phone number. I'd go home and get Simone's number and call her. She would know if Laurel was really in danger.

I drove home slowly, making sure I made a full stop at every stop sign, signaling at every turn, waiting extra long for oncoming traffic at every corner. I had the feeling that I was being watched. That if I slipped up even a little the police would descend on me and take me away. They'd take me away from Chloe.

When I got home I was so anxious to see Chloe that I ran into the house crying, "Mommy's home!" and found Peter sitting in the living room with Chloe in his lap. "Where's Vanessa?" I asked.

"I told her to go home," he said. He was giving me that sideways look. Examining me. I found myself patting my clothes to make sure they were all right.

"I thought you were playing golf," I said.

"Stan canceled," he said, his voice flat and cold. "Laurel's not well."

"No, she's not," I said. "Remember? I told you that."

"He said you came by."

"Yes! To check on Laurel, but he wouldn't let me see her. Listen, Peter, I think there's something wrong—"

"He said you've been telling Laurel stories about hurting yourself and Chloe."

"No!" I cried so loudly that Chloe whimpered. I went to comfort her, but Peter shielded her with his arm to keep her from me.

"You shouldn't be around her when you're like this," he said.

"I-I'm all right," I said, trying to keep my voice calm. "I'm just upset about Laurel. I think Stan is keeping her from me. I think he might be medicating her so she seems crazy." I almost said *poisoning her,* but I stopped myself in time.

Peter stared at me. "Do you realize how crazy that sounds?"

"Yes!" I said, again too loud. Chloe's face puckered, the way it does before she cries. I just wanted to hold her but Peter was keeping her from me. "I know that's how it *sounds* but it's what Laurel said the last time I saw her and now Stan won't let me in to see her."

"Because you've been feeding Laurel horror stories about harming our child." Peter kept his voice low but the anger curdled my stomach. Chloe looked from his face to mine and began to howl. The sound clawed at my nerves. I wanted to howl with her.

"I would never hurt Chloe!" I cried.

"Then why did you tell Laurel you think about dropping her from the top of the stairs? Why did you tell her you picture drowning her every time you give her a bath?"

Chloe was following every word as if she understood what they meant.

"They're intrusive thoughts," I said, but I could hear how lame the term sounded, how weak in the face of Peter's accusations. As if a bit of psychobabble could lessen the horror of picturing myself harming my own child. "I'd never act on them."

"I can't take that chance," he said. "You're seeing a doctor tomorrow. In the meantime, I'm not leaving you alone with Chloe. Either Vanessa or I will be here at all times."

"All right," I said, gulping back tears and reaching out my arms for Chloe. "Just let me hold her now."

"Not when you're this upset," he said, turning away from me. He took Chloe into the nursery and closed the door. I wanted to force myself in but then I thought of how much that would scare Chloe. I thought of calling someone, but who? Laurel was out of reach. Esta? She might side with Peter. There was no one. I was in this alone.

I came up here and wrote this all down, trying to make sense of it and calm myself down, but I have this horrible feeling that Laurel is in danger. I'm going to try emailing her—

I didn't email Laurel. When I opened my mail I saw I had an email from Schuyler Bennett. I was practically too scared to open it, but when I did, I could hardly believe my eyes. She'd written one line.

"When can you start?"

Chapter Ten

I stay up all night rereading all of Dr. Bennett's notes on E.S., keeping a sharp eye on Chloe, and by morning I understand why I put Chloe in the bathtub. It's the same reason Edith jumped from the tower. When she gave birth she was so traumatized she projected the experience onto her roommate, but because she still felt guilty for abandoning her baby she constructed a story that the child had been taken away from her. She had to find it and save it, which she did by leaping from the tower.

I understand also why I ran away. I transferred Laurel's fear that Stan was going to take her Chloë away from her to Peter. As Esta said, women with postpartum OCD "borrow" from other people's intrusive thoughts. Laurel was afraid that she'd harmed her Chloë and that Stan was going to take her away from her. So I started to think that Peter was trying to take Chloe away from me and that's why I made this crazy plan to run away. I even stole Laurel's identity to do it! My behavior was classic PPOCD! But now that I understand what I did, I think I can get better. I can explain to Peter that I'm cured and go home. Postpartum disorders are temporary, after all. At least, they usually are.

Edith Sharp wasn't suffering from a postpartum disorder; she had borderline personality disorder, which caused her to "mirror" the experience of her Favorite Person, who was her roommate.

I can see, also, how it fed into Sky's story about the changeling. The changeling isn't the baby at all; it's the mother!

I want to talk to Sky about my theory, but first I want to talk to Dr. Hancock and see if he agrees with my interpretation. After all, I'm not a psychologist, I'm just a librarian, although I think I have a special insight into this case because of my own experience.

When I see that it's almost morning I take Chloe up to the tower. I want to show her the sunrise. I put her in the baby Snugli carrier to make it easier to go up the spiral stairs with her. As I go up the stairs it's hard not to think about the dream I had, to imagine that bathtub full of bloody water and the woman and child inside it—

And for a moment on the second flight of stairs I think I *am* in that dream. My hands and Chloe's face are stained red as if we've been caught in a flood of bloody water. But it's only the light of the rising sun spilling down through the stairwell. When I get up to the top floor it's full of crimson light. Chloe opens her eyes and stretches out her little hands in the light, gurgling at it as if it were something alive. Then she looks right up at me and smiles. As if I had made this happen! My heart squeezes in my chest and for a moment I feel so full I'm afraid I might fly apart. Instead, I squeeze Chloe tighter to me and step closer to the window to watch the sun rise over all those acres of woods we came through to get here. I feel like the woman in Sky's story, only I've come through the woods with my real baby, not a lump of wood.

Now that I've made the journey once, I think I can go back.

Peter wasn't the culprit—although I think he could have been a little more patient with me. I needed to get away to understand what had happened to me. I hope that he'll understand now and that I can finish my six-month commitment to Sky. At the end of it I think I'll be ready to go back to my old life, but not as the *old* me. I'll never be that woman again. Becoming a mother has changed me. I feel like an entirely new person.

Daphne's Journal, August 8, 20—

Peter took me to see the new doctor today, Dr. Gruener. If he really *is* a doctor. I'm not sure of anything anymore.

For one thing, his office didn't look anything like a psychiatrist's office. It was in one of those medical buildings by the hospital but it looked like he'd just moved in. All the furniture looked like it had been rented from one of those office-supply companies. The carpet still smelled new—like cleaning fluid—and when I touched the front door I got an electric shock. I know none of that should be important—Peter says it's snooty—but I'm very sensitive to my surroundings. Besides, I didn't like Dr. Gruener very much.

For one thing, I could tell right away that he'd talked to Peter before I came and that he'd already made up his mind about me. He asked me a lot of questions about the "intrusive thoughts" I had about harming Chloe—how many times I thought about dropping her over the banister or drowning her in the bathtub. Had I ever acted on those thoughts? Say, held Chloe over the banister? Or dunked her under the water just for a second?

I told him of course not! I told him I'd do anything to keep Chloe safe, anything at all. He'd looked at me funny then, as if *that* were an admission of some kind of guilt. As if wanting to keep my baby safe was somehow suspect.

Then he asked me about my suicide attempt. Did I still hear voices telling me to hurt myself and Chloe?

"No!" I told him, but then I had to admit I did hear a voice saying, *What if she's better off without me?* but then I explained that was Laurel's voice and it wasn't talking to me; it was talking to Laurel. It was Laurel who was suicidal and I was trying to help her.

"Help her how?"

I almost told him about my plan, but even with doctor/ patient confidentiality I didn't really think I could trust him so I just said, "I'm trying to help her see her options."

"So you feel responsible for Laurel?" he asked.

"Well, yes," I told him, "because she's my friend."

"And are you afraid that Laurel might hurt herself? Or her baby?"

I didn't answer that right away because I was afraid suddenly of getting Laurel in trouble, so I asked him if what I told him was confidential.

He put down his pen and looked at me hard, like he was really seeing me for the first time. Then he said, "Yes, unless you give me information that involves you or someone else planning bodily harm to another person or self."

I had to process that for a few minutes. If I told him that I was afraid that Laurel would hurt herself or her baby, Dr. Gruener might call up Social Services and have Chloë taken away from Laurel. But if I didn't tell him and Laurel did hurt herself or Chloë, I would never forgive myself.

So I told him yes, I was afraid that Laurel might hurt Chloë and herself, but only because she was so sick. She would never mean to.

Dr. Gruener pushed a box of Kleenex across the table because I was crying. "Tell me this . . ." He had to look down to see my name. ". . . Daphne, if you were Laurel, what would you like to happen now?"

"I'd want someone to make sure that I didn't hurt myself or my baby," I said.

"Even if you didn't know you were sick?"

And suddenly I understood what was going on. I got up and grabbed my bag, but my hands were shaking so hard I dropped it. Laurel's wallet dropped out, open to the flap where she kept her driver's license. Dr. Gruener picked it up. I saw him glance at the license, but he must not have read the name because he didn't bat an eyelash.

"Is something wrong?" he asked. "You seem upset."

"I see what you're trying to do and no one is going to take my baby. Is Peter doing it now?" I demanded. "Is that why I'm here? So he can take Chloe away while I'm out of the house?"

"Perhaps you should sit down, Laurel. I don't think you should be driving while you're so upset."

"It's Daphne, not Laurel," I said. "You can't even remember my name. Where did Peter find you anyway? Rent-a-Shrink?"

I got out of there as fast as I could. I could see it all now. Peter had gotten this shrink to certify that I was crazy, that I was a suicide and infanticide risk. I was afraid he might already have a social worker at the house and that he was planning to take Chloe from me and have me put away. I couldn't let that happen. I couldn't let him take Chloe away from me.

I drove home as fast as I could without breaking the speed limit. That would be all I needed now, to get a speeding ticket. But as anxious as I was to get home, somehow I found myself driving to Laurel's house. Force of habit, I guess, or guilt that I should make sure that she was all right. But when I looked up at her dark and shuttered house I couldn't imagine that there was anyone home or that even if she was there I'd know what to say to make things better. To calm myself down I took out my laptop and wrote for a while in this diary, trying to put it all together. And it helps! It's in writing it down that I figured out what I have to do. I called Schuyler Bennett and asked if we could move up my start date. When I asked if I could come today she didn't answer right away and I was afraid that I'd ruined everything. She must think I'm crazy.

But then she said, "Of course. That would be perfect. Come right away."

I felt such a wave of relief I thought I might faint! I had to sit with my head down for a little while and I even fell asleep for a bit, which just shows how exhausted I was. When I woke up I didn't know where I was at first, which was scary, but then I remembered. I drove home as if in a dream. Now I'm in front of my own house. It's all clear to me now. I see that it's what I've been planning all these weeks. Maybe Peter and the shrink are right—I've been pretending the plans I was making were for Laurel when all along they've been for me. I'm the one in danger. I'm the one who needs to escape. I know what it will look like to everyone else, but what does that matter? After all these months of feeling like there was something wrong with me, that I didn't love Chloe enough, that I wasn't a good mother, I finally know for sure that I love her more than anyone in the world. And that I'd do anything to keep her with me. Anything at all.

Chapter Eleven

The guard at the gate is the same one who met me the first time. Ben Marcus, I recall. He's acquired a black eye since I last saw him. "Did Edith Sharp give you that?" I ask as he unlocks the gate.

"How do you know her name?"

"Sky Bennett told me," I say, omitting the fact that I'd looked in her file. "I've been reading about her in Dr. Bennett's journals. I thought you told me the wards were secure."

"I never said no one ever did a runner. Edith's been here so long she's learned all the tricks. She's crafty. When she decides she's had enough of the place she stops taking her meds, hides them in her cheek, and spits them out. Then she watches the nurses use the combination locks until she's memorized the combination. We change those once a week so she knows she doesn't have much time. She has to steal two keys—one to get out of C Ward, one to work the back gate." He cocks his thumb at the gate we've just come through.

"And then how do you find her?"

"We don't," he says. "If she makes it out, she usually comes back in a week or so. She always tells the same story—that she's been to check on her baby."

"Oh, then she really is . . . sick."

He glances at me, one eyebrow—the scarred one—raised. "Did you think she was here on vacation?"

"No . . . it's just that she sounded very intelligent in Dr. Bennett's journal."

"Do you think smart people don't go crazy? We've had Nobel Prize winners in here."

"I've seen *A Beautiful Mind*," I snap, tired of his condescending tone. "But it's different, hearing her voice . . . and besides . . ." I hesitate, unsure I should reveal what Billie said to me.

"Besides what?"

"Oh, it was just a rumor I heard—that she jumped from the tower and then was cured."

He barks a harsh laugh. "If jumping from a high window was a cure for madness the doctors would have tried it. The story the nurses tell about Edith is that she killed her own baby and she's always looking for it. That's why she tries to get out; so she can find her baby."

"That's awful," I say. "The poor woman."

He gives me an assessing look. "Most people aren't so sympathetic when they hear that she abandoned her baby in a dumpster. Some of the nurses call her Baby Killer."

I shudder. "But you don't. I saw how careful you were with her."

He shrugs and rubs the bruised skin around his eye. "A woman who abandoned her own child—I figure she's in hell every day of her life. That seems punishment enough to me."

THIS TIME AS we go up the elevator I pay more attention to the keys that he uses. He has five or six on a heavy ring clipped to his belt. How does Edith steal one off the guards? I imagine the careful watching and planning she must do—all to find a baby that is long gone.

Ben Marcus leaves me again in the reception office and tells the secretary to buzz him when it's time for "Mrs. Hobbes" to leave. When he turns to go I find the painting of the disembodied eye staring at me reproachfully. I find I dislike hearing my false name on Ben Marcus's tongue. He's been forthcoming with me; I don't like that I've lied to him. When I go home— when I stop being Laurel Hobbes—maybe I'll tell him who I really am.

Dr. Hancock seems a little distracted as he greets me, and a trifle cool. Perhaps he's not happy that Sky has instructed him to show me Edith's file. Instead of perching on the edge of the desk as he did last time he sits back down in his desk chair and folds his hands over the pale green folder, asserting his control over my access to it. "Before I show you Edith's file I'd like to know why you're so interested in her case."

"What do you mean?" I ask, taken aback by his blunt approach. "I've already explained that I'm researching the connections between Sky's writing and her biography."

"But that's not all there is to it, is there?" He smiles and I have the strange conviction that he is smiling at my discomfort. I see what this is about. Dr. Hancock likes to be in control and I have challenged his rule by going around him to get access to his patient's file. He doesn't like it. So to punish me he is going to make me uncomfortable about the request by imputing an ulterior motive. I remember that this is something I've always disliked about psychiatrists, always reading an ulterior motive into your behavior. I could, I suppose, demand that he just hand over the file as per Schuyler Bennett's order. I am not, after all, Dr. Hancock's patient. But I don't want to seem difficult.

"I only wonder," he goes on when I don't answer, "if you identified with Edith in some way. Sky tells me you have a baby yourself. I wondered if perhaps you had experienced any postpartum mood disorders."

I try to remind myself that even if he has looked me up, it's Laurel he's looked up. What could he have found out? Has he called Stan? The thought of him talking to Stan Hobbes makes me go cold all over. But even if Dr. Hancock has discovered my deception, what of it? It will be embarrassing, but I'm nearly ready to leave anyway. I'd like to finish out the job, but maybe Sky would let me continue it as Daphne Marist. But if Sky is angry at me for pretending to be Laurel then this might be my last chance to see Edith Sharp's file, so I may as well humor Dr. Hancock.

"You've caught me," I say. "I did suffer from postpartum depression for a few months after Chloë was born. But I went to a support group and I feel much better. I suppose that did make me identify with Edith Sharp. Maybe if she had had help earlier she wouldn't have ended up here."

"And is that why you want to see her file? So you'll understand how a woman might survive the experience of postpartum psychosis and come out whole?"

That strikes me as a strange way of putting it, but all I want to do now is put an end to this . . . *whatever* this is. "If you say so," I say impatiently. "Speaking of babies, I'd like to get back to mine sometime today. If I could just have the file—"

"I thought I'd give you something more," he says, rising to his feet. "Since understanding Edith is so important to you, I thought you might want to meet her."

"Meet her? But isn't she . . ." I can't hide my shock, which Dr. Hancock seems to be enjoying. "Isn't she . . . *dangerous*? I just saw the black eye she gave Ben Marcus."

"Oh, she's been sedated since then. She's placid as a lamb right now and twice as contrite. I thought it might interest you to talk to her, but if you think it will upset you . . ."

"No," I say quickly. Too quickly. There'd be no harm in admitting that the idea frightened me. Meeting a mental patient might make anyone upset. But Dr. Hancock is already getting out his keys, opening the door, barking orders to his secretary to hold his calls and let the on-call supervisor on C Ward know we're on our way over, and striding down the hall. I have to hurry to keep up with him. I feel like all the disembodied body parts that line the wall are watching me. What a gruesome assemblage for a mental hospital. It wouldn't surprise me if Dr. Hancock selected them. Right now, he's tapping the green file against his leg, like a treat he's using to lure me along. *Bastard*. He's doing this to punish me for getting *special privileges*. I wonder how he gets back at his patients.

He has to wait for me at the elevator. I watch him turn the two keys to operate it and then we go down, passing the first floor. The wards must connect in the basement.

When we get off the elevator it's as if we're in a different building. No plush carpet or framed pictures. The floor is water-stained linoleum and the bare walls are painted a noxious green. The doors of the rooms we pass have small frosted-glass windows that are covered over with metal mesh.

"We see some patients here." Dr. Hancock taps the corner of the folder on the windows as we pass by. I try to peer through the frosted glass and catch glimpses of shadowy shapes, like fish swimming in an aquarium. I feel like we're underwater.

We turn a corner and another. The floor seems to slope down. By the time we come to a door I'm completely turned around. I have no idea what side of the building we're on or how many floors beneath the ground. Dr. Hancock uses another key for this door and a slide card attached to a lanyard around his neck for the next one. How in the world did Edith get out of here? Perhaps I'll ask her—if we ever get to her.

At last Dr. Hancock opens the door to a small windowless room. "Here," he says, laying the file folder on a spare wooden table in the middle of the room. "Why don't you read this while I go get Edith." Before I can object, he leaves the room, locking the door behind him. The click of the lock echoes loud against the cinderblock walls. *It's to protect you*, I tell myself, sitting down at the table. But still I am besieged by claustrophobia, locked in this small windowless room. I open the folder as if it's a window that might let in some air, and begin to read.

The first thing I notice is that the page is full of black rectangles. Parts of the text have been blacked out by heavily inked boxes. Redacted. I flip the pages and see that the entire file has been altered in this way. As I begin to read, I see that the black boxes cover all references to the patient's name and any other identifying information. But why? I already know her name is Edith Sharp. The action seems hostile and unnecessary. Well, so be it; I don't need Edith's name. I can easily fill it in myself.

> ███ is a young woman from an affluent background who appeared to be a functioning young adult until the onset of severe dissociative symptoms in her early twenties. The one traumatic event of her childhood was the death of her parents in her early teens, but since she had already been in boarding school their deaths did not represent a major change in day-to-day life. She saw a school therapist and maintained a high grade point average and gained entrance to an elite college. To all outward appearances she seemed to be an organized, productive, well-adjusted young woman.

I look up from the page, hearing Laurel's voice in my head: *We tried to impose order on a world that had been torn apart.* No wonder I felt a kinship with Edith; her story had echoes in my own . . . well, except for the fancy boarding school. Still, the similarities make the next bit painful to read.

> The first symptoms of concern occurred in college. She formed an attachment with her college roommate that went beyond ordinary friendship. They shared clothes and began to dress alike. ■■'s roommate changed her major to ■■'s major. To outward appearances, it seemed that ■■'s roommate was the one who was emulating ■■, but when the roommate requested a room change in their sophomore year, ■■ became violently disturbed. She accused her roommate of betraying her and began spreading rumors about her around campus, accusing her of being obsessed with ■■ and stalking her. Because ■■ had no history of mental illness, and because of her charm, intelligence, and persuasive nature, the campus counselors believed ■■'s account of the situation. This may have been ■■'s first dissociative episode. She transferred her own emotions onto the roommate and began to "mirror" her roommate's repulsion about ■■'s obsessive behavior. The identification with her roommate reached a crisis when she discovered–

I turn the page and read:

> The worst crisis was precipitated by giving birth.

I turn back and forth twice trying to match the end of the page to the beginning of the next and then I check the page numbers. Page 3, page 5. There's a missing page. I rifle though the pages looking for page 4 but it's not in the folder.

"Goddamn you, Hancock!" I say out loud. He has deliberately removed a page. He's playing tricks with me. I'll complain to Sky.

In the meantime, I go on to read the rest of the file.

> The worst crisis was precipitated by giving birth. Soon after an uneventful pregnancy and childbirth ■ began to show signs of dissociation. She was not interested in caring for the child, claiming at one point that the baby was not hers.

I'm confused for a moment. This doesn't sound like the story I heard of Edith having a baby in college. Could she have had another child later? Perhaps after she was let out of Crantham? She *was* cured by the fall from the tower but she ended back at Crantham later after she had her own child. It makes sense, sort of. Her first crisis—her dissociative episode—was brought on by the shock of giving birth without any preparation and her second was brought on by having another child.

> She later denied that statement and said that she only meant that the baby felt like a stranger–

Once again I hear Laurel's voice in my head: *We're supposed to fall in love with this total stranger.* That's who E. sounds like, I realize. Laurel.

> ■ was sent home with her baby but her husband reported continuing problems: lack of interest in taking care of the child, periods of forgetfulness, leaving the

baby in inappropriate places, including a laundry basket,
an empty bathtub, the backseat of the car. ██'s husband
eventually urged ██ to see a psychologist and to attend
a mothers' support group. She seemed to make some
progress, but then she formed an attachment to one of
the women in the group that mirrored her relationship to
the college roommate. Once again, it appeared from the
outside that this woman was the one trying to emulate ██.
She began wearing similar clothes and had her hair dyed
the same shade as ██'s.

I feel a prickle on the back of my neck as if someone is standing behind me, even though the door is in front of me. Edith's
story is beginning to sound familiar—too familiar. It sounds
like Laurel and me. Has Dr. Hancock altered Edith's file to
mirror my own life? But to what purpose? And how would he
even get those details?

I remember, though, Esta's warning about reading myself
into other women's stories. Maybe that's all I'm doing.

██ even complained to her husband that the woman from
the group was becoming too clingy–

I cringe, but then tell myself that this is not about me and
Laurel.

–but when her husband suggested she spend less time
with the woman, ██ objected, saying the woman was her
only friend and the only one who understood her. When
██'s husband expressed concern over the intensity of
the relationship, ██ accused him of trying to isolate her.
She then became paranoid that her husband was trying

to have her declared incompetent so that he could gain
control over her money, which was tied up in a trust.

I no longer think I am reading about Edith Sharp. This is
Laurel's story. It's Hancock's way of telling me that he knows
I'm not Laurel. I've been found out.

In attempting to deal with her paranoia, ██'s husband
offered to have legal papers drawn up excluding him from
any benefits from the trust, but this only aggravated
██'s delusions further. When she attempted to voice her
fears to her friend, her friend rejected her claims, and ██
withdrew into a depressed state, refusing to get dressed,
wash herself, or care for her baby. She began to say that
she'd be better off if she had no money, like her friend.
She began letting her hair grow out to its natural color
and said she was going to take a job as a school librarian
(which had been her friend's profession). Her husband
became most concerned when she said that her friend
was a better mother, that at least her friend's baby was
not brain damaged as she had begun to believe about her
own child, and that she wished that she was her friend.
    When her husband brought her to see a psychiatrist,
██ admitted that she'd had thoughts of harming her
child and that she had suicidal thoughts. She ascribed
the suicidal thoughts to another personality, one that she
identified with her own name. To test the theory that she
now identified with her friend, the doctor called her by
her friend's name, to which she raised no objection. When
he called her by her own name, she accused the doctor of
forgetting her name and questioned his reputation. She
then left the office abruptly—

The words blur in front of me and I feel so dizzy I have to close my eyes and rest my head on the table. The report describes my visit to Dr. Gruener's office. But if this file is about Laurel, why is my visit to Dr. Gruener here? I remember Dr. Gruener calling me Laurel and then I *had* left abruptly, but that was because I was sure Peter was trying to steal Chloe, *not* because I was confused about who I was. I'd rushed home . . . no, I'd gone to Laurel's house first. But I hadn't gone in . . .

Or had I? I remember feeling dizzy, putting my head down . . . then I see myself getting out of the car and going up the front path, and letting myself into the house. But is it my house or Laurel's? I smell something metallic and hear the sound of water. The sound and the smell are coming from upstairs. Then I hear a baby crying. I begin to go up the stairs. My feet feel heavy—as if I'm in one of those dreams where you're trying to run and it's like you're swimming through molasses—only then I realize it's because the carpet on the stairs is wet. And it's a different color. Laurel's carpets are white, but this carpet is red—

The red seeps over everything, drenching my vision, blocking out the stairs and the open bathroom door at the top of the stairs. I don't want to see what's inside.

I open my eyes and I'm back in the green room at Crantham, clutching the folder. The door in front of me is open. Dr. Hancock fills the frame, watching me.

"Why do you have this?" I demand, shaking the file at him. "What happened to Laurel?"

Instead of answering, he steps in and to the side so another man can enter: Peter, his face square with barely suppressed rage.

"I know what you did!" I scream. "You and Stan! You murdered Laurel to get her money!" I turn to Dr. Hancock. "I can prove it. I've got a copy of Laurel's will that I found taped to the bottom of Peter's drawer. Why would he have her will unless they were planning to kill her for her money? There was a photograph with the will, a picture of Peter as a boy, but with another name. He's not even Peter Marist!" I jump to my feet just as a third man comes into the room. Stan Hobbes. "You killed her!" I scream. "You killed Laurel!"

Stan's eyes fill with tears. Perhaps he feels remorse, but I don't care. It's too late for Laurel. I can see her face now, looking up from the blood-filled tub, her sightless eyes staring at me. He opens his mouth and I steel myself for a lie—he will tell me that she killed herself—but I am unprepared for what he says.

"How can that be true," he asks, "when you're standing right in front of me, Laurel?"

And then Peter adds, "It's my wife, Daphne, who's dead."

PART II

Laurel's Journal, June 11, 20—

First meeting of the mothers' support group today. Stan *insisted*. Said it was either this or the hospital and I'd rather die than go back to the loony bin—even one of the posh ones.

Although this may be worse.

The leader is a gormless idiot. Esta—or Estrogena as I have dubbed her because she clearly has a serious case of estrogen poisoning. The women aren't much better, which I blame completely on Westfuckingchester. I'm sure there's a better class of loonies in Manhattan, but Stan also insisted that the city's too *stressful* for my poor delicate nerves, as if it wasn't stressful to be stuck out here with a bunch of lactating cows. One followed me out to the car like a fawning puppy, wanting to bond over our shared motherhood. What a doormat! She let her hedge-fund-manager husband bully her into not hiring a babysitter. Please.

Then I remembered that I'm supposed to be *bonding* with the locals, so I suggested a playdate. I thought she was going to jump in my lap. Seriously, you would have thought I asked her to a weekend in Paris. At least Doormat Daphne will be easy to schlep around, like that hideous diaper bag Stan bought for me. I mean, seriously, KatefuckingSpade.

Chapter Twelve

died.

That's the part I understood, the part I believed. The idea that I was Laurel—beautiful, accomplished Laurel—was not believable. But that Daphne had died and that this last week of leave-taking, driving through a dark forest, and starting a new life was all a kind of afterlife, that I could believe. Hadn't it felt unreal all along? I could feel the pieces of my reconstructed life flying apart like a broken mirror. Only one of those shards pierced my heart.

"Chloe!" I cried. "What did I do to Chloe?"

Stan and Peter looked at each other. Only Dr. Hancock kept his eyes on me. "Which Chloe?" he asked.

"*My* Chloe!" I screamed. But already I wasn't sure what that meant. I turned to Peter. "Your Chloe, then."

He flinched as if I'd hit him. "You took her," he said spitefully.

Stan stepped in. "But only because you were confused. We think you found Daphne drowned in the tub and Chloe there with her. Maybe in the tub."

The red-washed image floods my vision: a dead woman with a baby lying beside her—"No! She's not dead!" I could accept that I was dead, even that I had killed myself, but not that I would have killed Chloe.

"No, she's not." Dr. Hancock says almost regretfully. "You saved her. You rescued her from the tub and took her with you."

I want to scream that he's lying but I can see myself lifting the baby out of the bloody water, her face streaked with blood.

"Yes," Peter says stiffly. "I suppose I should thank you for saving my child's life, but it's been hell this last week grieving for my wife and not knowing if my child was alive." He's lying. I can tell by the way he turns his glance sideways to me.

Stan must see how transparent he appears. He steps between us. "But it's all right now," he says to Peter, his voice tight with suppressed anger. "Your child is fine. My wife, Laurel"—he looks at me—"took good care of her." Then to me he says, "You didn't want to hurt anyone. You were just confused."

Then it hits me. They are saying the baby I have been taking care of all week is not mine. They are saying that Peter is going to take her. "No," I say to Peter, "you can't have her." I turn to Dr. Hancock. "This is all a plan that Peter and Stan have cooked up to take Laurel's money."

"You mean your money?" Dr. Hancock asks.

"Laurel's money," I tell him. "That wasn't Daphne in the tub, it was Laurel. She told me she suspected something. She thought Stan was poisoning her. I should have listened to her but I thought she was crazy."

"You thought Laurel was crazy?" Dr. Hancock repeats. It's maddening the way he keeps repeating Laurel's name, like it's going to jar something in my memory. And it does. Laurel's will.

"They're both in on it," I say, looking from Peter to Stan. "Peter must have agreed to help if Stan agreed to invest the money in his fund."

"So both of these men colluded to defraud both of their wives?" Dr. Hancock asks with heavy irony.

"Why is that so hard to believe?" I demand. "Stan married a rich woman for her money. Peter was always looking for money. Who knows what he'd do to get it . . . I don't even know who he really is! His real name isn't even Peter Marist! He's someone named Thomas Pitt."

"And what about Stan?" Dr. Hancock asks. "Is he someone else as well?"

I shake my head, dismissing the distraction. "How the hell should I know? I just know he wanted Laurel dead so he could get her money. He was putting something in her water. He must have drugged her and drowned her in the tub. Only he had to change the will first or it would have all gone to Chloë."

"Chloë?" Dr. Hancock echoes. "Who was also in the tub?"

I splutter on this point, wanting to deny it, but I can see myself lifting a baby from the red water and wrapping her in a blanket—

The wet blanket in the car when I arrived.

"I don't know!" I cry. "I don't know how they planned to do it, but I have the will and the picture of Peter when he was Thomas Pitt. I hid them in the tower. I can show them to you." I take a step forward but Dr. Hancock blocks my way.

"In the tower where you think another mother plunged to her death?"

"Is there another tower?" I snap impatiently, trying to side-step around him. I can see now that there are two guards hovering just outside the door.

"Where you've been working as an archivist? A job you applied for as Laurel Hobbes?"

I can see where he's going with this. "I applied for the job *for*

Laurel, but then when she didn't want it I took it . . ." I falter, trying to remember the moment I decided I would take the job.

Dr. Hancock, smelling blood, dives in. "So you're doing a job Laurel was qualified for, using Laurel's credentials and her ID, which you showed at the gate—".

"I have her ID because we switched diaper bags," I say, trying to keep my voice calm. "I meant to give it back. I am not Laurel Hobbes. They killed Laurel Hobbes so they could get her money."

"Then why not just leave her dead?" Dr. Hancock says gently. It's this gentleness that makes me hate him the most.

"Maybe it's got something to do with the will," I say. "I'll go get it and you'll see." This time I'm too fast for him and I dodge past Dr. Hancock. Neither Peter nor Stan tries to stop me but the guards block my way through the door, presenting a wall of flesh and muscle I can't get through. "Get out of my way," I tell them. "I'm not a patient here. You can't keep me from leaving."

"Your husband has admitted you," Dr. Hancock says.

"He can't do that!" I cry, looking at Peter. He stares back at me blankly, like I'm a stranger. *He's* the one who's the stranger. Have I ever really known him? It suddenly seems more likely that I'm Laurel Hobbes than that I am married to this man. And Chloe—hadn't she seemed like a stranger too? They're saying she's Daphne's baby, so if I'm Daphne she shouldn't feel like a stranger. And she's not a stranger now. She's my baby and I have to get to her.

Dr. Hancock is saying something about a power of attorney and medical proxy and a writ of incompetence and past mental history. Stan is saying something about Peter dropping kidnapping charges if I'm admitted.

"After all," Peter says, "you saved Chloe's life. I'm willing to drop charges but I have to know that you'll never get near her again."

It's the hint of a smile on Peter's face that unravels whatever thread was holding me together. This is what he's wanted all along. To get Chloe, his perfect daughter, to himself, his imperfect wife out of the picture. I fling myself at him, nails aimed at those cold eyes, that smug smile. He sidesteps out of my reach, letting the guards take over. They meet my flailing arms with a wall of impassive muscle. My hands are caught and trapped as easily as tiny birds, but still I struggle, throwing myself against the hard wall of their bodies like that poor trapped sparrow had flung itself against the walls of Chloe's nursery. I can't stop myself. They're standing between me and Chloe. I'd rather die than let them keep me from her.

I feel a sting on my arm and then ice water floods my veins. Maybe Laurel *did* kill herself, I think as I feel myself sinking beneath cold water, a film of red washing over my eyes. Maybe Stan threatened to take Chloë from her and she chose to die with Chloë rather than live without her.

She was just trying to keep her safe, I want to say, but instead the words that slur out of my mouth are, "I was just trying to keep her safe . . ."

And then I drown. Again.

Laurel's Journal, June 18, 20—

Another day at the support group for lactating loonies. Estrogena went on and on about how we shouldn't feel guilty about not bonding with our babies like *normal* mothers when it was clear that what she was saying was that we're not normal. I'd like to know what's normal about any of this. What's normal about an alien growing in your body for nine months and then spending nine hours pushing it out? What's normal about being handed a shriveled sea monkey and being expected to love it immediately, especially when it proceeds to keep you awake 24/7 for the next three months? Who is supposed to be normal after that? Poor Doormat Daphne, though, was eating it up. Even after that ridiculous woman Estrogena mocked her last week as if it was a crime to worry about how things are supposed to be when everyone knows that's all that really matters in this world.

So I'm *supposed* to look at little Sea Monkey and feel a tug in my uterus when all I feel is those goddamned episiotomy stitches.

But that's how Doormat Daphne looks at her sea monkey. She trailed me out to the parking lot again. I could tell she wanted me to invite her home with me, but then that wouldn't really be fair to Simone who'd have to watch both babies, so I gave Daphne the name of the babysitter I used before I got a proper live-in au pair. While I was writing down the number she was cooing to her Chloe like she was God's gift, even though her Chloe isn't half as attractive as mine. So if she can act like a mother's supposed to, I don't see why I can't. Maybe I can learn it from her. And maybe I can teach her to grow a backbone.

She just texted me to say that skinflint hubby is willing to spring for a babysitter next week. I texted her back a few emojis. I think she may have wet herself. Just what I need. Another baby.

Chapter Thirteen

This is what it's like to drown.

Each time I rise to the surface a room swims into view, painted the same sea green as my dreams, and I gasp for breath. I try to stay afloat by stroking my arms against the surface, but I can't. My arms are held down. How can I stay afloat without my arms? Didn't I learn that once in a swimming class? I try to hold on to the memory—the smell of chlorine, the tight elastic hug of a swimsuit, the rough concrete scrape against my legs—but I am sinking before I can find myself in the memory. Who am I? Daphne or Laurel? The question is like a weight, like rocks in my pockets. *Maybe I'll walk into the Hudson with rocks in my pockets like Virginia Woolf.* Laurel said that. Or did I? Laurel's voice has been in my head so long I can't tell them apart. As Laurel said, *All the voices sound sensible at the time.*

SOMETIMES WHEN I surface I see a face hovering over me like a balloon. Women in bathing caps, men in white coats. Their mouths open and close like fish's, the sounds they make as echoing and hollow as sonar bleeps heard underwater. I try to reach for them, to hold on to something that will keep me afloat, but my arms are pinned. I try to cry out but my lips are parched and cracked, my throat burning as if I have swallowed gallons of seawater. *Chloe*, I croak.

"Your baby's fine, Mrs. Hobbes. Your husband, Stan, is taking care of her."

Not that Chloë, I try to say, but I've swallowed too much water. *You fool*, a voice says—Laurel's? Mine?—*you're supposed to put the rocks in your pockets, not swallow them!*

THE DEAD-MAN'S FLOAT. That's what they taught us in swim class. That's what you do to conserve energy. Stop struggling. Let yourself go limp. Fill your lungs with air to keep afloat. A suitable exercise for someone who has already died. The next time I surface I try it. I relax my legs and arms, I take a deep breath, I open my eyes.

Laurel's face is hovering over mine, bloated and distorted. I scream and scream until I've used up all the air and I sink to the bottom of the sea, where crabs pick at my flesh and gnaw my bones.

WITHOUT FLESH I am lighter. My bones have turned into coral, porous and buoyant. I can float longer at the surface. I listen to the nurses with the dispassion of the drowned.

"How are we doing today, Mrs. Hobbes?"

We? Is that the answer? Laurel and I are both here—or is it Daphne and I? What does it matter? Only Chloe matters. *My* Chloe.

Define "my," Laurel's voice challenges. It's a sensible point. She always was more sensible than me. Laurel would know what to do here. Laurel would know how to answer the nurses' questions so they would stop drowning us over and over again.

"We . . ." I begin.

Not we, you idiot, do you want them to think you're schizoid?

"I—I'm feeling a little better."

Not quite the Gettysburg Address, but a respectable start. The goal here is to get them to ease back on the medication a little. Try asking a normal question.

"Can I see my baby?"

Good! Way to play the concerned-mother card!

"You're not allowed visitors until you're doing a little better, but I'm sure once you are, Mr. Hobbes will bring in little Chloë."

"Not that Chloë," I say.

Careful, Laurel's voice warns, but I don't listen.

"I need to see *my* Chloe. I need to know I didn't drown her. I—" I taste salt. The sea is taking me again. I struggle to make the nurse understand. "I don't care that I've drowned, but I need to know she is all right."

The nurse gives me a puzzled smile and writes something down on her clipboard.

Patient exhibits delusion that she's dead. Up medication by a gazillion percent, Laurel snarks.

"I'm sure your baby's perfectly fine, Mrs. Hobbes. I've just written a note for Dr. Hancock to check in with you."

Then the nurse adjusts something on the balloon that floats over my bed and I'm sinking again. But this time I'm not alone.

At the bottom of the sea Laurel whispers in my ear, her voice the echo of my own bloodstream held in a conch shell.

They think you're me. You'll never convince them otherwise as long as you're doped up and lying around in unflattering PJs. You have to make them think you know you're Laurel Hobbes. So you had a teensy break with reality when you found your bestie floating in a pool of blood—

I didn't! I wouldn't!

Sure, if you say so. It's much, much more likely that rich, beautiful Laurel Hobbes offed herself than poor, pathetic Daphne Marist. Hey! No more tears now. We'll never get out of here if you can't turn off the waterworks. Of course, I didn't kill myself either. Someone killed me. Stan is my guess. But how are we going to prove that with you stuck in here? And the only way you get out is if you start acting sane—and to do that you have to pretend to be me.

But I don't know how.

My head fills with the sound of Laurel's laughter. *Excuse me? What have you been doing at Schuyler Bennett's house other than pretending to be me? Do you think these doctors and nurses are any smarter than Schuyler Bennett?*

No, but—

No buts! Shape up! Grow a backbone! Here, they're coming, you're on!

But—

I try to call her back, but her voice is lost in the roar of the surf. I open my eyes. Dr. Hancock's face floats over me, bobbing like a buoy. I swallow back the bile in my throat. He moves his mouth but I can't hear him. My ears are full of water. I shake my head to clear them and he frowns. He thinks I'm saying no to whatever he just said. He's turning away, motioning to the floating jellyfish, telling the nurse something.

"Please," I manage, "what did you say?"

He turns back, looks down at me, and this time I can make out his words. "I said, 'Good morning, Laurel. It's good to have you back with us.'"

I swallow back a gallon of saltwater and try to smile, but it must look like a grimace. I try speaking instead. "Good morning, Dr. Hancock," I say. The words echo in my head. I hear another voice far below me, calling to me, begging not to leave her at the bottom of the ocean, drowned.

I'm sorry, I tell Daphne, letting her go, watching her sink to the bottom of the sea. I lick the salt off my lips. "It's good to be back," I tell Dr. Hancock.

Laurel's Journal, June 25, 20—

If I hadn't already known that motherhood turns women into nut cases, I'd have the proof today. What a bunch of wack-jobs! They all sat around sharing their stories of losing their minds as if having a baby was an excuse for slovenliness. One woman confessed to walking around with her shirt unbuttoned. Another thought it was really funny that she had poured breast milk into her husband's coffee. They tell these stories pretending they're embarrassed while really they're reveling in their dysfunction. I saw the same thing in group therapy at MacLean. The crazies egg each other on, trying to top one another.

I noticed, though, that Doormat Daphne wasn't sharing. Instead, every time someone spoke she glanced over at me, as if wanting to see what I thought of it. I decided to try a little experiment. I told my own little story—I made up one about leaving the car keys in the refrigerator—and *quelle surprise!* DD let loose with an entire saga of coming to last week's meeting with the bottles she'd made up to leave home with her husband. Which only confirmed again what a sad sack she is.

But then she surprised me. One of the women said she heard voices and I thought, Oh good, at least now we'll get something a little juicy, but even the voices were boring, reminding her to buy orange juice and iron hubby's shirts. Estrogena said something soothing like the voices were at least sensible and Daphne whispered to me: *Sure, all the voices sound sensible at the time.* Ha! Maybe she has potential.

I invited her back here and gave her some wine, hoping she'd loosen up and let go of her nice-girl act, but instead she tells me her whole life story. And what a pathetic little life it is! Her mom was a drunk who killed herself driving home drunk from a bar. Daphne put herself through state school working, like, three jobs, got a library degree and a job in a dinky suburban library. Then she snags a hedge-fund manager, but the one hedge-fund manager in the world who isn't rich. And clearly he bullies her terribly. When I pointed that out, she wept all over my linen upholstery. I told her some crap about us both needing to find order in our lives and she cheered up a little. I thought she'd never leave! Finally I had to nudge Vanessa to remind her she needed to get going.

Stan came home when she was getting ready to leave. He put on his Old World banker manners for Daphne and you could tell she was lapping it all up. Her husband must really be a brute. It made me feel a little sorry for her.

I took a little nap while Stan gave Chloë her bath. After all, I'd been with her all day and all Stan does all day is golf and sit around thinking of ways to invest my money. He woke me up after she was asleep and brought me a protein shake "to keep my strength up." He's still worried about all the weight I lost after Chloë was born.

"Do you want me to plump up like Daphne?" I asked.

He actually pretended not to know who I was talking about for a minute, which told me he'd noticed her *just fine*.

"Oh, your little protégée," he said at last. "I predict she won't be plump for long."

I asked him what he meant by that, and he gave me his raised-eyebrow look. "C'mon, Laurel, you know what you do. You befriend some poor mouse of a girl who follows you around like a besotted cocker spaniel and then when you tire of her you drop her off at the pound."

"That's totally untrue," I told him, but not with a lot of energy.

"Your college roommate, that girl in Scotland, Roisin, your yoga instructor . . ."

"So I'm not good at girlfriends," I said. "I hadn't even thought of Daphne as a real friend. I'm just doing the mommy-bonding thing. Isn't that why you sent me to this group?"

"I didn't send you anywhere, Laurel," he said. "We both agreed it was for the best. And I only mention those other girls because you so often get . . . *disappointed* and I know you're a little fragile right now."

I hate it when Stan treats me like an invalid, but I felt too tired to argue. Daphne isn't anything like Carrie or Roisin or Monique. They'd all turned out to be phonies. Daphne, for all her simpering, isn't a phony. She's real. She might be the *realest* person I've ever met. She just needs a little tweaking.

Chapter Fourteen

Once I stop fighting being Laurel Hobbes my life gets easier. *Quelle surprise!* I can hear Laurel say, *It's easier being a rich heiress than trailer-park trash.*

I could point out that I did not grow up in a trailer park, but I'm trying not to argue with my voices. With all the meds I'm still on, I never know when I might blurt something out and talking to invisible people is just the kind of behavior to get you sent back to the Green Room. I still have bedsores from my three weeks there—three weeks of my life I'll never get back.

"We had to sedate you to keep you from harming yourself," Dr. Hancock explained in our first session together. I responded by throwing a chair at him. Turns out, that's another way to get sent back to the Green Room. I was there another week—at least, that's what I'm told.

The next time he brings up my sedation I channel Laurel's sangfroid. "I can see why that was necessary," I say, biting the inside of my mouth. And *voilà!* I was transferred to my own private room (courtesy, no doubt, of Laurel's trust fund) with a window. True, it has bars on it, but at least I can see the sky and a patch of grass and even a view of the tower. When I first saw that, I thought it must be a punishment of some sort, a taunt of what I've lost. And then I realized it was a test.

"Do you like your new room?" Dr. Hancock asks me at our next session.

"I'm happy to be in a room with a window," I say cautiously. "I missed being able to tell if it was day or night."

"I thought you might like a view of the tower," he says, "to remind you of your old life and work."

Asshole, Laurel says inside my head.

"It's something to work toward," I say. "Is . . . is . . . Chloe still there?"

"Which Chloe?" he asks.

Careful, Laurel warns.

I can feel the pull of the undercurrent tugging me down. "Daphne's baby. The one I brought with me. Did Peter take her home?"

"Yes," he says. And then, after a pause, "Don't you want to know about *your* Chloë?"

Caught you! Laurel crows.

But I'm ready for this. "I know Stan will be taking good care of her. That must have been why I was able to leave her behind."

"Do you remember deciding to take Daphne's Chloe?"

"No," I tell him honestly—and that one word of truth feels like a cut in my skin, exposing me to infection. *Maybe this isn't the best topic*, Laurel advises, but I need to know. "I have . . . *images* of going up a flight of stairs. The carpet is wet. At the top of the stairs is a bathroom . . ." *My bathroom*, I want to say, but I catch myself. "Where was she—Daphne—found?"

"In her bathtub," he answers. "Where else?"

"It's just . . . our houses look alike." *All those ticky-tacky houses.* "In my memory I'm in Lau—*my* house."

"I see," he says in that annoying way psychiatrists have of acting like they know you better than you know yourself. "But why would Daphne kill herself in *your* bathtub?"

Good question, Laurel says. *An even better one would be how did I wind up dead in your bathtub?*

It is a good question, but I don't have time to think about it before Dr. Hancock asks what else I remember. "Red," I say. "Red everywhere. When I walked into the bathroom, the floor was covered with red water . . ."

The water threatens to rise up and take me as I describe it, but Dr. Hancock urges me to go on. I can tell it's one of the steps I'm supposed to take on my "road to recovery." *Reliving the trauma*, Laurel supplies helpfully. *This is when you supposedly split and became me. Shrinks love this sort of thing.*

So I give him what he wants. I trace my steps through that bloody water to the tub and look down—

Into a woman's face floating below red water. A baby is crying—

"I picked up the baby," I say.

"From where?" Dr. Hancock asks. "Was she in the tub?"

I try to think. I see the red water and then I'm holding the baby wrapped in a blanket that's sopping wet. "I-I'm not sure," I admit.

"What did you do next?" Dr. Hancock asks.

"I walked downstairs. There was a suitcase by the door . . ."

A suitcase? Laurel asks.

I see myself walking out the door with a baby in my arms and a suitcase. "I had brought it over to Daphne's . . ."

Why? Laurel asks inside my head. *Why would I have brought my suitcase to your house?*

Don't you know? I want to shout at Laurel, but instead I say,

"I was leaving. I'd come to say goodbye to Daphne, but when I found her . . ."

Something snapped.

"Something snapped. I took Daphne's baby and I started to think I was Daphne. Daphne pretending to be Laurel."

Dr. Hancock sighs with satisfaction. "You experienced a dissociative break with reality brought on by the trauma of finding your friend dead by her own hand—her baby almost dead. The shock was particularly bad because of how much you identified with Daphne. You had to keep the baby safe so you had to *become* Daphne in your own head."

"I guess. It seems . . ."

Preposterous? Laurel suggests.

"Sensible," I say.

Dr. Hancock grins. "Exactly. You just did what you had to do."

"Yes," I agree, another moment of honesty that makes me feel dangerously exposed. "Now what do I have to do to . . ."—I stop myself from saying *get out of here* and say instead—"get better?"

"We keep talking," he says. "We figure out how you got here and then we find a path back."

"You mean we talk about Lau—my history?"

"Exactly."

Oh honey, Laurel says, *good luck with that.*

THE ONLY TIME I leave my room is to shuffle down a long hall to the bare, windowless room where I meet with Dr. Hancock once a day. I'm not allowed out into the "general population" yet. When I ask why not, Dr. Hancock tells me I'm still in a very impressionable state. "I want to limit your outside influences until you've established firm boundaries again."

It makes me sound like an orphaned duckling that will imprint on whatever it sees first. Or a blob of clay waiting for the potter's wheel. I *feel* like a blob. The medication they've got me on makes my mouth gummy, my hands and feet clumsy, my head full of cotton. I *need* to think clearly. There has to be some reason that Peter and Stan want people to believe I'm Laurel. But why? If they killed her for her inheritance why bring her back to life?

Good question, Laurel says.

"The money was tied up in a trust," I say, forgetting not to answer out loud, "so Stan won't have access to it whether you're dead or not."

He would have access to it as Chloë's guardian. But in that case, why do they need me to be alive? Why do they need you?

I'm about to answer when Dr. Hancock enters my room. "Laurel?" he asks. "Who are you talking to?"

They must have hidden cameras in the rooms. I'll have to remember that from now on.

"Myself," I answer.

THE NURSE BRINGS me three pills instead of the usual two with my dinner tray that night. That's what I get for talking to myself. I remember Ben Marcus saying that some of the patients "tongued" their medication, but I'm not sure how to do that. The nurse always makes me stick out my tongue after I swallow. But tonight, after I empty the paper cup of pills into my mouth, I kick the dinner tray off its stand. When she looks toward it, I spit the pills out into my lap and cover them in a fold of my pajamas. Then I quickly lift the water cup to my mouth and pretend to swallow the pills. The nurse is too angry at having to clean up the mess to bother checking my mouth. "*Baby Killer,*" she mutters under her breath.

I'm shocked. *It's not true!* I want to scream. *It was Laurel who tried to drown her baby.*

You don't know that for sure.

The blanket was wet, I answer in my head while peeling the damp, grainy pills off my pajamas. I hide them under my mattress.

Why are we hiding them? Laurel asks. But I don't answer her.

WITHOUT THE PILLS I stay up half the night. The hospital is different at night, full of sounds that are masked during the day by the voices of orderlies and nurses, the wheels of carts squeaking up and down the hall, the screams and shrieks of patients. At night I can hear a rhythmic thumping, like a giant heart powering the life of the building. I can hear, too, the wind moving through the pine forest. I remember the expanse of woods I saw from the tower. If I could get out of here I could hide in those woods.

I sit and watch out the window until it happens. What I've been waiting for. The light comes on in the tower. It flashes once. I flick my own light in answer. I don't know whom I'm signaling. In the stillness and quiet of the night hospital it feels as if I have slipped out of time and I am signaling myself weeks ago, sending a warning to myself.

Laurel's Journal, July 8, 20—

Project Doormat has been progressing quite well. I think I missed my calling. Organizing books and papers is not half as gratifying as organizing people. It's amazing what a little practical thinking can do for a person.

First I got Daphne to stand up to her husband and get some child care so we'd have some free time together. College student Vanessa is not as thorough as French Simone (which is why I didn't mind passing her on to Daphne—although I did make Vanessa promise she'd always babysit for me first if we needed her), but she's energetic and cheap once I explained to Daphne that she could tell Vanessa she could list the job as a child-care internship.

Then, with the money she saved on Vanessa's fees, I got Daphne to join a decent gym, one where you wouldn't get a fungal infection in the shower and that served an edible kale salad in the café. We've been going three days a week and you should see the change in Daphne! And it's not because I'm so shallow that I think looks matter more than anything else (although God knows they don't hurt), but anyone could see that poor squirrelly Daphne just needed to get some endorphins pumping into her system and stop obsessing over her baby 24/7 to feel better about herself. That brute of a husband told her he was "disappointed" that she gained weight during her pregnancy. I suggested she tell him she was disappointed he hadn't managed to grow a pair during the same time. I mean, what kind of man says that to the woman who's carried his baby? And what kind of woman puts up with it?

I guess it's a question of where you're from. Even though I lost Mommy and Daddy when I was young, I was brought up to think I was *someone*. Mommy always said that only weak women allowed men to bully them and that if you acted as if you expected people to treat you well, they would.

I remember once we were leaving for the summer on Cape Cod and my nanny was ironing some clothes that needed to be packed and she burnt one of my dresses. Mommy was so angry that she fired her on the spot and I cried because she'd been my nanny since I could remember. But then Mommy explained that burning the dress hadn't been an accident; it had been "an act of aggression against us" and we couldn't let people treat us that way. "Besides," she said, "won't it be fun for it to just be the two of us together this summer? We don't need fussy old Nanny with all her rules about bedtimes and meal times during our summer vacation."

Funny. I haven't thought about that for a long time. I guess Estrogena was right; writing in this journal is helping me get in touch with my feelings.

Chapter Fifteen

Fortunately, the part of Laurel's history Dr. Hancock is most interested in is her recent past—since Chloë was born, the postpartum depression, and her friendship with Daphne Marist—and I should, I think, be able to fill him in on all of that. Laurel and I talked endlessly about our pregnancies and childbirths. And the rest—well, I was there, after all.

"I had a difficult pregnancy," I begin, recalling what Laurel had told me. "I had morning sickness the first trimester and then preeclampsia and had to be on bed rest."

Dr. Hancock looks down at his notes and nods. I've gotten that right. After trying to convince everyone I'm Daphne, I find I'm doing much better pretending to be Laurel. "That must have been hard for you," he says.

"Yes," I agree, "because I . . ." *We both wanted to put the world in order after it had fallen to pieces.* "I like to have control and suddenly I felt like I had none. I have an unstable sense of identity."

"Oh?" Dr. Hancock looks up, interested. "Why do you say that?"

Because the Internet told you so, Laurel quips in my head. *Do you really think that trawling the Internet for a couple of hours and reading about a bunch of pathetic losers who like to broadcast their crazy to the world has given you a handle on me?*

"I guess it's what doctors have told me," I say, tossing my hair over my shoulder the way Laurel would have.

He smiles indulgently. "Let's leave your diagnosis to me. You just stick to your own experiences."

I blush, feeling chastened. Like when Esta told me not to share morbid stories. "Okay," I say, "but isn't that part of the problem? I mean, all my life I've been told who I am—by my parents, by the men I dated, by doctors. How can I help feeling that my identity is slippery?"

Whoa! Laurel says. *Where did that come from?*

I go on, ignoring her. "And it was worse during pregnancy—all those books telling me 'what to expect' and strangers coming up to me on the street telling me what I should and shouldn't do. Don't drink that coffee, God forbid I have a glass of wine, even touching me."

"You felt out of control."

"Yes! Wouldn't you? And of course gaining all that weight, my body changing. It felt like I was becoming a different person." I pause for breath, trying to remember what else Laurel had told me. "Oh—and then they had to induce labor! Like the little bitch didn't even want to leave!"

Does Dr. Hancock flinch when I say "bitch"? Have I gone too far? But he only keeps writing notes, so I may have imagined it.

"And then suddenly I have this crying, puking, pooping baby—this *stranger*—to look after and I'm supposed to love her and not care if she throws up all over me or pees on me." I realize I'm crying. I'd do anything to have Chloe here spitting up on me. How could I have been so ungrateful as to mind?

I thought we were talking about me.

I'm not sure who I'm talking about anymore, but I go on, because my experience here is close enough to Laurel's to serve. "Having a baby, it . . . it strips you down. Takes away who you were. I guess I wasn't handling it all that well, so Stan suggested I try the mothers' support group."

"And did that help?"

I remember how dismissive of the group Laurel had been. And I remember the story she'd told—my story about Esta. "I think the problem for me was that hearing all those other women's stories when I was in such a fragile state made me . . . I guess . . . be influenced by those stories. I started getting confused."

Dr. Hancock makes a noncommittal sound. "Tell me about Daphne."

I relax, relieved to be on firmer ground. "Well, the thing about Daphne is we had so much in common."

"Such as?" Dr. Hancock asks, his face impassive.

"Well, we had both lost our parents when we were young and we both went to library school."

"Aren't you being a bit self-effacing?" Dr. Hancock asks. "I'd hardly equate a degree in archival studies from the University of Edinburgh with being a school librarian."

Stung, I remember what Laurel had said when I pointed out the same thing. "We both needed to put order to the world. Besides, Daphne was thinking of going back to school for an archival degree."

Were you? Laurel asks but I ignore her. .

"Really? That doesn't sound like someone planning to kill herself."

"No, it doesn't." Then it occurs to me that this might be an opportunity to find out more about "Daphne's" death. "Are they sure that she did kill herself? I mean, have the police ruled out—"

Murder? Laurel says. *The word you're looking for is* murder.

"—any other explanation?"

"There was a note," Dr. Hancock says, keeping his eyes on me.

I want to scream that this is impossible. I never wrote a suicide note. But I only nod. "Well, I guess I didn't know her as well as I thought I did. She seemed . . . *sweet.* Maybe a little stressed, coping with a new baby. And, as I said, we had a lot in common. We even looked alike."

"Really?"

"Yes. Don't you have a picture of her?" Why haven't I thought of this before? If Dr. Hancock would just look at a picture of Daphne Marist, he'd know it was me. "I mean, wasn't there a picture of her in the paper when she . . . died?"

"I don't think so. Peter Marist wanted to keep it very quiet, especially with his daughter still missing. There were a couple of lines in the local paper."

That's all I warranted? There would have been more if it had been Laurel.

It was me, Laurel points out.

You know what I mean, I snap back.

To Dr. Hancock I say, "Poor Daphne. But yes, we *did* look alike. Especially after she dyed her hair and lost a few pounds."

"She dyed her hair to look like yours?"

"No . . . I mean, she—I—took her to my colorist, who thought it was a good color for her."

"And you didn't mind that she was imitating you?"

"It wasn't like that," I said. *Was it?* I ask Laurel, but she's gone quiet. "I mean, I encouraged her. I guess it was like a compliment to me that she wanted to be like me. And it wasn't all one-way. There were things about her I admired and wanted to emulate."

Such as? Laurel asks.

"Such as?" Dr. Hancock asks at the same time.

I search my brain. There were things Laurel had told me she admired—that I'd done so well on so little, that I'd put myself through school—but those weren't things she'd have wanted to emulate. Had there been any change in Laurel over the two months we knew each other that I could attribute to my influence? I thought of the last time I'd seen Laurel: pasty-faced, in baggy sweats, couch-bound. While I had gotten fitter, started dressing better, and applied for a new job, Laurel had sunk into despondency.

"No, I don't suppose she was a very good influence," I say, "but that wasn't really her fault."

Dr. Hancock clucks his tongue. "I know you must feel badly that Daphne killed herself, Laurel, but unless you're honest with yourself we won't get anywhere."

"I'm not sure what you mean," I say cautiously. "What part of what I've said hasn't been honest?"

"Your attitude toward Mrs. Marist, for one thing."

"What do you mean?" I say, genuinely surprised. "She was my friend!"

"Was she? Your journal tells a different story."

"My journal?"

"You don't recall keeping a journal?"

"No . . . I mean . . . yes. We were all supposed to in the support group. . . ." I want to say that Laurel had mocked the idea and I hadn't thought she had bothered, but Dr. Hancock is pulling a sheaf of printed pages from his folder. My heart beats harder.

"Is that Lau—my journal? I only kept it because Esta said we had to. I don't really remember what I wrote."

"Well," Dr. Hancock says, handing me the pages, "why don't you refresh your memory?"

DR. HANCOCK ALLOWS ME to bring the pages back to my room. It's the first time I've been allowed any reading material and it makes me realize how much I miss books. Maybe I can ask for books now—and to go outside. From my window I've seen patients sitting on benches reading. This place would be bearable if I could just go outside and read—and see Chloe. *My* Chloe. All I have to do is stay calm, keep playing the game that I'm Laurel, and eventually I will get out of here. Then I'll prove that I'm Daphne Marist. There must be a way—fingerprints on record, a DNA test comparing my DNA to Chloe's—and then I'll get her back. I just have to go through these steps that Dr. Hancock has laid out as my "road to recovery." Apparently one of them is reading Laurel's journal.

I move the pile of papers an inch to the right and then half an inch back to the left. Why am I so reluctant to read it?

Because it's an invasion of privacy? Laurel suggests. *Because it's ghoulish to read a dead woman's diary?*

No, I tell her, *it's because I'm afraid to find out what you thought of me.*

But I'm right here, she points out. *You could just ask me.*

You're not real. You're just a part of me. This is the real Laurel. What if she doesn't match . . . you?

Then don't read it, Laurel-in-my-head suggests, *and say you did.*

Dr. Hancock will ask me questions about the specifics. He'll test me on them. And besides, part of me is very, very curious—

I touch the first page.

Pretend it's a bit of archival record you're evaluating, Laurel suggests.

I turn the first page and note the date: June 11, the first day of our group. Like me, Laurel had gone home and begun the journal that Esta had asked us to write. From the first line I learn that Stan made her go just as Peter had made me. Also that the alternative for Laurel had been going back to a mental hospital, something I hadn't known. Poor Laurel. I can understand how scared she'd been to end up someplace like here. And then I realize that Laurel must have been in multiple hospitals, and all of that is part of *my* record now. No wonder Dr. Hancock is so ready to see me as a mental case; I have the history of one.

I read on and laugh at Laurel's name for Esta: Estrogena. But then I find her name for me. *Doormat Daphne.*

I'd only just met you, Laurel-in-my-head wheedles. *And you've got to admit, you were acting like a wuss, letting Peter push you around. And I was kind of a bitch. I'm even mean to Kate Spade!*

She's right—*I'm* right—I can't fault Laurel for thinking I was a doormat. Surely she must have felt differently about me as we started spending time together. I turn to the second journal entry. She still calls me Doormat Daphne but at least she thought Esta's shame-chant was as awful as I did. And though it still stings to read her say she thought her Chloë was prettier than mine—

What mother doesn't think her child is the most beautiful?

—I am surprised and touched that she envied how I looked at my Chloe. Of course I looked at her with love! I loved her even before I knew I did! I can feel that tug in my uterus now, just thinking about her. I feel bad for Laurel that she didn't feel that way and forgive her for that catty comment about wetting myself—

Gee, thanks!

—and turn the page to journal entry number three.

At first I'm heartened that she'd found something I'd said in group interesting, but then I'm startled to see that it was actually something she had said: *All the voices sound sensible at the time—*

Are you sure you didn't say it?

—and then I read her description of our first playdate. I had a *pathetic little life*, she couldn't wait for me to leave, I was "plump." Even Stan called me a mouse.

I say at the end that you're "the realest person I've ever met."

When I turn to the fourth installment (the last entry Dr. Hancock has given me) I find that it doesn't get any better. I was a "project" for her, a hobby to amuse herself with because she was bored in Westfuckingchester—

Maybe pretending not to care is my defense system.

—and she needed to look normal. Well, she wasn't. I see that now. All the time that I thought we were becoming friends—best friends—she was using me and making fun of me behind my back—

I was sick!

—and amusing herself by making me cut my hair like her and wear the same clothes.

No one made you do that.

The worst of it is that I was so invested in the friendship that I wanted to help her. I applied to the job with Schuyler Bennett to show Laurel her options.

Really? Are you sure you didn't apply for yourself?

And then she goes and kills herself in my bathtub! Why would she have done it in my house except to say one last fuck-you to Doormat Daphne? She must have known how devastating it would be for me to come home and find her in my tub, dripping bloody water all over my *ticky-tacky* house—

I thought we'd decided I was murdered.

—because she was a selfish, entitled, monster!

I throw the pages of Laurel's journal into the air and get up so quickly the chair falls back to the floor with a loud bang. As the pages flutter down I grab them and tear them into pieces, tossing the bits into the air so that they rain down like confetti. Ripping feels so good I decide to keep going with my sheets and pillowcase, which are so thin and threadbare they tear easily. Where are your gazillion-thread-count pima sateen sheets now, Laurel?

I stop at the mirror, which is metal, unbreakable. It reflects back a distorted picture of a bloated face. The face of someone who has drowned. A monster. "Look at what you've turned me into!" I scream.

It wasn't me—

"Shut up!" I shout, covering my ears with my hands. "Shut up! Shut up! Shut up!"

I'm still screaming it when the orderlies come in to restrain me. They have to wrench my hands away from my ears. Hanks of hair come with them. Blood and bits of flesh. I don't care. I will rip my ears off before I listen to any more of that bitch's lies. But when I'm finally pinned and lying on the floor, one cheek pressed to the cold tile, the other under an orderly's knee, all I hear is the roar of the ocean as the tide comes in to claim me. Laurel is gone.

Laurel's Journal, July 9, 20—

I've been thinking a lot about that summer on the Cape, the one when Mommy fired my nanny and we were supposed to have all this mother-daughter time together. Only I don't remember spending that much time with Mommy. She slept late in the morning, so I would get up and go down to the beach myself. The morning was the best time for shell collecting. I would walk for miles, looking at each shell that had washed up overnight, squatting beside it, deciding whether or not to pick it up. Some shells would look perfect until you dislodged them from the sand and you'd see they were broken. I didn't want any broken ones. There were pebbles that looked shiny when they were wet but which turned dull when you took them away from the water. I liked the long dark-blue shells, but they smelled. My favorites were the curved conch shells that you could hold up to your ear and hear the ocean, but I hardly ever found any of those that weren't broken. I liked the idea that I was becoming a collector the way Daddy collected antique cars and Mommy collected matchbooks from fancy restaurants that she kept in a big brandy snifter in the foyer.

By the time I got back to the house, Mommy would be up and reading the *New York Times*, which she had delivered from the local grocery store. There'd be coffee but not much else because Mommy was on a diet and only drank special shakes she mixed up, so I would bicycle into town and buy doughnuts at the grocery store and eat them all in the parking lot because if I brought them home Mommy would tell me I was going to get fat.

Only that was the summer I got really thin. All that walking on the beach and bicycling to town, I suppose.

When I got back Mommy would be napping so I'd go down

to the beach for a swim. I had an inflatable raft that I'd take out. It was always a challenge to get it out beyond the breakers and sometimes I'd get hit by a wave and suddenly I'd be under the water, turning over and over again like a shirt in the washing machine. Later I'd find bruises and scratches on my arms and legs and a gallon of sand in the crotch of my suit.

Once I was past the breakers I would belly flop on the raft and ride the waves in. I became really good at judging just the right moment to catch the wave, but sometimes I misjudged and got pummeled in the surf. One time I was just lying on the raft daydreaming about something—I used to make up stories in my head about wild horses or living in the woods and how I could survive on my own in a tree house in the Adirondacks where Grandma and Grandpa had a "camp"—and suddenly I noticed that I'd drifted far away from the shore. I could barely see the lifeguard station. Usually the lifeguard would have blown his whistle if I went out too far but he must have been talking to one of the leggy girls who hung around the lifeguard station all day and not noticed me.

At first I wasn't scared. It was kind of peaceful drifting on the water with the sound of the surf like the sound I heard inside the conch shells and the people on the beach looking soft and blurry like old pictures. I figured eventually the lifeguard would notice how far out I was and come get me and then I'd be that girl who was rescued and Mommy would come running down from the house and make a fuss and she'd feel bad for leaving me alone so much.

But the people on the beach got smaller and smaller, the sound of the surf fainter and fainter, and still no one blew a whistle or came swimming for me and I realized that I'd better start paddling in. It was harder than I thought it would be. There was a current pulling me out to sea that I had to fight against and if I let up for a second I drifted backward. Every time I looked up the shore looked just as far away and the people on it just as small and blurry. Finally, I just gave up. I lay back on the raft and looked up at the sky and watched the clouds and thought about what Mommy would think when I didn't come back and how she would cry and feel bad and wish she'd spent more time with me . . . and then all of a sudden the surf was loud again and I was being pulled under the water and thrown around like a piece of trash.

I finally dragged myself onto the beach and up to the house and when my mother saw me she screeched. I thought she was upset because I'd almost drowned. But it was because my hair was so tangled. "Look at her," she cried, waving her glass at me. "That's what comes from giving her a Jamaican nanny; she's got dreadlocks!"

The truth was Nanny was the one who always brushed my hair. I didn't know how to. When Mommy tried she pulled my hair so hard I screamed, which only made her slap my leg with the brush.

I learned to stay in the shadows during cocktail hour when Mommy had her friends over. They'd sit on the deck, drinking G&Ts and rum & Cokes and pitchers of margaritas the hired girl made up. I'd sit under the deck in the sand, drinking plain Coke and eating the raw vegetables—crudités, Mommy called them—and potato chips that the guests sometimes brought. I'd listen to the swells of conversation and laughter drifting across the sand and out to sea. Sometimes the hired girl would slip out to smoke a joint with her boyfriend and I'd watch them from my hiding place, pretending to be a spy. I was reading *Harriet the Spy* that summer and I liked the idea of being a spy, of watching people to figure out how to speak and act and dress.

It's funny thinking about that now because it's kind of what I've been doing with Daphne. I like to watch her with Chloe because when I see her acting so natural with her baby I think that I could be like that too. It even helps, I think, that she looks a little like me—even more now that she's gotten her hair cut like mine, lost some weight, and started wearing better clothes. At first it kind of annoyed me, but now it makes me happy, like we're both helping each other become better people.

Which I know sounds really sappy. It must be the postpartum hormones or all this thinking about the past, I guess. I haven't thought about that summer for years, because it was always painful to think about after Mommy and Daddy died. It was the last summer on the Cape before the accident, and I feel like I should have better memories of them. What I remember most about that summer, besides almost drowning, is throwing all those seashells back into the sea at the end and that when I got back to the city Mommy had to take me to Vidal Sassoon and have all my hair cut off. When I try to picture Mommy and Daddy they're small and blurry like those people on the beach when I was drifting out to sea.

Which is strange because they're the ones who died, not me.

But sometimes I feel like it was me who died that summer. That I floated farther and farther out on the tide until a wave took me down to the bottom of the ocean and I drowned.

Sometimes I wish I had.

Chapter Sixteen

It's quiet in the Green Room without Laurel's voice but I'm not there long before I have another visitor. At first I mistake the man in pressed khakis and golf shirt for the crazy golfer, but then one of the nurses says, "Your husband's here to see you, Mrs. Hobbes," and I realize it's Stan.

He looks older than I remember, his skin sallow under the fluorescent lights, the flesh around his jaw looser. There's a patch of gray hairs on his chin and a dab of shaving cream on his earlobe. He's really gone to seed since Laurel's death. For a moment I feel sorry for him, but then I remember he's the reason I'm here.

And a potential ticket out. I remember that there are hidden cameras in the rooms. While Stan thinks no one is listening I have to make him say something that reveals he knows I'm not Laurel.

"Stan," I say, or try to. What comes out sounds more like *Thaarrggh*. The drugs they've given me have numbed my lips and swollen my tongue.

Stan stares at me as if I'm a piece of dog shit he's just noticed on his Tod's loafers. Surely the nurses must notice that he's not looking at me with the loving indulgence of a husband.

I lick my lips, swallow, and try again. "Thstan," I manage this time. "I'm sorry about Laurel."

His eyes widen and he looks around nervously for the nurse, but she's left the room.

"I should have realized she might kill herself," I continue carefully, my speech starting to come more easily. "You warned me that she'd tried before."

Stan clears his throat. "Did Daphne tell you that I told her that?" he asks, adding a rather loud and stagey, "Laurel." Surely anyone listening can hear how fake he sounds.

"No, Stan. *I'm* Daphne. You know that. The woman in the tub was Laurel."

He leans forward and touches my manacled hand. I'm sure he's going to confess the truth. I only hope he's loud enough for the sound equipment to pick it up.

"Dr. Hancock explained to me that when you saw Daphne in the tub you had a dissociative psychotic break. You recognized your own 'death wish' and saw yourself in the tub, like looking into a mirror. That's why you think you're Daphne."

I almost laugh. All this psychobabble coming out of Stan's mouth! He must have spent hours memorizing it. I decide to switch tactics. "How's Chloë?" I ask.

To his credit he doesn't ask "Which Chloe?" "She's fine. I hired a new nanny."

"What happened to Simone?"

"Don't you remember? You fired her. She went back to France."

I shake my head. "Laurel would never have fired Simone. What happened, Stan? Were you afraid she'd identify the body in the bathtub as Laurel? Who *did* identify her?"

"My God, Laurel, it was Peter, of course. It was *his* wife, in *his* home. Thank God it wasn't you. You have a child to think about. I can't imagine what could have driven a mother to do such a selfish thing. Or what possessed you to take her baby and drive to the middle of nowhere—" He breaks off, breathless, looking around him as if remembering where we are.

I search in my head for something to say that will make him slip up. "I suppose if it had been Laurel, you would have inherited all her money."

"My God, Laurel, what a terrible thing to say. As if I'd care about that. Besides, you know your money's all in trust for Chloë."

Something about this tickles at my brain. Something Laurel said to me the last time I saw her about the money being all in trust—

"So it wouldn't have actually been convenient for you if Laurel *had* killed herself?" I ask. A muscle pulses in Stan's jaw and I think I may have stumbled on something. "Is that why you had to pretend the body was me, not Laurel? Because you still need to have Laurel alive?"

"I can't do this, Laurel," he says, getting up.

And then I remember what Laurel told me. "You're her mental-health conservator. That's why you can keep me in here. You have more control over Laurel alive than dead. Is that what happened? Did Laurel kill herself and you realized you'd lose control of her money? Is that why you had to pretend the body in the tub was Daphne? I should have believed Laurel when she said you were trying to poison her. When I get out of here I'll tell the police."

He looks down at me with an expression almost like pity. "I'm afraid that won't be happening anytime soon, darling. I couldn't take the risk of you hurting yourself—or Chloë. I'd never forgive myself if anything happened to her."

I believe this last part. "Then who put her in that tub, Stan? Who risked your baby's life?"

He looks unsure for a moment, then says, "Perhaps you imagined that part. Perhaps poor Daphne's baby was in her car seat all along. At least, that's what I'd like to believe of Daphne."

He turns away. I struggle against the straps holding my arms and legs. "Please," I say, all bravado evaporating at the thought of being left alone in here, "if you let me out of here I won't tell anyone I'm Daphne. I—I'll go away with Chloe—"

"Oh, I don't think Peter would like that," Stan says. Then he walks to the door. As he opens it I see Dr. Hancock standing in the hall. Of course he's been listening—and watching on the hidden cameras, I hope. Did he hear anything to make him suspect I am really Daphne Marist?

"I'm sorry," Stan says, a tremor in his voice. "She insists she's Daphne Marist. She even made threats against our child. I—I can't trust her home with Chloë."

"No," Dr. Hancock agrees. "She needs to stay here as long as she thinks she's Daphne Marist."

"What about shock treatment? It helped the last time."

"ECT? It's a possibility . . ." Their voices grow fainter as they step out of the room. I strain to hear what they're saying. Are they really considering giving me shock treatment? But whatever they're saying is drowned out by the sound of someone pushing a cart—the meds trolley, I realize—down the hall. As the sound of the trolley grows closer, though, the two men step back into the doorway to my room, apparently less worried about me overhearing them than that the nurse in the hallway will. I catch Stan saying, "But I'm her conservator. I can give consent."

"That's true, but I still need to get two psychiatrists to sign off."

"Then get them. Anyone looking at her will see she needs help."

"Most likely, but there are the side effects to consider."

"Such as?" Stan asks.

"Long-term memory loss, retrograde amnesia." Dr. Hancock lists these side effects as if they're of no more concern than the minor effects listed on a bottle of aspirin. "Most patients lose at least several weeks before the procedure, sometimes months."

"So she might not remember these last few weeks?"

"Yes, it's likely she'll lose her most recently formed memories."

"So she might forget all about Daphne Marist," Stan asks.

"Yes," Dr. Hancock says. "That's one possibility."

"Then let's try it," Stan says, looking back at me. "Let's hope it gets rid of Daphne Marist for good."

Laurel's Journal, July 10, 20—

We had dinner at Daphne's tonight. I was surprised Stan went along with it, since he didn't like any of my girlfriends in the city and he'd made all those mouse comments about Daphne. But he said he wanted to "encourage my bonding with other mothers in the support group." Sheesh. Ever since he was named my conservator when I had that teensy postpartum breakdown he's had this patronizing attitude toward me. I did a little research today on the Internet and found out that mental-health conservatorships usually expire after one year, but I also found out that I could apply to have it overturned if I can demonstrate that I'm doing better. And clearly I *am* doing better.

I talked to Stan about ending the conservatorship on the drive over to Daphne and Peter's. I told him it made me feel infantilized for him to have that power over me. At first he was very defensive. He asked me what choice had he had. He reminded me that I was raving, trying to harm myself and Chloë. I couldn't really argue with that, because I don't remember those couple of weeks after Chloë was born at all. When I was hospitalized they gave me shock treatment and it pretty much wiped out my memory for the whole first month of Chloë's life. I told Stan how angry it made me that I couldn't remember the first month of our daughter's life and he told me I was lucky I couldn't remember it. He said it was a nightmare.

Which made me want to cry but I knew that if I cried he would just tell me I was acting hysterical so I stayed calm and said, "Well, that's over. It was just a postpartum thing and now I'm better and I'd like to have the conservatorship dissolved."

He didn't say anything for a few minutes. He just looked straight ahead at the road. Finally he said, "Of course if that's what you want, that's what we'll do. You do realize, though, that you'll have to have a psychiatric evaluation. Are you sure you want to go through all that right now?"

I told him I could handle it and he asked if I'd like him to call the lawyer to set things in motion or did I want to do it? I told him I'd call my parents' old lawyer and Stan said that was fine and squeezed my hand. I felt so relieved!

When we got to Daphne and Peter's I felt like celebrating. Daphne had gotten all the ingredients for Expats because I told her I used to drink them in Edinburgh, which was really sweet of her. She's really got a lot more to her than I thought at first. I saw all the books on her shelves and noticed that she'd read all the classics (the Brontës, Dickens, Hardy, all those nineteenth-century books I loved in college) and even though her decorating ideas were pretty plebeian (framed prints of museum posters, Pottery Barn furniture), her house was really cozy. After the Expats she opened a bottle of Prosecco and I made my "Better Prosecco than Prozac" toast, which maybe wasn't the best choice after the conversation Stan and I had had in the car, but what the hell! I feel like I've been living in this prison since I got back from the hospital. No wonder I've had trouble bonding with Chloë when our first weeks together were fried out of my brain. Things are going to be different now. Motherhood is so much better when you're not doing it alone. As Hillary Clinton said, "It takes a village."

I could tell that Stan was a little annoyed, though, by how he started looking at his phone. He said this bullshit about the Asia office when I know full well that he hasn't had any consulting work for months. He *says* that's because he's had his hands full with taking care of me but I think that's an excuse. I think this whole conservatorship thing has been more about giving him a sense of purpose than about my mental-health is-

sues and that's why he became defensive when we talked about
it. He's using it as an excuse not to find other work, which isn't
good for him either.

Maybe he could get some deal going with Peter. They
seemed to hit it off really well, which surprised me because
Peter, quite frankly, has all the charm of a used-car salesman.
He was so obviously trying to impress Stan with his financial
acumen. The two of them vanished into Peter's study for ages
to "talk business." Which I figured was Peter trying to get Stan
to invest in his fund. Ha! I bet Peter was surprised to find out
Stan doesn't control the purse strings. When Stan came out he
had on his Grinch face, which he gets when he remembers the
money's *my* money. He always compensates by getting bossy.
So while Daphne was calling the taxi for Vanessa he went into
the nursery and was fussing with Chloë in her portable crib.
He said he wanted to make sure she was all right, like I wasn't
capable of putting her in her car seat. I got a little mad and he
left in a huff.

I stood for a few minutes to get my bearings and looked
around the nursery. It's really too frilly for my taste but I could
see all the work Daphne had put into it. There's a whole bookshelf of children's books and all the pictures of Chloe in her
first few weeks and a Baby's First Year calendar on the wall.
I flipped through the calendar and saw all the silly things
Daphne had written down in it, like Baby's First Bath! And
Baby's First Trip to the Park! And then I started to cry because
I couldn't remember any of that with Chloë. It made me want
what Daphne had so badly!

Which maybe explains what happened next.

I took Chloë out of the portable crib that Daphne had set
up and put her in the car seat. My eyes were all blurry from
crying, so maybe I just couldn't see very well. But you'd think a

real mother would know her own baby just by touch and smell. But I didn't. When we were ready to leave Daphne noticed that the baby I'd taken was *her* Chloe. I was mortified. I tried to make a joke of it but you could tell everyone was shocked. Stan just stared at me. When we got in the car he said, "Are you sure you're ready to be evaluated by a psychiatrist right now?"

I cried all the way home.

Chapter Seventeen

In the days leading up to my evaluation I am given more free-dom than I've had yet. I'm released to my own room and given permission to spend time in the recreation lounge. I'm even allowed to go outside with an escort. At first I don't know what to make of the sudden change in treatment but then, as my meds are reduced and I can think clearly again, I realize that Dr. Hancock must be worried about how the outside evaluators will look at my treatment.

Which tells me two things. One, my treatment so far—isolated, confined to the Green Room, and doped up to the gills—has not been standard. The question is, why has Dr. Hancock treated me differently than he would another patient? The answer must be that someone wants me kept here. Stan, no doubt. But how has he been able to influence Dr. Hancock? With money? Laurel's money?

It scares me to think of the power of Laurel's money mar-shaled against me. But then I realize the second thing: if Dr. Hancock is worried about my evaluation, there is a chance I can convince the two other doctors that I'm not crazy. Maybe I can even convince them I'm *not* Laurel Hobbes.

I work on my strategy while sitting in the recreation lounge, a large, sunny room on the ground floor with big windows and glass doors overlooking the lawn and gardens. It resembles the lobby of a resort hotel, complete with bucolic watercolor landscapes of the grounds and surrounding mountains. Anyone visiting Crantham would think it's a model of humane treatment for the mentally ill, albeit one with a rather strange clientele. My fellow patients look harmless enough, lounging in wicker chairs, playing cards, doing jigsaw puzzles at folding tables, or strolling back and forth on the terrace. Only when I get closer do I see the flaws in the scene. At the card table a young unshaven man in his twenties keeps shouting, "Go fish!" to the complicated bridge bids of a gaunt old woman with owl-like eyes. The sullen teenager writing in a journal is writing the same line—*I HATE EVERYBODY*—over and over again. The professorial gentleman reading on the terrace never turns a page of his book. When I get close enough to overhear conversations I learn that the bridge player thinks she's at her country club waiting for her husband to finish a round of golf, her unshaven partner is telling an invisible companion that the train will arrive in Seattle soon, and the professor thinks he's J.R.R. Tolkien.

And then there's Edith Sharp.

I almost don't recognize her, she's so diminished since the day of her attempted escape. Shorn of her dandelion-puff hair, she sits listlessly on a sofa near the French doors, gazing longingly at the lawn. I only recognize her when I sit down next to her and she turns her haunted eyes toward me. "Is it teatime yet?" she asks in a wispy Southern drawl.

"Oh," I say, startled by those wide green eyes. "I don't know. I'm new here."

"Are you a transfer?" she asks.

"A transfer?" I repeat. Does she mean from another mental institute?

"I transferred from Sweet Briar," she tells me, "for the art history department. They have the best art history department here. You see these paintings?" She gestures at the landscapes on the walls. "They were done by a famous painter. The college's art collection is one of the very best, only . . ." She looks around nervously and then leans toward me. Her breath smells like copper pipes. "Only some of these Northern girls aren't the friendliest."

I remember Dr. Hancock saying that Edith had her breakdown her sophomore year at Vassar. She's even fit the paintings on the walls into her fantasy. That's where she is now. Vassar circa 1971.

I realize that everyone here thinks they're someone—or somewhere—else. If I try to tell my evaluators that I'm really Daphne Marist, they'll chalk it up to delusion and certify that I'm incompetent. But if I pretend to be Laurel Hobbes I'll be saddled with Laurel's history of mental illness—and successful ECT therapy. I'm caught in a Catch-22.

On my third day in the recreation lounge I'm sitting on the sofa next to Edith. She's flipping through a stack of homemade cards—color copies of famous paintings pasted on cardboard. Edith keeps them together with a piece of red ribbon that she ties around her wrist when she's flipping through them.

"Would you help me study for the final?" she asks when I sit down near her.

I hold up each card and she recites the name of the artwork, the artist, the date it was made, and a few comments. She does surprisingly well. We've gotten to the Baroque when Ben Marcus walks past the terrace. Seeing him startles me, and my first instinct is to hide. The distance I've fallen since we met—from professional archivist, dressed in nice clothes, to bedraggled mental patient in pajamas—is too great. I'm embarrassed for him to see me like this.

Then I feel Edith's hand in mine. "Is that a boy you like?" she asks in her girlish voice.

I start to object but when I look into her green eyes I'm startled by how keen they are. For all her delusions, Edith is surprisingly observant. "You should talk to him," she says. She's right, I realize. He may be my best way out of here.

I get up and walk quickly out the French doors. I can hear an orderly calling me, but I ignore him. He catches up with me quickly, though. "Where are you going so fast, Laurie?" he asks, his meaty hand gripping my elbow.

"It's Laurel, not Laurie," I say in exactly the same imperious tone Laurel would use when someone got her name wrong. For a moment my—Laurel's?—reaction stops me cold. How am I going to convince anyone I'm Daphne Marist when even I have stopped believing it?

The orderly turns me around as Ben Marcus vanishes over the hill behind the golf course. I allow myself to be meekly led back into the lounge. Edith is waiting for me on the sofa, a sad look on her face. She pats my hand when I sit down beside her. "Don't you fret," she says, kindly. "I see that boy walking by the golf course all the time. He must be on the golf team. You'll get another chance. Now, here, help me with these Madonna-and-child paintings. I never can tell my Fra Angelicos from my Fra Filippo Lippis."

The next day I abandon Edith and find a seat on the terrace. I can see she's hurt—I've become another unfriendly Northern girl—but I need to watch for Ben Marcus.

It's colder than I expected outside, which makes me realize how long I've been at Crantham. It was summer when I arrived at Sky Bennett's house but now the leaves are turning. I'd like to go inside and get a sweater, but I don't want to risk missing Ben Marcus, so I sit shivering on a lawn chair, my arms wrapped around my chest. I'm watching so intensely that I don't know anyone's behind me until I feel hands on my shoulders.

I flinch, but then I see it's just Edith draping a crocheted afghan around my shoulders. She sits down beside me and takes out a piece of paper and pencil. "Why didn't you tell me it was time for sketching class?" she says, sweeping her pencil across the paper. "I love drawing landscapes, don't you? And I love our new drawing teacher. Don't you think he's handsome?"

I agree that our drawing teacher is handsome and to keep Edith happy I accept a piece of paper and one of the cardboard-backed art photographs to lean on, and begin sketching the line of trees and the house and tower rising above them. It's the perfect excuse for being out here, and once again I marvel at Edith's canniness. It's also oddly soothing to draw the rough outlines of the landscape, even though I've never had much artistic talent. And this time I see Ben Marcus as soon as he appears on the rise.

I stand up and call his name in as clear and loud a voice as I can muster. It comes out sounding like a hysterical plea, but at least it captures his attention. He stops and shields his eyes to look at me as if I'm too bright to look at. I imagine a crazy aura around me, like the picture I saw once in an Intro to Psychology textbook of a drawing of a cat made by a schizophrenic.

Ben Marcus lifts his hand and waves back at me. Then he turns to go on his way.

I break into a run, screaming his name, and flailing my arms over my head. I hear the thud of feet behind me and guess that the guards are in pursuit, but I've gotten enough of a head start to reach Ben Marcus before they do. I skid to a stop a few feet before him and hold up my hands. "I just want to talk to you," I plead. "Please."

His eyes narrow and his brow furrows as if he's angry, but I can see a slight quirk of his mouth that might be a sign of indulgence. He looks past me as one of the guards roughly grabs my arm. "Easy, Connor, Mrs. Hobbes just wants a chat. I've got it from here."

"But she doesn't have grounds privileges," Connor says, his hand still gripping my arm.

Marcus fixes his eyes on Connor's hand. "Then I'll walk her back to the lounge," he says slowly, as if speaking to a child. "You'd better get back to your post, Connor, the professor is heading for the trees again."

We all turn to watch the professor shambling across the lawn, waving his arms at the trees as if he were hailing an army of Ents. Connor swears and takes off running. "Go easy!" Marcus calls after him. "He's an old man." Then he turns to me. "What can I do for you, Mrs. Hobbes? I hope you don't expect me to escort you off the grounds. You know I can't do that."

The reference to our former relationship stings, but at least it gets right to the point. "You know I didn't seem crazy when you met me," I say. "I'm not. I'm being kept here under false pretenses and I need your help."

Instead of looking surprised at my statement he looks weary, as if he's heard this sort of thing before.

"So you didn't claim to be someone else when your husband showed up?"

I know my safest path out of here is to convince everyone I know that I'm Laurel, but looking into Ben Marcus's eyes I remember how I'd disliked lying to him the first day I met him.

"I did," I tell him. "But that's because I'm not Laurel Hobbes. I'm Daphne Marist."

"The Westchester woman who killed herself in the bathtub?"

"Yes. That's me. The woman they found in the bathtub was Laurel Hobbes, my friend, and she didn't kill herself. She was murdered. That's why they need to keep me here, because I know something . . . or would if I could just stop taking these drugs and remember."

It all sounds so crazy when I say it out loud. I expect Ben Marcus to escort me straight back to the hospital and remand me into the care of the doctors, but instead he leads me to a bench beneath an oak tree. "Okay," he says, sitting down beside me. "Why don't you start from the beginning?"

THE SPOT HE'S chosen is peaceful. We're facing an unmowed meadow of gold and purple grasses. The leaves above us cast deep violet shadows. I have the feeling Ben Marcus has chosen this spot for its calming effect, but the signs of autumn are alarming. Time is slipping away from me, summer gone, and autumn tipping into winter. I have the feeling that once winter comes I will be trapped here, snowbound in Laurel's body and name.

Start from the beginning, he said, but what was the beginning? When Chloe was born? When Peter found me drowning in the bathtub? When he sent me to the support group? When I met Laurel—

That's where I begin. I tell him about making friends with Laurel, how good it was to find someone who understood what it was like to be all alone with a baby.

"What about your husband?" he interrupts. "Wasn't he around to help?"

"Yes," I say, "actually Peter was really helpful. He adores

Chloe. Only that sometimes made me feel even more alone. . . ." I falter, unsure how to explain. Instead I ask him if he has children.

"A six-year-old daughter," he says, looking away. "She lives with her mother. Tell me what happened after you met Laurel."

So I'm not the only one who has things she doesn't want to talk about. But I *am* the one confined to a mental institution and about to get her brain fried so I tell him about Laurel. "She is—was—one of those people who draws people to her. You know? Like all the light in the room gravitates toward her. It's so crazy anyone thinking I'm her. I'm nothing like her."

"You were pretty lit up when I met you."

I blush at the compliment—if it is a compliment. "Maybe because I was pretending to be Laurel," I say. "I bet I don't look very 'lit up' right now."

He looks at me and I wish I were wearing anything other than pajamas. I look down at my hands, at the chipped polish on my nails and the ragged cuticles. Those days at the salon seem a lifetime away.

"You're all right," he says. "No one looks very shiny at Crantham."

"Laurel didn't look very shiny the last time I saw her," I say. "She looked like all the light had been sucked out of her."

"She sounds like someone with bipolar disorder," Ben Marcus says. "You say she thought her husband was poisoning her?"

As I describe Laurel's theories I can feel Ben Marcus's gaze on me. They sound paranoid and delusional, like something a woman in a mental institution would come up with. Even I had thought they were crazy. But they don't sound half as crazy as the situation I find myself in now.

"I suppose she could have killed herself, but why do it in my house?" I finish.

"Maybe she wanted you to save her," he suggests.

"Then I let her down," I say, thinking of the time I wasted sitting in my car writing in my journal while Laurel was bleeding out in my bathtub.

For the first time I realize that it's my fault that Laurel is dead. I can't say anything for a few moments. Ben Marcus lets me be quiet as if he knew what I was thinking. Then he says, gently, "But you did save Chloë—her Chloë."

As he says it I realize that he believes me. I have to stop for a minute to keep myself from crying. "But I might not have," I say at last. "And I can't believe Laurel would have risked killing her."

"Even if she thought she was somehow saving her from something worse?"

I consider that, remembering the woman who jumped from her window with her baby strapped to her chest because she thought it was better if he died than lived life broken. Would Laurel—perfectionist, high-strung Laurel—have done such a thing? Would I?

"I have to tell you something," I say. "Right after Chloe was born I-I wasn't doing so well. I took too many pills and wound up almost drowning in the bathtub. I would have drowned if Peter hadn't found me. I don't remember planning to kill myself, but that must have been what I was trying to do."

"Or at least that's what your husband says."

"You don't sound surprised," I say. Does Ben Marcus think I'm so crazy that nothing is impossible?

"It was in the paper," he says, pity on his face. He reaches into his pocket, takes out his phone, and taps in a few words, then hands the phone to me. My heart pounds at the sight of my face on the screen and I quickly scroll down past the photo to the headline: WESTCHESTER MOM SUICIDE. The print swims in front of me, random phrases surfacing like bloated fish rising to the top of toxic water . . . history of mental illness . . . treated for postpartum depression . . . previous suicide attempt . . .

I scroll back to the picture, hoping at least for proof that I am Daphne Marist. The picture is an unflattering one taken in my third trimester of pregnancy. My face is round and bloated, my hair growing out from an ill-advised pixie cut, my eyes squinting against the sun. Even after weeks in a mental hospital I think I look better now. For a minute I'm angry at Peter for choosing such an awful picture, but then I realize that's the point; he gave the newspaper a picture that no one would connect with how I look now.

"I know this doesn't look like me," I say.

"Not much. And I couldn't find any other pictures online. Not one for Facebook, eh?"

I laugh. "Peter said it was tacky and a lure for pedophiles so I took it down—Oh!" Our eyes meet.

"He was either planning this for a while or he's just a controlling prick," Ben Marcus says.

I should be glad he's taking my side but hearing him call Peter that stings. It's true that Peter was controlling but I'd always thought that was because his parents were so strict. But if he really has planned this, he's not just controlling, he's a monster. And what does that make me, a woman who married a monster? How could I have been so stupid? So spineless? Laurel was right. I was a doormat.

"Or both," I say finally, looking into the narrowed eyes of the pregnant woman in the picture. She looks like such a stranger that for a dizzying moment it seems more likely that I am Laurel Hobbes than her.

"Daphne?" It's the first time Ben Marcus has called me that, and it brings me to my senses. It brings me to *myself.*

"Yes?"

"Is there anyone who could identify you? Someone I can bring here?"

I try to think. Friends from college and library school appear in my mind, but I'd only been close to a few people and I've been out of touch with them for years. Peter had never been interested in socializing with my old friends.

I shake my head and a tear comes loose. "Laurel was the first real friend I'd made in years." How did I end up like this? How did I end up so alone?

"What about the other women in the group?"

I try to imagine Alexa Hartshorn driving upstate to stare at a bedraggled woman in a mental institution. . . . "Esta," I say. "The group leader. She'll know I'm Daphne."

"Okay," Marcus says with a nod. "What's her last name?"

For a moment I can't remember, and it makes me doubt everything. Isn't it more likely that Laurel would forget our group leader's name than I would? But then I hear Laurel's voice—for the first time since I read her journal and got angry at her.

Esta Greenberg, sweetie. And just for the record, I never forget a name.

"Greenberg," I tell Ben.

He taps the name into a notes app on his phone. Then he turns the phone around and takes a picture of me. "To show Esta Greenberg," he says. When he turns the phone back around so I can see the picture I wish he hadn't. I don't recognize the woman on the screen at all.

Laurel's Journal, July 23, 20—

I'm worried about Chloë. Ever since that night at Daphne's house she hasn't seemed herself. She cries all night long. Simone says it's just teething, but I'm afraid she might have caught something from Daphne's Chloe. I made Stan get up last night and take us to the emergency room. They couldn't find anything wrong with her, but what can you expect from a little podunk suburban hospital? I told Stan that we need to take her into the city to see a specialist. He told me I was projecting my fears about my own health onto our daughter and that he wasn't going to let me turn her into a guinea pig. I told him I was glad to see he'd gotten a medical degree so now maybe he could get an actual job. He asked me what I thought managing my money and me was if not a job? Then I threw a baby bottle at him and he left, saying he'd be back when I calmed down.

He slammed the door going out and it woke up Chloë. The sound of her crying felt like sandpaper rubbing at the inside of my eyeballs. I went in and picked her up but she just screamed louder. What kind of baby screams more when her mother picks her up? It's like she doesn't recognize me. I jostled her up and down, the way I'd seen Daphne do with her Chloe but she just screamed harder. It felt like she was screaming *inside* my head, like the sound had gotten inside and was scraping out my brains like a serrated spoon scooping melon out of its rind. I thought that if it went on any longer I wouldn't have any brain left, so I gave her a shake—just a little one—and screamed, "Stop it!"

And she did! But just for a second. Her eyes got really wide and surprised. And then she started crying again only it sounded different, weaker and thinner. Like I had broken something inside of her. Which made me cry. That's how Simone found us when she came in: sitting on the nursery floor, both of us crying.

SIMONE SAID I needed to go out and take care of myself, so I made appointments for mani-pedis at the spa for me and Daphne. I thought it would make me feel better, doing something for someone else, but as my mother used to say, *No good deed goes unpunished.* I was telling Daphne about how much Chloë's been crying and that I'm afraid something is wrong with her. I said she had rolled off the bed because I was too embarrassed to admit I'd shaken her, but Daphne looked at me funny as if she knew I was lying. Then she gave me this really patronizing look and told me I ought to have Chloë *checked out.* Which was practically like saying I'm a horrible mother and I've ruined my baby's life.

Daphne's just like all the other mothers at the support group with their whining about how sensitive they are. They're all just looking for someone to pat them on the head and tell them that whatever they do is normal and that their baby is the smartest, prettiest, best-behaved baby in the world. I'm glad that Peter said that Daphne and I don't need to go to the group anymore (not that I need *his* permission!). But at least now I don't have to see backstabbing Daphne anymore. Stan didn't even argue when I told him I wasn't going to keep going. He said that maybe hearing all those women talking about their problems wasn't good for me, that I've always been "suggestible." Then he finally agreed to take Chloë to a specialist in the city.

So, we went to this fancy suite in Sutton Place, all neutral grays with modern abstract statues of mothers and children and fertility goddesses—that sort of crap. Stan told me that the doctor wanted to talk to me while he took Chloë for some tests, so I told the doctor everything I've noticed about Chloë's behavior and my theory that she got something from Daphne's Chloe. He started writing down a lot of notes and asking me questions about Daphne, like what we talked about, and whether I started acting differently after we became friends, and did I often compare myself to other mothers? It was only when he asked if I hadn't done the same thing in college with my roommate that I realized we weren't there for Chloë; we were there for me. This was my psych evaluation to determine if Stan should still be my mental-health and financial conservator.

I was so mad that I started yelling at him that I'd been brought in on false pretenses and what kind of doctor went along with that kind of ruse? and he just sat there, cool as a cucumber, writing down everything I said and asking questions like did I often think people were plotting against me? Did I sometimes think I was someone else? Had I been experiencing any blackouts? Lost time?

"Like the forty-five minutes I've just spent in here?" I asked.

Needless to say, I didn't score high on the psych evaluation and Stan's conservatorship has been renewed. When I accused Stan of tricking me he said I'd asked for a psychiatric evaluation.

I was so upset that I had to take two Valiums when we got home. Then of course Stan gave me a lecture about taking too many pills and not taking care of myself. He even made up this vitamin drink that tastes like shit but I've been drinking it just to shut him up.

That was yesterday. Today Daphne came over and I tried to explain to her what I was up against but she's so naïve that she compared the conservatorship to her officious husband getting her to sign a power of attorney. Like they're the same thing!

Then she started acting condescending to me again, pulling that passive-aggressive bullshit, pretending to be concerned for me but really implying that I'm nuts and can't take care of myself or Chloë.

So I asked her to leave.

But when she left I realized how alone I am. There's really no one I can turn to. When Mommy and Daddy died, they didn't even have anyone to leave me to, except their stodgy old lawyer, Ronald "Call me JB" Jones-Barrett, who doles out my allowance and pays the bills for boarding school, college, and mental hospitals. Even then they didn't trust me to take care of my own money.

It's bad enough that it's all in trust, but at least I had control over my own allowance before Stan got the conservatorship. If I die, Stan will have complete control of the money because he's Chloë's guardian.

Unless I do something about that.

So I just called JB and asked if I could change Chloë's guardianship. After a lot of gobbledygook, which I was paying, like, a gazillion dollars an hour for, he finally told me how I could do it. I'm meeting him in the city next week to go over the details. For the first time since Chloë was born I feel like I'm in control. I feel like myself again.

Chapter Eighteen

Knowing that Ben Marcus has gone to find Esta should make my days at Crantham easier. All I have to do is behave myself, swallow my pills (or at least appear to; I continue to stockpile them instead), and busy myself with some harmless pursuit in the recreation lounge.

Since our sketching session on the terrace Edith has decided to switch her major from art history to studio art. "My roommate, Libby, says why should I study what a bunch of dead white men painted when I can make my own art?" she explains.

Libby sounds like a bit of a tool, I think, remembering from Edith's files that it was her roommate who turned her into the administration when she had the baby. But I can't argue against sitting outside on the terrace drawing side by side, wrapped in afghans against the cooler weather.

My own attempts are clumsy, but Edith clearly has—or had—talent. She captures the contours of the landscaped grounds, the meandering paths, gently rolling lawns, dark woods, and the tower rising on the ridge above it all. She draws the tower again and again. "Libby says I need to work on perspective," she says, "and an octagonal structure is perfect. It's

like the temple in Raphael's *Marriage of the Virgin*." I remember
that was one of the pictures in her stack of art cards. She's put
away the cards now that she's changed majors, but she keeps
the piece of red ribbon tied around her wrist.

"You like your roommate?" I ask.

"Oh, Libby's the best!" Edith gushes in a girlish voice totally
at odds with her lined face and white hair. "She's actually been
to all the places we study in art history. She's so . . . *worldly*.
She gets all her clothes at B. Altman's in the city and has her
hair done at Helena Rubinstein's. She's going to take me the
next time she goes in." She gives me an uncertain look. "I could
ask if you could come too."

"Thanks," I say, "but I wouldn't want to intrude."

Edith looks relieved. "Well, maybe that's best. Libby can be
a little finicky, if you know what I mean. She might not like a
change of plan."

I'm so taken up in Edith's fantasy world that the next time
we meet on the terrace I ask her how her trip to the city went.

"Oh!" she says, her face lighting up, "it was wonderful! We
had lunch at the Lotus Club and went to the Metropolitan Museum. Libby bought me a book on perspective at the Met and
I drew this. It's modeled on Raphael's *Marriage of the Virgin*."

She takes out a piece of paper and hands it to me, as if to
prove that the excursion really happened. It's a sketch depicting
two figures in classical garb, a man and a woman, standing in
front of a round temple. It actually looks very much like the picture from the card. Mary's face is tilted, her eyes cast modestly
down at her hand as Joseph puts the ring on her finger. A perfectly proportional classical temple stands behind them, giving
the scene a sense of order and balance.

I look up from the drawing into Edith's wide green eyes. "It's
very good, Edith. You're very talented."

A shy smile tugs at her mouth. "Thank you. Libby says I should do my junior year abroad in Italy and go to the Slade after college." Her eyes are so full of hope that for a second I am seduced into imagining Edith studying art in Rome and London. Then I remember that that will never happen. She will give birth alone in a dorm room and throw the child into a trash bin. She will be expelled from college and go crazy, tortured by that irrevocable act. She will be locked away in this place, her youth and talent burned out of her by drugs and shock treatments, her mind so haunted by the memory of that lost child that she'll climb to the top of the tower and throw herself over.

This is what will happen to me if Ben doesn't find anyone to prove I'm Daphne Marist. They'll give me shock treatment and I'll forget what's happened in the last few months. I'll forget Chloe. I'll forget myself. I'll become an empty hull, a shadow.

I wipe away a tear and Edith's sketch, which I've been blindly staring at, swims in front of me, the pencil shading of the temple blurring into shadows. There seems to be something in one of the windows.

I look closer. Yes, there's a figure in the center window of the temple, a shadow of a shawled woman, one hand lifted in a wave. It's only the briefest of sketches but Edith really is talented: I could swear the woman is signaling for help.

Laurel's Journal, August 1, 20—

I went to the city to see JB today. It had been so long since I'd gone down to Manhattan. When we moved here Stan said I could go in every day if I wanted, lots of people commute. I did go in at first but then when I was pregnant I hated the crowded trains, so many bodies pressing in around me.

At first I was excited to be making the trip. I put on a new dress and heels. I'd have lunch at a nice restaurant after the meeting, do some shopping. I thought I'd walk along Fifth Avenue for a bit, look in the shop windows, but it was so hot that by the time I got to the law firm I felt wilted and tired. Then JB kept me waiting for half an hour in an overly air-conditioned waiting room, listening to the receptionist making wedding plans on the phone.

When JB finally saw me he made a big fuss and apologized for the wait—he'd had to squeeze me in on such short notice, he hoped nothing was wrong? Then before I could answer he called to his secretary to bring us coffee and he had to go out to handle something and I had to sit there in his office, looking at all the silver-framed photographs of JB's grandkids and his sailboat and the house on Martha's Vineyard and it all made me want to cry. If Mommy and Daddy hadn't died on that plane I'd have all this: I could talk to my family about what was happening with Stan, Chloë's picture would be on Daddy's desk, and I'd be on the Cape right now instead of in sweltering, dirty Manhattan.

When JB came back he perched on the edge of the desk and gave me a cup of coffee, which I let sit on the table beside me because I was afraid my hands would shake too hard if I picked it up. I told him I wanted to change the terms of the trust to protect Chloë's interests.

"You want a new trustee? Is there anything wrong between you and Stan? Should I call Arnie in from Matrimonial?" He said all this in his lockjaw patrician drawl. His white hair and tanned skin reminded me of Stan. But then, that was because JB looked like what I imagined my father would look like now and I'd married someone who reminded me of my father.

That thing I said to Daphne, about us wanting to put the world back together, was bullshit. You can't put together something that's broken. It's like trying to glue together a priceless Ming vase. In the end it's just a piece of broken trash.

"No," I told him, "I don't need Arnie—at least not yet. I just want to make sure that Chloë's money is protected."

When I told him what I wanted to do, he made a face. He tried to talk me out of it, to get me to at least wait and think about it, but I did what Mommy would do when one of the servants made excuses. I just smiled and repeated what I wanted.

"Of course," he said. "I'll have the papers drawn up right away and send them to you." Then there were a lot of details about notaries and witnesses. I started to feel jittery from the coffee and as soon as we were done I went to use the ladies' room and threw up. When I came out of the stall the receptionist was standing at the sink. She asked if I was okay and I told her I was fine and that she was picking the wrong colors for the tablecloths at her wedding. Salmon would make everyone look sallow. She should go with peach.

I fixed my hair and makeup. I looked awful but I figured it was just the bad lighting. For what JB charges an hour you'd think the firm could afford better lighting.

I didn't feel like sitting alone in a restaurant or trying on clothes so I took a cab back to Grand Central. I got sick *again* on the train. Maybe I've got the flu. Probably something I picked up from Chloë. Babies are like germ factories.

All I wanted to do was sit quietly on the train and stop think-ing about how crappy I felt when of course this woman shoves her face right up in front of me and screeches, "Laurie, is that you?" And would you believe, it's Esta, with a bunch of Eileen Fisher and Saks bags, wearing one of her tent dresses and big macramé earrings. Last person on Earth I wanted to see. She sits down across from me and starts braying away: why'd I quit the group, I was doing so well, she'd been worried about me, blah, blah, blah. Then she sticks out her waddled neck and peers closer at me and says, "You really don't look so well."

"Just a summer cold," I told her.

"Oh, those are the worst!" Then she sits back with a smug look on her face and says, "Is that what was wrong with Chloë?"

"What?" I asked her.

"Daphne called me to say she was worried about you be-cause you've been fretting about Chloë."

I couldn't believe it! After all the times we had made fun of Esta together and I defended Daphne when Esta was mean to her, Daphne goes and rats me out to Esta! I was so mad, I could barely pay attention to anything Esta was saying. She was going on about Daphne and how she was afraid she had that postpartum OCD thing where she over-identifies with other women's stories so I asked her if she wasn't betraying patient-therapist confidentiality by talking to me about Daphne. That shut her up.

When I got home I was so chilled that I changed into Stan's sweatpants and crawled onto the couch. Stan mixed up a drink with electrolytes and I was so dehydrated that I drank two big bottles of it. I was just feeling a little better when Daphne showed up, basically to tell me that I looked like shit. Then she started going on about these jobs I could apply for—as if *that* was the answer to my problems!—and about how I had *lost myself.* I took a good look at her then and I saw how much she's copied about me: my hair, my clothes—she's even got the same fucking Kate Spade bag that Stan gave me—and I realized she's been making herself into a little mini me. Which is so pathetic it made me feel even sicker.

But the worst thing was Daphne got this saccharine sweet I'm-so-worried-about-you look on her face and asked me if I was thinking about killing myself. She said Stan told her I'd tried when I was pregnant. She was blubbering about how she'd tried to kill herself too, like it made us blood sisters or something and I suddenly understood what's going on. I've been such an idiot.

Stan's been telling everyone that I'm crazy and suicidal. So if I really *did* kill myself everyone would think, "Oh, poor Laurel, we should have seen it coming."

When what we all should have seen coming is that Stan is planning to kill me and make it look like I killed myself.

Chapter Nineteen

A week goes by and there's no sign of Ben. I begin to wonder if he ever believed me at all.

Or maybe I imagined the whole conversation. I remember Ben Marcus saying that this place could drive a sane person insane. Take those watercolors on the walls in the lounge. From a distance they looked like ordinary landscapes—the kind of thing you'd see in a country inn—but I've been looking at them more closely and they're not so ordinary. They're all of the same view, for one thing, of that bench where I sat with Ben Marcus with the hill and the tower in the distance. In some of the paintings the bench is empty and then in some there's a young woman sitting on it, and in a few there's a man and a woman. It's in the paintings with both figures that the landscape gets a little odd. The trees seem to be moving, like there's a wind thrashing them about, but when you look closer you can make out figures in the trees, writhing men and women who look like they're in the throes of passion . . . or madness. I doubt the staff has ever looked at them closely enough to notice or they wouldn't keep them on the walls. There's something weird about the tower too. It grows taller in the later pictures and emits a weird light. In one of the pictures there's a giant eye on top of the tower as if the tower itself is watching the couple on the bench. The most disturbing picture is the one in which only the man remains on the bench. But the woman isn't gone. If you look closely you can find her body parts littered among the foliage.

I wonder if the painter—"C.S.," he signs himself—was crazy to begin with or if he became crazier as he stayed here. Being surrounded by crazy people makes you feel like there's no solid ground, no baseline of sanity to balance your own thoughts against. It's like trying to hang a shelf on a wall that's crooked. Nothing lines up.

I can see the frantic desire to make things line up in Edith's increasingly chaotic sketches. She has become obsessed with drawing *The Marriage of the Virgin* over and over again, seeking to find balance in the classical proportions of the Renaissance master. At first she satisfies herself by drawing diagonal perspective lines from the figures in the foreground across the paving squares to the round temple. "See," she says, "they're all connected."

Then she decides that the temple should be taller and the people smaller. As the temple grows into a tower the woman in the window becomes more distinct. I can see now that she's holding something in her arms. "She needs to be connected too," Edith says, drawing lines from the central window in the tower to the figures in the foreground. She still calls them perspective lines but I think she means to represent the sight lines of the woman in the window. They look, though, like rays of light emanating from the tower. As if the tower had become a lighthouse and the woman in the window its beacon. Perhaps she's gotten the idea from the watercolor of the tower with an eye atop it.

The scene in the foreground changes too. The crowd of suitors and handmaids disappears, leaving only two figures, who are no longer Joseph and Mary, but are instead two women. One holds a baby; she is offering it to the other woman, who is wearing an outfit that looks like an old-fashioned nurse's uniform.

"Who's that?" I ask, pointing to the nurse.

"Nurse Landry," she says. "She's nice."

I haven't met a nurse named Landry here, or any that are particularly nice. I point to the man who stands in between them. He is a bearded old man, like the priest in the original painting, but now he brandishes a meat cleaver in his hand.

"Who's this?" I ask.

"Solomon," Edith tells me, plucking at the red ribbon on her wrist. "He's telling the women that he'll cut the baby in two if they can't agree who's the mother." I shiver. It's getting far too cold to be out on the terrace.

"Of course, it's only a trick to find out who the real mother is," I say.

Edith looks up, her green eyes so piercing on this gray, overcast day that I can almost see rays of light shooting out from them like in the picture. "Is it?" she asks.

The next day it snows and I'm relieved to have an excuse not to go out on the terrace to sketch with Edith. Instead Edith sits at a card table, covering page after page with pictures of women and babies and men with cleaving knives. She steals glue from the arts-and-crafts table and hangs the pages up on the windows. Then she steals red yarn from the knitting circle and strings yarn from picture to picture, creating an intricate spider web. She strings yarn from the landscapes on the wall to her pictures too.

"Don't you see," she says, when I try to lead her away, "they're all connected—the tower, the baby, the man . . . here, hold this—" She hands me a ball of yarn and walks around me in a circle. When she's wrapped me up she goes on to one of the other patients and when he tries to stop her, she darts around the room, trailing red yarn behind her in bright lassos, until orderlies, patients, and nurses are all bound in her web. Finally, one of the orderlies restrains her and drags her out of the lounge, and we all unwrap ourselves.

I'm picking yarn fuzz off my arms when Dr. Hancock comes to tell me that the doctors are here to do my psych evaluation.

"What about Ben Marcus?" I ask as Dr. Hancock leads me down the hall to the elevator.

"What about him?" Dr. Hancock asks without turning around.

"He—he was getting something for me. Something that I need to show the doctors."

Dr. Hancock stops abruptly and turns on me. "Guards are not allowed to bring presents to patients," he says. "Marcus's behavior was completely inappropriate. He's been fired."

"Oh," I say as Dr. Hancock gives me a slight push onto the elevator. I can feel tears welling in my eyes. Ben Marcus was my last hope. How will I convince these doctors I'm Daphne Marist without any proof? I catch a glimpse of myself in the convex mirror in the corner of the elevator, my face elongated like the figure of Edvard Munch's *The Scream*. My hair is tangled with yarn, my face smudged with glue, my pajamas covered with fuzz. I look like I should be institutionalized.

The elevator lets us off on the floor of Dr. Hancock's office. It's strange being in this hall again after so long and I wonder why the evaluation is here. "Can I use the restroom?" I ask.

"I don't have a female matron to supervise you," he says. "You'd have to go back downstairs, and the doctors have been waiting already."

I want to object that they can wait but Dr. Hancock strides

on ahead. As I walk behind him I glance at the pictures on the wall. I notice that they're signed "C.S." They're by the same artist who did the landscapes in the lounge. Here is where the body parts of the woman on the bench have ended up. It's not a particularly cheerful thought to have as I make my way to Dr. Hancock's office. It makes me feel as though parts of my own body are coming loose.

Inside Dr. Hancock's office are a man and a woman. The woman is dressed in a smart knit suit that instantly makes me feel slovenly in my fuzzy pajamas. The man is wearing baggy corduroys and a plaid shirt. The lines of his shirt remind me of Edith's perspective lines. He's got a stray thread on his sleeve that I have to keep myself from plucking off.

They introduce themselves but I forget their names immediately and I'm afraid if I ask again they'll think I'm scatterbrained. I sit in an upholstered chair that's so soft I sink into it. They sit in hardback chairs lined up across from me. I imagine perspective lines stretching from me to them. I am clearly the focus. The vanishing point.

"Do you understand what the purpose of this meeting is?" the man asks in a voice that manages to be kindly and terrifying at the same time.

"To determine if I'm competent enough to refuse electroconvulsive treatment," I say, proud that I've remembered the correct term for the procedure. "I *am* competent, and I do not want the ECT."

"Why not?" the woman asks, opening a file. "I see here that you had ECT six months ago and that it lessened the symptoms of postpartum depression."

"That's not me," I say. After days of indecision I've decided on the spur of the moment to tell them I'm Daphne Marist. It may be reckless, but I am beginning to see how easy it is here to fall into delusions, like Edith's delusion that she is a college student in 1971. I am afraid that if I tell these doctors that I am Laurel Hobbes I will begin to believe it myself. If I'm going to fight for my life, I want to do it in my own name.

"You're saying you don't recall having the ECT?" the woman doctor says.

"No, I'm saying I didn't have it. Laurel Hobbes had it and I'm not Laurel Hobbes. I'm Daphne Marist."

There's a moment of silence, followed by a quick whispered consultation. I hear "mirroring," "dissociative break," and "schizoaffective disorder." I will myself to stay calm and wait for them to return their attention to me. When they turn back to me I begin talking before they can ask any questions. I need to get ahead of the story that I am Laurel Hobbes. "I'm asking that you consider for a moment that I am Daphne Marist and *not* a deluded Laurel Hobbes. Consider that you have no real proof that I'm Laurel. No DNA test, no fingerprints. You have only the word of two men, Stan Hobbes and Peter Marist, both of whom profit financially by my being Laurel. Stan because he's Laurel's conservator and has control of her money as long as Laurel is deemed incompetent, and Peter because I believe Stan is investing that money in his fund."

I take a deep breath, pleased at how reasonable the argument sounds. The doctors' faces are impassive, but at least they haven't interrupted me. I go on.

"I don't know whether Laurel killed herself or someone killed her or why she ended up in my house, but I think whatever happened, Stan and Peter realized they needed Laurel to be alive to use her money. Laurel said something to me a few days before she died about changing the terms of Chloë's trust. I think that would have kept Stan from controlling her money after her death. But if Laurel was alive and incompetent, he could access her money. So they needed me to become Laurel."

The woman doctor tilts her head and starts to say something, but I talk over her. I feel like I'm running a race and I have to get this all out before they trip me up. "Unwittingly, I played into their hands. I assumed Laurel's identity to take the job with Schuyler Bennett. I didn't plan to at first; I applied to the job for Laurel, but when I accidentally switched bags with her I got the idea of using it to go away myself. At least, that's what I told myself." I pause, feeling the tension of the lines I've drawn sag and fray.

Seeing my uncertainty the woman doctor probes. "You see it differently now?"

"Yes," I say, glad that she is at least following the story. "I think I was jealous of Laurel. I wanted to be her—or at least *like* her. I also think I was afraid. I must have sensed what was going on with Peter and Stan and when I came home and found Laurel . . ."

I stop. This is the part I can't really explain. The part that makes me sound crazy. The part I still don't really remember. When I try to think of it, my vision goes red, as if a red veil has been dropped over my eyes.

"That must have been traumatic," the woman doctor says.

"Yes!" I agree gratefully. I've decided I like her. "All I can remember is going up the stairs. The carpet is wet. It reminds me . . ." I hesitate, realizing I've entered a trap.

"Of what?" Woman Doctor asks.

Do I tell her about the bathtub incident? For the first time it occurs to me that even if I convince them I'm Daphne Marist I may not be let out of here if they decide that Daphne Marist is crazy. But I've come too far. I'm convinced that Woman Doctor will know if I don't tell her the truth.

"A couple of weeks after I gave birth I was very depressed. I took some pills and got in the tub. I don't think I meant to kill myself, but I was so . . . tired. I think I just wanted to sleep. My husband found me . . ."

I recall Peter's hands on my shoulders, pulling me to the surface, but now it occurs to me that if he were really pulling me up to the surface his hands would be on my arms, not on my shoulders. He wasn't pulling me out; he was pushing me down.

Woman Doctor is still watching me, waiting patiently.

"I think my husband, Peter, tried to kill me," I say, tears rising to my eyes. "He said I tried to drown myself, but I wouldn't have done that. I think he wanted me gone and when he had the chance to say I was the woman in the bathtub he took it. That way he and Stan got control over Laurel's money and he got me out of the way."

"Why would your husband want you out of the way?" she asks. "Daphne Marist didn't have a big inheritance too, did she?"

I almost laugh. "No, I don't have any money. I—I don't know why. Peter's very . . . *particular*. Maybe it was too difficult having a wife with postpartum depression. But I think that's why I don't remember finding Laurel in the tub. I was going up the stairs, remembering when Peter found me in the tub and then when I got to the bathroom . . ."

The red veil descends. I can't see anything else.

"When you looked into the tub, who did you see?" the male doctor asks. His voice is deep and persuasive.

I keep my eyes closed. I watch myself crossing the bathroom floor. The tiles are wet and stained red. Red water is dripping down the sides of the tub. I look down. I see—"Me," I say, opening my eyes. "I saw myself. That's why I ran."

The woman doctor gives me a small, sad smile. "That's why you had a dissociative break. You saw yourself in your friend's dead face, so you 'died.'" She holds up two fingers on each hand and wiggles them like bunny ears. "You became your friend."

"You became Daphne," the male doctor says. He turns to Dr. Hancock. "I think the patient is making progress with talk therapy. Is ECT really necessary?"

"She still thinks she's Daphne Marist," Dr. Hancock replies. "She'll persist in the delusion until something jolts her out of it."

"Perhaps," the woman doctor says, "we should consider the possibility that she's telling the truth, that she *is* Daphne Marist."

Dr. Hancock barks a short, rude laugh. "Are you really buying this outlandish conspiracy theory? You're feeding into the patient's delusion."

The woman glares at him. "Could it hurt to have outside verification? A friend or relative of Daphne Marist?"

"Well," Dr. Hancock says, "in fact, we do have one. I was going to wait until after the evaluation, but since this has come up again . . ." He leans back toward his desk and hits the intercom button on his phone. "Rose, would you please send in Ms. Greenberg?"

Ms. Greenberg? "Esta's here?" I say.

"Yes. After Ben Marcus was fired he contacted her and asked her to come up here to identify you. I told her it wasn't necessary, but she insisted." He makes a face and I can imagine how unpleasant Esta has made herself. I feel like cheering. Sour, disagreeable Esta! I can't think of anyone I'd rather see right now.

The door opens and Esta bustles in. She's wearing flowing layers of linen and wool and carrying an enormous tote bag. Her face is turned down in a scowl, her hair standing up in spikes. Miniature crystal chandeliers sway from her earlobes. She looks like Mary Poppins in Eileen Fisher. I could hug her.

"Esta!" I say, standing. "Thank God. Tell them who I am."

Esta gives me a long, assessing look. Then she turns to the three doctors. "I can't believe I drove three hours for this. This woman is Laurel Hobbes."

Laurel's Journal, August 2, 20—

I've decided that I have to leave. And I can't trust JB anymore, which means I can't depend on drawing my monthly allowance from the trust.

After Daphne left, Stan came home and sat down on the couch with his "concerned" look on his face. He said that JB had called him to say I'd come into the city and that I sounded "irrational."

I was furious. "That's a complete breach of client-lawyer confidentiality," I told him.

"I think JB was acting as a friend, not a lawyer," Stan said. "He didn't even tell me what you wanted . . ."

His voice trailed off like I was going to volunteer what I was there for, but I was damned if I was going to tell him what I wanted even if Daphne was right. I mean, if he knew he'd no longer profit from me dying then I suppose I'd be safer but it's not like I'm going to let him *do* anything to me and I'm leaving anyway. Daphne's provided me with the perfect solution. I reread Daphne's last email to me about the job in the Catskills. I'd ignored it at first because it sounded dull but now it occurs to me that it's the perfect place to hole up until I can have my money transferred to another lawyer and divorce Stan. I'm going to send Schuyler Bennett an email and apply for the job. If I weren't so mad at Daphne I'd call her up and thank her.

August 8, 20—

The papers came yesterday and I went to the notary to sign them and then express mail them back to JB. I also took out as much cash as I could. Weirdly, I find that I can't leave without saying goodbye to Daphne. I've really been wrong about her. When I emailed Schuyler Bennett, she wrote back asking if I'd changed my email address and was I still planning on arriving on the fifteenth. *Quelle surprise!* Daphne applied for the job for me! I need to thank her. And I guess I should apologize for how I acted. I can see now that she couldn't possibly be in on Stan's plan. Now that I've stopped drinking that "vitamin water," I'm thinking much clearer. I'm going over there right now.

I'M IN FRONT of her house right now, but Daphne's car isn't here and Chloë is sleeping in her car seat, so I thought I'd pass the time by reading over these entries. What a bitch I've been! It's like I've been someone else since Chloë was born and I think I know who—my mother. It's like as soon as I became a mother I thought I had to be like her. Well, I can be better than that.

I feel bad about letting Simone go. She cried and said she'd lose her visa. I gave her all the money I'd taken out of the bank. She tried to give it back to me but I told her I didn't need it where I was going. And I don't. I see that now. I can see everything more clearly now.

For instance, I've just seen Esta coming out of Daphne's house. *Quelle surprise!* I think I'd better go in and find out what's going on. If Peter's there, I'm going to give him a piece of my mind. I'll bring my suitcase in so he can see I'm serious about leaving and that he'll never see a penny of my money. And I'll tell him what I think of how he treats his wife and that if he keeps bullying Daphne I will personally pay for a divorce lawyer who will make sure he never gets to see Chloe again. That will be my parting gift to Daphne.

Chapter Twenty

I remain calm. I don't make a scene. I don't fall to pieces. Because that is clearly what they expect of me. I can see it on Dr. Hancock's face. He's watching me like a boy watches an ant under a magnifying glass, waiting for it to go up in flames.

"Esta," I say calmly, "look at me closely. I'm not Laurel; I'm Daphne. I know we look alike and you aren't expecting to see me."

Esta gives me a long, steady look, giving me a chance to observe her. She's looking good. Laurel used to make fun of her shapeless hippie clothes but I notice she's given them an upgrade. Eileen Fisher instead of J.Jill. She's gotten a younger, sharper haircut. The crystal earrings might actually be diamonds. Her skin glows like she's recently had a salt scrub at a spa.

"Actually," she says, "I never thought you looked all that much alike. Daphne, poor thing, had a sweetness in her face that you never had." Then she turns to the trio of doctors. "Forgive my tone. I can't help blaming Ms. Hobbes for Daphne's suicide, although perhaps I should blame myself. I saw how Laurel was influencing Daphne, first in how she dressed but then also in how she thought. She filled her head with horror stories. I saw that Daphne was suffering from postpartum OCD and was internalizing Laurel's stories. I warned Laurel not to tell them—"

"*No!*" I shout, unable to stay silent any longer. "That was *me* you told."

The doctors all look from Esta to me. Dr. Hancock smiles. The woman doctor quickly jots down a note. I bet she's thinking she can get a paper out of this: "The Woman Who Thought She Was Her Own Best Friend."

"Of course it was you," Esta says, smiling a dazzling smile. Has she had her teeth capped? "I just said it was you. But you didn't listen, did you? You told your horror stories of women jumping from windows with their babies, women drowning their own children, women leaving their babies in the backseats of running cars in closed garages—until poor Daphne was so afraid she would kill her child that she took her own life." She shakes her head and then turns back to the doctors. "Classic borderline personality disorder. You should be careful who you expose to her."

"I'm afraid I have to agree," Dr. Hancock says. "I gave her greater freedom this past week and the patient she's been spending the most time with just had an episode in the lounge."

"That wasn't my fault," I object. "All I did was sit by her as she drew."

"Here's one of those drawings." Dr. Hancock takes a sheet of paper out of a folder and passes it to the other doctors. The woman doctor flinches and gives me a look of horror.

"That's not fair," I say. "I'm not responsible for what Edith Sharp draws."

The male doctor holds up the page. There's the same scene Edith's been drawing all week: the tower, the group of people below. But now a woman is dangling a baby out the window of the tower and the people below are shouting up at her. Poor Edith, I think, she's descended into a nightmare world.

But so have I.

The doctors are all looking at me with stony faces, as impassive as the face of Edith's Solomon. They are ready to sacrifice me, to cleave the part of me that is dangerous from my own brain.

I look away from them to Esta, who has the same stony look on her face. For a moment the mask slips and I can see a look of satisfied pleasure beneath it. It's like she's an entirely different person beneath that mask. It makes me wonder if anyone really knows who anyone really is.

AFTER ESTA LEAVES, Dr. Hancock tells me that they'll confer on my case and let me know when they've come to a decision. "But rest assured," he adds in a grave, paternal voice, "whatever we decide will be in your best interest."

Yeah, right, Laurel quips, *like volts to the head is in our best interest.*

"Just please," I say, ignoring Laurel's voice, "consider that Esta's been paid off to say I'm Laurel. Get someone else. Vanessa Lieb, my babysitter, or one of the other mothers in the group . . . Alexa Hartshorn or . . ." I can't remember any other names. Why wasn't I friendlier with the other mothers?

Because I was more fun, Laurel answers.

"We're not having fun now." I say it out loud. The woman doctor picks up her head and I see the look of certainty on her face: I'm a nut job and I need to be treated. I certainly can't be trusted with making my own decisions.

I see heavy-handed Connor hovering outside the door, waiting to take me back. If I struggle he'll hurt me. And what's the point? I'll only convince them that I'm crazy and a menace to myself and others.

I go peaceably to my room. Not the lounge. There will be no lounge privileges for me for a while, at least not until I've been made docile with electroconvulsive treatment and pills. I wonder how Edith is doing. *Was* I a bad influence on her? I'd been happy to encourage her drawing because it gave me an excuse to sit outside waiting for Ben Marcus. There's another person I've harmed; Ben's lost his job trying to help me. How many others have I let down? Laurel? By not believing her? By letting her get killed? And Chloe—my Chloe—whom I abandoned because I was so traumatized I took the wrong baby?

It's thinking about Chloe that undoes me. I sit on the edge of my bed, staring out the barred window as the light leaches out of the sky, imagining what Chloe will be told about me when she grows up. I remember when I got the news that my mother had been in a car wreck, driving home drunk on a Saturday night. I'd thought about her getting in that car drunk, never thinking that she was leaving me behind, never thinking that I was worth staying alive for.

Just before dark, Dr. Hancock comes to tell me that the other two doctors have concurred in his assessment that I should receive electroconvulsive treatment. "You needn't be afraid," he says, kind now that he's won. "You'll be anesthetized for the treatment. You won't feel a thing. And when you wake up, you'll feel like a new person."

I smile at that. "You'd like that, wouldn't you? For me to be Laurel. Much better to have a rich patient than a poor one."

He ignores my comment and pats my knee. "Get some rest," he suggests.

As if.

I agree with Laurel that there's no point in trying to sleep. I sit on the bed, watching the window, waiting—

And there it is. The light in the tower comes on and then goes off again. A signal, but from whom? What good does it do me? I turn my own light off but I don't turn it back on. Let that be my response to whoever is signaling. Over and out. I have nothing more to add.

At some point I fall asleep. I'm not sure for how long. I'm awoken by the sound of a key in the lock. Is it morning already? Have they come to get me? It's still dark but I imagine they like to start early. Nothing like electroshock in the morning to get the day started right. I curl into a ball, hugging my knees to my chest, head tucked, trying to make myself small. Trying to disappear, so they'll go away—

A hand touches my shoulder, so gently it's like a bird brushing against my skin, and I open my eyes. Edith is standing above me, her spiky hair standing out around her head like a halo in one of her beloved Renaissance paintings. She's holding up a ring of keys. "Come on," she whispers, "let's go find your baby."

PART III

Edith's Journal, September 6, 1971

I'm finally here! After all the shouting matches and tears, all the forms and sitting in offices, and hours on the train and running through Pennsylvania Station with all my bags like the Keystone Cops were after me, I've finally made it! Vassar College! And what do I discover when I get here? My clothes are all wrong, the girls are all snoots, and my roommate, Libby, is crazy. Since I got here all she's done is lie in her bed, read French poetry, and smoke, smoke, smoke. When I told her I'd come here to study art history she snorted like a pig and asked what I was going to do with that, was I just looking to have some polite dinnertime conversation with my husband's boss?

I could've asked her what she planned to do with French poetry, but I couldn't stand the smell of smoke a minute longer. I spend all my time in the art history library, where they hang copies of the slides we're supposed to know for the midterm and final. After every class there's a whole slew of new pictures hung up in a long hallway. The girls line up chairs all in a row so you can sit in front of each one and test yourself. If you have a friend you can test each other. I don't have anyone to test me, though.

If you're on your own you have to decide when it's time to get up and move to the next chair or the girls behind you get annoyed. It's like musical chairs, only instead of music it's dates and painters and temples and churches. I had a dream last night that I was sitting on the line and when I got up the girl to my right wouldn't give up her chair and the one to my left had already taken the one I'd been in but when I went to step back out of the line I saw we were all balanced on a narrow bridge between two buildings and below us was a bottomless pit. Then one of the girls said, "You don't belong here," and gave me a shove.

I woke up screaming and there was Libby, lying awake, staring up at the ceiling, smoking. "Who's Cal?" she asked.

Chapter Twenty-One

Edith leads me to a doorway I've always assumed was a broom closet, but when she unlocks it I see it's a stairwell. It smells like cigarette smoke and sex.

I hesitate to follow her. As scared as I've been here these last few weeks, the hospital has become my routine, an orderly place where I know what to expect. Once I enter this door I may never get back.

But Edith is pushing me through. I hear why; the squeak of rubber on linoleum heralds an approaching orderly. Edith has timed our exit perfectly to get us to this door in between rounds.

Edith draws the door closed behind us, holding the lever so that it doesn't make a sound. I have just time enough to admire her skill before we are plunged into darkness.

I follow Edith down the stairs. When she stops at a door I'm pretty sure we're not on the ground floor yet, and sure enough, when she unlocks the door I can tell right away from the carpet and soft yellow walls and the creepy paintings that we're on the floor with Dr. Hancock's office. "What are we doing here?" I whisper.

"We have to get your record from the dean's office to find out what they've done with your baby."

I try to stop her. I know where my baby is—a hundred miles away in Westchester with my lying, no-good husband. But she's already creeping down the hallway, one hand on the wall trailing over the framed paintings. I follow, anxiously peering under doors for a telltale scrap of light that would reveal a late-working doctor. What if Dr. Hancock is here? But no, he said he commutes from Garrison.

At the end of the hall Edith has paused in front of the painting of the disembodied eye. "This is when it happened," she says.

"When what happened?" I whisper, afraid that the paintings are triggering her psychosis the way that drawing the tower had. What will I do if she starts to fall apart here?

"When Solomon took his ax to us," she says. "When he cleaved us apart."

"You mean when Solomon said he'd split the baby in half?" I ask.

She nods, her eyes glassy in the dim fluorescent light.

"But remember? He doesn't do that. The real mother says she'd rather give up her baby and that's how he knows she's the real mother and he gives her back her own baby."

Edith gives me a look like I'm the simpleminded one. "We tried that," she says with heavy patience, "but it didn't work. They still cut us up in little pieces."

I shiver at the image. This is what years in a mental hospital must feel like to Edith: as if a bunch of all-powerful men had taken knives to her poor bewildered brain and cut it into little pieces. This is how I'll feel in twenty years if I don't get the hell out of here.

"We're still whole," I say, laying my hand over Edith's. "And my baby is still out there somewhere."

Edith nods and squares her jaw. "And so is ours," she says, taking the keys out of her pocket. They are each wrapped in red yarn. She selects one and opens the door to Dr. Hancock's office like she's done this before. How many times has she escaped, I wonder as I follow her into the office, only to come back again? Why should the outcome of my escape be any better?

Because you're not crazy.

I'd like to agree with Laurel, but the fact that I'm hearing her voice undermines her message.

Edith finds the key to the filing cabinet in Dr. Hancock's desk and opens the middle drawer. "Here's mine," she says, plucking out the pale-green folder. "It's just as I thought. Nurse Landry has taken our babies to the tower." She shows me the drawing that she herself made earlier today, the one that Dr. Hancock demonstrated as proof of my corrupting influence. This is how madness works, I think, it's a self-perpetuating loop. One delusion proof of another, the crazy voices confirming the crazy theories—

Don't forget to get our file, Laurel says.

I pull out the file labeled Laurel Hobbes. *Our file,* I think as I stick it in the waistband of my pajamas. I've started thinking in the first person plural just like Edith. I suppose she's right. It may have started out as Laurel's but I've added to it now. We have become inextricably merged, as connected as the figures bound in Edith's red yarn. It should frighten me that my allies are a dead woman and a crazy woman. But as I leave the office with Edith I find I feel less alone than I have in months.

Edith's Journal, September 29, 1971

I don't feel so alone anymore. Things have been better since the night I woke up calling Cal's name. I told Libby all about him. How even though he was just a waiter up at the lake he was saving up to go to college and he and I were going to elope and both get jobs as teachers in Richmond. I told her how we'd meet at the boathouse and lie out on the pier on a bed made of life vests, looking up at the stars and talking about . . . well, *everything*. Our favorite children's books and the names of our first pets and what we'd name our children. I felt so much better spilling it all out to Libby, even the bad parts when Mama and Papa found out and forbade me ever to see him again because he was poor and "not the right religion," so they sent me up North so we couldn't meet in the fall.

"So you didn't come here for the art history after all," Libby said when I was done.

"No," I admitted. I was afraid she was going to make fun of me again but when she laughed I could tell it wasn't *at* me. It was this low, smoky laugh, like we were sharing a secret. And then she told me all about her fella and how her father didn't approve of him so he sent her away, first to a French boarding school and then, when she came home last summer and took up with him again, away to college.

"Why doesn't your father like him?" I asked, because I couldn't imagine Libby going with any poor waiter or her folks caring what religion her boyfriend was.

"Because he's an artist," she said, blowing smoke out when she said *artist*, "and no one understands artists. That's why you understand. I've seen those sketches you do in class."

I only did the sketches to help me remember the art slides, but it made me feel so good that Libby thought I was a real artist that I told her I was thinking of changing my major to studio art.

"You should," she said. "Why should you study what a bunch of old, dead white men made when you could make your own art?"

She told me she was going to be a writer and live in Paris with Clive. That's her artist's name. It's so much more romantic than Cal's plan for us to buy a house in Richmond, but still, I feel like everything has gotten *bigger*. Like I was looking at a beautiful painting and suddenly it became real and I stepped inside it. And that I was one of the beautiful, fascinating people you see in those paintings. Libby makes me believe I could become someone special, someone completely new!

Chapter Twenty-Two

E dith knows a back door out of the building and a path that will take us to the back gate. She tells me this way we'll avoid the searchlights and *white angels*. Apparently that's what they called the dorm matrons at Vassar. I assume for our purposes she means the guards.

The path we take goes through a garden that she calls Shakespeare's Garden and past a Tudor-looking building she refers to as the infirmary.

"That's where Nurse Landry works, but the lights are out so she must not be there yet."

I remember looking down from the tower that first night and thinking that the hospital looked like a college campus; for Edith, the hospital *is* the campus of her memories.

She takes me to a spot where the electrified fence traverses a steep ravine. We scramble down, clutching saplings to keep from sliding headlong into the fence. Improbably, I begin to feel like a college sophomore out on a lark, ducking curfew to drink a few beers or smoke a joint in the woods. The longer I spend with Edith, I realize, the more I enter into her delusion.

At the bottom of the ravine Edith clears armfuls of dead leaves, revealing a gully where the ground has fallen away beneath the fence. There's a gap about two feet wide and two feet deep. Edith flattens herself against the ground and squirms under it like an otter. When she pops out on the other side her face is smeared with dirt and leaves stick up from her hair like a wreath. She looks like a slightly demented Puck. "Come on," she urges me. "It's easy."

Maybe if you've been eating hospital food for more than forty years. Not only is Edith thinner than me, she also has the bones of a bird.

She's a sixty-year-old woman, Laurel says in my head. *Are you really going to let her outdo you in the gymnastics department? Why did I bother taking you to all those Pilates classes?*

Shamed by Laurel's rebuke, I lie down on the ground, my head facing the gap, and crawl. It feels like I'm burrowing into my own grave. The soil is damp and cold and smells like worms—

Don't think about worms.

But of course now I am. Worms and snakes and spiders. Something slithers down my neck and it takes every ounce of my willpower not to thrash out and impale myself on the electric fence.

That would be ironic, Laurel coolly observes, *electrocuting yourself while running away from electroshock.*

I feel a laugh bubbling up inside me and then I'm crying, tears turning to mud in the dirt. It's not my grave I'm digging, I realize, it's Laurel's. Snarky, carping, bitchy Laurel. The taste of dirt in my mouth is her death, the first time I've grieved for her. Laurel is really dead—

But you're not, she points out.

Not yet, I reply, *not if I can help it.*

Then I feel hands gripping my arms, pulling me out of the grave I've dug for myself. "I've got you," Edith says, holding me to her as I sob. For Laurel. For me. For both our Chloes. For Edith's lost baby.

Edith pats my back. "It's okay," she says. "We'll get her back." She wipes my face with the sleeve of her pajamas and helps me to my feet. She leads me by the hand into the woods. It's only when we've been walking a few minutes that I think about that "her." According to Dr. Bennett's notes, Edith's baby was a boy. So, who, I wonder, is she talking about?

As WE WALK up the hill I try to make a plan. Should I run or should I go to Schuyler Bennett and try to convince her that I'm really Daphne Marist? If could get my ID and Laurel's will and the photo of Peter from the tower, maybe that would convince her. On the other hand, if I show up at Schuyler Bennett's house covered in mud and with a delusional woman, Sky will call the police. She has no reason to protect me. I lied to her about who I was and took advantage of her trust and hospitality. Also, I'm technically an escaped mental patient. But hers is the only house for miles. Where else can we go? What I need is to find a car so I can get someplace where I can prove my identity.

I'm so lost in my thoughts that I don't notice at first that we're no longer climbing upward. We've been walking on a level path for some time, along the ridge Sky Bennett's house sits on but not toward the house itself. Given her obsession about the tower, I had assumed that's where Edith was leading us.

Before I can ask where we're going, we arrive at some kind of garden shed. A rather decorative one, with a pointed eave, gingerbread trim, and faded green paint. A storybook cottage in the enchanted woods. Maybe I really *have* gone crazy. When

Edith opens the door, will we find the witch from Hansel and Gretel or a family of dwarves?

What's inside is nearly as surprising. A cot covered with a faded flowered quilt and embroidered throw pillows, an armchair, a table made in a rustic bent-twig style. There's even an old-fashioned lantern, which Edith lights with a box of kitchen matches. A china teapot and two teacups are set out on the table as if for a tea party, but there's clearly no way of heating water. There are books everywhere. I pick one up and see it's a children's book of fairy tales.

This is some kind of playhouse, clearly, perhaps Sky's when she was little. But it's in too good shape for it to have been disused since Sky's childhood. Perhaps Billie's grandchildren use it when they visit, or Sky has preserved it as a writing room. "What is this place?" I ask Edith.

She lies down on the padded bench, cushioning her head with an embroidered pillow, and sighs. "Home." Then she closes her eyes. Within minutes she's snoring.

I stand there, not sure what to do. Go to Sky's house and try to steal a car? But instead I sink down into the armchair. As I sit I feel the edge of the file folders I stuffed in my pants rub against my back. I pull them out and lay them on the broad, flat arm of the chair on top of an illustrated collection of Norse myths. I can see by the light filtering in through the cottage's one window that it will be daylight soon. I should be trying to get as far away from Crantham as I can. Once they discover that Edith and I have escaped, the woods will be filled with searchers. How hard could it be to find this place?

But as I look around I notice the pictures on the wall. I'd assumed they were fairy-tale prints to match the books, but I see now that they're reproductions of paintings and sculptures, temples and cathedrals. All the art that Edith studied in

Art History 101 at Vassar and then some, so many that they've been layered on top of one another. Clearly Edith has spent considerable time here. It must be at least relatively safe.

Still, I want to run, to get as far away from this place as I can. But running blindly into the woods is *not* a plan. I need to get to the tower to get Laurel's will and Peter's photo to prove there's a conspiracy going on. I need my own ID to prove that I'm Daphne Marist. But I can't just leave Edith here. I'll have to wait until the morning and then go to the tower. In the meantime it might be useful to know more about Edith. I pick up her file and begin reading.

Edith's Journal, October 3, 1971

Being friends with Libby is the best thing that's ever happened to me. Better even than Cal. I mean, that was romantic, sure, but Libby has shown me this whole other world I didn't even know existed. A world of art and culture and ideas.

I was surprised at first that Libby didn't want to marry Clive. "Marriage is so bourgeois," she said. "I'm going to travel. See the world. Live life. How else can I become a writer? We could travel together. You can paint and I'll write."

That wasn't at all like the plan I'd made of getting my teaching certificate and settling down in Richmond with Cal. "I don't think my parents would give me the money to do that," I said.

"I've got money," Libby said. "My mother left me loads. Enough for both of us to start out and then we can get jobs—waitressing or modeling. You've got a face like a Pre-Raphaelite angel. All the boys in Paris will want to paint you."

I looked up the Pre-Raphaelites in the art history library. Some of those women looked a little strange and when I read about the models I learned that one of them died from an overdose of laudanum. Her name was Lizzie Siddal. There's a picture of her lying in a flower-covered pond, looking up through the water with dead eyes, that made me feel queasy. I read that the painter made her lie in a bathtub of cold water while he painted it and she got sick from the chill.

"You have to suffer for your art," Libby says.

Sometimes I think Libby is *trying* to suffer. She hardly eats and I hear her throwing up in the bathroom sometimes, which makes me feel like I have to throw up too. She barely ever leaves Main Hall, and she huddles in those oversized shirts and sweaters of hers—I think they're Clive's—and sleeps through her classes.

I've been so worried about her that I went to the infirmary and talked to one of the nurses there. Nurse Landry. She was really nice. She's a small-town girl like me and just a few years older. After I told her about Libby she asked me how I was adapting to college and I told her that it was hard at first making friends but it was much better now that I was friends with Libby. She said Libby was really lucky to have a friend like me and I told her she had it all wrong. I'm the lucky one. Libby's turned me into a whole new person.

Chapter Twenty-Three

This is what I find out from Edith's file: On December 10, 1971, a newborn male infant was found in the dumpster outside of the Vassar College infirmary. The on-call nurse saw Edith Sharp, a nineteen-year-old sophomore from Fredericksburg, Virginia, deposit the baby in a dumpster. When the nurse questioned her, Edith said that she'd given birth in her dorm room and that she had taken the baby to the dumpster to get rid of it because she thought there was something wrong with it. She became agitated when asked who the baby's father was and had to be sedated, after which she was taken to Vassar Brothers Hospital and examined by the psychiatrist on call. Believing that she was Lizzie Siddal, model and mistress of the Pre-Raphaelite artists, she told the doctor that she'd been made to lie in a bathtub full of ice water. She'd made a drawing of herself giving birth in the bathtub.

The drawing was attached to the file. When I looked at it I instantly recognized Edith's drawing style. Here she had taken a painting by John Everett Millais of Ophelia drowned in a woodland stream, flowers scattered on the water's surface, and reinterpreted it so that the woman is in a bathtub and a baby, still attached by the umbilical cord, is lying on her chest. It's a

disturbing image but even more disturbing is the picture un-
derneath: the same woman in the bathtub but with the baby
floating over her, attached by a long red string, along with other
body parts—ears, eyes, a heart—also attached to the woman
in the tub by red strings.

Like the red ribbon that Edith wore around her wrist and
the red yarn she had strewn around the rec lounge yesterday.

At Vassar Brothers Hospital, Edith was diagnosed with borderline schizophrenia and transferred to the Crantham Psychiatric
Center. The admitting notes, made by Dr. Bennett, confirmed
the diagnosis.

> Patient continues to harbor delusion that something was
> wrong with her baby, representing a dissociative break
> with reality. Patient continues to search for the lost baby,
> convinced that it is alive.

I turn back to the original report from the hospital in Poughkeepsie. It doesn't say whether the baby in the dumpster was
found dead or alive. I look up from the file, thinking about that,
and find myself staring at the pictures on the wall. They've
been layered on top of one another like a collage. A red line—
like Edith's red yarn—catches my eye. I get up and peel away
another picture to uncover the rest of it. It's a painting of a
woman lying naked on a hospital bed. Blood stains the sheets
beneath her bent legs. She holds a handful of red threads that
attach to a half-formed fetus, a snail, a severed torso, exotic
flowers, and some kind of gray contraption I can't identify. I
recognize the face of the woman on the bed, though, from a
million tote bags and coffee mugs. It's Frida Kahlo.

I look back at the picture in Edith's file. It's less disturbing when you realize that she was mirroring a painting she might have known from her college art history classes.

As I'm staring at the picture I hear Edith stirring. I quickly put the file away. Edith blinks at the room for a few minutes, then looks at me. "I think we missed breakfast in the cafeteria," she says brightly.

My stomach growls as I'm reminded of how long it's been since I ate. We've got no money. Where are we going to find food?

"Good thing we've put in supplies," Edith says. She reaches under the bed and pulls out a red plastic bin full of candy bars and bottles of water. I'm afraid the candy will be moldering remnants left over from the seventies but when Edith hands me one I see that it's a protein bar with a recent sell-by date. I eat it gratefully and wash it down with the bottled water.

"Edith," I ask, "who got all of this?"

"My roommate," Edith mumbles through a mouthful of granola bar. "She buys it all at the college store because she doesn't like going to the cafeteria anymore."

"Do you . . . um . . . *see* your roommate bring it here?" I ask. How do you ask someone if they're having hallucinations?

"Of course, silly . . . only . . ."—Edith looks confused for a moment—"only she hasn't really been herself lately. She stays in bed all day . . . or takes long baths in the hall bathroom. Nurse Landry says she sounds like she's suffering from depression." She gets up and paces around the tiny shed. "We have to go now," she says. "We have to find the baby."

"Okay," I say, getting to my feet and wiping chocolate crumbs off my pajamas. "Where should we look?"

"In the tower, of course," she says, plucking the red ribbon on her wrist. "That's where I left him."

Edith's Journal, November 2, 1971

Libby asked me last night if there was anything I wanted to tell her. I didn't know what she meant. It was so funny the way she said it, like how Mama used to put it when she thought I'd taken something or I had gotten a bad grade at school. Then I was afraid that she knew I'd talked to Nurse Landry about her. I was so ashamed that I blushed hot pink.

"Ah! So there is," Libby crowed like it made her happy. I was so embarrassed. And then I noticed she was staring at my belly and I turned even pinker. The truth is I *have* gained weight this semester. The freshman fifteen, they call it, even though I'm a sophomore. It's the starchy food at the cafeteria and all the candy bars Libby keeps in the room.

"I thought you didn't mind me sharing your candy bars," I said.

"I don't," Libby said, "I just didn't know you were eating for two. I thought you said you and Cal were careful."

I could hardly believe she would say such a thing. I told her I wasn't pregnant and then she asked me why I hadn't used any of the tampons I'd brought with me, and I had to explain that my periods had always been irregular.

"So how do you know you're not pregnant?"

I didn't have an answer to that.

Chapter Twenty-Four

In the light of day I see that we're not far from the house. I can see the top of the tower over the tree line. I'm sorry now that I didn't come at night and climb to the tower to retrieve Laurel's will, Peter's picture, and my ID. I try to suggest to Edith that we come back later but she shakes me off. "We have to get to the baby now. Can't you hear it crying?"

I sigh, but then I *do* hear it. Faint at first. It might be a blue jay or a mockingbird, but as I follow Edith toward the house the sound grows louder and it tugs at something inside of me the way Chloe's cries used to tug at my womb. I can feel that pull now, like the cry is a red thread reeling me in. Even if I could convince Edith to turn back now I couldn't do it myself.

When we get to the edge of the trees I see we're only a few yards from the north end of the terrace. The tower is to our right. To our left the terrace wraps around the back of the house. That's where the sound of the baby is coming from, the area where I ate dinner with Sky and Billie and where Chloe would sit in her bouncy chair or portable crib. But it's not Chloe; Chloe is in Westchester with Peter. This must be one of Billie's grandchildren. Instead of going there I should go into the tower and up to the top room where I hid my ID, the picture of Peter, and Laurel's will.

I lay my hand on Edith's arm. It's as rigid as steel, tensed against the sound of the baby crying. As much as she's drawn to the sound she's also terrified by it. I wonder what she is reliving. I remember how Chloe's cries would grate against my skin and imagine a lifetime of hearing that without being able to *do* anything to comfort that poor baby.

But now I'm going to use that fear. "Edith," I say, willing my voice firm and steady, "we have to go into the tower before we can go to the baby." I wait to see if she'll question my shaky dictum but she turns her tear-stained face to me and nods. Poor Edith, I think as I lead her around the base of the tower, she must have been a very tractable young woman, easy to influence, easy to lead. First some boy got her pregnant, then her upper-class snoot of a roommate convinced her to hide her pregnancy and get rid of the baby when it was born. Now she's blindly following me. She follows whoever has the strongest voice, the most convincing story—

Just as I fell into Peter's stories of someday riches and let him bully me. Just as I eagerly copied Laurel's clothes and carped with her about the indignities of motherhood. What I wouldn't do to suffer those indignities now. To go back in time—

When we come around the tower I think for a moment I *have* gone back in time. Parked in the driveway is my Ford Focus, the car I arrived in. Why hasn't Peter taken it back? Is it too shabby for him now that he's gotten Laurel's money? Maybe he sold it to Billie or gave it to Sky in thanks for sheltering his errant wife. Whatever the reason, it's the first stroke of luck I've had, because along with my ID, Laurel's will, and Peter's picture, I hid a spare car key in the tower because the fob had my initial on it. All I have to do is get to the top of the tower and reclaim it.

Then I can drive home. Find Chloe. Find someone to confirm my identity.

The next stroke of luck is that the door to the tower apartment is unlocked. I'd been afraid that Sky might have hired another archivist, but she must have been too reluctant after her last one turned out to be crazy. Still, I open the door to the apartment warily in case someone has taken up residence.

At first I think no one is staying there. Nothing is out of place, no mug on the kitchen counter, no book on the coffee table, not even a dent in the couch cushions. In the bedroom, though, a suitcase sits on the bench at the foot of the bed. A Louis Vuitton roller bag. It takes me a second to recognize it as the one I arrived with—

Because it was never yours.

I run my hand over the embossed leather surface. I have never owned anything so fancy. Why didn't I question where I had gotten it?

But I can picture it now, sitting at the bottom of the stairs, all packed and ready to go. I'd simply picked it up on my way out. I open the suitcase and see the neatly folded clothes. Laurel's clothes. Why hadn't I wondered how I'd ended up with them?

Because you didn't want to remember I was dead.

The red veil begins to fall but I blink it away. I see myself walking up the stairs, my feet sinking into the wet carpet. I can feel myself going back in time, to the moment when I woke in the tub with Peter's hands on my shoulders. I shy away from it—

Because he tried to kill you.

Yes. I force myself not to retreat from the thought now. I watch myself walk up the stairs and into the bathroom. There's blood everywhere, pouring over the rim of the tub, staining the bath mat and the baby blanket—

The baby blanket.

It's lying on the floor and Chloë is lying on top of it. She's crying. I pick her up. Her playsuit is soaked. The blanket is soaked. I hold her to me and look down into the tub and see—

Myself.

Because you thought you were back in the moment when Peter tried to kill you.

I blink and my face becomes Laurel's face. Her eyes are open, staring sightlessly at me, her lacerated hands float palms up in the water as if she were holding her arms out for the baby I hold in my arms. She doesn't want me to give her the baby, though. She wants me take her, to save her. She's telling me that if I have to think of her as my Chloe to save her, then that is what I should do.

"That's why I took her," I say, turning to Edith. "That's how I could think of her as my own. I had to in order to save her."

But Edith isn't looking at me. She's looking past me to the doorway, her green eyes wide as if she too has been confronted by a ghost from her past. I turn around and find Sky Bennett in the doorway.

"I thought you'd show up," she says. But she's not talking to me, she's talking to Edith.

Edith steps forward with a smile on her face. "Of course I came back to you!" she says. "I always come back to you, Libby."

Edith's Journal, November 7, 1971

Libby says if I go to Nurse Landry at the infirmary she'll have to call my parents. "And besides," she adds, "it's probably too late to do anything about it. When was the last time you were with Cal?"

I think back to that night at the lake—our "last" and only time—and tell Libby the date in June.

"Over five months," she says. "That's too late. They'll send you home to have the baby. Will your parents be cool with that? Aren't they kind of religious?"

I tell her no, they will *not* be cool with me having a baby out of wedlock. And yes, they are religious. Papa is a Baptist preacher. Mama teaches Sunday school.

"So they'll probably ship you off to some home for fallen women," Libby says. "Then they'll give the baby away. Maybe your fella, Cal, could help out."

I started to cry then because in my last letter to Cal I told him I was thinking I might want to go to Europe after college and I hadn't heard back from him since.

"What a wet blanket," Libby said. "But don't worry. We'll go away somewhere where you can have the baby and then we'll find some nice people to raise it. You don't want it, do you? I mean, we can't very well travel to Europe with a baby."

I told her I didn't want it. It made me feel sick saying it, like the baby might hear me, but I could tell that's what Libby wanted me to say and I need Libby to help me. And she does want to help me. When I asked her why, she said a true friend helped you when you didn't even know you needed help.

She says we have to wait for Christmas break so she can go home and get some money hidden at her house. She's says she's got some money hidden away up in the old tower. We'll go get it and then we'll hide out in the Catskills until I have the baby. There's an old cabin on the property where we can stay. She's friends with some of the guards at the hospital, who will bring us food. When I asked her if she wasn't afraid of living so close to a mental hospital she said that was a very close-minded question. A lot of people in mental hospitals were just misunderstood creative geniuses. Hadn't I read *One Flew Over the Cuckoo's Nest*? She was friends with a lot of the patients and many of them were great artists who simply didn't fit into bourgeois society.

That's when I guessed that her "artist" must be one of the patients. No wonder she didn't want to marry him.

Chapter Twenty-Five

I wait for Sky to deny that she's Libby but instead she opens up her arms. Edith rushes into them and they embrace. There are tears in Sky's eyes when she lets Edith go. "I'm so glad you came to visit, Edie. Your room is all ready for you." Then she looks at me. "I see you've brought a friend."

Edith looks nervously between me and Sky. "Is that all right? She knows all about the baby."

"Does she?" Sky raises one eyebrow. "And does this friend have a name?"

"Daphne," I say, stepping forward. "Daphne Marist."

"Funny," Sky says, "I could have sworn I knew you under a different name."

"And I could have sworn your name was Schuyler."

"Silly," Edith jumps in. "Her middle name is Schuyler. That's her mother's maiden name but she hates it because it's too . . . what did you always say, Libby?"

"Too bourgeois," Sky says with a wry smile. "Oh, the conceits of youth! I thought my first name, Elizabeth, was too snooty too, so I went by Libby."

"And you were Edith's roommate, the one who—"

"Let's not rehash old history while the two of you are so clearly in need of baths and a good meal," Sky interrupts.

At the word *bath* Edith tenses. I imagine I do too.

"We'll start with lunch then," Sky says, "which is being served on the terrace. Come along. There are some other guests I think you'll be pleased to see."

WHEN I WALK onto the terrace and see Peter, I freeze. I want to turn and run. But then I hear a baby's cry. It's coming from a portable crib. An infant is standing up, holding the bars of the crib. I walk straight toward her, the world around me blurring. She's wearing a pink-and-orange playsuit. Blond, wispy hair; blue eyes; wide, chubby face—the details don't matter. They could belong to any baby of eight months. Even the strawberry mark on her nose could belong to any baby. And who am I to know my own baby when I took another woman's?

But when she holds up her arms, I pick her up. Her body feels stiff at first, resistant, but then I feel her muscles relax and she molds to me. *Chloe, Chloe, Chloe.* I know it's her. The fact that she knew me first is only a little bit chastening.

I feel a touch on my elbow and I spin around, tightening my hold, but it's only Billie leading me to a chair. I sit down warily, holding on to Chloe so tightly she begins to squirm. Carefully, I place her on my lap. She looks up at me, waves her arms and smiles. I laugh, smile back, order myself not to cry.

I feel another touch on my arm and look down to see Edith crouched on the flagstone, beaming up at me. "See, I told you we would find her."

I shake my head, unable to parse the delusional logic that led us here. I'm reminded of something my mother used to say: Even a broken clock is right twice a day. But was this just chance?

I look around the circle of chairs on the terrace. Peter, stone-faced; Edith, beaming; Sky, looking at Edith, her face rapt with some strong emotion. I pick up that thread first. "You were Edith's roommate. Is that how she ended up here after—"

"After the incident," she says quickly. Did she think I was going to blurt out *after Edith tossed her baby in the trash*? "I thought it was the best place for her, where she could best be taken care of. She always knows I'm here for her, right, Edith?"

Edith tears her eyes away from me and Chloe to look at her friend. "We have secret signals," she says. "Like in *Nancy Drew*."

"The light in the tower," I say. "You use it to signal to Edith. But how . . ." I look down at Sky's legs and notice now that she's not using a cane. She'd walked from the tower to the terrace without one.

"My arthritis comes and goes," Sky says. "And if I can't make it up to the tower myself, Billie sends a signal. I make sure that Edie is well taken care of, just as Peter wanted to make sure that *you* were well taken care of."

I laugh. Chloe looks up at me expectantly. I smile at her and temper my response. "I don't think Peter's motives were quite as altruistic."

"He was only trying to protect you and Chloe," Sky says. "You have to admit you were acting erratically."

"You were going to take her from me," Peter says. The first thing he's said since I've arrived. "You were looking at jobs on the Internet."

"For Laurel," I say.

He laughs. "That may be what you told yourself, but you know the truth. You always meant to take the job yourself. You jumped at the chance when you saw the ad from Schuyler Bennett, your *favorite author.*"

I look at Sky to see how she responds to his mocking tone, but she is staring at me with a grim expression. "Did you put the ad online *for* Peter?" I ask.

"It was my idea," she says. "I didn't want to believe that a mother would take her child away from its father, but Peter told me you were delusional, that you'd concocted a story of abuse that wasn't based on reality. He was afraid you were going to run away with Chloe and then hurt yourself and Chloe. I said, Why don't we see? I placed the ad where you'd see it and you jumped at it, using that poor Hobbes woman's CV. I saw then that Peter was right and that the best thing I could do was make sure you had a safe place to come with Chloe. I didn't know that your delusion was so developed you would lead your friend into suicide."

"I didn't!" I object. "I don't even think Laurel *did* kill herself. It was Stan and Peter's plan to get Laurel's money."

"But why would they kill Laurel when her money wouldn't even go to Stan?" Sky asks reprovingly.

I shake my head, confused and beginning to feel frightened. Chloe, sensing my fear, begins to fret in my lap. "Maybe they didn't know until it was too late," I say, wishing I sounded more sure of myself. The story had sounded more sensible when I worked it out in my head.

All the voices sound sensible at the time.

"And then you conveniently played into their plan by picking up Laurel's baby and driving here?" Sky asks, one eyebrow raised, lip curled.

"You didn't even take the right baby," Peter says. "What kind of a mother doesn't know her own child? I would never not recognize my own child."

He's staring fiercely at Chloe and I think, *That's true.* Since she was born Peter has reveled in their similarities: the same square face, red-blond hair, blue eyes. I look from Chloe's face to Peter's. Then I look to Sky and, just like that, as if a key has turned in a lock, I understand.

Edith's Journal, December 9, 1971

I just wish it would all be over. Every day I feel like I'm dragging an enormous weight. And I *am*. Libby said I might as well
eat as much as I want since I'll lose it all later. So that's what
I've been doing. She's been buying boxes of the chewy chocolate chip cookies the bookstore sells and bags of candy bars. In
the cafeteria I eat macaroni and cheese, slabs of meatloaf,
pancakes, ice cream. I barely taste any of it. When I sit in
the chairs in the art history library I feel my stomach pressing
up against the fold-down desks. I can feel the other girls staring at me, whispering about me. The only class I go to is art
history, where it's dark and everyone's eyes are on the slide
screen. We're up to the Renaissance. When I look at the
rounded bellies of all those doleful Madonnas, I touch my own
swollen belly.

All finals week Libby and I haven't gone out at all. It's been
snowing all week. The sky is white, like a blank canvas. The
only class I'm studying for is art history. Libby has made up
cards with all the art slides and quizzes me on them. With
each card she tells me about the city the painting or church is
in and describes what we'll do when we go there. She tells stories so well it's as if we're there. When I look out our window
I see us on that blank canvas, eating crepes at a café in Paris,
wading through fields of sunflowers in the south of France, lying
on beaches on Greek isles. There's no baby in these stories, but
sometimes I pencil him in, strapped in a backpack, toddling
at the water's edge, floating above us like an angel in a Renaissance painting.

Tomorrow is the art history exam. Once I've taken it I'll be
done with this place. I've decided I'll go to Nurse Landry and

tell her about the baby. I know she'll help me. It may mean getting in trouble, but I'm scared and I'm not sure that Libby really knows best anymore. I think she could use help too. I feel better now that I've made a decision. I'm going to go to bed now and try to get some sleep before the big exam.

December 10

So much has happened since last night and I don't have long
to write it all down, but I'll do my best for Libby's sake and for
the baby's sake.

I had gone to sleep but something woke me up. I noticed
that Libby's bed was empty. I thought she must be in the bathroom, but when a half hour went by and she didn't come back
I started to worry. I put on my robe and slippers and went out
into the hall. Our room is at the end of the hall, right next to
the bathroom. Most of the girls on the hall use the bathroom
at the other end because it has showers, but Libby likes the one
at this end because it has a big old-fashioned bathtub and she
likes to soak for hours. I thought she might be taking a bath. I
opened the door to the bathroom and saw that the lights were
off in the sink area, but there was a light under the stall with
the bathtub. I heard water dripping. The room smelled like old
copper pipes and tampons. I thought Libby had a bad period
and was taking a bath for cramps.

I left the outside light off and padded softly to the stall door.
I knocked and called her name. I heard a grunt that sounded
more like an animal than a person and I was suddenly very
afraid. I wanted to turn around and run back to my room but
the stall door had cracked open a bit because it wasn't locked
and I saw Libby crouched in the tub, a washcloth stuffed inside her mouth, her face purple. At first I was afraid she was
dying, that she'd had some kind of fit or attack or that she'd
been attacked. When I got closer to the tub I saw the blood,
gallons of it. So then I thought this must be some kind of
stunt, someone had tied Libby up and poured pig's blood over
her. I took the gag out of her mouth and grabbed her shoulders
and shook her. When she looked at me she didn't seem to rec-

ognize me. Then she let out a moan and her body shook and there was more blood. It was coming from between her legs. I reached there—not even thinking about being embarrassed to touch her there, just wanting to stop the blood—and my hand touched something round and hard.

My first thought was that Libby had somehow found a way to have the baby for me.

And then it was like I'd floated up out of my body and I was looking down. I could see two girls, one in the tub, one crouched over the tub, and I couldn't tell who was who. The girl outside the tub was helping the girl in the tub to have a baby. They were both covered in blood. When the girl outside pulled the baby out of the inside girl they were connected by a long bloody rope. They will be connected by that red string forever. What difference does it make who is who?

Chapter Twenty-Six

It was your baby," I say to Sky. And then, looking at Peter, "It was you."

Peter smiles. I haven't seen him look so pleased with me since the minutes after I gave birth to Chloe. "You see the resemblance, don't you? I saw it the minute I saw Sky's picture on the back of your copy of her book."

"You never even told me you were adopted," I say.

He shrugs. "I stopped telling people years ago. They treated me differently, like there must have been something wrong with me for my mother to abandon me." Sky makes a sound and Peter reaches over to touch her hand. "I don't blame you," he says. "I understand now that you didn't have a choice."

"My father made me give the baby away," Sky says. "He was very strict and I was only nineteen."

"What about Peter's father?" I ask.

Sky turns pale. "He was dead."

"But you let people think it was Edith's!" I look down at Edith, who is playing peekaboo with Chloe, apparently oblivious to our conversation.

"Edith thought it was hers," Sky says softly. "She took him from me after he was born. I think she meant to take him someplace safe, but she must have gotten confused and left him in the dumpster. Luckily a nurse at the clinic saw Edith leaving the baby. She realized that it wasn't Edith's baby and so she went to the dorm to make sure the real mother was all right. I might have bled to death if she hadn't."

"That was some nurse . . ." I catch Billie's eyes and she smiles. "It was you, wasn't it? The nurse who found the baby . . . but her name was something else."

"Landry, my maiden name. That was my first job. Dr. Bennett helped me get it. He wanted me to keep an eye on Sky. When I saw Sky's roommate with a newborn baby, I had a feeling it was really Sky's. I went back to the dorm and found Sky bleeding to death. I brought Edith and Sky and the baby to Vassar Brothers Hospital, where Dr. Bennett was on call. He took care of Sky *and* Edith. He was able to sign off on Edith's mental state—"

"He lied! He said Edith was the mother."

"She thought she *was* the mother," Sky says. "Confronting her with reality would have just made her more upset. He took care of her." Sky lifts her chin defiantly. "She's never had to pay a dime for her care at Crantham. My only regret is that I let him convince me that my baby would be taken care of as well." She looks at Peter and that defiant chin wobbles. "If I'd known . . ."

"I should have been adopted right away," Peter says, "a white male baby. But there were complications because I was premature. I was hospitalized for several months and then by the time I was ready for adoption, I was older than what people wanted. So I was in an orphanage for two years. Then the people who adopted me—the Pitts—weren't well suited for parenthood, and they gave me back. You can imagine how things went for me after that."

I'm picturing the boy in the photograph. The unsmiling face. The vacant eyes. "I'm sorry, Peter," I say. "I wish I had known."

"You would have thought there was something wrong with me. When you started talking about taking Chloe—" He breaks off, looks away. I see a tear well in his eye and remember how he cried when Chloe was born. I understand now; it was the first time he'd ever seen someone he was related to."

"It's all right, darling." This time it's Sky who reaches across to squeeze *his* hand. "I think Daphne understands now. After all, Daphne, you're a mother who's just been reunited with her child. Imagine how I felt when Peter found me. How could I refuse his pleas for help?"

"Even if it meant locking me up under a false name?" I ask.

Sky frowns. "You came here under that false name."

"After my friend died," I say. "Is that okay with you? That a woman died in my house and Peter told the police she was me? Don't you think that seems . . . *suspicious?*"

"I think he was confused and upset. He didn't know where you and your friend's baby were."

"Until I arrived here and you could tell him I was safe. Why not clear it all up then? Why would Peter let me go on as Laurel unless it was because he and Stan needed Laurel's money?"

"Peter doesn't need anybody else's money now," Sky says. "He's my heir."

"Then tell the police I'm Daphne Marist. Tell them you made a mistake."

Peter laughs. "Right. So I can go to jail and you can take Chloe from me."

"No one's sending you to jail, Peter," Sky says, touching Peter's hand again. This time I see him flinch. "I have excellent lawyers. You found a dead woman in your own bathtub. Of course you thought she was your wife. You barely saw Daphne at Crantham. It will be on Stan that she was identified as Laurel."

"But why do any of that?" Peter snaps irritably. "Why not let things stay as they are? She's clearly unhinged. She belongs in a mental hospital."

Even though I thought I'd faced the worst about Peter—that he tried to kill me, that he was content for me to spend the rest of my life at Crantham—the anger in his voice shocks me. It must surprise Sky too. She looks at him as if she's seeing him for the first time. The adoration in her eyes falters. I can't imagine what it's been like finding her long-lost child after all these years, seeing her own features in his face. I can hardly blame her for wanting to help him. What wouldn't I do for Chloe in the same situation?

"Darling," she says gently, "I think we can leave that assessment for Dr. Hancock. But he should have all the facts—"

"Like he's had all the facts about her?" He jabs his finger at Edith so violently that Edith cowers and whimpers. Chloe, who has been happily engaged in peekaboo with Edith, begins to cry.

"As a matter of fact," Sky says, the doubt in her eyes hardening into ice, "he knows all about Edith. I told him everything when he took over, after my father died. If there were any way Edith could live outside, I would have her here with me. If there were any way I could go back and undo what I did forty-five years ago, I would. But remember, I was all alone. Your father was dead."

"So you said. A tragic car accident. Still you could have fought harder to keep me."

I notice that Sky looks away from Peter when he says "car accident" and then looks at him sideways the way Peter looks when he's lying. That single eye reminds me of something—

I look in through the window to the parlor, where I can see the portrait hanging over the mantel. The bright primary colors look familiar. I picture the landscapes in the lounge at Crantham, those two figures on the bench, then that disembodied eye outside of Hancock's office—

"Peter's father was a painter, wasn't he?" I ask Sky. She gives me a warning look but I go on. "And a patient at Crantham."

Peter whips his head around to stare at Sky. "You told me that you met him in France."

"I was sent to France after we fell in love," Sky says gently. "My father wanted to separate us."

"He was a mental patient?" Peter asks, aghast.

"He was a talented painter," Sky says reprovingly. "A misunderstood genius. His paintings still hang at the hospital."

"They do," I say, thinking of the landscapes in the lounge and then what the paintings turned into when the woman disappeared. "He put all his sorrow at losing you into his paintings."

Sky gives me a grateful look. "Yes, you understand. When I came back from France I saw how much he loved me. He painted that portrait of me." She looks through the window into the parlor at the painting over the mantel.

"And then you went away again," I say.

A shadow passes over Sky's face. Edith reaches up to stroke her cheek, as if to banish her sadness. "You were so sad those first months at college," Edith says. "I didn't understand at first. You had been broken apart."

"That's how he painted you," I say, "broken into pieces. And then . . ."—I remember what Dr. Hancock said the first time I commented on the paintings—"he killed himself."

A tear rolls down Sky's weathered cheek. She looks toward Peter. "I didn't want you to know."

"My father was a suicide," he says, his voice curiously flat. I remember what he said to me after I almost drowned in the tub: *What kind of a mother kills herself, leaving a child behind?* Even after all he's done I recognize the anguish of being left and want to spare him.

"He must not have known you were pregnant," I say to Sky.

"I never had a chance to tell him," Sky says. "By the time I knew, he had killed himself. I've always regretted that I let my father send me away and that I let him convince me to give you up. That's why I don't want you to saddle yourself to one wrong decision. Believe me, son, you don't want to live with that kind of regret."

I think she has used the word *son* deliberately, but what she doesn't know is that Peter once told me he hated when his father (his adopted father, I realize now) called him that. *He did it to make me feel small,* he'd said, and my heart had bled for the boy who had grown up feeling so unloved. Now I see his jaw stiffen. "What do you suggest we do?" he asks in a tight voice. He's taken the pain and shame of learning that his father was a suicide and turned it into anger against Sky.

"I suggest we sleep on it," Sky says with an easy smile that tells me she has not heard the threat in his voice.

"Under the same roof as two lunatics?" he asks.

Sky frowns. "Edith is harmless, and as for Daphne . . . if you thought she was dangerous, why did you send her to me?"

A vein pulses at Peter's temple. He doesn't like to have people question him. He is going to explode. For a moment I am hopeful. Then Sky will know he is the crazy one. But before he can get out a word, another man announces himself on the terrace.

"I see you've found them." Dr. Hancock says, two orderlies in tow. My heart sinks. "I'll take them back to the hospital now."

"There," Sky says. "Problem solved. We'll discuss the matter tonight. And we'll talk about your father. Perhaps tomorrow we can go look at his paintings together." She pats Peter on the knee, then turns to me. "Don't worry, dear, just one more night and it'll all come right if I know my boy."

But she doesn't, I think, she doesn't know him at all.

Edith's Journal, December 10, 1971 (cont.)

I think I lost a little time after the baby came. The next thing I knew, I was holding the baby wrapped in the college blanket I'd bought from the bookstore my first week. A pair of bloody scissors lay on the floor. I didn't remember getting them or the blanket from the room. Had Libby gone for them?

"You have to get rid of it," Libby said.

She was sitting next to me on the bathroom floor. There was blood on her nightgown and mine. Blood on the baby's face. Everything was red except for the blue of the baby's eyes, which were staring up at me. I understood then why the Virgin was always dressed in red and blue; those are the colors of a new-born baby.

"You have to get rid of it!" Libby screamed so loud that I was afraid she'd wake up the other girls.

"But where should I take him?" I asked.

"I don't care! Someplace no one will see you. You have to go now, while it's still night. Go out the back door, past the laundry and the power station, to the lake. No one will see you there."

"And just . . . leave him?"

Libby looked like she was going to yell again but instead she put her hand on my arm and spoke softly. "It would be the kindest thing. You can see he's not . . . *right*, can't you? He came too early. He won't live—or if he does he'll be stunted and ugly."

I looked down at the baby. He *was* very small, his face pinched and wrinkled, his skin nearly transparent, as if it hadn't quite finished forming. He had come too soon. It was only seven months since I had been with Cal . . .

"Are you sure?" I asked Libby.

"Yes," she said. She squeezed my arm. "Go. Take it down to the lake. Leave him . . . someplace pretty. And then everything will be the way it was. We'll go to Europe. We'll lay a wreath for him on Keats's grave in Rome and Elizabeth Barrett Browning's in Florence. You'll paint pictures for him and I'll write for him. Whatever we make will be for him. But if you don't go now, there will be no paintings and no books."

I didn't know what to do. *Find someone who will know,* a voice said inside my head. The voice sounded like Libby, even though Libby was sitting right in front of me and she wasn't saying anything like that. But maybe it was what she really wanted. Once she had said to me that a true friend helped you when you didn't even know you needed help.

And then I knew what I had to do.

Chapter Twenty-Seven

Run, Laurel told me. *Fight*.

But how could I do either with Chloe in my lap? Where could I run and take Chloe with me?

Edith buries her head in Sky's lap. Sky strokes her hair. "It will be all right," she tells her. "Dr. Hancock will take care of you and you can come visit again."

"But what about the baby?" Edith wails.

"The baby will be fine," Sky says. "I'll make sure."

Edith nods, appeased, but I'm not. I can't hand Chloe over to Peter. Billie stands, waiting to take her just as she must have taken Peter from Sky all those years ago. How easy she made it for Sky to give up her own baby!

I get up. Both of the orderlies take a step toward me. Do they think I am going to dash my baby's brains out on the flagstone? What kind of monster do they think I am?

One who abandoned her baby, Laurel provides helpfully.

I ignore her and walk toward Sky. I don't want it to be easy for her this time. I want her to know what it feels like to give up a baby. I look down at Chloe, hold her blue gaze for a moment, and then hand her to Sky. Sky stiffens and presses herself back in her chair, recoiling from Chloe's touch, but then Edith takes both of Sky's arms and pulls them around Chloe. Sky resists a moment longer and then softens, shaping herself to Chloe— her *grandchild*.

"I'm holding you responsible for her care until I can come back for her," I say. "And I'm holding you responsible for telling the truth."

Sky looks up at me, her eyes wide and vulnerable. This is a Sky I haven't seen before. For the first time I think she really understands what it feels like to give up a child. She nods once and before I can change my mind—before I melt into a puddle of blubbering goo on the flagstone—I turn and let the orderlies lead me from the terrace.

THE ORDERLIES LOAD Edith and me into the back of a van that has a Plexiglas divider, so we can't jump the driver, and a locked back door. One of the orderlies sits with us; the other drives. Dr. Hancock sits in the passenger seat. For all her acquiescence on the terrace, Edith is trembling now. "Let me sit next to her," I ask the orderly. He shrugs his consent and I move next to Edith and take her hand. "It's okay," I tell her.

Edith pats my hand, as if I'm the one in need of reassurance. "I'm just glad we found your baby. That's what matters. Libby will look after her. Only . . ." A flicker of doubt crosses her face. "Only I didn't like that man. He reminded me of Solomon."

"Peter?" I ask, wondering what Peter could possibly have in common with the bearded Old Testament judge. "I'm not sure I like him much anymore either, but he does love Chloe. You can tell by the way he looks at her."

Edith nods. "Yes," she says, but she still looks uncertain. "But some kinds of love are as dangerous as hate."

The words chill me and we ride the rest of the way in silence. I think about kinds of love that are dangerous: sexual passions that lead to envy, possessiveness, and jealousy. Protective love that leads to blindness. Sky's father thinking it was better for her to be sent away. Peter's father painting his beloved in pieces because she had left him. Loving a child so much you can't bear the thought of anything happening to her so you wall off your heart from loving her. Hadn't I done that with Chloe? I was so afraid of the things that could happen to her, of all the horrible pictures that popped into my head, that I had closed my eyes to her. Yes, it's scary to love someone that much, and dangerous, like wearing your heart on the outside of your body.

I squeeze Edith's hand, thinking of how she loved her roommate so much she'd taken on her own shame of giving birth. I'm still holding her hand when we arrive back at Crantham.

When the back door of the van opens, Dr. Hancock is already out, waiting for us. I can feel Edith tense. Connor grabs her by the arm and hauls her off the van. "Hey!" I cry, but the orderly who rode with us restrains me.

"Search them for anything dangerous they might have picked up," Dr. Hancock barks.

The orderly runs his hands over my body as impartially as if I were a piece of meat he was tenderizing. "This one's clean," he calls.

Connor is treating Edith to a rougher pat-down. When he touches her leg she screams and bolts, running so blindly she careens into me and nearly knocks me off my feet. Connor tackles her and brings her to the floor. The other orderly grabs me and drags me into the building, into the elevator. I don't fight or struggle; I don't want to end up in the Green Room again.

He takes me to my room and pushes me inside. "If you know

what's good for you, you'll behave," he says as he closes the door. I hear the lock click into place.

When I'm sure he is gone I unclench my fist to examine what Edith pressed into my hand: three keys wrapped in red yarn.

I HIDE THE keys under my mattress. When they bring me my dinner and meds on a tray I placidly tip the Dixie cup full of pills into my mouth. As soon as the nurse leaves I spit the pills out into my hand and tuck them with the others I've been stockpiling. So that I could kill myself if it grew too painful to live without Chloe. Being separated from her is like having a part of my body gouged out. But now I realize that turning off the pain is not an option. Not when Chloe needs me.

I rinse my mouth out with water, and spit. Then I sit at the edge of the bed watching the sky grow dark and waiting for lights to come on in the house on the hill. I keep thinking about what Edith said about Peter reminding her of Solomon. I can't think of anything Peter has in common with Solomon, but then apparently I don't know Peter very well. I think back to things he told me about his childhood: his parents were strict but they had taught him self-reliance; when I wanted to keep Chloe in bed with us he said his mother always said that would spoil a child. But what mother had he been talking about? He'd been in an orphanage for two years. All the parenting books I read said that babies learned how to love by their attachment to their mothers. What happened to a baby who didn't have that?

They treated me differently, like there must have been something wrong with me for my mother to abandon me.

Or, it occurs to me now, maybe they treated him like a monster because they thought that's what someone becomes when they've lived in an orphanage for as long as Peter did.

I feel chilled by the thought, and guilty for having it. If Peter had told me about being in an orphanage for two years might I have hesitated to marry him? What if I'd known his father was in a mental hospital and had killed himself? Might I have feared he was a monster?

But no, he *loved* Chloe. I could see that from the moment she was born. He doted on her. Every burp, every smile was a sign of her intelligence and similarity to him. He loved it when people told him she looked like him. It must have been like looking into a mirror—

Something about that idea bothers me. I get up and move to the window. There are lights on at the house now. Perhaps Sky and Peter are sitting in the ornate parlor watching Chloe crawl on the rug, play with her toys. It gives me a pang to think of them in the warm circle of lamplight while I sit here in the dark. How often had Peter felt that, I wonder, growing up in foster homes? He must have always felt like he was on the outside looking in. No wonder he had reacted so badly when he thought I was going to take Chloe away from him. I remember how he had looked at her—

Not so much as if he loved her, but as if he wanted to *consume* her.

Some kinds of love are as dangerous as hate.

What would Peter do if he thought he was going to lose Chloe? It would be like losing himself. Like looking into the mirror and seeing nothing.

I think of the pain I feel being separated from Chloe, the stash of pills hidden under the mattress. I think of that woman who jumped from a window with her baby strapped to her chest because she thought he would be better off dead than living damaged without her. I think of the moment when I thought that it might be better to take Chloe with me if I killed myself. I rub my arms and blink away a tear. My vision blurs, turning the lights in Sky's house blurry. They swell and flicker. I rub my eyes, but the light has only grown, reaching up to the sky like—

Flames! The house is on fire. With Chloe inside.

I grab the keys from under the mattress, find the one to unlock the door, and run down the hall to the stairs. Once again I hear Edith's voice telling me that Peter reminded her of Solomon. But it wasn't Solomon she really meant; it was the false mother, the one who would rather see the baby split in two than let anyone else have it.

Edith's Journal, December 10, 1971 (cont.)

It was snowing when I got outside. I'd wrapped the baby in the blanket and tucked him inside my coat, but still I worried that something so small wouldn't survive outside in the cold very long. I could feel him like a second heart beating against my chest.

There was no one around but I headed toward the service buildings like Libby had told me to. The old laundry was there and the powerhouse, but neither was used anymore. It was the least pretty part of campus, so no one much came here. I walked toward the big smokestack of the powerhouse. If I turned right there, I would come to the lake. I stopped on the path and looked up at the smokestack as if it could give me a sign. Miss Mayhew told us in her lecture on St. Peter's that when a new pope is chosen people wait in the plaza to watch the smoke come out of the Sistine Chapel's chimney. Black smoke meant they were still undecided; white meant they had chosen a new pope.

But the powerhouse wasn't used anymore, so I didn't know how to choose. If I went right I would take the baby to the lake. I could lay him in the reeds at the edge of the water like Moses, only I didn't have an "ark of bulrushes daubed with asphalt and pitch" and it wasn't warm here like it had been in Egypt. And there was no pharaoh's daughter washing clothes downriver to find a baby and bring it up as her own.

That's what I needed: a pharaoh's daughter. Then I could leave the baby and know he would be all right and Libby and I could go to Europe together. Later, when Libby was herself again, I would tell her what I had done and she would be glad that I hadn't left the baby to die. But where could I find a pharaoh's daughter?

I looked left, away from the lake. I saw a building on a hill with a light on: Baldwin, the infirmary. There would be a nurse on call there. A nurse would know what to do. I could put the baby on the doorstep and knock on the door, then run and hide. I'd watch until someone came and then I'd run back to Main.

I took one look back at the powerhouse—and saw that there *was* white smoke coming out of the smokestack! It was a sign that I was making the right decision. I couldn't risk going on the path, though, because it was getting light and someone might see me. So I climbed up the gully behind Baldwin. The snow made it slippery, and the baby put me off balance. Just before I reached the back door I fell. I kept my right hand on the baby and put my left out to brace my fall—and landed so hard I felt something crack. I felt nauseous and had to sit for a few minutes to catch my breath. It was light and the snow was coming down harder. It was pretty, like being inside a snow globe, and part of me just wanted to stay there. I unbuttoned my coat to make sure the baby was all right. He looked right up at me and then he looked up at the sky, at the big heavy flakes falling down, and I thought it was such a perfect moment, why not just stay in it forever?

But then he began to cry, so I got up and kept going up the hill. There was a light on at the back door and a car parked in the lot. That would be the visiting doctor, I thought, and I was glad because he'd be able to make sure the baby was all right. I walked across the lot and unbuttoned my coat. The baby stared up at me as if asking me what I was doing.

"It's all right," I told him. "Someone will be here soon."

And then the door opened. I looked up, expecting the doctor, but it was a woman. It was Nurse Landry. Thank God, I thought. She was just the right person to help me.

Chapter Twenty-Eight

I am out of the building before I can even think whether I should be trying to alert someone that there's a fire. But if I call for attention they'll hold me and I can't bear that. Chloe is in a burning house. Already she could be breathing smoke, already she could be—

I can't even think of her engulfed in flames. But of course, now I *have* thought of it and the thought renders my body as weak as water. I stumble but somehow keep upright, racing past the buildings that Edith had called the infirmary and the one she'd called the powerhouse, all parts of her make-believe college where forty-five years ago she carried her roommate's baby to the infirmary. How she must relive that trip every day of her life! Will I remember this trip the same way? With remorse that I hadn't been able to save my baby?

No! I won't let that happen!

I look up and see an orange glow above the tips of the pines and smell smoke. I scramble down the gully, careless of the branches that whip against my face, and dive into the gap beneath the fence.

He hasn't left Chloe in the house, I tell myself, *he loves Chloe—*

He only loves her because she's his.

It's such a strange thought that I flinch—and something catches at my hair, as if the thought itself has reached out and grabbed me. *What does that even mean?* I plead. *Of course we love our children because they are ours—*

Is that why you love Chloe? Because she belongs to you? Would you stop loving her if she didn't belong to you?

No, I think. Even if I had to hand her over to Peter, I'd keep on loving her.

That's not how Peter loves her. If she can't be his, he won't love her anymore. He'd rather see her dead than with you. So hurry—

I surge forward, but my hair is tangled in a vine. I struggle, ripping handfuls of my hair out from my scalp, and then I feel someone's hands on my arms, pulling me through. For a second I think it must be Edith, but then I see it's a man. I struggle out of his grip, afraid it's one of the orderlies come to stop me, but then I hear his voice.

"It's Ben. I was heading to the house and saw you."

I'm relieved it's him, but I'd rather that he was at the house saving Chloe.

"You should have kept going to the house. It's on fire—and my baby's there!"

I see something pass over his face and then he turns and runs up the path. I take off after him, keeping pace behind him until we reach the ridge and he stops. I try to keep going but he throws out his arm to block me. A wave of heat hits me at the same time so that for a moment I think he's somehow thrown up this wall of heat to stop me.

I push past him and run into a wall of fire. The house is ablaze. Flames leap out of broken windows. The terrace we sat on this morning is scorched. I spy the playpen Chloe stood in earlier today and cry out.

An answering cry comes from the edge of the terrace and a woman comes flying at me, hair singed, face blackened by soot, the whites of her eyes glowing red in the glare of the fire. She's a Fury come to wreak her vengeance on me for leaving my child behind. She's every mother who ever lost a child through neglect or madness. She's me if I don't save Chloe.

"Do you have her?" The Fury transforms into Billie. "Do you have Chloe?"

How could I have her? I open my arms wide to show her I don't.

"What happened?" Ben asks, grabbing Billie by the arms and shaking her. "Where are Ms. Bennett and Marist?"

I want to scream that they don't matter, but he's right. Chloe hasn't gone anywhere on her own. Either Peter or Sky has her.

"They fought," Billie gasps out, turning to me. "After you left. Sky asked him some questions and he grew . . . *resentful*."

I can well imagine.

"And Sky grew willful. She doesn't like to be crossed."

I can imagine the two of them, mother and son, pitting their wills against each other, stoking the flames—

We don't have time for this. "Did she say something to make him think he'd lose Chloe?"

Billie nods, tears streaming down her face, carving white streaks in the soot. "She told him that if it was true he killed Laurel, she'd make sure he never saw Chloe again. She said *she* would take custody of her. That shut him up. She thought she'd carried the day."

I knew that quiet well. "He was just biding his time."

"We went to bed—I've been staying over to take care of Chloe—but I woke up to find that she was gone. Then I smelled smoke. I called the fire department and ran up to Sky's room, but she was gone and when I checked Peter's room so was he."

"Is his car gone?" Ben asks.

Billie begins to say something but it's drowned out by the sound of approaching sirens. "The gates!" she cries. "I have to unlock them for the fire trucks."

Both Billie and Ben run toward the front of the house. I'm about to follow them when something makes me look up. There's a light on in the top floor of the tower. At first I think it's the fire, but the fire hasn't spread to the tower yet. I squint and look more closely. Yes, the light in the tower is on and someone is standing in the window. A man, holding something in his arms.

I let out a cry and run toward the tower door, which blessedly isn't locked. I bolt up the first flight of stairs. On the second floor I smell smoke. The door to the library is ajar, a chair toppled over, books strewn everywhere. Sky's cane on the floor. She must have risen from her sleep, smelled the smoke, gone to find Chloe, and seen Peter take her.

I can hear voices coming from the top floor. Sky followed Peter here and somehow hauled herself up the stairs. I grab the cane and close the door that connects the tower to the house, hoping to keep the fire at bay for a few extra minutes. I begin up the stairs slowly and quietly but then I hear Chloe cry and sprint the rest of the way up, heedless of hiding my arrival.

Sky is standing in the middle of the room in flannel pajamas, hair sticking up in crazy peaks, eyes wide and frightened. She's staring at something behind me. I turn.

Peter is perched on the windowsill, legs stretched out and crossed indolently as if he were having a convivial chat with a colleague. He's pushed the window out and broken the rod that keeps it from opening too far. There's nothing but empty space behind him, and a three-story drop to the flagstone terrace beneath him. He holds Chloe balanced on his knee with one hand. Her face is red and puckered as if she's been crying, but otherwise she looks all right.

I take a step toward them and Peter pulls Chloe closer to him—and to the open window. "What's the matter, Daph? Isn't this one of your fantasies? Dropping Chloe from a window?"

I swallow the bile rising in my throat. "It's one of my nightmares, yes," I say, "but even in my worst nightmares I never believed you could hurt her. You *love* her."

"Of course I love her," he says, his voice catching as he looks down at Chloe. "I did all this for her." He waves his hand in the air and I flinch to see him take it off Chloe. He's holding something, a piece of paper floating in the breeze from the open window.

I look down and see that the floorboard I'd hidden my ID under has been pushed aside. My driver's license and the picture of Thomas Pitt, age three, are lying on the floor. It's Laurel's will that Peter's brandishing in his free hand.

"Do you know how rich we would have been? Stan promised to invest all of Laurel's millions in the fund. He showed me the will. He gave me this copy of the will to prove that he'd have control of Chloë's money if she died. How was I to know Laurel had changed the damned thing?" He crumples the paper up and tosses it out the window. "The only way to hang on to the money was for everyone to think that Laurel was still alive. Chloe—*my* Chloe—would have been an heiress. Now what will she be? The daughter of a convicted criminal and a crazy mother? Imagine the life she'll have. What the other kids will say. Bastard. Reject. Trash. Children can be so cruel."

He aims the words over my head—at Sky—but I don't turn to see her response. I can't take my eyes off him and Chloe. I have to hold them on the edge of the windowsill with the power of my gaze.

"I never meant to take her from you," I say.

He snorts. "As if I'd ever have let you. But the police will take me away. Once everyone knows you're Daphne Marist and the woman who died is Laurel."

I can hear the sirens getting closer. Billie must have gotten the gates unlocked. They'll start putting out the fire in the main part of the house. Will they realize that we're here in the tower? Is anyone coming to help? If they saw Peter at the window they could set up a net to break his fall, but will they do it soon enough? I have to talk him away from that ledge.

"It could have been a suicide," I say.

Peter's smile chills me. "That bitch was too selfish to kill herself. And too stupid not to take a drink from a man she was lecturing on spousal abuse. You should have heard the things she called me. Thought she could run off her mouth in my house and I'd just stand there and take it."

"So you drugged her," I say.

Behind me I hear Sky say, "I'll get you the best lawyers. You'll plead insanity—"

"So I can wind up like my father?" Peter scoffs.

"You're nothing like your father," she says. I think she means to reassure him that he's not crazy like his father was, but it comes out bitterly.

"Then like you?" He points in Sky's direction, but I'm afraid to turn around and see what he's pointing at.

"What does he mean?" I ask.

"I believe he's referring to my leg, an injury I incurred jumping from the very window he's perched on now."

"*You* were the one who jumped from the window? But I thought it was Edith. Wasn't it Edith your father saw in the tower?"

"Yes, but one day she escaped from Crantham and came up

here looking for the baby. She'd gotten it into her head we were keeping him from her. I saw her from my window and followed her up here. I tried to stop her and we both fell. I landed first and saved her from the worst damage. I broke my leg—so badly that it never really healed right—but something inside me had healed. I was better after that."

So it was Sky Billie had been talking about. No wonder she hadn't wanted me repeating the story in front of her.

"How nice for you," Peter says bitterly. "Did you think of going to find your son then?"

"I thought you'd been adopted. That's what my father told me."

"That's what you wanted to believe so you could go off to Europe and write your books. You abandoned me like you'd have me abandon Chloe. But I won't let her grow up without a father the way I had to."

"She won't have to grow up without you," I say. "I'll pretend to be Laurel. I'll go back to the hospital. I'll never say a word. Neither will Sky." I risk a second's glance back at Sky. Her face is so drawn she looks like a skeleton of herself, but she nods stiffly. Then she steps a few inches to the right. Why? I wonder, where is she going? Then she silently mouths something to me. *Take . . .* I can't make out the next word but I realize now that she's moved so that I am blocking Peter's view of her. She's trying to tell me something. *Take . . .*

A sharp crack makes me pivot back to Peter. He's half-turned on the ledge and is holding Chloe up to the open window with one arm while he points with the other. "Look at the pretty lights," he says.

But Chloe isn't having it. She's in full-on tantrum mode, stiffening her arms and legs, making of herself an unholdable weight. I've nearly dropped her a half dozen times when she does this and she didn't weigh as much then as she does now.

The trick is not to fight her, but to sit on the floor with her and let her have it out. But Peter doesn't know this—or he's unable to give in. His face is taut with anger, the loving expression he had a few minutes ago wiped clean. The look he's giving her now is how he looks at me when I've disappointed him. When I've crossed him. Love changed to anger as easy as flipping a switch.

"Stop it!" he yells at Chloe, shaking her. She goes still for a second and then suddenly flails her whole body, arms and legs out, head back. Peter loses his grip. She's slithering out of his hands, falling out the window—

I am there to catch her without knowing I have moved. And as soon as my hands are on her, Sky rushes past me, bumping my shoulder. I make myself fall backward instead of forward, landing hard on my rump, keeping my arms around Chloe. *Take Chloe*, that's what Sky had said, *when I rush him*.

As I watch, she throws herself at Peter, her arms open wide, as if she means to embrace him. He is surprised into opening his arms. On his face is an expression I've never seen. How often, I wonder, had he dreamed of this as a child: his mother returned to him to take him in her arms? *Maybe it's not too late*, I want to tell Sky. For either of them. For any of us.

But the force of her embrace tips Peter over the ledge. I lay Chloe on the floor and lunge at Sky's leg, but it slips out of my grasp. They are falling, out the open window, propelled by Sky's headlong rush. I glimpse her face against Peter's cheek, her arms cradling him as if she meant to lay him down softly in his bed—

And then they are gone. I gather up Chloe in my arms and stand, holding her tightly as I inch closer to the window, hating to go so near the drop, needing to see—

In the light of the fire I can see Peter splayed out on the

pavement, Sky curled by his side, her arms still holding him. A fireman comes rushing around the house, sees the bodies, then looks up at the tower and sees me. He shouts something at me, but I can't make out what. *Come down? Stay put?*

I turn around—

And see smoke rising from the stairwell. While I've been up here the fire has jumped from the main house to the tower. I hear voices below me—shouts, roars—no, the roar is the fire. Holding Chloe to me, I take a few steps toward the stairwell, peer over, and see flames leaping up, seeking the open air of the window behind me. The firemen can't make it up here on the stairs.

The floor is hot beneath my feet. The air is thickening with smoke. Chloe begins to cry. I step backward to the window and look down. There are several firemen now. One points a bullhorn at me and shouts: *Go to the other side! We're getting a ladder.*

I move to the other side, to the window facing the driveway, and try to wrench it open. It's painted shut and I can't get it open while holding Chloe and I'm not willing to put her down. She could crawl to the open stairwell. I could lose her in the smoke, which is thicker on this side of the tower with all the windows closed.

I look down at the truck backing up to the tower. If I wait, they'll break through the glass, but how long do I have to wait? Chloe is coughing, gagging on the smoke. I can feel it filling up my lungs. If I lose consciousness, I'll drop her.

I cross back to the other side of the tower, to the open window. The emptiness that yawned so threateningly before now beckons. Is this how it felt for the woman who jumped from a window with her baby strapped to her chest? Like the only choice left to her?

But she was deluded. Crazy.

And yet . . . her baby lived.

She had a baby carrier, though. I look around the room, hoping for a Snugli to materialize, but there's nothing but smoke here now. But that's okay. I can make a Snugli. I take off my pajama top and button Chloe into it, knotting off the bottom and tying the sleeves around my chest. Then I take off my pants and wrap them around us, securing Chloe tight to my body. Then I look down.

Three stories. Sky and Peter are lying motionless on the flagstone. The fall killed both of them, but then, they both landed on the pavement. If I go straight backward, Chloe won't hit the pavement because she's tied to me.

You'll die. It's Laurel, her voice flat, unjudging.

But she may live, I answer back.

There's no reply. I don't need one. I know what to do. I've always known.

I look across to the other window. If the firemen break through now . . .

I count to ten but no rescuing fireman breaks through the glass. I can barely see the window. Is it the smoke or am I blacking out? Chloe has gone still against me, her breath rattling against my bare skin.

I sit on the windowsill. I check the knots on my makeshift Snugli. I wrap my arms around Chloe and tuck my chin down and draw my knees up, making myself into a human egg crate.

Then I fall back.

Chapter Twenty-Nine

When I wake up I think I am back in the Green Room. Not that the room is green. It's white and blindingly bright—near-death-experience bright.

Dead is my next hypothesis, but then the pain kicks in and I decide death can't hurt this much. Every cell in my body is crying out like a million screaming babies who haven't been held or fed or changed in days.

Chloe. What happened to Chloe?

"Chloe," I manage to croak out and someone, a man, says, "She's all right. She wasn't hurt . . ." Something catches in the man's throat. "You took all the damage."

I feel my face turn wet and my body convulses, which turns up the volume on all those other babies. *What about us? What about us?* they cry. I can't possibly help them all, so I slip away, out of that blinding light, into the dark.

THE NEXT TIME I wake the light is a little more bearable and I can turn my head a little. *Not paralyzed then*, a voice says in my head, *at least, not from the waist up.*

"Shut up," I murmur.

The man sitting by my bed startles awake. "Was I snoring?" he asks.

I laugh and every cell in my body cries out in pain. "No, sorry, I wasn't talking to you."

Way to get yourself recommitted.

The man seems unalarmed. He leans forward so I can see his face. It's Ben Marcus, only Ben Marcus with stubble and dark rings under his eyes. "Your daughter is okay," he tells me. "You've been calling her name."

"Where is she?" I ask.

"Billie Williams has been looking after her."

I nod—realize that's not a good idea—and lick my lips. I trust Billie to take care of Chloe, but the thought that I may never be able to take care of her myself terrifies me. "Am I . . . *paralyzed?*"

His eyes widen. "No! The firemen got an inflatable cushion in place before you jumped. You still broke three vertebrae, your right leg, and your shoulder. You'll be in here for a while but you will recover. When you can sit up I'll ask Billie to bring Chloe to see you."

My face is wet again. Each sob sets off a ripple of pain and some beeping from a machine. A nurse comes in and adjusts something on my IV. I can feel myself sinking, but before I do I need to ask. "Sky? Peter?"

"Both dead. I'm sorry." He squeezes my hand. The pressure of warm flesh sets off a mini quake in all my injured cells.

So, not paralyzed from the waist down either, I hear Laurel quip before I slip away again.

IT'S LIKE THAT for a spell of time that I later learn is three weeks: waking and sleeping, drifting on a sea of pain and drugs to curb the pain. Slowly I stay awake longer and make incremental progress. I sit up, I drink from a sippy cup, I form new words. I've become my own baby. Soon I'll have to learn to walk.

Ben Marcus is there every day, his devotion a mystery I can't begin to parse.

"We hardly know each other," I say one day when he brings me grapes and a newspaper.

"You don't know me but I know the woman who broke her own back to save her child. That's enough to make me want to stick around and learn more, but if I'm being a pest . . ."

"You believed me when no one else did," I say. "That's enough for me to want to stick around and get to know you better."

"Not that you have much choice," he says.

We both laugh at the same time.

"Exactly," I say.

To DISTRACT ME as I begin physical therapy, Ben brings me news from the outside world. Stan Hobbes and Esta Greenberg have been arrested for aiding and abetting the murder of Laurel Hobbes. Although she was cremated, DNA has proven that I'm Daphne Marist so the police are going on the assumption that the woman found drowned in my bathtub was Laurel. They've also found Laurel's journal on her laptop, which reveals she was planning to confront Peter at my house.

"Peter hated to be confronted," I say.

"Apparently," Ben answers. "What I don't understand is why Laurel would take a drink from him."

"Stan was already drugging her," I say. "She must not have been thinking clearly—"

That's sweet, Laurel says, *but when are you going to start saying what you really think?*

"—and she was kind of arrogant. She'd never suspect Peter would drug her, let alone kill her."

Who would? Nerdy Peter Marist in his Izod golf shirts and Dockers? Besides, I thought I'd taken care of that.

"She changed her will," I say, "so that Stan wouldn't inherit when she died. She thought . . . she *must* have thought that would keep her safe. But maybe she didn't get a chance to tell Peter that she'd changed it. He thought killing her was the best way of getting to her money. And then when he and Stan found out that she'd changed her will they realized they'd messed up." I imagine how angry Stan would have been at Peter and how poorly Peter would have handled that. "The only way they could still access her money was if she were alive and crazy. And I played into their hands by running away to a mental institution."

"Thank God you ran away," Ben says. "Who knows what Peter would have done to you if he had found you there. The man's clearly—"

But before he can finish what he's saying, the nurse comes in to say it's time for my PT. The exercises I do feel like I'm stabbing myself over and over again with steak knives, but right now that's preferable to contemplating how stupid I'd been not to know I was living with a sociopath.

TRUE TO BEN's promise, once I am well enough to sit up, Billie Williams brings Chloe to visit. She's so big I barely recognize her, but she recognizes me. She greets me with an angry howl and then turns her head away from me, refusing to look at me.

"She's angry that you've been gone, but don't worry," Billie says consolingly as she bounces Chloe on her knee, "once you're back on your feet and able to take care of her she'll come back to you."

"Thank you," I say, although I'm not sure I believe her, "and thank you for taking care of Chloe."

Billie turns red. "It's the least I could do after . . . well, after going along with Sky's plan."

I had wondered about that. "So you knew all along I wasn't Laurel Hobbes?"

Billie nods and busies herself wiping some drool off Chloe's chin. "She told me she'd found her lost baby and that he needed her help. I've always felt bad about the part I played in Sky losing her baby. If I hadn't gone to Dr. Bennett that morning, Sky would have had a chance to decide for herself whether she wanted to keep the baby. Then when Peter came back into her life so many years later she seemed so thrilled that I didn't want to say no when she asked me to help her. She said you weren't in your right mind and that you were trying to steal Chloe away from her son. We were to keep you and the baby safe until he could make sure you were better. I knew it wasn't lawful, exactly, but I've seen women go a little crazy after they gave birth."

"Like Edith?" I ask.

Billie looks up at me. "Edith hadn't had a baby," she reminds me. "Her problems were different. But Sky . . . after the doctor brought her back from Poughkeepsie, she was in an awful state. He hired me to watch her—just as he'd hired my mother to watch Sky's mother after she gave birth. I guess postpartum depression must run in their family. Dr. Bennett thought it would be better for Sky if the baby was taken away from her, but I think that it only made it worse. When she saw Edith going up into the tower she thought she was hiding her baby from her. She ran up into the tower and attacked Edith. They both fell out the window."

"That's not what Sky told me," I say.

"It's not the way she remembered it afterward," Billie says, "which I thought was a blessing."

"That's why you didn't want me to talk about E.S. jumping from the window in front of her."

Billie looks embarrassed. "I only told you about it to let you know it was possible to get better from postpartum depression. But now I wonder if she was ever truly herself again. Losing a child like that . . . even if she thought she didn't want it . . . you're never the same. She coped by writing, though she really just told the same story—her story—over and over again. When Peter found her, she thought she could make up for what she'd done, to both him and Edith. And I thought . . . well, if we were only keeping you until you were better, what harm was there?"

"I can see that," I say, willing to forgive her because of how well she's taken care of Chloe. But Billie isn't ready to forgive herself. "But then she asked me to move Chloe to the bathtub during the night."

"You did that?" I ask, both relieved it wasn't me and horrified that she'd crept into my room at night.

Billie nods, biting her lip. "Sky said we needed you to see you were unwell, but I didn't feel right about it, playing a trick like that. Of course I made sure Chloe was safe. I stayed right by the door to hear if she cried. I heard when you got up to get her. That's when I realized that you were a perfectly good mother."

"It wasn't even my own baby," I say, looking regretfully at Chloe. Perhaps she should be angry with me. She's not even a year old and I've already abandoned her twice—once for another baby.

Billie shakes her head. "Oh, but that's what being a good mother really means. That you have so much love for your own it spreads out to all the other children in the world who need you." Billie looks down at Chloe with such a clear expression of love that I feel a pull inside me, like that red thread Edith wears on her wrist.

"How is Edith?" I ask.

"Sky left a trust for her care and . . ."—Billie's voice wobbles—"she split the rest of her estate between me and Peter, which means that half will go to you. Of course, the house is gone but the land is still quite valuable and there's plenty of money to take care of Edith. I've been taking care of her at my house . . . I hope you don't mind that she's staying with me while I watch Chloe."

"Why would I mind?"

"Some mothers might worry if their children were living with a former mental patient."

I start to object, but then I realize that this is *exactly* the kind of thing that would have thrown me into a paroxysm of dread a few months ago. But when I think about Edith, I find I don't have the least anxiety about her being near Chloe. "I can't think of anyone *less* likely to hurt Chloe," I say, feeling a swell of gladness at the thought of Edith free of Crantham. If loving our children connects us to other children, it also connects us to all who love them, shouldn't it? And for a moment I don't just forgive Billie, I forgive Sky for doing what she thought she had to for her long-lost child and, picturing that little boy in the photograph, I forgive little Thomas Pitt, my husband.

AFTER BILLIE LEAVES, I ask Ben the question I've been dreading. "Where's Chloë? Laurel's Chloë. Laurel didn't have any family . . . or many friends."

Way to make me sound pathetic.

"I believe the Department of Social Services has taken custody of her," Ben says. "But a lawyer has been wanting to talk to you, a pretentious prick from Scarsdale who talks like he's got a hockey puck in his mouth. Nurse Goodnough and I have been fending him off."

"Why does he want to talk to me?"

"Something about an amendment to Laurel's will. Do you want to talk to him?"

I wait for Laurel to fill me in, but all she says is, *Sheesh, you know I'm not the real Laurel, don't you?*

"Yes," I tell Ben, "I think I'd better."

LAUREL'S LAWYER IS like a parody of a John Cheever character. He has white hair, tan skin, and a lockjaw WASP accent that reminds me of Thurston Howell from *Gilligan's Island*. I feel bad for Laurel that her welfare was entrusted to this man when her parents died. The thought that Chloë will be raised with him as her legal guardian turns me cold.

I'm grateful that Ben suggested we meet in the solarium. I would not want this man to see my rumpled hospital bed. I've gotten dressed for the occasion, in clothes that Ben bought for me at Target. Pull-on sweatpants and a Jets T-shirt. I can see Ronald Jones-Barrett (or JB, as he tells me to call him) eyeing them as if he could read the Target labels. Good, I think. I'm tired of pretending to be someone I'm not.

"First of all, Mrs. Marist," he says in a deep baritone, "I would like to express my regret for not detecting the egregious fraud perpetrated on you and my client, Laurel Hobbes. If I'd known—"

"All you had to do was visit her in the mental hospital," I say, angry less on my own behalf than on Laurel's. "You would have seen I'm not her."

"Yesss." He draws out the word as if it contained multitudinous meanings and interpretations. "I meant to visit, but I was away and I had no reason to suspect foul play. Laurel *was* acting erratic and unstable when she came to see me the week before her disappearance."

"Before her death, you mean. What do you mean by erratic and unstable?"

"She wanted to change the terms of her will, but she refused to tell me the basis for the change. She seemed unwell and . . . well, frankly, *paranoid.*"

"Her husband was drugging her and plotting to put her away in a mental hospital to take control of her money. Did it occur to you that she might have grounds to be suspicious?"

"Well, I did consult her husband . . ."

"Great," I say, "an impartial source."

"And who else would you have had me consult, Mrs. Marist?" He's stern now, annoyed by my tone. "You have to remember that Laurel had a history of mental illness and had been unstable since the birth of her daughter. She was clearly suffering from some kind of postpartum mood disorder. And then her request . . . well, it was very unusual."

I swallow the remarks I'd like to make about Jones-Barrett's diagnostic abilities and ask instead, "What was so unusual about it?"

"She wanted to change the trustee in charge of Chloë's trust. To remove Stan and place someone else in the position, someone I had no knowledge of . . . in short, she named you as Chloë's guardian and executor of the trust."

"Me!" I am sure I have misheard him. Laurel hardly knew me, and from the journal entries I read she didn't even think all that well of me.

"Yes, well, you can see why I questioned her judgment. No offense. A woman she'd only known for a few months, whom she'd met in a support group, a woman with her own history of emotional problems—"

"How did you know that?" I ask. I do not say that, in my opinion, the qualifier "no offense" is usually followed by offensive comments.

"I spoke with Stan. He told me that your husband had mentioned that you'd tried to kill yourself after your daughter's birth."

"I didn't," I say. "Peter just tried to make me believe I had."

Jones-Barrett shrugs. "How was I to know? At any rate, despite my reservations I complied with Laurel's request."

"You did? But why? If you thought she was crazy and I was unfit . . ."

"I thought . . . well, frankly, I didn't think the issue would come up. I also assumed once Laurel had recovered her senses she would change her will again. But I'm also not in the business of going against my clients' wishes. I see a lot of troubling behavior in my line of work . . . although perhaps none as troubling as the behavior of your husband . . . and if I started choosing whose orders to follow and whose not . . . well, I wouldn't be in business very long. Laurel chose you as Chloë's guardian. When I asked her why, she said it was because you were a good mother and she trusted you to take care of Chloë." He pauses, as if expecting me to say something, but I find that I can't. Not unless I want to blubber in front of this patrician man. After a moment he nods as if I had spoken. "In any event, she was proven correct. You took Chloë with you. You made sure she was safe."

Leaving my own child behind, I want to say, *and then giving Chloë up when I wound up in a mental institution.*

"Where is she now?" I finally manage.

"In a foster home. I will await your instructions for her care as soon as you are able to advise me."

"And if I don't . . . if I don't think I can take care of her?" My head is swimming. Before all this began, I could barely manage one baby, never mind two.

"Then she will be made a ward of the state and appointed a guardian. There are funds to take care of her—plenty of money, actually . . . though as we can see by Laurel's upbringing, money alone doesn't guarantee a high level of care. Sometimes it's just the thing to bring out the worst in people. But the decision is yours." He picks up his briefcase and stands up. I struggle to stand too, but he puts out his hand to indicate I shouldn't bother. "Save your strength," he says. "You'll need it. Good day, Mrs. Marist."

I sit in the solarium, frozen despite the warm sun coming in through the windows. *How could you?* I ask Laurel. *How could you leave me with this decision? What made you think I could handle this?*

I wait for a response for so long that the sun moves across the room, climbs a wall, and vanishes. I wait long enough to know that Laurel isn't going to answer, that she has said all she has to say to me. *Of course I'll take Chloë*, I say to her, *I'll raise her like she's my own*. I don't need to hear Laurel's voice to know what she would say if she were here.

Edith's Journal, December 12, 1971

Nurse Landry took me and the baby and Libby to the hospital, where Libby's father Dr. Bennett has been taking care of us. He's been very kind. When I told him I wanted to finish writing in my journal he asked Nurse Landry to go back to the dorm and bring it to me. He let me write down everything that happened and now he's letting me write this last entry. Then he's going to put my journal away for safekeeping. "You wouldn't want it to fall into the wrong hands," he said to me. "You wouldn't want the wrong people to find the baby, would you?"

He told me that if anyone knew who the baby's father was, it would be bad for him. I tried to tell him that the father was an artist, but he told me that wasn't true. He was a patient in the mental hospital. A very serious case. He should never have let his daughter anywhere near him. When Elizabeth Schuyler went away to school he killed himself. Would you want the baby growing up to know that about his father?

No, I wouldn't.

And if people knew the mother was Libby, she'd lose her opportunity to finish college and continue her career. Did I want that?

No, I didn't.

It was easier, he told me, to say the baby was mine. Would that be okay?

I told him it was. I already thought of the baby as mine. We were connected—Libby, the baby, and I—by that red thread. We'd always be connected. Dr. Bennett has given me a red ribbon to tie the journal closed when I am done writing. That way we will all be safe—Libby, the baby, and I. Dr. Bennett says I can have a red ribbon to tie around my wrist too, so I'll always remember to keep quiet. So I'll always remember why I have to be. I told him he could count on me. I'd do anything to keep Libby and our baby safe. Anything at all.

Acknowledgments

I'd like to thank my always elegant and inexhaustible agent, Robin Rue, and her wonderful assistant, Beth Miller, for their support and encouragement. Thanks to Margaux Weisman for acquiring this novel, and to Kate Nintzel for becoming its adoptive mother and guiding it into maturity with insight and grace. Thanks to all the nurturers of this book at William Morrow.

Researching and writing about postpartum mood disorders has been challenging and at times daunting. I want to thank the women who have shared their stories with me, starting with my mother, who told me that when she experienced depression and suicidal thoughts after the birth of her second child she was unable to tell anyone what she was going through. I also want to acknowledge the women and their families who have experienced postpartum mood disorders. The story Daphne hears about the woman who jumped out of a window with her baby in a Snugli is loosely based on a real-life story. Postpartum mood disorders are a terrible, under-discussed mental illness that I hope we can begin discussing more honestly. There are ways to get help if you think you are struggling. I found Teresa Twomey's book *Understanding Postpartum Psychosis: A Temporary Madness* informative and inspiring. Thank you, Teresa, for continuing the conversation with me in the P.S. Section of this book and for recommending www.postpartum.net as a resource for struggling mothers and their families and friends.

In writing this book, I was transported back to the period when I first became a mother. While it was in some ways an isolating experience, I was fortunate to have a world of support in my parents, Marge and Walter Goodman; my husband, Lee Slonimsky; my step-daughter, Nora Slonimsky; my brothers, Larry and Bob Goodman; my sister-in-law, Nancy Goodman; and my friends Gary Feinberg, Connie Crawford, and Scott Silverman. As a wise woman once said, "It takes a village to raise a child." I've been fortunate to have a village of wise women. Thank you to the other mothers who have shared the journey: Eileen MacDonald Amon, Roberta Andersen, Amy Avnet, Laurie Bower, Juliet Harrison, Alisa Kwitney, Lauren Lipton, Mindy Ohringer, Wendy Gold Rossi, Cathy Cole Seilhan, and Ethel Wesdorp.

And thanks, finally, to my daughter, Maggie, who has made being a mother the best thing that ever happened to me.

About the author

About the book

Read on

Insights,
Interviews
& More . . .

Meet Carol Goodman

Franco Vogt

CAROL GOODMAN is the critically acclaimed author of twenty novels, including *The Lake of Dead Languages* and *The Seduction of Water*, which won the Hammett Prize. Her books have been translated into sixteen languages. She lives in the Hudson Valley with her family, and teaches creative writing at the New School and SUNY New Paltz. ∽

An Interview with Teresa M. Twomey

In researching *The Other Mother*, I found Teresa M. Twomey's book *Understanding Postpartum Pyschosis: A Temporary Madness* informative and inspiring. I spoke with Ms. Twomey so that she could shed more light on the experience of postpartum mood disorder.

CG: What first inspired you to write a book on postpartum psychosis?

TT: I had a mood disorder crisis after my first pregnancy, but I didn't hear the term postpartum psychosis until I was on bed rest during my second pregnancy. I knew something was wrong, but in spite of having problems and telling people I could not cope, I didn't get professional help. I had to piece it together on my own. My initial reaction after I'd recovered was that I wouldn't tell anyone what had happened. But then when I read about Andrea Yates, the Texas mother who drowned her five children while suffering from postpartum psychosis, I knew someone had to write a book about the subject. It took me some time to decide that that person would be me. I thought that the book should come from someone who had nothing to gain and everything to lose—unlike a woman in prison who might be accused of being self-serving. While I realized that going public with my own experience with postpartum psychosis would be opening myself up to professional and personal stigma, I knew it would be an important book. When I learned how serious this ▶

3

An Interview with
Teresa M. Twomey *(continued)*

illness was and that I was fortunate to get out alive with a child alive and marriage intact, I saw writing this book as an act of gratitude.

CG: You include first-person stories from women who have experienced postpartum mood disorders in your book. Without giving away any confidentiality, how did you make contact with these women? What common threads did you find in their stories? What was most surprising to you? Do you think that the process of telling their stories was helpful to them?

TT: At first, having been told that a book specifically on postpartum psychosis did not have a good chance of being published, I embarked on a book that covered the spectrum of postpartum mood disorders. I created a website, gave talks, and reached out to family and friends for stories from women who had experienced postpartum mood disorders. I was surprised at many of the women whom I knew who related having had PPMD, some of whom were older women who had never shared their stories with anyone. Although I had been told that women with PPP would be reluctant to tell their stories, I heard from so many of them that I realized I had enough for a book. When I saw that another book had been published on the full spectrum of PPMDs my friends and family reacted with dismay that someone else had written the book I was working on. I took this however as an opportunity to write the book I really wanted to write—one that focused on PPP.

I corresponded with the women who volunteered to share their stories by mail and email, going back and forth with them to "polish" their stories, not in a literary sense, but in order to gain clarity. Many of these women related that sharing their stories was healing for them. The process of reading the stories was healing for me. The overwhelming feeling was of not being alone; this had happened to other women. The willingness of other women to share their stories bolstered my own courage to share my experience.

CG: Having written a book on postpartum psychosis, what kinds of responses have you gotten from the public? Have any of these surprised or disconcerted you?

TT: Often people ask if I am a mental health professional. When I say I am not, they usually seem puzzled and ask why I wrote it. When I say that I had PPP it seems people do not know what to say. Or sometimes the reactions are startling. One woman loudly exclaimed, "You mean you were crazy?" Another confided that her husband didn't believe in "things like that." I realized that he was fortunate not to have had experiences in his life where he had to learn otherwise.

Although usually my talks have drawn larger than expected crowds, at one library talk, shortly after my book was published, I was initially disappointed to see that only three people had come. Before any event I say a silent prayer putting it in God's hands that my talk will help someone, even if it is just one person. At the end ▶

An Interview with
Teresa M. Twomey *(continued)*

of the talk, a woman shared that she had had postpartum psychosis decades earlier but had never told anyone besides her family and doctors. If there'd been a bigger audience, she might not have felt free to share that.

CG: What do you think is most "misunderstood" about postpartum mood disorders? What preconceptions would you like to correct?

TT: There are three main misconceptions I encounter:

1. Once crazy, always crazy: Once a person has a psychotic break, they are forever tainted by the experience. In fact, psychotic breaks are more common than we think, and can be caused by a variety of factors.

2. The mind is "gone"—that the person is "absent" during a psychotic break. We treat people roughly when they're having a psychotic break, as if they don't register what they're experiencing. Whereas these women are often traumatized by how they are treated during PPP.

3. "It cannot happen to me." There is a misconception that this illness only happens to "other" people—women who already have problems like drug addiction, poverty, abuse, and existing mental illness. People do not understand, or perhaps believe, that it really can be random and happen to *any* pregnant or postpartum woman.

CG: One of the most intriguing parts of your book to me was the warning to women who might have postpartum OCD; in fact, I use that warning to begin this novel. As a writer with a very overactive imagination (and one who experienced "intrusive" thoughts postpartum) it occurred to me that this might leave a woman very vulnerable to influences. Can you tell me any more of what you've learned about this element of postpartum mood disorder?

TT: "A little knowledge is a dangerous thing." As PMADs become better known, women—and even professionals— may assume that if a woman has OCD symptoms she cannot have PPP. That is incorrect, they can co-occur. Conversely, a woman with OCD may fear she has PPP when she does not—this could increase her risk of suicide. And then, of course, there is the tendency of women with OCD to "borrow" images. That is, they can be highly suggestible so when they are told or read of another woman's intrusive thoughts about "X" they start having intrusive thoughts about "X" as well.

CG: What advice would you give to a woman who suspects she might be suffering from a postpartum mood disorder? What advice would you give to her family and friends?

TT: Get help. There is no virtue in suffering. You deserve and your family deserves the best possible start to a life together—that cannot happen with a ▶

**An Interview with
Teresa M. Twomey** *(continued)*

mood disorder in the way. ALL perinatal mood disorders are identifiable, diagnosable, and treatable, and with proper care you will be yourself again.

To family and friends: Care for those you love. Help her get help. Help her help herself. If she cannot help herself, act for her. Do not wait for her to ask. Do not wait for a crisis to occur. If something seems wrong, it probably is. Whatever she does, keep in mind that she is suffering from an illness. Don't take things personally. Be her ally. She is not to blame. She did not choose to be ill. And with proper care, in time she will be herself again.

CG: What resources are available for women experiencing postpartum mood disorders?

TT: Probably the best resource in the US is www.postpartum.net. From there you can locate other resources. If you don't find what you need on the website, call or email them.

CG: Is there anything else you would like to add?

TT: Women with this illness are not evil and are not to blame—even those who harm others. Blaming the woman is a step *away* from what we need, which is more efforts to prevent such tragedies. We need increased education and awareness that can lead to prompt action and proper care.

Also, I appreciate your contacting me in an effort to "get it right." Too often articles and stories about this illness simply reinforce common misconceptions—even when the writer is well-intentioned. This is such a problem that I actually devote part of a chapter in my book to address those in the media.

CG: I'm glad that I did. Also, that chapter, "Postpartum Psychosis Across History and in the Media Today," was very helpful. Throughout your book, the distinctions you make between what people used to refer to as "baby blues" and specific postpartum mood disorders helped me think about what my characters were experiencing and about stereotypes that I wanted to move beyond. I remember vividly that my mother told me that after she gave birth to her middle child (my older brother) she had suicidal thoughts. I was the first person she'd ever told about what she experienced because she still had a deep sense of shame about the feelings she'd had. I'm grateful to you, and other writers, for shedding light on these experiences in a compassionate and nonjudgmental manner. Thank you for your book and for doing this interview.

TT: Thank you. ∾

Reading Group Guide

1. Describe the setting of the novel. How do the surroundings create a mood or reflect the thoughts and actions of the characters in the story?

2. What was your first impression of Daphne? Did you think she was a good mother? What about Laurel?

3. When did things first appear to be off with Sky? Can you point to a specific moment in the story when you felt that she wasn't quite who she seemed to be?

4. Describe and compare the narrative voices between the three journal writers (Daphne, Laurel, and Edith).

5. The connection between women and madness goes back a long way. Indeed, the term "hysteria" originates from the Greek word for uterus, *hystera*. And throughout history, women who have rebelled against patriarchal control and the demands for respectability were considered "deviant" or "mad." How do the female characters in *The Other Mother* play into this historical narrative? Are they acting out against male control? How so?

6. Do you think Peter is a good husband? Why or why not?

7. There's a lot of doubling—groupings of two characters who appear to resemble or switch places with each other—throughout this story. Describe these groupings. In what

ways do the characters double each other?

8. Take a moment to think about the significance of myths in this story, particularly those about Solomon and the changeling. What do these myths suggest about motherhood? How do they inform specific moments in the novel?

9. What is postpartum depression? How much did you know about this condition going into the story? What did you learn?

10. Comment on the story's narrative structure. How does the nonlinear format engage with the story's themes of psychosis, depression, and mental illness in general? If the narration unfolded from start to finish, how would the reading experience change?

11. When Billie first tells Daphne about the woman who jumped from the tower, what did you make of the story? Did you suspect it was Sky or somebody else?

12. The story relies heavily on first-person perspective and written documentation (such as the journal entries and doctors' files). How does this intimate method of storytelling challenge stigmas against mental illness? To what extent do you consider the characters depressed or neurotic?

13. Are you satisfied? What do you envision the future will look like for Daphne and the other characters? ◡

An Excerpt from *The Widow's House*

Chapter One

WHEN I PICTURE the house I see it in the late afternoon, the golden river light filling the windows and gilding the two-hundred-year-old brick. That's how we came upon it, Jess and I, at the end of a long day looking at houses we couldn't afford.

"It's the color of old money," Jess said, his voice full of longing. He was standing in the weed-choked driveway, his fingers twined through the ornate loops of the rusted iron gate. "But I think it's a little over our 'price bracket.'"

I could hear the invisible quotes around the phrase, one the Realtor had used half a dozen times that day. Jess was always a wicked mimic and Katrine Vanderberg, with her faux country quilted jacket and English rubber boots and bright yellow Suburban, was an easy target. *All she needs is a hunting rifle to look like she strode out of Downton Abbey,* he'd whispered in my ear when she'd come out of the realty office to greet us. You'd have to know Jess as well as I did to know it was himself he was mocking for dreaming of a mansion when it was clear we could hardly afford a hovel.

It had seemed like a good idea. Go someplace new. Start over. Sell the (already second-mortgaged) Brooklyn loft, pay back the (maxed-out) credit cards, and buy something cheap in the country while Jess finished his book. By country, Jess meant the Hudson Valley, where we had both gone to college, and where he had begun his first novel. He'd developed the superstition over the last winter that if he returned to the site where the muses had first spoken to him he would finally be able to write his long-awaited second novel. And how much could houses up there cost? We both remembered the area as rustic: Jess because he'd seen it through the eyes of a Long Island kid and me because I'd grown up in the nearby village of Concord and couldn't wait to get out and live in the city.

Since we'd graduated, though, 9/11 had happened and property values in exurbia had soared. The rustic farmhouses and shabby chic Victorian cottages we'd looked at today cost more than we'd get for the sale of our Brooklyn loft and Jess had immediately rejected the more affordable split-levels and sixties suburban ranches Katrine showed us.

"They remind me of my dismal childhood," he said, staring woefully at the avocado linoleum of a Red Hook faux Colonial.

"There's one more place I think you should see," Katrine had said after Jess refused to get out of the car at a modular home. She'd turned the Suburban off Route 9G toward River Road. For a second I thought she was driving us toward the college and I tensed in the backseat. Jess might want to live in the area where we had gone to school, but he didn't want to *see* those young hopeful college students loping along the shaded paths of Bailey College. At least not until he'd finished the second novel and he was invited back to do a reading.

But Katrine turned south, away from the college, and I heard Jess in the front seat sigh as we entered the curving tree-lined road. *This* was what I knew he had in mind when he talked about moving to the country: dry-laid stone walls covered with moss, ancient sycamores with bark peeling off like old wallpaper, apple orchards, clapboard Victorian farmhouses, and, through the gaps in the trees, glimpses of stately mansions and the blue ridges of the Catskills beyond the river. The road itself was filled with the light of a Hudson River school painting. I could see it reflected in Jess's face, replacing the sallow cast it had taken on this winter as he'd labored over his long-unfinished work. Or the "unborn monster," as he'd christened it. If only there were something we could afford on this road, but ▶

even the dreary farmhouse I'd grown up in was surely out of our price range.

When we pulled into a weed-choked driveway and parked outside a rusted gate, though, I immediately recognized where we were and thought Katrine had misunderstood our situation. Lots of people did. Jess was, after all, a *famous* writer. The first book had done well enough—and he'd been young and photogenic enough—to get his picture in *Granta* and *Vanity Fair*. He'd gotten a high-six-figure advance for the second novel—but that was ten years ago. The advance was long gone; the second novel was still incomplete.

But Jess had already gotten out, drawn by that golden river light, and gone to stand at the iron gate to gaze up at the house. Silhouetted against the afternoon light, so thin and wiry in his black jeans and leather jacket, he looked like part of the iron scrollwork. *How thin he's grown this winter,* I thought. The late afternoon sun turned Jess's hair the red gold it had been when we first met in college, banishing the silver that had begun, not unattractively, to limn his temples. His eyes were hidden behind dark sunglasses, but I could still read the longing in his face as he gazed up at the house. And who wouldn't long for such a house?

It stood on a rise above a curve in the river like a medieval watchtower. The old brick was mellowed with age and warmed from centuries of river light, the windows made from wavy cockled glass with tiny bubbles in it that held the light like good champagne. The sunken gardens surrounding an ornamental pond were already cool and dark, promising a dusky retreat even on the hottest summer day. For a moment I thought I heard the sound of glasses clinking and laughter from a long-ago summer party, but then I realized it was just some old wind chimes hanging from the gatehouse. There hadn't been any parties here for a while. When the sun went behind a cloud and the golden glow disappeared my eyes lingered more on the missing slate tiles in the roof, the weeds growing up between the paving stones of the front flagstones, the paint peeling off the porch columns, and the cracked and crumbling front steps. I even thought I could detect on the river breeze the smell of rot and mildew. And when Jess turned, his fingers still gripping the gate, I saw that without that light his face had turned sallow again and the look of longing was replaced with the certainty that he would always be on the wrong side of that gate. That's how he had become such a good mimic, by watching and listening from the other side. It made my heart ache for him.

"No, not in our 'price bracket' I think."

If Katrine noticed his mocking tone she didn't let on. "It isn't for sale," she said. "But the owner's looking for a caretaker."

If I could have tackled her before the words were out of her mouth, I would have, but the damage was already done. Jess's face had the stony look it got when he was getting ready to demolish someone, but as he often did these days he turned the rancor on himself. "I've always fancied myself a bit of a Mellors."

I was about to jump in and tell Katrine that Mellors was the caretaker in a D. H. Lawrence novel but she was laughing as if she'd gotten the reference. "That's just the sort of thing Mr. Montague would say. That's why I thought you two might get along."

"Montague? Not Alden Montague, the writer? This is his house?" Jess looked at me questioningly to see if I'd known it was the old Montague place, but Katrine, ignoring—or perhaps not noticing—Jess's appalled tone, saved me.

"I thought you might know him, Jess being a writer and since you both went to Bailey. He's looking for a caretaker for the estate. A couple, preferably. He's not paying much, but it's free rent and I'd think it would be a wonderful place to write. It could be just the thing for your . . . circumstances."

I glanced at Katrine, reassessing her. Beneath the highlighted blond hair and fake English country getup and plastered-on Realtor's smile she was smart, smart enough to see through our dithering over the aluminum siding and cracked linoleum to realize we couldn't afford even the cheapest houses she'd shown us today.

"But you wouldn't get a commission on that," I pointed out, half to give Jess a chance to get ahold of himself. The last person who'd mentioned Alden Montague around him had gotten a black eye for his trouble.

"No," she admitted, "but if someone was on the grounds fixing up the place it would sell for a lot more when the time came—and if that someone planted a bug in Mr. Montague's ear to use a certain Realtor . . ."

She let her voice trail off with a flip of her blond hair and a sly we're-all-in-this-together smile that I was sure Jess would roll his ▶

An Excerpt from
The Widow's House (continued)

eyes at, but instead he smiled back, some
of that golden light returning to his face.

"In other words," he said in the silky
drawl he used for interviews, "you don't
give the old man much longer to live and
you want an accomplice on the inside."

To her credit, Katrine didn't even sham
surprise.

"I wouldn't put it quite like that. But the
word around town is that Mr. Montague is
a pretty sick man. I have no intention of
taking advantage of that, but I did think
the situation might be mutually
beneficial . . ."

Jess grinned. "Why then, by all means,
set up the interview. I'd give good money
to see Old Monty on his deathbed." ⌣